THE JOURNEY

The Quest for Meaning

"A Modern American Fable"

A Transcendental and Metaphysical Journey
Through Time and Space

Gregory G. Abati
2014

THE JOURNEY
The Quest for Meaning

"A Modern American Fable"

Gregory G. Abati
2014

ISBN: 978-0-9915029-1-2
Direct Purchase: www.amazon.com/dp/0991502914

1st Edition
Yale Publishing House / Transitions
1831 Yale Drive, Louisville, Kentucky 40205
1-502-314-9371 / gregory2560@att.net

Contents

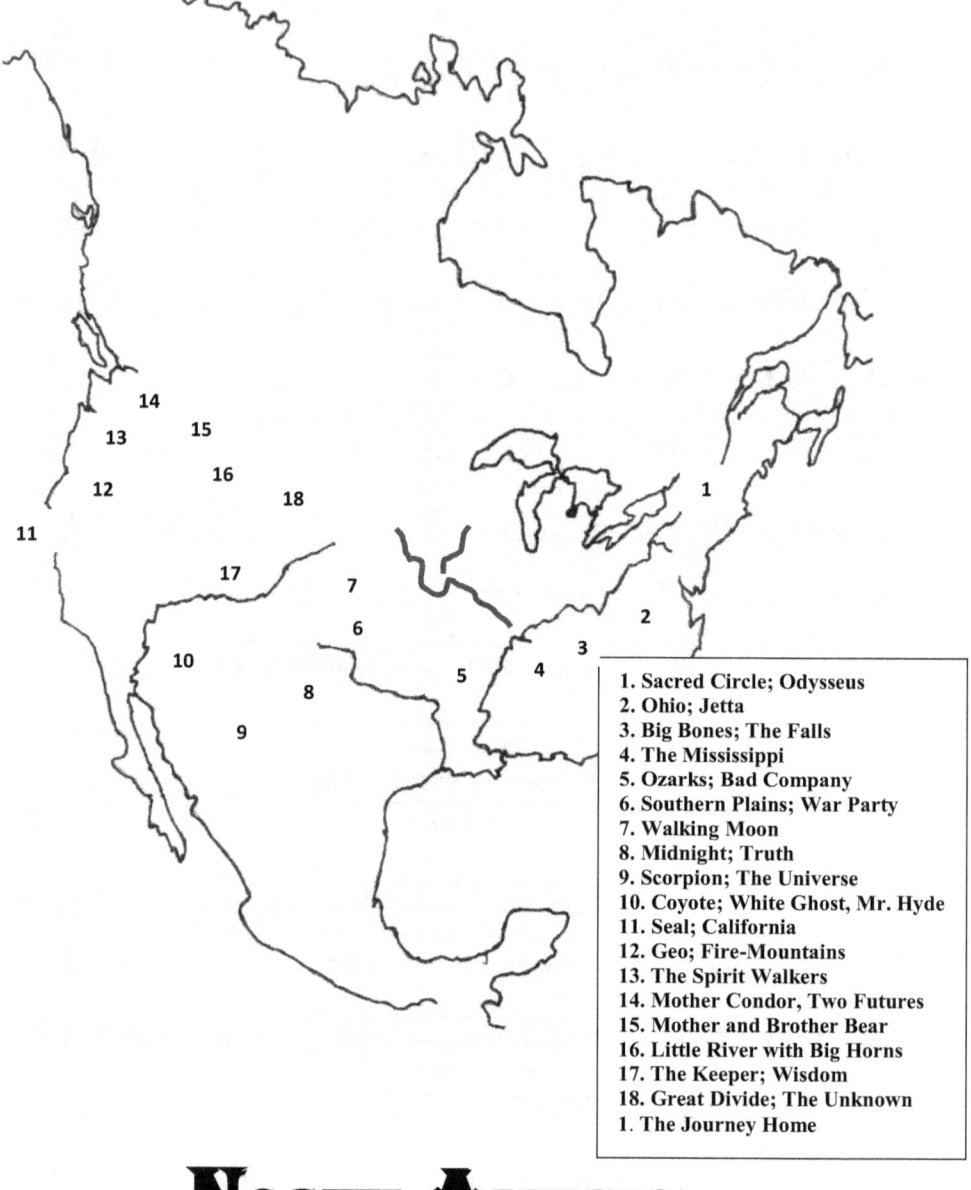

1. Sacred Circle; Odysseus
2. Ohio; Jetta
3. Big Bones; The Falls
4. The Mississippi
5. Ozarks; Bad Company
6. Southern Plains; War Party
7. Walking Moon
8. Midnight; Truth
9. Scorpion; The Universe
10. Coyote; White Ghost, Mr. Hyde
11. Seal; California
12. Geo; Fire-Mountains
13. The Spirit Walkers
14. Mother Condor, Two Futures
15. Mother and Brother Bear
16. Little River with Big Horns
17. The Keeper; Wisdom
18. Great Divide; The Unknown
1. The Journey Home

NORTH AMERICA
The Journey

Introduction

Marcus

This story is about a young raccoon by the name of *Marcus* who leaves home and sets out to explore the world around him. He lives with his family under the protection of an *Old Oak Tree* in the middle of a vast forest. He is full of curiosity and wants to know the answers to his many questions.

He wants to know who he is and why he exists. He wants to know about the *Earth* we live on, the moon and the stars. He knows it rains and his family and other creatures depend on the rain water to satisfy their thirst, but where does the rain come from and what is the sky? *"Why does it rain? Why does the rain water disappear? Where does the rain water go when it dries up? I need to know!"* With every question answered, he wants to know more.

His parents want Marcus to stay within their circle of love to care and protect him from the many dangers they face in *Nature*. Not satisfied with the answers given by his parents, he sets out on his own to explore the world and find the answers to his questions. Defiantly, he begins his journey.

During his travels Marcus learns the basics of survival. He learns more and more with each passing day. He travels through many regions of North America and comes into contact with other creatures. He has accomplices, friends, teachers, and enemies. He quickly learns that in the fragile balance of life, Nature can be unforgiving. One misstep can throw you into the *abyss*; existence without life; the darkest regions of the *Universe*; below *Absolute Zero*.

After traveling thousands of miles and experiencing many adventures he discovers many of Nature's basic truths. He gradually grows weary and finally discovers the deepest meaning of life. Marcus not only gains an understanding of himself, *he develops a profound reverence for the Earth and like all life forms he discovers that he and Nature are inseparable; he is a physical being in a physical Universe.* With the passing of time he ends where he started, life and death being a perfect circle in a Universe of perfect circles. With courage Marcus ventures into the *Great Unknown.*

A Metaphysical Journey

This journey like no other carries Marcus far-far away from his home. Once beyond the *Sacred Circle,* like a leaf in the wind, he has little control over his destiny. He is on a *metaphysical journey that transcends reality* where most things are not what they appear to be. There are layers and layers of distortions and abstractions hiding the truths he seeks. He must search and struggle to find purpose and meaning. Marcus wanders endlessly to uncover the answers to his many questions.

This is a journey where the past, present and future are entwined and where history and the fabric of reality are folded into each other. It's a story about our country, its high ideals, natural wonders and manmade tragedies. Like the Civil War, where brother fought against brother to end slavery only to continue the struggle against hatred and injustice until this very day. Or like the demise of the planet which began during the prehistoric age. Once man's capacity to exploit the Earth's natural resources extended beyond meeting his basic needs; survival turned into the raw lust for more, no matter what the costs to the health of our planet and its wildlife. We have yet to stop this naked need for more. To the contrary we are moving in a reckless direction to have more than what we need or what the Earth can provide.

The characters Marcus encounters share human and animal traits possessing the best and worst qualities of both. The characters speak and act like humans, but their wildness makes them more intense, more believable. They wish to never leave the wild and take on the persona of being human to tell their stories. They are members of the animal kingdom forced to act out their parts as directed by the humans. They flow back and forth between these two states, human and being wild, to deepen this tale and reveal Nature's basic truths. Many of them change their being to protect Marcus.

For example: The prairie dog villages are metaphors for the Plains Indians of North America (Sioux, Cheyenne) during the latter part of the Nineteenth Century with their revered warrior chiefs being Red Cloud, Sitting Bull and Crazy Horse. The hounds of the east are symbolic of the US 7th Cavalry which was determined to subdue the Plains Indians, destroy their culture and confine them to the reservations. Strong Wolf personifies George Armstrong Custer and the defeat of the Seventh Cavalry at the Battle of the Little Big Horn. The Keeper takes on the roles of Socrates and Aristotle in helping Marcus to deepen their discussions and discoveries concerning the meaning of life, the essence of being and the wonders of the Universe.

The Narrative

The narration of this story is fluid and flows back and forth between myself, the author in the third person and Marcus, the main character in the first person. At times the narration crosses over, one to the other within the same passage.

Nature's Truths (Science)

Copernicus, Galileo, Newton, Darwin, Einstein, Leaky and many others have taken us far in our understandings of the *Cosmos*, the planet Earth and the evolution of life. Will we accept these truths as to our existence or continue to deny our natural beings which are directly connected to the Cosmos and the formation of our planet?

The Setting (North America and the Earth)

North America at this time is a *pristine*, *untouched wilderness* that stretches thousands of miles north, south, east and west from Marcus's home; the Sacred Circle. It is a vast region that covers millions of square miles of the Earth's surface. This continent is one of Earth's seven great land masses and is joined to its sister, South America, by a large land bridge known as Central America.

The natural wilderness that encompasses North America stretches from the eastern woodlands westward across the Mississippi River into the Great Plains. The Great Plains continue west by northwest along the Rocky Mountains to the forest and pines of Canada. This vast grassland joins the Rockies at its eastern base, stretching up into the sub-arctic and arctic regions of Canada and Alaska where snow and ice dominate the landscape and life struggles to survive.

To the south and southwest of the Rockies this wilderness crosses the great basin country into the drier and desert regions that run north and south of the Colorado River. The Colorado River drains these arid lands flowing through

Mexico out into the Gulf of California. The Mojave and Sonora Deserts continue south by southwest into the Sierra Nevada Mountains and the northern portion of Mexico. The great Mississippi River and its many tributaries drain the heartland of North America forming the vital arteries that keep this landscape teeming with life. Scores of rivers on both sides of the continent drain the coastal highlands adding to the bounty and beauty of this country. Before man, North America was one of Nature's true gardens inhabited by a vast array of animal species.

Forces of Nature

Although Marcus does not fully understand the totality of the ever changing seasons and weather, they play a key role in his ability to adapt and survive in the wilderness. The northern and southern extremes of the Earth cool the warm waters that flow north and south from the *Equator*. These cold regions are known as the *Poles* and with the warmth of the equator are the Earth's hot and cold engines that drive our oceans, atmosphere and weather. This swirl of wind and currents bring movement and life to this planet and affect every living thing on Earth.

In addition to finding food and water Marcus must learn how to adapt to the extremes in the weather to survive his journey. He must seek and find shelter daily. He must protect himself not only from the blazing heat and freezing cold but also from the dangerous predators that are always stalking him. Called forward, his journey seems endless.

On his journey he discovers that *there are great geological forces shaping this planet*. These geologic forces are constantly moving the continents and the oceanic floors, pushing and pulling these land masses into each other as the

Earth spins on its axis. This constant motion gives rise to the *great mountains* of the world: the Andes, Himalayas, Rockies and the deepest spots on the planet, the *vast rift valleys* found in Africa and the Pacific Ocean. The inner core of the planet generates the magnetic shield which surrounds the planet further protecting the Earth's atmosphere and wildlife. Marcus discovers that a giant ring of geological motion surrounds the Pacific Ocean giving rise to America's western mountains and volcanoes. He travels into these mountains and wonders at their formation and beauty.

Marcus learns that the Earth is a living planet constantly in motion, constantly in flux from within its interior; in its oceans and atmosphere. Motion and change are without end. Even when the air appears still it is forcefully moving somewhere on the planet. The atmosphere, oceans and continents; and indeed the Earth itself are in constant motion. When there seems to be calm and all appears still, the tiniest of animals, seen and not seen, are moving about; in the stillest waters and within the ground itself these tiny creatures move and play. It is on this active planet he lives.

Marcus seeks to be with others and in that experiences many adventures and misadventures. Through his travels, misjudgments and teachings he learns and grows. His greatest challenge lay within himself. Although he wears a mask, he is a good guy who at times is led astray. His drive to know takes him to the edge, an edge we all must face, to a place we all must go.

North America would remain unspoiled until the arrival of man. The ice age would expose a land bridge between Asia and Alaska allowing the first massive migration of humans to North America about fifteen thousand years ago. With the arrival of the Europeans in the fifteen hundreds the fate of North America would be dramatically changed. The natural pristine beauty of the continent would be forever altered. Over time mankind will take the wild-lands away from the animal kingdom and bring the Earth to its near destruction. Marcus learns that if we fail to alter our reckless path the natural world that gave us life will be lost forever.

Dedication

This story is dedicated to my children; the warm breeze that confirms my existence. It is further dedicated to my children's children, may they inherit a better world. Finally, I wish to dedicate this story to all those who work diligently every day to keep our natural environment healthy and to those who want to teach our children a better way; a path connected to Nature and the truth as to our real purpose on this planet. *"We are its Keepers."*

Recognition

I wish to thank all those who assisted me with this book. I want to extend a sincere and special thanks to my dearest friend April for her careful reviews and insights. Her readings were a major contribution to this work. I further wish to thank my niece Kirsten for her review and suggestions; they were helpful in many ways. My nephew Ron's encouragement and faith in this story was and is dear to me. Andy Albatys' insights and careful review further the completion of this work. Sara Crutchfield's final review assisted me greatly with the necessary finishing touches to the story. Their collective input and support helped me to improve and better tell this story.

Prologue

Join Marcus on this epic journey through time and space as he travels across America to discover Nature's basic truths. On this journey he experiences many adventures. It is a metaphysical journey that starts and ends where it all begins. This is a journey through a Universe of circles that sets all things into motion and fills our lives with awe and wonder; ***Birth-Death, With Life In Between***.

Born on the Allegany Plateau he heads west. Marcus travels through a vast forest, down its mighty rivers into the Great Plains and across the deserts. Marcus learns many lessons on his journey and commits himself to follow Nature's narrow path.

This is a story about a young man's ***quest for meaning***. Through his travels he meets many characters; some who will lead him astray and others who will teach and guide him toward a ***higher state of being***. There are the ***hollow ones***, the ***spirit warriors***, the ***controlling elite***, the ***seekers-teachers-keepers*** and ***seers***.

On his journey Marcus will meet many of Nature's wild creatures: Eclipse the raven, Odysseus the frog, Jetta the black widow, Badger the outlaw, Justice the white buffalo, Walking Moon the warrior chief, Midnight the bat, the black scorpion, Coyote, Heckle, Jekyll and Mr. Hyde, Seal, Geo, Rahoo and the voices from the forest, Mother Condor, Mother and brother bear, the Keeper, Chaos, and many others. His encounters with these beings teach him much.

He has dreams and visions and at times he is not certain if he is awake or asleep. The real world, he soon finds out, is often confusing with dreams and nightmares occurring both day and night. He discovers that we often disregard our dreams making the nightmares more real than they really are. And that we too often destroy what we build and pass the ruins of our destruction on to our children.

America at this time is not ready for the humans. It is the animal kingdom that will teach this young man his greatest lessons. He will choose and live with bad company. He will fight in an unnecessary war and engage in criminal behavior. There are those that will warn him about the coming future and the corruption of mankind in its callous relationship with the Earth. There are those that seek to destroy Marcus and those who will give their lives to protect him. He falls in love and has wonderful children and grandchildren. His wanderlust will lead him into the unknown. *Chaos* will pursue and catch up with him. He will be saved by the ones who love him the most.

He learns about the Universe and the natural wonder we call Earth. He gains a profound reverence for the Earth, our home, and ceases to believe in the gibberish handed down through the ages. He embraces the truth that we are of and from this Earth. He will discover the balance of Nature, the miracle of life and the inescapable reality of death. He will seek out and discover the unknown. His greatest teacher will be Nature herself.

Marcus is a human who has disguised himself as a raccoon to better fit into the natural world. Although a good guy, he hides behind a mask to cover his true identity and misdeeds.....

Where are you in terms of your state of being? In the quest for truth we seek knowledge and the acquisition of knowledge gains us wisdom. The highest state of being, a ***Seer***, is reserved for the few, but opened to all. Only those who are willing to travel far from home and learn through the passage of time become seers. Will you look within yourself and join Marcus on this journey? I warn you if we fail to find our way the world as we know it will be lost. There is a war going on; and that war is within ourselves.

"From a mighty oak tree a leaf will fall to fill this Earth with wonder. A strong wind will carry this leaf far from its home to discover the unknown."

The Journey
The Quest for Meaning

1. The Great Forest

Emerald Green

There once was a vast wilderness that stretched unbroken across North America. In the east an expansive forest embracing the shores of the Atlantic Ocean spread its emerald green bounty over a thousand miles north, south and west. From the coast this great forest reached westward beyond the banks of the Mississippi River. In the south this mighty forest surrounded the warm waters of the Gulf of Mexico stretching northward to the snow and ice of what is now northern Canada.

In the northeast the forest was filled with beautiful hardwoods: giant elms, hickories, ash, maples, sycamores and oaks. In the far north up into Canada the hardwoods gave way to the spruce, cedars and pines, to the south the cypress and mangroves. For generations without measure the leaves and needles of these great woodlands covered the forest floor, feeding the Earth the nutrients it needed to regenerate this majestic forest over and over again.

This ancient forest formed a green blanket over the Earth, protecting the plants and animals below. The sun's summer light illuminated the forest canopy, accentuating its green leaves. In rhythm with the sun and clouds, the leaves would become a living mosaic of emerald greens flowing across this canopy in every direction with the breeze. In the fall the sun's light would again ignite this great forest with millions of red, orange and yellow leaves covering the landscape with colors akin to fire. For eons without measure and in *harmony* with Nature, all was as it should be; unblemished.

In the summer the forest was alive with movement. During the day the sun would find its way through the branches and leaves illuminating the ground below. With the motion of the trees, the sun's piercing beams of light danced here and there on the forest floor. As the winds pushed from the north, south, east and west they filled the forest air with the noises of the wild. These winds would carry the ever present animal calls and bird songs through the air, accentuating their residence in the forest. The chirps, whistles, grunts, growls and nightly hoots and howls affirmed Nature's command of these woodlands. The forest was alive with smells and sounds. The combined presence of the plants and animals filled the forest with life and a sweet fragrance found only in Nature.

From the unseen microorganisms to the mammalian giants the forest was alive with life. The invisible world of minute creatures sustains the productive lives of the larger creatures and in turn the larger creatures provide nutrients for the little ones to thrive; creating a natural recycling of the minerals necessary to keep Nature in *balance* for all. *"Life and death are in rhythm. Nothing including this Earth lasts forever."*

The invisible and visible creatures of this world are here to keep company with the Earth on its journey through space and time. The insects, fish, amphibians, reptiles, birds and mammals, live with and off of each other to give birth to their off-springs. They seek to survive and reproduce to exist beyond their *mortal lives* and live in the future with the

Earth. *"We have been born of and from this Earth as the living extension of its being; swirling in a solar system to keep up with the Sun."*

These creatures live and thrive in special niches. Many of them seek nourishment and shelter from the soil while others thrive above ground amongst the plants and trees. There are creatures that live entirely in the creeks and streams, in the canopy of the trees, and yes, up into the sky; where birds of prey and other flying creatures search for food and shelter.

In the winter the northeastern woodlands rested bare, with snow and ice covering the ground. Food was scarce and the animals sought shelter and rested during the coldest days. Some of the animals took refuge for the entire winter months and withdrew into their dens for an extended sleep. But even on Nature's coldest day, life moves.

A squirrel could travel hundreds of miles in any direction through the trees never setting its paws on the ground. Leaping from one branch to another, from one tree to another, a squirrel could travel across this land and leave no visible trace of its presence on the forest floor.

The sun's daily march across the sky framed the beauty of this forest bringing light and warmth to its domain. The moon, planets and stars illuminate the night's sky giving wonder to all those who ponder its thousands and thousands of lights.

The Beginning (The Mighty Oak Tree)

At the center of this great forest stood a mighty oak tree. This massive oak was taller than all the other trees in the forest. It towered over two hundred feet and reached above the forest canopy into the sky; a rich green canopy that covered the Earth for hundreds of miles in any direction.

The roots of this giant tree stretched out a great distance from its trunk; forming a protective circle for all the creatures living within its shelter. The squirrel, the chip-monk, rabbit and raccoon could readily take refuge under its thick roots when Nature threatened.

During the day the oak leaves above brought shade to the surface beneath its branches; giving comfort and shelter to all the creatures that flourished under the tree's care.

The Mighty Eagle

One bright summer day a dark shadow gently drifted from the west over the forest. This shadow glided slowly above the tops of the trees creating great excitement for the creatures below. The animals of the forest felt threatened and knew to hide. *It was the unknown that scared us the most.*

As the shadow gave way to the creature that created it, a majestic eagle landed in its place on the tree's topmost branch. The eagle folded its wings to his body and came to rest. The mightiest of birds, the American Bald Eagle, had been drawn to the upper branches of the forest's tallest tree. There was something familiar about this tree; something profound. You could see the curvature of the Earth as it arched from horizon to horizon; a perfect circle surrounding a perfect perch. It was a perch where the coming night fuses into the day; (dawn meets dusk), and the past and present join to embrace the future; a place where we share Nature's splendor. The eagle's sharp sight pierced through the leaves and his shadow fell on me. With a clear and powerful voice he asked: *"Who's that child hiding in my shadow?"*

Realizing where he was and where he had been, with a great flap of his wings the mighty eagle flew off into the Cosmos never to be seen again.

The creatures below chattered with relief. My parents had warned me, *"Watch the skies."* I was in awe and trembled with fear and wonder.

Born in the middle of this vast forest I lived with my family beneath the branches of this giant oak tree. We too lived within its protective circle. Where life and death were in *harmony* with Nature and the bounty of the Earth belonged to all of us equally.

This forest and the wilderness beyond stretched from *sea to shining sea* and covered thousands of miles: east to west and north to south. Living within the *balance* of Nature, the creatures of this land struggled to survive.

Life and death were in *balance* and the rhythm of both was governed by Nature. It was the dawn of time and humans had not yet left their footprints upon the forest floor. Humans had not yet arrived and our lands remained untouched.

My Family

My parents were poor and humble creatures who raised six children within the protective shield of the tree's roots. We had opposable thumbs and wore masks to hide our identities. To survive we learned to eat almost anything and could find food in the most unpromising places. My father and mother were very young when a violent storm rolled across the

Allegheny Plateau. My parents were hiding under the roots of the oak tree when the storm began to crackle with lightning and thunder. A lightning bolt flashed from the storm striking their tree. This bolt of lightning burned a deep hole into the tree's trunk creating a pocket of burning embers illuminating the night sky for miles.

My father was drawn to its glow. He watched it carefully as the hole expanded deeper into the tree, creating a perfect hiding place. The smoke from the lightning strike filled the air and rose into the heavens. My father saw the rising smoke as a good omen; as the embers cooled the light within faded. The strike occurred just above a broad branch, creating a perfect perch from where to view the world below. He decided to make this spot, marked by the heavens, our home.

A few days passed and my father returned to the tree determined to hollow out a nest for his future family. My father and mother would raise, love and protect two litters of kits in this tree. This mighty oak tree and the roots that anchored it to the Earth would become our home, our Sacred Circle. It stood in the center of the Allegheny forest and from its top branches you could see unbroken sky for miles. My parents would have the tree's roots to protect us, and the nest in its trunk to give birth to and raise their family.

My father's name was **Solomon** and my mother's name was **Sheba**. First born were **Romulus**, then came **Remus** and **Patricia**; triplets. They were the first litter born to my father and mother. The next and last litter born to our family was: **Isabella**, myself; **Marcus** and our baby brother **Brutus**.

Romulus and Remus were great warriors and hunters and moved to the north and south sides of the great oak to start their own clan. My eldest sister Patricia married a mighty chief and moved to the east of the circle. We had family on the four corners of our world. We were allowed to visit our older brothers and sister during the day but warned to always be home before dark and to never stray from the Sacred Circle that protected us.

Descendants of David

Legend has it that years and years ago, one of our forefathers slew a hideous giant name *Golith* in a great battle between the humans and the wild ones. Golith, fighting for the humans, was a foul smelling monster covered with coarse red hair standing over nine feet tall. He ate his victims alive. The warrior who killed Golith was a young brave by the name of *David*. To escape the humans after the battle, David migrated from the far west to the shores of the Atlantic Ocean and started a new life for himself and his family. My older brothers, Romulus and Remus, always claimed that we were the direct descendants of this courageous warrior king. My father, while not denying it, would always say: *"If the elders say it's true; it must be true. These are the sacred words that have been passed down through the ages."*

Eclipse

When we were still nursing, a family of ravens built a nest in the tree next to ours. These two trees were so close that their branches intertwined with each other, one branch overlapping the other, binding the trees together. Although our tree towered over the other they both shared the same destiny; being a safe haven and home for wild families.

As we grew older one of the newly hatched fledglings caught our attention. We named him *Eclipse* in honor of his coal black feathers. We soon became dear friends. At first it was all play. Eclipse would hop along the branches of his tree and call out as if teasing us. Brutus and I would scramble from our hiding place and take on the challenge. He would call out again, move to the tip of his branch, flap his jet black wings and retreat back to his nest.

When we demonstrated a chase across our branches he would dart under his parents, who would loudly protest our charge, stopping us in our tracks. At the fringes between the two trees the branches were very thin. As we approached this edge the branches would bend under our weight.

Eclipse would always retreat at the final moment to see how far he could pull us toward oblivion. Brutus would always take it too far, nearly snapping the branch in half.

Eclipse, Brutus and I became constant companions. Each morning Eclipse would call us to play. We would play this dangerous game of chase in the tree tops with Brutus always on the fringes of flight.

We learned to rely on each other's natural skills, sharing our adventures and mishaps in equal proportion. We learned to watch each other closely to benefit from the other's discoveries. We shared our successes and food and became the best of friends. Eclipse's excellent vision and our sharp claws served each other well. We became partners in survival. From up high he would spot a fat grub and call our attention to his find. We would scurry to the ground, dig the grub out from under the roots and share our catch with our friend. The grub's oblivion was our dinner.

By his first year Eclipse had grown into a very large raven; the largest in the Allegany Mountains. His perfectly formed feathers were jet black wearing an iridescent deep blue and black collar to accentuate his beauty.

At mid-morning he would show up to taunt us with his power of flight. He would soar through the sky perfectly positioning his body between us and the sun to cast his shadow down on us and laugh. *"I am the master of the Universe and your souls; the ruler of your destinies."*

Hovering for an instant he would blot out the sun, catching us in his shadow. He would then abruptly fly off, blinding us with the bright light that had been shielded behind him. Vanishing into this glare he would disappear from our sight into the forest. *"Caw, Caw, Caw, Master of your souls."* He would call as his taunts faded in the distance. *"Your souls, your souls,"* the forest would echo, crowning his dominion over our spirits. Fearless and with super keen eyesight Eclipse held us in awe. As he soared into the wind, the power of flight made Eclipse special. Brutus craved his approval and would do anything to get his attention.

Eclipse was always there to tease, always there to spur us on; he was our best friend. Earning his name he would completely eclipse the sun to demonstrate his power over gravity and our feeble and mortal beings;

"Marcus and Brutus the sons of Solomon and Sheba were born in the forest to live wild and free upon this Earth. In motion, our lives are but an instant in time marked in a vast ocean of space stretching beyond the Universe itself."

Eclipse would tease Brutus to the extreme and Brutus would always accept his challenge. One morning he dared Brutus into a base jump that almost cost Brutus his life. Folding his wings next to his body, Eclipse dove from the top of our tree, daring my rash baby brother: ***"Follow me!"***

The two of them jumped to a branch twenty feet below. If Brutus missed, it spelled certain death for my little brother. At the last instant Eclipse opened his wings while Brutus flew passed him, smashing into the branch with his body barely breaking his fall.

"That's not fair!" Brutus cried. *"Raccoons can't fly."* Eclipse laughed.

My brother and I would play in the tree branches and climb into the sky to watch the stars and days go by. We played catch, jumping from limb to limb in perfect **balance** with the elements. We would wrestle on the fringes of gravity with only thin branches keeping us from a tragic end. My brother would take this edge to the extreme, seemingly immortal. I thought myself invincible; but he thought himself a demigod. Eclipse would always be nearby just waiting to goad us on.

My older siblings didn't have much time for foolishness and were annoyed by our constant misbehavior. By the time we were teenagers we were really up to stuff; testing their limits.

My brother and I would find our way to the edge of the Sacred Circle to play and horse around. It was a point of mischief; we knew we should not be there. Brutus was always daring me to step across. I would say: *"Remember what mother and father warned us about; it's dangerous beyond the circle."*

He would giggle like a girl and place one of his paws beyond the point of no return and say: *"See; nothing, absolutely nothing. I told you they were just trying to scare us!"*

I would retort: *"If you are so brave, jump over!"*

Brutus: *"You are just a sissy, always doing what mother tells you to do. Marcus, you are afraid of your own shadow!"*

He purposely left father out because we all knew to never question our father's voice. His words were sacred to us, handed down from one generation to the next. He was our first teacher. Mother's words were strong and she often backed it up with a paw if necessary, but our father's words were absolute. I finally would say: *"Remember what father warned!"*

On a clear sunny day he dared me again. I retorted: *"I dare you!"* And in one leap, oblivious to thought, he jumped out into the other world. He looked bewildered himself when nothing happened.

"SEE I TOLD YOU, THEY'RE JUST TRYING TO SCARE US!!!"

When I did not join him he yelled: **"S-I-S-S-Y!"**

"Sissy, Sissy, Sissy!" Eclipse called; hiding in a tree always spying on us; following us around ready to mix things up.

I stood my ground and obeyed the wishes of my parents.

Brutus: *"I'm a holy warrior and this proves it! You better not tell!"*

Mother would insist that father stop our reckless play, believing one of us would go too far. But our father encouraged the play telling mother: *"They must learn the hard way by hurting themselves or the lesson will be hollow. Besides they are developing the skills they will need in the future to survive. What's the point of life if they don't survive to have children? We are just sparks in a sea of darkness."*

My younger brother Brutus was the most reckless of the bunch always accepting a dare; always challenging his limits to the edge. He was pure muscle from head to toe and possessed an iron grasp. He demonstrated a ton of wit and loved the attention of the crowd.

One day on a dare, Brutus climbed to the very top of the mighty oak to attempt a leap across its branches, hundreds of feet above the forest floor. I tried to stop him, but he would not listen.

Eclipse showed up to call him on: *"Jump Brutus; you can do it! Jump; I double dog dare you, chick-chick-chicken!"*

Like the blackness to come, Eclipse called my baby brother on: *"Jump; see if you can fly!"*

I pleaded: *"Don't do it Brutus; it's too far!"*

With a devilish grin he said: *"Just watch me brother!"* Then Brutus leaped into oblivion, the emptiness beyond space.

Brutus reached for the branch. His mighty grasp failed him when his claws ripped through the bark, sheering the bark from the hardwood beneath, causing him to lose his grip and fall to his death.

I watched him free fall through the air; in silence my dear brother fell to the Earth. There was a sickening crack as his bones smashed into the ground below. Drawn by gravity into the void - death was waiting to claim his life; darkness beyond measure was now his constant companion.

My mother grieved out loud in anguish as my father turned and whispered *"Oh, my dear son, what have you done? My baby boy, what have you done?"*

His wit and strength carried him far but his grasp proved too powerful for the tree. The physical world had reclaimed him. He was our baby brother and we felt lost without him. At night I frequently call out his name, knowing he has been lost to me forever and won't answer any more.

Eclipse teased and taunted Brutus to the extreme. The extreme being the one place Brutus loved the most; playing on the fringes that separated life from death. In shame and grief Eclipse flew off into the *shadows*, never to be seen by Marcus again. Seeking redemption, Eclipse disappeared into the unknown.

*E*CLIPSE

My sister Isabella married a reckless fool and never recovered. She eventually moved south to join Remus' clan. At an early age she became ill and passed from this Earth before her time.

The mighty oak tree and its Sacred Circle did not protect us from everything. Foolery is not much tolerated by Nature. Some creatures get away with more than their fair share. I was the last, of the last litter.

The Warning

My parents warned us not to stray too far from the center of the mighty oak tree and to always, always stay within its protective circle. The older four children yielded to this warning; faithfully obeying our parents.

I was a little fellow with a million questions. *"Who was I and what was my relationship to all the other creatures that lived in the forest? Where did the forest come from and how did it all start? Why did the sun march across the sky and what were those shining twinkles of light in the sky when the sun goes down? What is life and why do we exist?"*

I was very playful and could not keep my mind focused. I asked: *"Why?"* all the time. One of the most difficult questions to answer, I asked why anyway. I needed to know: *"Why does the oak tree reach so high into the sky? Why does the night chase away the sun only to have it return the next day and chase away the night? Why are there so many creatures and how are they related to me?* I noticed that some of them are covered with fur too and have to find things to eat every day: *"If we have the same needs, why are we not all identical?"*

My parents would scold me and say: *"Silly little boy, the world is what it is and what it will always be. You ask too many questions and don't pay attention to the important things. We all walk a different trail to the same ending. It's the trail you travel that defines who you are."*

My parents in frustration would say: *"The important questions are; where and what are we going to eat today, how can we avoid danger throughout the day, and where will we sleep safely tonight? It is the where, what and how questions which are most important, not why. Marcus, you ask too many silly questions, that can't be answered. Stop this silliness and find us something good to eat."*

The echo of why, caused me to wander. I would always find myself at the edge of the Sacred Circle pondering what lay beyond? *"Are there other mighty oaks, and does the forest go-on forever? Are there others like me? Does my mate live somewhere else in the forest? Is she waiting for me? Will I be a great warrior and hunter like my two older brothers? Is there something wonderful for me to discover?"*

"Where does the horizon end? Can you walk off into the night and keep ahead of the sun, or walk off into the daylight and never witness the night again? Is the night sky a blanket that covers us to aid our sleep or a great pond that we can sail across? Does the Earth end and where it ends can you step off into space and float into the heavens? Why am I standing here waiting?"

The Get Away

I planned my escape. I would pack enough food for two weeks, one week to reach the edge of the world and one week to get back home. I would see the world and marvel over the Universe and life itself in fourteen days. In half of the Lunar Cycle I will return home. Mother and father won't even miss the food and would easily forgive me once I told them of my great adventures and all the things I discovered.

I woke up well before dawn and eagerly packed my *haversack* with food. I slipped out of the den and quietly crawled over and under the roots to make my escape. I pretended that I was a prisoner of some great war and soon would be free from the chains of tyranny. I was a revolutionary ready to change the world. I was a great explorer that would discover a new continent, a scientist to find a new species to add to my collection and answer the riddles of the Universe; all in fourteen days. I would find the answers to all my questions, to explore, to travel until my soul burst with the joy of discovery. ***"I would become a great teacher and keeper of the truth."***

I was not half way when I stopped for food. I opened the *haversack* and greedily ate my fill. A pool of water caught between the roots satisfied my thirst. I pondered what existed beyond the mighty oak and could not wait to get to the edge of the Sacred Circle and truly be on my way. I thought to myself I would take a short nap, and with that I closed my eyes for a few moments and fell into the world of dreams.

MARCUS

2. Beyond the Sacred Circle

The Great Watersheds

While I rested on the forest floor, my mind wandered to my father's lessons. My father would teach us about our home and the surrounding forest. He said we lived in the middle of the Allegheny Plateau just west of the Appalachian Mountains. He said that this area was part of the western watershed flowing southwest from the highlands. He taught us that the eastern watershed flowed from the Appalachians eastward to the Atlantic Ocean. The larger of these rivers were the St. Lawrence, Hudson and Delaware. These rivers teemed with life providing needed nutrients and minerals to the Atlantic Ocean.

The real mystery concerned the **western watershed**. No one knew for sure where its waters flowed and what streams and rivers drained this region. It was referred to as **the great unknown**. When I asked my father what **watersheds** and **oceans** were, or what the word river meant, he said he did not know. Since a little boy my father had never traveled very far beyond the Sacred Circle. These were holy words that had been handed down to him to keep for his children. These words came from the ancients, the old ones, but nobody knew or remembered what the words meant. He said he was told by his father **Ra**, that the Atlantic Ocean meant; waters without measure, but beyond that the words had lost their meaning. There were always small creeks, and pockets of water trapped within the roots of our tree, but my father had no memory of ever seeing a river or an ocean.

When pressed to tell his story, all my father could remember was crossing the Appalachian Mountains when he was a very young boy and losing his family in the great firestorm that almost destroyed the forest. He did not like talking about those early years. He spent nearly his entire life under the protection of this mighty oak tree. He was an orphan who grew to rely on and trust its Sacred Circle; the oak tree and roots that protected him. My father's reverence for this tree was without bounds.

My father said: *"Son there are things you just must believe and accept on faith. These are sacred words handed down through the generations. Who are we to question their meaning or truth?"*

Father continued: *"Marcus, you ask too many questions. You're going to get yourself in trouble. You are spending too much time in the clouds. Slow down. Everything you do, including thinking, you should do in moderation. Don't sleep or think too much, it just isn't good for you."*

"Remember all things need and feed off of each other. It is the order of things, the grand design of Nature. As it has been and as it will always be. We come and go with time; that is the way it is. It's a dangerous world. Stay within the Sacred Circle *and believe in its power to protect you. There are hungry creatures out there waiting to eat you.* **Beware!"**

Abandoned in the Forest

When my father was a young man, he too challenged fate and stepped across the Sacred Circle, but fear of the unknown drove him back. For an instant curiosity had gotten the best of him, but within that same moment the stories of the wild (the unknown), passed from one generation to another; forced him back to the safety of the known. The thick and near indestructible roots of the mighty oak protected all those that stayed within its shelter. The known appeared certain while the unknown was full of dangerous creatures determined to devour you; bite by vicious bite.

For his time he was considered the bravest of the brave. He had climbed the highest branches of the mighty oak spending weeks gazing at the stars and horizons to ponder their mysteries. He noticed some stars moved while others seemed forever fixed in the black emptiness of space. He watched the sun rise and set, each day unique from the other.

My father journeyed to the very edge of the Sacred Circle and like Brutus dared to step across only to scurry back in fear. One day where the Sacred Circle touched the roots of another giant oak tree, he heard a soft whimper. Daring to cross over he found my mother, Sheba, his future wife. My mother had been abandoned, left alone to die from a strange fever. As she grew weaker by the day and appearing beyond help, fear and grief drove her family away. Sick, frightened and near starvation my father found her and quickly returned with her to the protection of the mighty oak tree. My mother was but a little girl left alone and sick in the forest to die.

The Cricket

Initially my mother's fever took a turn for the worse. My father in desperation again ventured beyond the Sacred Circle in search of a **black widow** to learn my mother's fate. ***Black widows were renowned for their ability to see into the future.*** With only a few hours on the trail he ran across an old cricket that looked lost and confused; bewildered. Looking my father in the eyes the cricket in a clear and trusting voice said: *"My name is **Vision.**"*

Vision went on to say: *"My friend you look so troubled and sad. Maybe I can help, what troubles you?"*

My father: *"I found a young girl in the forest and she has a fever that will not break. I barely know her, but I love this little girl and want her to get well. Can you please help me? I am looking for a black widow?"*

Vision: *"A black widow is a seer, not a healer. I come from a large family of famous medicine men and women. Their wisdom has been handed down through the ages. Does she have cold sweats, and in spite of her high fever are her paws cool to the touch?"*

My father: *"Yes, it is exactly as you say!"*

Vision: *"Most likely she has eaten some poison blueberries. She must purge this poison before she can recover. I want you to fill this pouch full of clovers. Mash the clovers in a cup of saltwater and make her drink all of it until she vomits and defecates. Once the poison passes she will recover."*

My father: *"What do I owe you for your kindness?"*

Vision: ***"A kindness to another. Remember, a kindness given is a kindness earned."***

Vision's Story (Visitor from the Future)

Vision: ***"I am from the year 2525 and mankind did not survive.*** *I have been sent down this trail to help you, help us alter our futures. In my time the skies are yellow and the sun's light seldom touches the ground. Only a few species of insects and some reptiles have survived. In our world the atmosphere reaches extreme temperatures and at times*

34

climbs above 150 degrees. *The clouds that sweep across this empty landscape are dusty brown. These dusty brown clouds are filled with toxic chemicals; water too poisonous to drink. During the day the* **purple rain** *that falls from the sky dries before it hits the ground. At night when the atmosphere and Earth cools, the rain reaches the ground and floods. By noon it is so hot again, that the pools of purple rain evaporate leaving patches of* **acid dust** *everywhere. When the winds are up we must retreat deeper into the darkness of the caves to stay alive.*"

Vision: "*We have learned that our futures are tied directly to the actions of the humans. The biosphere has been so corrupted, that in time, even the insects and reptiles that made it are doomed. Only by hiding in the crevices and caves have we been able to last this long.*"

Vision: "*I found a passage through one of the dark caves that led me here. The world I am from is dying. Nature as you now know it, no longer exists. In my time, outside of the caves the land is dry and barren. Only the water filtered through the sandstone is drinkable. We insects survive off fungus and the reptiles survive off us.*"

Vision: "*I just barely made it through a narrow passage when I entered your world. The blue skies and wet lands filled with life are beautiful. I am in awe at this wonder. It will not always be so. Unless stopped the humans will have their way and take the Earth pass the point of no return.*"

Vision: "*My voice and skills have been sent down this worn out trail to save the planet. This message will echo through time but the humans will not listen. In saving ourselves, we must save them."*

Vision: *"This little girl, you have taken in, will give birth to a child that will bring forth the light which will illuminate our paths and save the Earth. He will pester his parents with questions, but in the end he seeks the truth. One thing connected to another, to another, to another to ensure a safe and prosperous future for all of Nature's children."*

Vision: ***"The humans don't understand it yet but they will become the keepers and guardians of Nature's garden, the Garden Before Eden, or they will forever fade from the memory of the Earth."***

Solomon was confused by the cricket's story. He respectfully listen to what surely was a riddle spoken by a voice he could see but could not hear. He seemed confident about Vision's remedy to help the little girl, but Solomon confused the truth about the future with the idle ***gibberish*** that most creatures speak when they have nothing else to say.

Either way Solomon realized Vision's remedy was the only hope he had to save the little girl. Besides, she was just a baby girl. It would be years before she would be ready to marry and have babies. Who knows what the future holds?

The Storm (Our Nest in the Tree)
With that they parted company. My father rushed back to her side and did exactly what the cricket had commanded. Under the loving eyes of my father, my mother soon became well.

Just a young man, my father took her in and with the compassion of a saint brought her back to good health. This saintly care, pure in form, grew into love. Years passed and she blossomed into adulthood, two of Nature's own fell wildly in love; her with him and him with her. They married with joyful passion under the protection of their mighty oak tree. In the wild they whispered their vows and were joined for life. Before the great storm they pledged their love and fidelity to each other. They were wild things and set out to have and raise their wild children. Before the storm they found shelter under the roots of the mighty oak and like nomads moved about nightly searching for food while during the day they hid in the upper branches of their oak tree. After the storm they would take shelter in the nest created by the heavens and raise their children. They would prove to be the models of parental love faithfully protecting and guiding their children through life. My father's disapproval was discipline enough. His disappointment set boundaries we could not bear to cross. My mother's quick and sharp paws stopped us in our tracks and redirected our behaviors without further comment. They were wonderful parents. I hadn't even reached the edge of the Sacred Circle and already I missed them dearly.

The Perfect Storm

THE PERFECT STORM

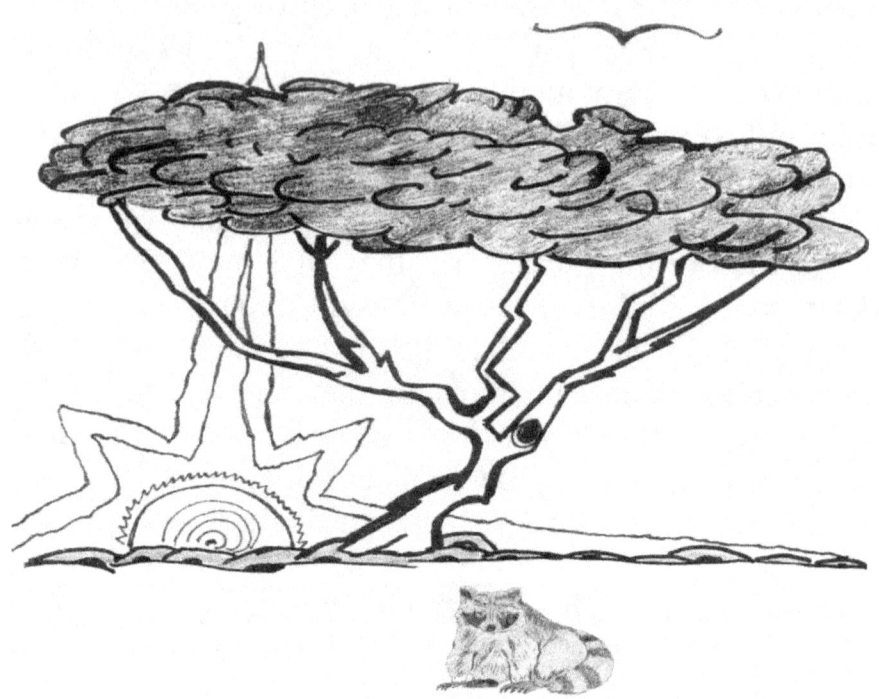

THE MIGHTY OAK TREE / SACRED CIRCLE

Day Dreaming

I woke up. The sun was not fully up when I reached the edge of the Sacred Circle. There I stood under the mighty oak tree that had kept me safe all of my life. I was poised to step off into the unknown; possibly never to return. I heard the familiar sound that had teased me so many times; a sound of something rushing over something else. A sound I never heard unless I was on the edge of the Sacred Circle. It was a soft sound, yet there was strength and motion in its lyrics, foreign lyrics that seemed to bubble in my ears and beg for my attention.

I paused and looked back; the sun was edging above the horizon with its light spraying through the trees; illuminating my path forward. The morning sun seemed to bless my journey and beckoned me on. The music out in front of me danced through my head and had to be known. Where does this tune come from; who or what is responsible for its grace? With apprehension I took my first step into the wilderness; my first step toward the light and into the unknown.

Without looking back I rapidly hiked forward in the direction of the sound ahead of me. Unlike the ground under the oak tree the forest floor rapidly fell before me. I found myself walking at a fast pace; nearly running downhill.

The ground became broken and for the first time in my life I saw rocks and boulders. The ground became saturated with water and was covered with thick moss. The forest floor angled downward and was punctuated here and there with beautiful ferns and other exotic plants I had not seen before.

The sound grew louder and louder as the day seemed to disappear before me. I had journeyed throughout the day without discovering the source of the magical lyrics. In my quest I had lost track of time. I suddenly realized it was rapidly turning dark and I was alone and far away from home. Suddenly fear overcame my quest for discovery.

Sleeping alone in the forest was my first true experience with raw and naked fear. As it grew darker I realized I had not thought through the process of making camp. Where exactly should I locate the camp site? Where should I store away my gear? What did I need to sleep under? And what would be crawling around me when I lay down to go to sleep?

My mind exploded with unimaginable creatures united in their one desire to kill and eat me; eat me while I was still alive. The calls and sounds of the night were new, strange, horrifying; keeping me awake.

The piercing howl of one animal drove me into the trees. Instinctively my paws and body leaped into action. I grabbed my *haversack* and climbed to the upper branches of the closest tree. Up, up I climbed until a few branches and stars were all that separated me from space.

The Source of All Life

The night had grown thick with moisture. Dew began to gather on the leaves, gradually filling their pockets with droplets of water. The weight of each leaf increased as these pockets filled with water. In turn the leaves would bend spilling out their tiny pools of water, dripping from one leaf to another down to the forest floor.

I slept through the early morning hours to be awakened by the drip-drip sound of water falling from one leaf to another. In my sleep my soul captured the rhythm of each water droplet hitting the forest floor; I was called into action by an unbelievable thirst. I suddenly realized how thirsty I was and drank myself full. Once my thirst had been satisfied my senses returned and my hearing grew sharp again. The lyrics from that unknown source sang in my ears. "I must be close!" I gathered my gear and moved down the trail without pause.

The slope grew steeper, the boulders were harder to climb, the moss thicker; saturated with water. Then I saw it and fully comprehended its meaning. It all flowed together and made perfect sense. The water from the leaves dripped onto

40

the ground, the saturated ground carried the water downhill to the boulders. Under the boulders the water gathered to form pools, these pools spilled over to form streams, the streams spilled over to form creeks and the creeks spilled over to form rivers and the rivers flowed down hill to the edges of the world. The water, rushing over the stream beds and rocks, sings with joy as it fills the Earth with life and wonder.

I followed the streams and creeks traveling southwest from the Appalachian Mountains steadily moving downhill until I reached the edge of the Allegheny Plateau. I marveled at the beauty of the great forest that spread out before me.

Their waters joined with each other as all the streams and creeks before them, flowing downhill to moisten the land; from rain drop to ocean and back again.

The waters of this region were pulled downhill by gravity to cut a pathway through the landscape, a landscape covered by forest. It was a forest that stretched north, south, east and west for hundreds of miles. The flow of these streams, creeks and rivers would over time form hills and valleys covered with a vast variety of plants including a multitude of trees.

I had been born within the Sacred Circle of a mighty oak in a vast landscape covered with trees. I had embarked on a life long journey which would take me far, far away from my home.

I would travel through vast woodlands and stop to live on the Great Plains. I would journey into the desert and visit the Grand Canyon. I would bathe in the ocean and stand on the Great Divide. I would meet and live with many creatures. I would take risks and do foolish things. I would love others and be loved in return. I would discover nobility and find courage. I would learn many lessons and have great teachers. My greatest teacher would be Nature and all she possesses.

Survival

I had been out beyond the Sacred Circle for several weeks before I ran into trouble. The first week was easy I had packed plenty to eat for my journey. I thought I would see the world in a week and be back home before my food ran out. I was shocked when I ran out of food and had not traveled very far in a forest that seemed to go on forever. Fourteen days came and went and I realized I would not see home again for a very long time. I was committed to my journey and had learned enough to survive. My food supply had long been eaten and I learned to live off meager rations.

My *haversack* was empty of food; handed down from father to son for generations. I would keep it safe and by my side always. Like my soul it carried the story of my family. The haversack, the journal and the eagle feather I found on the forest floor were now my greatest possessions.

I began to search for food. I found scraps from others and without much of an effort caught a few crawdads and small fish. I found that if I stayed perfectly still for long periods of time the fish and crawdads would come out of their hiding places and swim right into my hands. I soon discovered that I was not the only one wading in the creeks for food and the easy catch was getting harder and harder to find. I found I had competitors, and in that the struggle for life.

Water, food and shelter became the order of things and at times my single mission. I knew I must adapt to this order or

I would not survive. I stayed close to the water and followed the creeks downstream. At times I felt like something was watching me. I cannot explain exactly why I had this feeling but it was there. There were no new sounds in the forest and no new scents in the air. I would place my nose into the wind and tilt my head left, then right; nothing new. But every once in a while it would grow eerily silent in the forest and I knew; *"something was watching me."*

My father and mother had warned me of the dangers in the forest beyond the Sacred Circle. I had heard the howl of a strange creature and camped in the trees for protection. The howl was always far off in the distance and late at night. This was something else, dark and sinister. *"Close and from the shadows something was watching me!"*

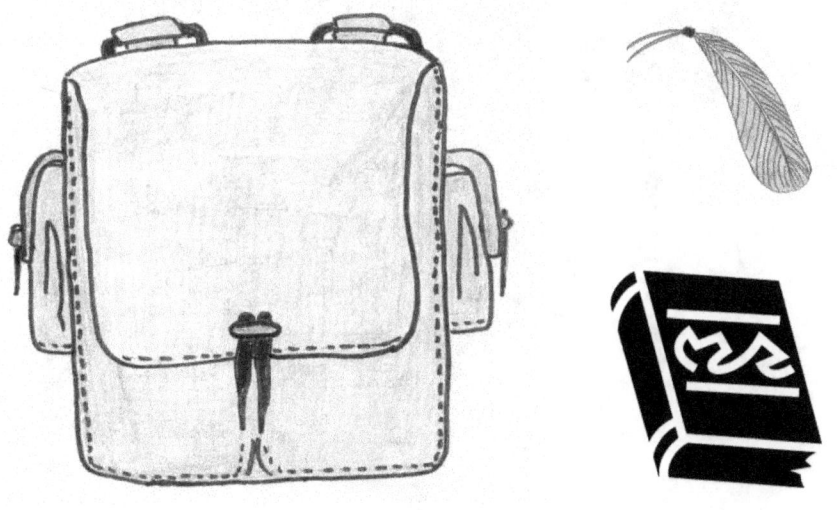

JOIN MARCUS ON THIS METAPHYSICAL JOURNEY ACROSS SPACE AND TIME.

WE ARE WATCHING YOU,
WATCHING YOU!

YOU WILL BE TESTED, TESTED,
TESTED!

The Trek South (The Frog and Turtle)

Marcus took out his journal and started taking notes. "One stream flows into another, all flowing toward lower ground, they must lead somewhere."

I traveled down the Allegany Plateau to what appeared to be the start of a river. There were many small brooks and creeks merging together, each larger than the previous one. The creeks and streams spilled over the plateau forming a gorge. The streams flowed into one another growing wider and deeper until a small river poured out from the gorge.

I entered the gorge and was awed by its beauty. After exploring the surrounding cliffs and forest I got back on the trail along the river; again heading southwest. I had been on the south side of the Allegany River for a few days finding nothing to eat. The trail was worn and well-traveled; so well-traveled that the path cut a groove into the soil and bedrock below. The gorge and the forest around it had been depleted of its food. I would have to move quickly and find something to eat if I was going to survive.

I would have to be extremely careful and travel only at night. The signs of black bears, wildcats and eagles were everywhere. They too were desperate for something to eat and to feed their young. Their scents were strong and fearfully close. I spent most of my days up in the higher branches of the trees until darkness provided the cover I needed to move down trail. I was falling behind schedule; I would have to make up some ground and scavenge for food on the move.

The high branches of the tall trees did not always guarantee safety. I could snooze but I had to be mindful to keep my eyes and ears open for danger whether coming from the ground below or the skies above. Eagles could snatch you from your perch without making a sound; just food for thought.

I dozed off for a minute waking to a repetition of clicking sounds moving around the tree coming toward me; click, click, click… a large armored worm with hundreds of legs stopped in his tracks and looked me in the eyes. In words you could see but not hear, in the language of the wild ones he said: *"My name is **Crawler**. I have a hundred legs and officially they call me a centipede. I guess with that haversack you're a traveler; a seeker of the truth, one who loves the quest for knowledge."*

Crawler: *"You must visit the past before you can embrace or see the future; **"legend-myth, myth-legend, legend-myth, myth-legend,"** always seeking the truth. You must dabble in fantasy before facing reality. Things are not always what they seem; before the physical there was the supernatural; the metaphysical. Before there was science there was superstition. **Before there was recorded history there were myths and** legends."*

Crawler: *"Be careful of the friends you make and those you trust. Appearances can be deceiving. Put your faith in what you know to be true and question everything else."*

Making a steady clicking noise the centipede continued down the tree. I grabbed my haversack and followed him but he quickly disappeared into the thick brush. My ears shot up, twitching, searching for any sound or scent that would give him away. He was gone. What did his riddle mean, myth-legend, legend-myth? Puzzled, I headed down river.

THE CRAWLERS

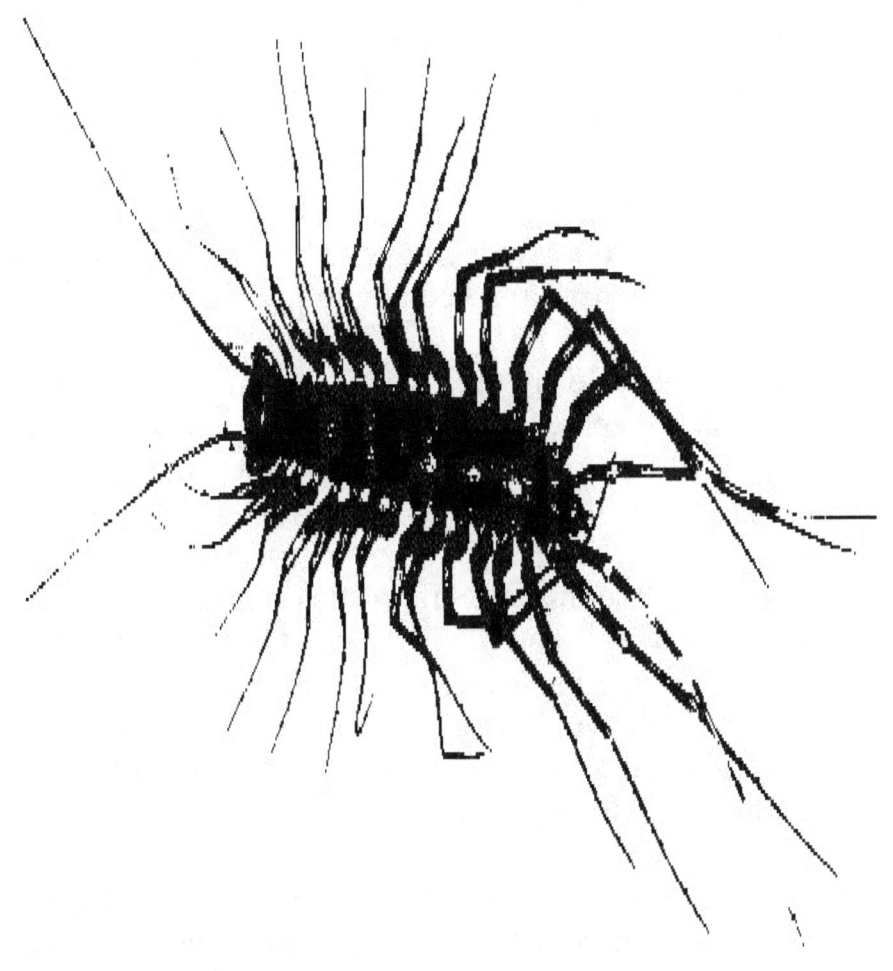

*THEY CAN SEE THE PAST AND
FUTURE BUT CANNOT SEE
THE PRESENT*

I came upon some shallows that stretched across the river to the other side. At these shallows the river's water rapidly washed around a string of boulders creating white caps and ripples. Like stepping stones the exposed boulders offered a safe crossing. What should I do; face certain hunger or cross the river and try to even the odds?

I decided to cross expecting to find another run of shallows on the north side of the river. I believed I could cross back over somewhere downstream, keeping to my plan.

Once on the north side of the river I was more successful with the smaller creeks, catching plenty of crawdads and minnows. I ate myself silly, climbed a tall tree, found a wide smooth branch and instantly fell asleep.

I was certain there would be a safe place down river where I could cross back over. I had plenty to eat, trees to rest in and I was steadily moving southwest on the more giving side of the river, seemingly void of predators. With less and less danger lurking about I became embolden spending more and more time traveling during the daylight.

One mile led to two, two to three and before I knew it I had covered over one hundred miles with the river growing faster, deeper and wider; no crossing this river today, too far to turn back now, just maybe tomorrow my luck will change.

I was scared back to my senses when I found myself trapped on the north side of the river. I could only accept my "self-imposed" dilemma and moved forward hoping in vain that there had to be another crossing somewhere down river.

I finally came to a point of land that made it all too clear. Where the trail opened to its widest view, in the distance I could barely see the forest to the southwest. At this juncture another river joined the Allegany from the north and I finally realized the trouble I was in. What started as a small creek in a limestone gorge now was a raging river I had no hope of crossing.

I had traveled a few hundred miles on the wrong side of the river meaning going back to the shallows would take weeks. There was no turning back. The fast flowing river pouring into the Allegany was as wide if not wider than the Allegany itself. The final blow to my well thought out plan was if I decided now to follow this trail I would be headed due north, not southwest; north to the great unknown.

Again at a small creek I found plenty to eat. It had been a long night and mostly a sleepless day. As routine, I scouted out one of the taller trees and found a branch where I could get some sleep. Reviewing my dilemma, facing a fork in the rivers, what should I do; should I immediately head back up the Allegany, or gamble again and follow the trail leading due north up the new river? Either way I was exhausted and quickly fell asleep. As I began to drift off the crickets and frogs blasted the night with noise. It sounded like they were intent on keeping me awake. The frogs and crickets were competing with each other for air space and they filled that space with nerve racking sounds.

I slept through most of the night waking to a symphony of sounds and finally the music of Nature broke through the noise of a few. Although still night in the distance dawn was breaking and my eyes picked up two dimly lit lights flashing off and on at the base of my tree. It was still too dark to make it out. So I waited.

Blinking On-Off (Odysseus)

Off-on, off-on, left-right, left-right, one-eye-opened, one-eye-closed, one-eye-opened, one-eye-closed; there was something under the arch of a root with flashing eyes. One-eye-opened, one-eye-closed, one-eye-opened, one-eye-closed; the flashing of the bullfrog's red and yellow eyes pulled me into a hypnotic rhythm and I waited for his voice, the scripted language of Nature, words you can see but cannot hear. This is the voice Nature that the humans may never see or hear.

Knowing that others were watching, the frog dragged himself from under the root. It was pitiful watching the crippled frog crawling on the ground. Dragging his broken legs behind him he sadly looked up at me. In rhythm, one-eye-closed, the other eye-opened, he said: *"My name is **Odysseus** I am from the land of Ithaca. I have been traveling ten years and given up all hope of ever reaching home."*

Odysseus: *"I once was a Greek soldier and fought alongside **Achilles** and **Ajax** against the city of Troy. Together we fought two of Troy's greatest warriors; **Hector** and **Paris**. The city of Troy was protected by a massive wall and a fierce army that had never been defeated. We, Greeks were just too proud to admit that we had finally met our match.*

On my voyage home from this meaningless war I was shipwrecked and seriously injured. I have been pulling my useless legs behind me trying to get home. My wife and son have been waiting for me all these years."

When the toad blinked again a tear rolled down his face. *"My name is Marcus. What do they call this river?"*

Odysseus: *"The natives of this forest call it the Monongahela which in their language means; the River of Sticks. At times the river floods and the water level gets so high it kills many of the trees. Over the years these trees die leaving their bare branches (bones) sticking out of the water. At night these dead trees give the banks of the river an evil look, as if the ghosts of the dead are watching you; moving toward you in motion with the flow of the river and moonlight."*

I continued: *"Does this river have a shallow where I can cross up ahead?"*

Odysseus: *"Not that I know of, but on the trail at a fork in the road I ran into some travelers who said there was a ferry crossing upriver. There are no passable trails along the edge of the river. From here running forty miles north it is too steep and covered with thick foliage and underbrush. It would be impossible to make it to the ferry crossing on foot. The trail north leads inland east, before it starts to break west. We would have to follow a few rough trails gradually turning west back to the river upstream. We will need to find the boatman to guide the ferry across the river. We have to know his story and pay his fee before he takes us across."*

I continued: *"You mean you would travel with me? It would take us forever. With you having to crawl all the way we would barely cover a mile a day. I have been traveling alone for a long time. I would love to travel with you, but with your legs being severely broken like they are we would never make it to the ferryboat."*

The Travois

Odysseus: *"You could build a travois and easily pull me along the trail. I know the best creeks and streams and given my seamanship I am a pretty good navigator, especially on trails like this one with multiple forks. If you are not careful, you could find your hungry and tired ass going in circles without end; circles within circles, into oblivion. If you always turn left you must come back to where you started. If you always turn right you are lost on the same trail. "*

Marcus: *"What is a travois?"*

Odysseus: *"The natives of this region are nomadic and frequently move their villages from one area to another. They do this to be in rhythm with Nature's food cycle; the seasons of the year when certain plants and animals are more abundant. These natives created a triangular frame from young trees, weaving the smaller thinner branches to form a tightly woven pocket to hold their belongings. With my guidance we could easily build a travois."*

Odysseus directed Marcus in the building of the travois. Marcus secured the help of two beavers to cut down the tree branches needed to build the frame. Odysseus worked on the pocket that would be attached to the travois. Odysseus used his strong hands to tightly weave the thin limbs and flexible bark holding the pocket firmly together. The soft pocket was suspended in the center of the travois by flexible plant stems absorbing the bumps making for a near perfect ride; a ride fit for a king.

Two main posts were joined together to fit around Marcus's neck. These two posts formed the upper collar while the third post was used at the base to spread the two outer posts apart to form a triangle. Balanced by the two main posts the weight was evenly distributed on each of Marcus's shoulders. The weight of the travois was then transferred equally to the two main points of the posts. When level with the ground the travois was easy to pull. Cutting grooves in the trail the two sharpened points at the end of the posts minimized the drag. With all of their gear loaded, including Odysseus, Marcus was surprised how easy it was to pull the travois down the trail.

Marcus noticed that the small creatures that helped build the travois seemed joyful, chattering and giggling as they worked. A joke being played on the unsuspected seemed to float through the air. The struggle to survive in Nature is nonnegotiable. The union between species in the wild is rare.

It was a joy to work together; freeing ourselves for the moment from the competition and violence of raw survival. *Survival of the fittest,* took a back seat to advance a noble cause; greed and selfishness were placed on hold. A crippled old sad toad with no promise of ever returning home, offering to guide a lost raccoon through the wilderness, and a family of wildlife with their many skills and talents eager to help the two strangers along. The *prophet* would be proud.

There was a good chance had Marcus and Odysseus not worked together and gained the help of their wild brothers and sisters they would have perished somewhere along the trail. They both benefited from this union. They joined together to make the impossible-possible.

Marcus and Odysseus with the help of their new friends quickly built the travois and fashioned a harness from fiber stripped from the bark of young tree branches. With the harness completed they were ready to move out. Around Marcus's neck and resting on his shoulders the harness was a perfect fit. Once loaded they said their goodbyes and headed down the trail. Marcus merrily pulled all of their gear and his new trusted friend. The little wild ones rejoiced with glee.

They initially traveled east away from the River Styx. Once Marcus was under Odysseus' spell, Odysseus began to work him; Off-on, on-off, left-right, right-left, one-eye-opened, then one-eye-closed; hypnotic, hypnotized, spell bound, entranced; his mind no longer his. A pale gray haze captured and clouded Marcus' mind; a slave to repetition, monotony, mile after mile.

After several hours on the trail, looking over his shoulder, Marcus said to Odysseus: *"Let's take a break. I bet we have covered over five miles this morning."*

One-eye-opened, one-eye-closed, Odysseus to Marcus: *"Let's make it to the first fork in the road; it's only a little ways further."*

Now under Odysseus' complete control; Marcus responds: *"Anything you say boss."*

It was pushing dark when they finally came upon the first fork in the road. Marcus was exhausted.

Marcus: *"I am exhausted. We must have covered thirty miles today. There is no way I can pull you and all of our belongings that far again tomorrow."*

Appealing to Marcus' vanity; blinking one-eye-opened one-eye-closed, Odysseus: *"Marcus you're so strong and determined. You made great time today. I bet you can do it again. I know you can do it. I believe in you. I have faith that you can max out at forty miles tomorrow if you try. By the way we just crossed a creek, can you run back to that stream and fetch us some water? Oh, while you're at it, catch us some crawdads and fish. I am hungry."*

One-eye-opened, one-eye closed; Marcus skipped down the trail headed back to the stream.

First Night on the Trail: (Story Telling)
Odysseus: *"Marcus what is your story? Why are you way out here on your own? Where are you headed? Where did you come from?"*

Marcus: *"I am a great explorer and I am dedicated to learn as much about our planet as I can. I keep a daily log of my discoveries and adventures in a journal that I carefully store in my haversack. I have chosen to travel alone to minimize logistics and conflicts. I am headed west and may be the first creature to traverse the Earth. I was born in the Alleghany forest."*

Marcus, changing the subject: *"Do you really believe the world is round?"*

After joy riding all day Odysseus was full of energy. They made camp and settled in for the night. Full of excitement that he was finally headed north, Odysseus began to tell the story of Troy. Marcus could barely keep his eyes open.

Odysseus: *"Yes. We started our voyage to destroy the city of Troy and headed east toward Persia. After the war we headed west for home. Keeping a westerly course a violent*

55

storm blew our ships passed the Pillars of Hercules. One storm followed the other and before we could adjust our sails we had traveled thousands of miles out into the northern ocean. One ship after another went down. Near a coast covered by forests stretching as far as one could see our ship finally ran aground and was smashed against the rocks. I was the only survivor. I woke up on a rocky shore with two broken legs."

The Trojan War

Odysseus began his tale. He said it took him several months to heal. He was befriended by a centipede who nursed him back to health. The centipede affirmed that the world was round and that he could communicate with other centipedes and a few spiders around the world. Those with this ability were known as **seers** and could see into the future. Like other centipedes, **One Hundred Legs** was a **seer** and a **healer**. His compassion for others had no boundaries.

Odysseus thanked the centipede for his kindness and help and started his trek around the world. Odysseus crawled inland from the coast with only the memory of his family and home driving him forward. Now that he knew that the world was round, if he headed west toward the setting sun, he would find his way home.

Odysseus claimed he fought in the **Trojan War** alongside of **Achilles** and **Ajax** the greatest Greek warriors of all time. The Greeks amassed a fleet of a thousand ships to fight against the Trojans. **Hector** and **Paris** princes of Troy, assembled a large army to protect their city. Thousands died over the foolish love between Paris and **Helen**. Helen was the most beautiful toad ever. Her perfectly aligned lumps and slimy wet texture drove her husband and his army crazy.

Helen hopped after Paris, the King hopped after Helen and his army hopped after their King. The army became delirious, and followed their king across the great Mediterranean Sea to Troy. Helen could not be resisted and like all males before them the soldiers made fools of themselves. She was the prize of their kingdom and everyone wanted to join her at the pond. They were eager to serve their king and win his beautiful queen back. The king's army was too small to defeat Troy by itself so Helen's husband, *Menelaus* joined forces with his brother, *Agamemnon*. Thousands of toads left their homes to serve in this righteous cause never to return again.

Sometime in the telling of Odysseus' story Marcus began to snore. Initially Odysseus didn't notice and was finishing his story when Marcus ran out of air and snored so loud he woke himself up. Looking into the dark Marcus and Odysseus heard a disturbing scream, like a crazed wounded animal. Both were scared and pulled closer to each other. After a long silence and in rhythm, there came a; *knock-knock ------ knock-knock-knock,* from the forest - then again; *knock-knock ------ knock-knock-knock.* Something was out there. Something was watching, threatening them. The forest went silent. They were unnerved by this strange knocking. It took them hours to fall back to sleep.

Second Night on the Trail

With a sparkle in one eye and dirt in the other, Odysseus woke up barking orders to Marcus. One-eye-opened, one-eye-closed: *"We did not cover a lot of ground yesterday. We should do better today."*

Marcus: *"Did the Greeks win Helen back? What happened to Achilles, Ajax, Paris and Hector? What about those strange noises we heard last night from the forest?"*

One-eye-opened, one-eye-closed, Odysseus: *"Could you fetch me some fresh drinking water from the creek? Are there any leftover crawdads? Could you fold my blanket...?* Eager for the story *Marcus, the puppet, jumped to the tasks.*

Odysseus: *"We won the war. Achilles killed Hector, tied him to the back of his chariot and dragged his torn body around and around the city of Troy for everyone to see. In another battle, Ajax put up a courageous fight but in the end was overwhelmed by the Trojans. Brought down like Hector; Ajax was cut to pieces."*

Odysseus: *"We had suffered the loss of many warriors. I convinced King Agamemnon that there was no way we were going to breach the walls of Troy. Many armies tried and failed. I laid out a plan for King Agamemnon to trick the Trojans into believing they had defeated us. We would leave them a gift too self-gratifying to pass up."*

The Greeks would build a wooden horse to honor the Trojans warriors and pretend that they had abandoned the war and sailed away. A small number of us would hide inside the horse. The Trojans believing this rouge pulled the wooden horse into the city of Troy to celebrate their victory. Too many Trojans had too much to eat and drink and let their guard down. Climbing out of the wooden horse I led the attack on the guards to take command of the gates. Once inside the City of Troy the gates were opened and we easily defeated the Trojans."

THE TROJAN HORSE

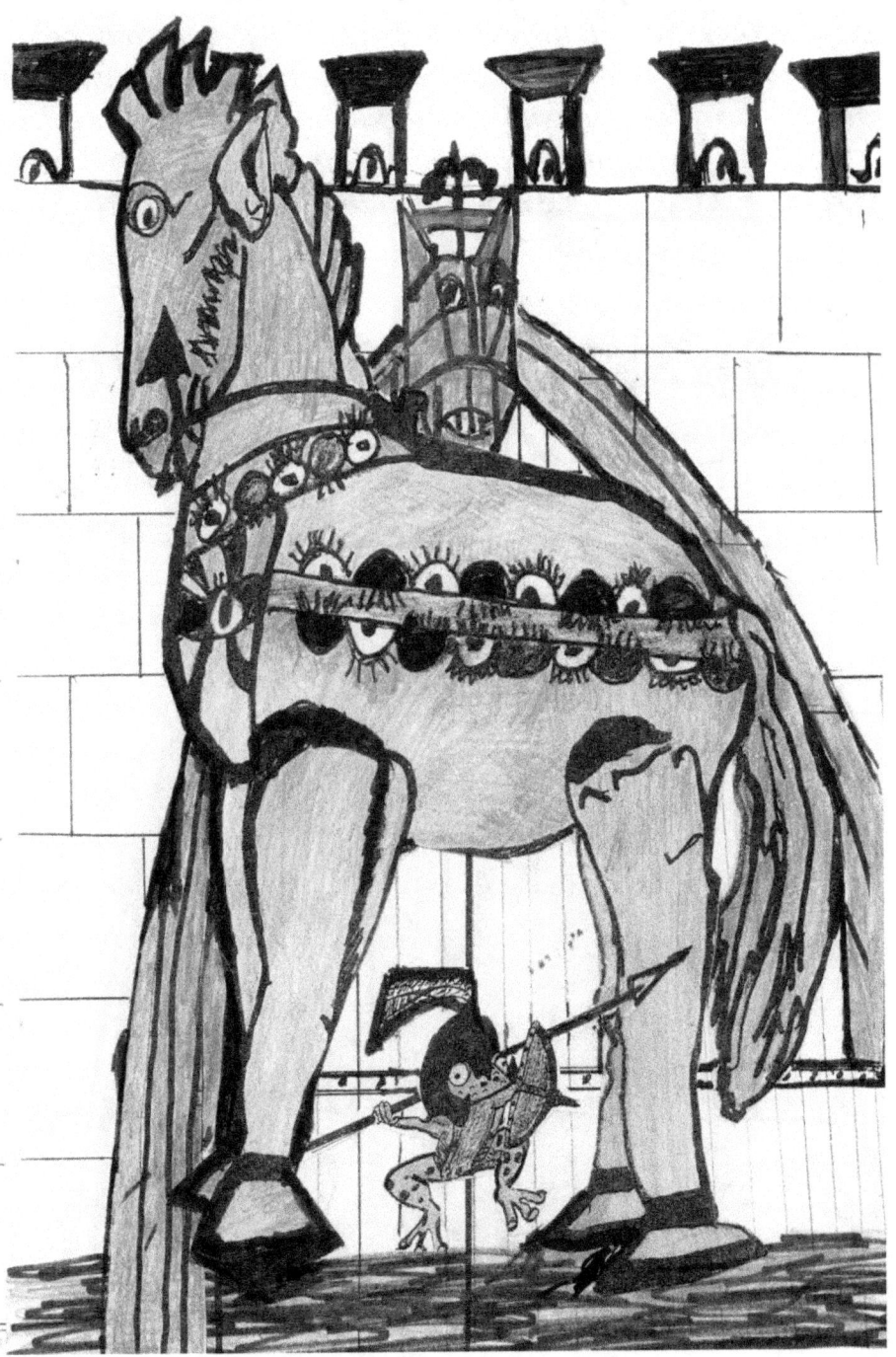

Odysseus: Paris drove an arrow through the back heel of Achilles' foot, crippling Achilles. Paris then drove several more arrows into Achilles' chest. Achilles bled out before collapsing to the ground. Once the Greeks were inside the walls of Troy they easily defeated the Trojans. Paris and Helen were separated during the battle and were never heard from again. Some say Helen dumped Paris and ran off with a pack of horny toads."

ODYSSEUS THE WARRIOR

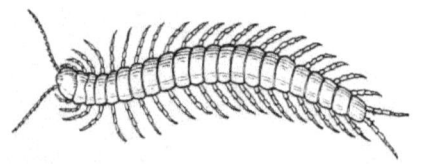

Marcus: *"And what about those strange sounds from the forest?"*

Odysseus: *"Remember the deserted village we passed through yesterday; and the rancid nasty tasting water you and I drank from that well. We got so sick we crapped ourselves raw and vomited all over the place. That well was intentionally poisoned. Last night we just imagined the weird screams and knocking sounds. My ass still burns; and my head is still spinning! We have to be careful about the water we drink. That old centipede warned us not to drink from that well; something about bending time and space, three wicked brothers from the badlands, college students protesting a war,* **LSD 'and the pill you took today.'** *The old crawler said in the future the humans will finally achieve peace by chemically programming each individual to serve their masters. With the exception of one frigid landmass at the bottom of this planet, six kingdoms will rule the Earth. With no sense of being the minions will be mindless (void of thought) and yield to every whim and desire of their masters. The* **lab humans** *from this point in time will be cloned."*

With the gear packed away and Odysseus firmly fixed on the travois, Marcus placed the harness over his now aching shoulders and down the trail they went.

Odysseus: *"Here's the first fork in the road. We should be headed roughly due north. The next fork should turn us northwest and if we are real lucky by the third turn we should be headed due west certain to reach the River Styx and the boatman. Depending on the pace you set and keep we should be there in two days."* One-eye-opened, one-eye-closed, left-right, right-left; in a trance Marcus continued on.

Third Night on the Trail

They had traveled until late afternoon when they reached the second fork. Confirmed by the position of the sun they were defiantly headed northwest.

"The moon is full tonight let's keep going;" insisted Odysseus. His eyes blinked, Off-on, On-off, Open-close, Close-open.

Like the walking dead Marcus struggled on. The dawn dimly illuminated the eastern sky still full of stars when Marcus gave out. Like it or not Odysseus made camp and snuggled next to Marcus to keep warm. In his dreams Marcus chased his brother Brutus through the old oak tree, the Sacred Circle that protected them.

A pitiful howl from the future woke Odysseus from his nightmare. With flashing canine teeth snapping at Odysseus' face, a wild dog trying to protect Marcus invaded Odysseus' dreams. The creature from the future would protect Marcus with his life from those that would do Marcus harm. Odysseus burrowed deeper into Marcus' warm coat to escape the nightmare and the small wolf determined to protect his dear friend Marcus.

Back on the trail with both eyes wide open, Odysseus to Marcus: *"Marcus let's take it easy today. We covered a lot of ground yesterday and last night. One more fork and we will be within striking distance. Marcus, can I fetch you some water, something to eat?"*

They just passed the third fork in the road when Odysseus called to Marcus to stop and make camp for the night. Brain washed, Marcus: *"There's plenty of daylight ahead of us, let's keep moving;* one-eye-opened, one-eye-closed, left-right, right-left...

The Story of Rex:

Odysseus had his way and after traveling several more miles they set up campsite for the night. Marcus gathered wood for the fire pit, unloaded the travois and started scrounging for food; tonight it will be grubs and snails. Odysseus seemed eager to tell Marcus the story of **Oedipus Rex** and how Rex became the boatman who ferries *"travelers"* across the River Styx; myth-legend, legend-myth, one-eye-opened, one-eye-closed; where does the truth hide/Hyde?"

Odysseus: *"Oedipus Rex was a young shepherd who was raised by his parents just below a mountain ridge running southwest along the Monongahela River. The mountain sides were covered with broken rocks and gigantic boulders, one on top of the other. Over time these natural pockets were filled with rich soil and covered with grass becoming a perfect feeding ground for wild sheep and goats."*

Odysseus: *"Oedipus Rex was a robust and perfectly formed river turtle protected by a beautiful coat of armor. Black patterns outlining golden pentagons illuminated his presence. If threatened Rex could use the brightness of his shield to blind his enemies. In this mountain country his strength was unmatched. The few who dared to challenge him found themselves on their backs pinned to the ground. In jest his good nature would not allow Rex to hurt others and with a smirk and a wink he would declare defeat."*

Odysseus: *Over the years his long ventures into the mountains added to his endurance and strength."*

Odysseus: *"When just a toddler Rex knew he was different from his parents and older siblings. One day Oedipus asked his mother and father why he was so different from them. He*

63

said although he had a beak it was much smaller than theirs. He went on to describe the other features that set them apart. He continued that he did not have feathers or wings; he had four feet, a hard shell and could not fly."

Odysseus: "*Being thoughtful and reflective parents they told Rex his story. At one of the highest points on the mountain range his father while checking on their herd spotted what appeared to be a stone of gold. In rhythm with the clouds this stone caught the glare of the sun light and flashed beams of light back into the sky. His father to be, swooped down to see what could possibly cast such beautiful beams of light.*"

Odysseus: "*To his joy, father had found a beautiful turtle abandoned on a cold and isolated mountain. The baby turtle's legs had been purposely tied together and it was clear he was left on the mountain top to die.*"

Rex: "*Do you think my **real parents** left me to die?*"

Father and Mother: "*No we would never abandon our baby. You belong to us and from the moment we saw you, you were our child. **We are your real parents. Those that care, provide and protect you are your real parents.** Those that leave their babies are pretenders and will be condemned to the **Frozen Lake** forever. They will cross the River Styx and Never Return. Their misdeeds and pictures will be posted in the heavens and their names recited over and over again in prayer.*"

Odysseus: "*Rex had been raised by his adoptive parents to be courteous and respectful toward others. His parents being golden eagles marveled at his endurance and ability to watch over and protect their sheep and goats. For weeks on*

64

end in quiet solitude Oedipus would glory over the beauty of Nature and stand guard over his family's herd."

Odysseus: *"His watchful eyes seldom missed a movement. Rex was determined to face any threat and if necessary position his armor into the sun to blind his enemies. He mastered the art of throwing stones. He discovered that flint stone could be fashioned into sharp circular projectiles. Its weight and rounded edge made it deadly accurate. When still a boy he became the family's hunter of small game; at thirty yards he could take down a rabbit, even a small bird."*

While Odysseus continued to tell Oedipus' story, Marcus began to doze off to sleep, waking every few minutes to catch bits and pieces of the legend of Oedipus Rex.

Odysseus: *"As Rex grew older his father began to encourage Rex to return to his place of birth and become familiar with the natural habitat where he was born; the River Styx. Several weeks went by when Rex approached his father."*

Rex: *"Father I love these mountains and our family. I have tormented over your guidance to return to the River Styx and reclaim my rightful place in Nature. I understand the wisdom of your words and now know what I must do."*

Odysseus: *"His father replied; it is the natural order of things. From unique settings we have evolved and within those settings we thrive. You are my son and are always welcome here. Our love for you is eternal. From the skies we will watch over you."*

Odysseus: *"Rex gathered his belongings, his staff, sling and pouch of throwing stones, kissed his mother and father*

65

goodbye and headed down the mountain. It took several days before Rex reached the Road Royal that connected the North and South Kingdoms."

King Philip

Odysseus: *"**King Philip** was returning from the Northern Kingdom forcing all those traveling upon the Road Royal to step aside and give his chariot passage. The obedient commoners yielded to their king and walked in the muddy ditches on both sides of the road. The poor travelers would curse under their breaths and bear the weight of their heavy bundles and children to obey their vile and selfish king.*

Odysseus: *"Weeks earlier King Philip had traveled north to reaffirm his rule over the Northern Kingdom. There was bad blood between the two kingdoms with the noble estates owing their allegiance to King Philip over their rightful lord **King Harold**. Once Philip became king he sponsored an annual chariot race at King Harold's expense to reestablish his dominance over Harold's kingdom in the north."*

Prince Philip and Prince Donte

Odysseus: *"When Philip was a young prince he was known throughout his father's kingdom as a great charioteer. Being good friends at the time,* Phillip's father, ***King James,** agreed to allow Philip to train Harold's son. In good faith King Harold entrusted his only son, **Donte'** to Prince Philip's care and training in the art of racing chariots."*

As Odysseus continued Marcus fell to sleep, only to move about occasionally, convincing Odysseus he was still listening. Marcus drifted into the dream world and joined Odysseus' story in his sleep.....

Odysseus: *"Philip's and Donte's beautiful chariots were pulled forward by two powerful dragonflies the size of coyotes. Donte was an excellent student and soon rivaled Philip's mastery over the chariot. Donte's team of emerald dragonflies was more challenging to handle, but Donte's chariot was newly built and one of the fastest chariots in the kingdom. Donte quickly gained mastery over his dragonflies and turned their wildness into speed."*

Odysseus: *"Prince Philip was jealous of his student's new and beautiful chariot. Donte quickly gained control over his dragonflies and with the new chariot had the edge. Philip was afraid that the youth he schooled just might defeat him on the race track; bringing dishonor to Philip's family."*

Odysseus: *"Donte was determined to win back his father's honor. Philip would be humiliated if defeated by anyone especially by the son of Harold. Vain and arrogant, Philip had to win the tournament. The tournament had been ongoing since spring with the best of the charioteers eliminating each other. The day set for the final tournament was announced. Before the first leaf fell the ultimate match between the two best charioteers would take place at King*

Harold's palace. Philip and Donte steadily advanced toward the championship, becoming the finalists in the tournament."

Donte would prove himself worthy of the title Charioteer; a titled earned, then wrongly stolen. Unlike his father King James, who ruled with generosity and kindness, Phillip projected the image of a depraved and hedonistic tyrant.

Odysseus: *"Determined not be defeated, the night before the race, Prince Philip slipped into the race track after dark. At the far turn of the track he dug a shallow pit close to the inner wall covering the pit with loose soil and rock. Only if Donte was in the lead would Philip attempt to drive Donte's chariot toward the pit. Once in the pit Donte's chariot would be pulled off the track into the inner wall."*

Odysseus: *"The palace and stables were at the other end of the track across from the finish line where King Harold, his Queen and guests would watch the race. The commoners and peasants would view the race from the back of the track; across from where Philip dug the pit."*

Odysseus: *"Philip was unaware that the stable keeper's daughter saw him as he left the race track that night. She noticed that Philip's trousers and leggings were covered with dirt. Believing Philip was seeing to his jet black dragonflies and his chariot, at the time the keeper's daughter did not question Philip's visit."*

The race drew crowds of spectators from near and far to witness this event. The great lords and nobles took their places with King James, King Harold and their wives at the center; having the best view of the track.

A great feast had been served and then the race was on. Donte and Philip were at their marks. They would run three laps. The bugles played and they were off.

With little control over his emerald dragonflies Donte fell behind and Philip easily took the first lap. Once contained Donte's stallions caught up with Philip's sweaty nags and pulled ahead. The second lap was Donte's. The crowd cheered and laughed at Philip who was falling behind.

Enraged Philip fiercely whipped his dragonflies forward. Fearing defeat Philip closed the gap and moved to clip Donte's right wheel. Donte attempting to pull away from Philip's chariot catches the rut. Donta's left wheel digs in, hits the outer edge of the pit causing the chariot to flip over and break into pieces. Holding tightly on to the reigns Donte is pulled forward in front of the chariot. The chariot breaks away from its harness and crashes into the wall. Donte is dragged under the chariot and crushed to death.

The crowd screamed out in horror. Donte's right shoulder and arm had been ripped from his body. His face and head was crushed flat. Donte bled out in seconds soaking the ground around his body.

The people held their breaths as the royal family made it to the site. Seeing the rut in the track King Harold immediately had the stable and track keeper brought forward and publically executed.

Vain Glory

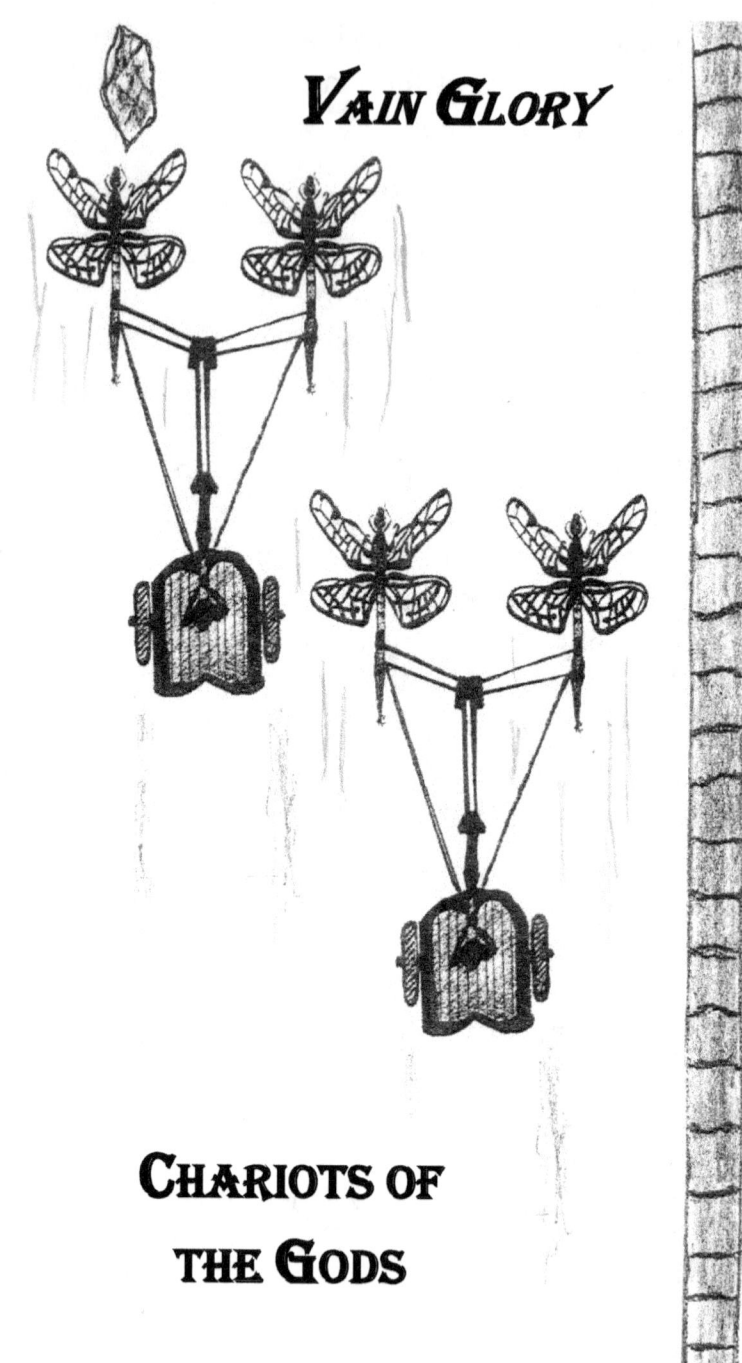

Chariots of
the Gods

Wrongfully Accused and Executed

King Harold to the Keeper: *"Your neglect of this track killed my son. Your entrails and gutted body will hang at the front gate and your head will be posted at the entrance to the palace; food for the ravens."*

The Sable Keeper: *"My honor and my duty have never failed you my King. I have served you faithfully without complaint. These sacred grounds were placed in my care. No matter what ultimately caused this blemish upon this kingdom it was my duty to check and sanction the track. I believed I did my duty and cannot account for the rut. In that I failed and willfully embrace your judgement."*

The Keeper's arms and legs were tied to four dragonflies and his head to the post marking the finish line. In cold silence King Harold signaled the dragons. In an instant the Keeper was torn apart; sent to the Frozen Lake for a crime he did not commit.

After the execution of the stable keeper, King James immediately returned to the Southern Kingdom. Sadden by Harold's lost King James dressed in dark purple to dignify Dante's royal status and the loss of Harold's son. With his son laid out for burial and the royal black flags raised, the people moved forward to express their sorrow and bid King Harold and his Queen well.

With tearful eyes the keeper's daughter approached the King and quietly whispered: *"My lord you have executed the wrong man. I saw Prince Philip on the south end of the track last night. At the time I did not give it much thought. But after today, I know the truth. Hidden under the straw of his dragonflies' stall I found a small shovel and bag of gravel. I realized that moment it wasn't my father's neglect of the track that caused Donte's chariot to flip over. But instead my lord, it was Prince Philip's criminal actions that caused the death of your son. My father was always faithful in his service to you, his king."*

King Harold called two of his guards and sent them to Philip's stable to confirm the keeper's daughter's claim. The guards soon returned and reported that the claim was true.

Immediately King Harold called out: *"Everyone with the exception of Prince Philip clear this royal and hallowed hall. Darkness has fallen on our families and evil is with us."*

When the hall was clear, King Harold: *"I have grievously condemned an innocent man to death. What I am going to say you already know is true. You, not the Keeper killed my son! We found these items in your dragonflies' stable. Do you deny this?"*

Philip stood arrogant and with no regret retorted: *"So what, if you dare raise your hand against me or spread this story to bring dishonor to my family, my father will destroy your kingdom and kill thousands of your people."*

King Harold to Prince Philip: *"If you were more like your father, this veil and corrupt act would not have taken place. Your father's compassion for others is without measure. Even during times of war your father was always eager to listen and share the burden of compromise and bring peace back to our land. Out of love for your father we have too often covered for your lewd and rancid being. I will follow King James example and not let your foul behavior cause the suffering of so many."*

After a long pause, King Harold: *"No I will not bring war to my innocent people. But hear this: Your first born will rise up and take your life; you will be brought down by a single stone. Being ignorant of your actions, your family will innocently be corrupted and disgraced. The darkness from your son's eyes will be eternal. I curse you and your family. Because of this horrid deed your family will suffer much sorrow. The boatman will carry you across the River Styx. Frozen in ice; at the feet of Lucifer you will dine on your children's rotting souls."*

KING HAROLD'S REVENGE

THE GUARDIAN OF EVIL

King Phillip

Odysseus: *"Many years passed after the wrongful death of Donte. King Harold lived in pain and humiliation having to sponsor the chariot race year after year to honor King Philip's rule. King James had died and Harold had to withhold his anger as King Philip gloated and taunted him about Harold's curse. Philip would make fun of the old king as to the curse; 'that Philip's future family would pay a terrible price for the death of Harold's son, Donte."*

Taunting, Philip to Harold: *"Your curse has not reached me yet. I am the wealthiest and most powerful king in the land. Too much wind and not enough muscle in that big bag you carry; making fun of Harold's large belly and unwillingness to go to war."*

The Road Royal to Oblivion

Odysseus: *"After his day of glory King Philip headed home to the Southern Kingdom. Philip was dressed in his finest armor and carried Iberian weapons crafted by the most renowned blacksmiths of their time. Riding on a beautiful chariot, pulled by two emerald stallions Philip proudly trotted down the Road Royal back to his palace. Forcing many travelers off the road and into the mud he craved their submission. 'I am the Master of this road and all the kingdoms it touches. Those who dear stand in my way will be plowed under! To forward this point, King Philip would threaten; 'The fat of your little ones will grease the axles of my chariots."*

Odysseus: *"Phillip gloated over his wealth and power. Two of his most trusted warriors flanked their king as he basked in his dominion over his kingdom; driving his stallions forward with his wild subjects scrambling for the safety of the ditch."*

An Obstacle in the Road

Odysseus: *"Reining in his dragonflies the king pulled to a stop, stunned by the courage that stood in front of him. 'How dare you stop our King?' One of the warriors shouted as he charged out of the chariot intent on killing Rex."*

Odysseus: *"Rex, a shepherd raised by two golden eagles on a mountain top did not know that the man in front of him was King Philip; the ruler over all the lands in the eastern forest. Rex did not know that the man he dared to challenge was King Philip, his father."*

Odysseus: *"Philip's vain lust for glory led to the death of his student, Donte, the murdered son of King Harold. Harold's curse tied the fatal* **Gordian Knot** *that Philip's innocent family, including Oedipus, could never see. For Philip's evil misdeeds and lifelong vanity would destroy them: leaving an infant son on a mountain top to die, a son who would kill his own father and unknowingly marry his mother while his lustful sisters pursued their mother's young and handsome husband; tragically their brother, Oedipus."*

Odysseus: *"Rex fell in love with one of his sisters only later to discover the twisted circumstances surrounding his life. Even knowing this truth he could not temper his lust for his sister. Their love-lust tore at his mother's heart but they could not restrain themselves. Through no fault of his own Rex uncovered his tragic story. Philip's arrogance and pride had taken Rex (An innocent baby), up a jagged trail to a foot path with a vertical cliff on either side. A tragedy Oedipus Rex could not bear to see. He loved his mother and his only to discover this tragic truth."*

The Fatal Attack

Odysseus: *"The first warrior charged out of the King's chariot and threw his spear at Rex. Rex stepped aside and the spear passed doing no harm. In that instant a golden eagle took the first warrior to the ground, gouged out his eyes and ripped open his throat; the warrior's passage into oblivion well earned. The second warrior charged forward. Another golden eagle in three strokes sent this warrior on his way to the unknown. Rex stood his ground proud and bold; with the body and demeanor of a god."*

Rex was a simple shepherd and measured conflict in simple terms; Rex to the King: *"This is the people's road born from the heavens and time. No one, no matter their lofty title, can claim this road or any of Nature's holy ground as theirs. I am your equal. I love and will protect my friends and my family. I will respect those who respect me. I will stand against evil. I mean you no harm, please let me pass."*

Odysseus: *"He was the righteous son of two proud parents when wicked **fate** corrupted his journey. From the heavens his parents cried: 'Your future is yours. We will always be just out of sight; watching you. Your soul is pure yet fate has dealt you a tragic and sad end that we cannot bear to see."*

Crossing the trail leading down the mountain a centipede scripted these words to Oedipus. *"Today you will be confronted by an evil king. Having the sun to his back the king will believe he has the advantage. Rub dark clay under your eyes to lessen the glare of the sun. When the king attacks use your polished shield to blind him. Your honor and bravery will be tested, tested, tested....;*

Odysseus: *"With the sun to his back like a lion Philip charged Oedipus Rex. Reaching into his pouch Rex clutched his heaviest flint stone. Like a Greek warrior Rex took his stance to throw the stone. At the last moment he turned his shield into the sun blinding King Philip. Like a catapult Rex launched his missile."*

Odysseus: *"With only a stone, Rex brought Philip the mighty warrior king down. Perfectly placed through the helmet's visor the flat sharp piece of flint pierced Philip's skull killing him instantly. King Philip, face down crashed to the ground. The peasants and merchants cheered. 'You have killed the king and you must leave this land or lose your life! Come with us and we will help you get away."*

Odysseus: *"Oedipus Rex wanders for several years finally returning to the place of his birth. He takes a noble wife; the rest is a sad, sad story of unintentional incest and betrayal."*

A Dream within a Dream

Falling to sleep Marcus enters Odysseus' story: *"Seeing the ruin of his family Oedipus Rex is summoned before the city's elders. He is stripped of his crown and condemned to eternal darkness. He was summarily blinded. Oedipus is beaten with stocks of thorns and paraded around the city without rank; naked. He is to suffer this eternal darkness chained to the ferryboat that carries the lost souls of the world across the River Styx to account for their sins. All the evil and confused souls crossing the river will suffer a long and painful journey to the **Frozen Lake,** the center of Hell where their mortal bodies will live forever under the mighty wings of Hades. Locked forever in ice they will be forced to act out their sins over and over again from a place they can never escape."*

To the Elders, Rex: *"I cannot bear to see my horrid deeds. I killed my father, slept with my mother and lusted for my sister. Please give me darkness and condemn me to Hell. Let tears of puss flood my cheeks while swarms of flies infest and lick my hallowed (sacred) wounds; leaving their hungry children behind. As I cross the River Sticks let the ferry's rusty chains cut deep into my flesh; my sins forever etched in my soul."*

Odysseus: *"Found guilty, Oedipus was bound to a post where upon his eyes were gouged out with a rusty spoon. Then he was beaten with thorns until his flesh was gone. After many hours dragging the pole behind him Oedipus finally reached the ferryboat landing. With titanium hooks and chains he was shackled to the guideline that crossed the River Styx. His chain was then attached to the ferryboat with hordes of sinners waiting their turn to cross over. The strongest turtle in the land was condemned to ferry all the evil ones across the River Styx to Hell forever."*

Descent into Hell (The Hollow Ones)

Odysseus: *"As those condemned to Hell approached the river bank it drew dark and cold. Black and gray clouds poured out of the swirling storm filling the landscape with horror. Those on the ferryboat could see thousands upon thousands of blemished souls chasing after something in the distance; tormented by the storm that now consumed them. As those condemned to Hell fled the ferryboat they too suffered the raging storm. As the sinful minions ran up the river banks hornets the size of humming birds dove at them again and again inflicting deep and painful wounds."*

Odysseus: *"Fleeing from the hornets the hollow ones ran up the river bank and joined the chase for the flag without*

78

meaning; a flag without color or an emblem, a flag representing nothing, a flag that they would kill and die for."

Odysseus: *"The spirit warriors, those who cry the loudest for* **war**, *carry their empty banners into the cold darkness that surrounds them. The cries and screams of the lost souls echoed through the forest of charred and dead trees, frozen in time and space they hopelessly run in circles. They are destined for the Frozen Lake where one evil doer eats the remaining flesh of another before puking up their victim's remains to devour his/her soul again and again. Oedipus was condemned by a twist in fate for eternity to carry the evil ones across this river. Under this dark and vicious cloud the boatman labors to deliver his cargo."*

THE HOLLOW ONES

THE SPIRIT WARRIORS

Day Four

Marcus fell asleep but continued to fade in and out absorbing some of the remaining story of Oedipus Rex. Odysseus started to mumble and soon fell to sleep himself.

When Marcus and Odysseus finally woke up they found themselves at the last fork in the road, the one headed due west to the Monongahela. Marcus packed away their gear and gently placed Odysseus on top. After a short hike they stopped at the base of a very steep and rough looking trail. The sign pointing up the trail read, **Misery Mountain**; better known by the locals as **The Iron Man** or more simply, **Mt. MFer**…. the trail narrowed at times and at these narrows the trail was covered with broken bits of sharp rock.

One-eye-opened, one-eye-closed, one-eye-closed, without thinking; Odysseus: *"We are almost home! Let's stop, take a breather and then get going. One little hill to climb. This will be a piece of cake. Marcus, you can do it!!!!"*

Still under Odysseus' spell, Marcus headed straight up the mountain. After several grueling hours with hardly any skin left on his feet, Marcus pulled the travois loaded with gear and Odysseus to the crest of Misery Mountain. In the distance there she was, the great Monongahela. One-eye-opened, one-eye-close; Odysseus: *"It's all downhill from here. Let's get going!"*

The Monongahela (The River Styx)

When Odysseus and Marcus approached the ferryboat Odysseus hopped off the travois and headed straight toward the river. Dragging the travois and all their gear Odysseus knew that Marcus could not follow him; Odysseus leaped from the travois and made a dash for the Monongahela.

Marcus was perplexed, puzzled, confused, baffled, dumbfounded... as to seeing Odysseus hopping down the trail to the river. Marcus cries out: *"You're going to hurt yourself and break your legs again!"*

As he hopped away, Odysseus: *"I was just pulling your legs, get it, legs; ha, ha, ha..."*

Odysseus said: *"The **Odyssey** and **Oedipus Rex** were just stories a vagabond told us while on the trail. We call him **Homey. Homey told us many stories to confuse myths and legends with the truth.** He said that those in power wanted us to stay ignorant of our true origins; so they made up hundreds of stories to distort the past."*

Odysseus: *"I am not really a warrior. I wouldn't hurt a fly unless he got within range of my tongue. I have to get to our breeding pond to join in on the orgy. I just need to make sure that the next generation gains a pool of genes from me; genes that they can rely on getting them through some tough times in the future. Unless you are a famous painter like **Picasso**; if you don't mate you have nothing to leave behind to confirm you ever existed. In Nature, trickery works. Nature has her toys. The problem is she plays for keeps."*

Odysseus: *"When have you ever heard or seen a dragonfly the size of a coyote. And the closest thing we have to a chariot is a travois and what in Hades is a wheel? Just eat a few wild berries left over from the future and who knows what to believe in."*

Odysseus: *"You'll see when you get to the ferry I was just pulling your tail. My name is really not Odysseus and I never took part in the Trojan War. They call me* **Ody** *and I live but a few creeks up river from the crossing. The boatman's name is really Rex, but he is not blind and did not marry his mother or kill his father."*

Ody: *"Rex is not shackled to a titanium chain and is paid for his service by the gifts he receives from those who cross. The cord that stretches across the river to guide the boat is made of heavy hemp rope woven by slaves hundreds of years from now. These proud and great people will be brought to the Americas in chains from a place called Africa."*

Ody: *"Many will wring their hands and cry for this wrong. The nation that rises from slave labor will be bought down but never really cleansed of this sin. The stars and bars on their revered flag will proudly leave statues dedicated to the leaders of their tragic rebellion mocking a civil war that costs thousands of lives."*

Ody: *"My clan loves gathering bundles of this hemp to start our campfires; man do we get a big kick out of eating, singing and just enjoying life dancing in the smoke."*

As Ody laughed and hopped away: *"I just like to heckle travelers with my version of these stories. Get it, heckle? Who in the hell knows what you will find when you cross that river? Life can be pretty unpredictable.* **'Hey fiddle-diddle life is but a riddle; the crow flew over the lagoon,'** *pretty good don't you think? The River Sticks, the Monongahela, Homer Lucifer's Frozen Lake the ferry boat, oblivion ,,,"*

Marcus stood there with his mouth wide open near tears of absolute disbelief when the frog said: *"I was just kidding. They are just old tales that nobody really believes anymore; thanks for the ride."*

Rex (The Boatman)

Marcus makes it to the landing and finds the boatman. The boatman is a strong and handsome young turtle who has ferried passengers across the Monongahela for years.

Marcus reaching the ferryboat: *"Are you Oedipus Rex?"*

The boatman seeing the travois and the bewildered look on Marcus's face responds: *"Has that damn toad been telling lies about me again? My name is Rex Tiller and I was not raised by two golden eagles on the top of a mountain."*

Rex to Marcus: *"Ody is a master of deception. Every year he finds a sucker to build a travois to haul his lazy ass down to the Point where he basks in the sun during the day and croaks at the pretty girls all night long."*

Rex: *During mating season he finds another sucker to haul his phony ass back to the ferryboat landing. He is after one thing and one thing only. He claims to be in love with Helena, the most beautiful toad in the pond and challenges all the other toads that get too close. When it comes to Helena even the horniest toad cannot get pass Ody."*

Rex: *"Ody gets his stories all mixed up; then blames it on a vagabond they call Homey. Homey is a centipede who claims to be a noted poet from a prestigious school. Homey brags that he can see into the past and future. This time of the year this place is just crawling with centipedes."*

83

Rex: *"Ody tells Homey's stories as if they were his own. Ody claims the centipede with one hundred legs can hear voices from around the world; something about air space and radio waves, and that someday our planet will be encased in a digital cloud. No one knows what he is talking about; gibberish, words spoken but not seen or understood."*

Rex: *"Remember, Ody is a freeloader and takes advantage of everyone he meets. The little ones at the Point were happy to get rid of him. That's why they were so eager to help you build the travois. Marcus, that frog is a real trickster and gets others to build him a travois pretending he was crippled during the Trojan War."*

Rex to Marcus: *"Get your gear and climb aboard. No matter what, when we get across the river do not go straight into the forest (west) or turn north upriver. You must follow the trail and go down river. If you go into the forest or upriver you will suffer an eternity of madness. You will enter* **Hell**, *for your sins. You have disobeyed your parents, led your brother astray, and have been naïve, gullible and foolish. You have engaged in enough foolery to spend half of eternity in* **Purgatory** *just out of reach of the* Frozen Lake; *the coldest place in the Universe. If you are not careful you will find yourself frozen in space, at the feet of* **Lucifer**.*"*

Rex: *"If you follow a righteous path you may find redemption and avoid ending up in Hell. Remember stay on the trail from the ferry landing heading southwest where the Allegany and Monongahela rivers flow together to form the Ohio."*

Rex: *"My Fee, When you are standing on the margin that separates life and death, (the Great Divide), do not falter; embrace eternity, you will be going home."*

Crossing the Monongahela

Once across the Monongahela River Marcus took the advice of the boatman and headed southwest. After surviving Odysseus and the River Styx, Marcus finally reached the Ohio River. Following the north side of the Ohio he seeks a river crossing to the blue grass country known as Kentucky.

Marcus pondered the deeper meaning of Crawler's words: *"You must visit the past before you can embrace or see the future. You must dabble in fantasy before facing reality. Before there was science there was superstition. Before there was recorded history there were myths and legends. Things are not always what they seem. Be careful of the friends you make and those you trust. Appearances can be deceiving. Put your faith in what you know to be true and question everything else."*

Marcus reflected on his encounters with the wild ones he met north of the River Styx and the stories Odysseus shared with him. How the wild ones were eager to help him build the travois to get rid of Odysseus, the freeloader. And how Ody pretended to be crippled, allowing Marcus to haul his lazy ass to the ferryboat landing.

Marcus thought to himself: *"I must be more careful as to the friends I choose. What is friendship anyway and who can you really trust? Was Odysseus ever a true friend of mine? What about Eclipse who flew off after my brother's death never to be seen again? Brutus and I just loved Eclipse, our best friend."*

A few days earlier a severe storm had hit this region and there were many trees floating downstream. Still north of the Ohio, again Marcus gambles and with some luck, swimming from tree to tree he finally makes it across the river.

ODY, THE TRICKSTER

ODYSSEUS

ONE-EYE-OPENED, ONE-EYE-CLOSED

3. The Ohio River

The Seer

I followed the southern banks of this river and quickly learned to stay close to its shores. I depended on the river for the basics using what I learned to keep me going. With the river being close there was always plenty of water to drink.

The first basic rule of Nature; where there is water there is life. Crawfish, minnows, fish and clams sustained me. I traveled by the river during the night catching food where I could, moving south by southwest with the river. During the day I mostly took shelter in the trees.

I spent weeks and weeks alone and learned how to survive. I stopped at a stream that joined the Ohio to find something to eat. There in the mud was a strange new set of tracks. They were tracks that I had not seen before. The paw print was much, much bigger than mine with four clear digits; each possessing long sharp claws. The left paw of this creature was missing a claw and half of its inner toe. I paused, and again I felt like *"something was watching me."* I quickly scurried down the stream putting several miles between myself and the tracks. I finally felt safe and slowed my pace.

As *Happenstance,* (Luck, coincidence, accident, fluke, happenchance) would have it this part of the stream was crawling with crayfish. I ate myself full and stopped for a nap; *"survival of the luckiest."*

With my sleepy eyes half opened I noticed in the branch above me a black spider. She wore her glossy black dress with a red hourglass marking with pride. She seemed to radiate knowledge and glowed in the shade of the tree. A voice came from around the tree that appeared to come from nowhere. The voice echoed between my ears. The black spider seemed to speak to me in tones I could not hear, but could see. I thought I was dreaming.

*"I am **Jetta** the seer of the near and far future, the seer of tomorrow. I know all and everything that will take place. I hear voices rippling in the wind; radio waves from the future. Marcus, I am your friend and mean you no harm."*

Jetta: *"I see a time when the Earth will suffer; it has already begun. There are beings in the east that have fallen from Nature. They have created tools to cut down the forest and kill our kind. They call themselves humans. **The humans discount our worth and are at war with Nature and the animal kingdom.**"*

Jetta: *"They squabble and fight with each other and are coming our way. They create gods and religions and kill each other over their beliefs. They build walls and structures to hide behind."*

Jetta: *"They are selfish and greedy and lust for more. They don't know contentment and are never satisfied. They seek control and have grown indifferent to Nature. They want what they want, at any cost!"*

Jetta: *"Their gods, religions and ideals are driving them crazy. Their religions and ideals are taking them in circles and are keeping them from us. They are in denial of their humble origins. Their belief systems are greater than their intellect and they are not rational beings. Logic and reason escape them."*

"Are they from the Earth?" I asked.

"Yes," Responded Jetta. *"They once walked in **harmony with Nature** and are members of our family. They have been with us for millions of years."*

Jetta: **"Like us, they were born of and from this Earth,** *but believe otherwise. They have confused their origins with the teachings of their religions. They cannot tell fact from fiction and have lost touch with Nature. Once part of the natural world, now they don't care. They would not recognize a spider unless it bit them."*

Jetta: *"They will bring death and destruction to our kind and drive us into hiding. They will kill our kind for profit, stripping some of us of our fur to make hats.* **"They are thousands of years away, but they are coming."***

Jetta: *"A great nation will rise and its people will claim that they were born from the **Age of Reason.** **They will quickly leave reason and enlightenment behind, enslave their own kind and corrupt this land.** They will steal the land from the older humans, those who use stone points, and sell the land for profit. They will hunt out our forests and many of the great mammals will be driven off the land in the east. **The greedy elite will fool the masses who will bow down and recite the elite's gibberish. Capital Gain** will rule their reality and their reality will bring ruin to this Earth.*

Jetta: *"They are intelligent and gifted beings full of ideas and conflicts. They will one day reach for the stars while they wage war on each other and pollute the Earth. They will land on the Moon and Mars and a distant comet yet not raise a hand to save the elephant. When they could be healing the*

Earth they will choose to further cause its destruction. Their greed will spread and corrupt. Once they created tools; there was no stopping them!"

Jetta: *"They have **tipped the balance of Nature** to their advantage and stand poised to destroy the world. They will divide one of Nature's smallest particles and destroy themselves. The Earth will recover, but many of us including the humans will be gone. Ten thousand radioactive mushrooms will cover the Earth."*

Jetta: *"If they continue to challenge Nature with their science they may create a hole from which there is no escape. They may yet destroy the Earth and the solar system in which they/we live; like all the other black holes in the Universe created by other civilizations too arrogant to respect Nature...I cannot see this end, but I fear it."* **"They are coming! Be Warned, They Are Coming!"**

"What about me? What will my tomorrows bring?" I asked.

"It is dangerous to know your own future. Do you really want to know? I am frightened by the future; in the end it all ends!" As a seer I know all and knowing all scares me." Jetta said.

"I need to know!" I claimed.

Jetta said: *"You are a **seeker** and thereby restless. You will travel far from your home but will return. You will do bad things and seek redemption. You will carry deep wounds from your youth that will never heal. You will hurt others that you yourself cannot forgive. You will fall in love many times and be reckless with your soul and their hearts. You* *will wonder over your children and thank life for their blessings. "**You will be a student, seeker, teacher, and keeper; a vagabond and a fool**. You will love all that is natural and rise into the heavens from where we all came; never to return."*

"What does all this mean? I asked.

"Sleep and you will know." Jetta whispered.

I woke and the branch above me was empty. It must have been a dream. I must have eaten one too many crayfish.

JETTA

Big Bones

I followed the Ohio for several weeks down to a region called "the dark and bloody ground," Kentucky. There are many creatures drawn to a particular area along the Ohio River known as the Big Bone Lick. They are attracted to this place for its pools of saltwater.

This mineral is much favored by the herd animals. The herd animals that are drawn to the saltlicks attract predators that follow and hunt them. These predators include wolves, mountain lions, wildcats, and bears. The large predators tend to travel alone or in small packs. All of the predators stalk the movements of the other animals in their search for food. They are the meat eaters who daily track and chase down other animals to survive.

The predators seek out the young, old and weak and show no mercy for their prey. They separate the weak from the herd to satisfy their hunger. When attacked, the stronger in the herd often try to defend the weak and chase the predators away. The struggle for survival in the wild is without right or wrong and is intense. **Happenstance** and **Chaos** are the order of things. **Existence** and **Nonexistence** are bound together in Nature, and **Nature has no favorites**.

For thousands of years animals have come here for the salt. Ages and ages ago, when animals before our time existed, they came to the Big Bone Lick to get this mineral. These animals were very large and included an elephant like creature called the mammoth and the giant sloth. The mammoth and sloth have long since disappeared from this Earth with only their big bones left to tell their story.

The Falls of the Ohio

I moved further south along the Ohio until I came upon a rocky area of the river known as the Falls. The river was shallow there exposing the rocks. There was a curious little bird hopping from rock to rock pecking at the stones. Almost as if he was looking for something. He seemed most interested in the layers between the rocks, intently hopping from layer to layer exploring the cracks in between.

He was an oddly shaped little bird. From the distance I could not make out its details. The other animals referred to these birds as the *"Watchers of the Night,"* for they are nocturnal doing most of their hunting and research in the dark. He had big eyes and could turn his head completely around on his shoulders; an odd little bird.... I made camp in the trees for the night and set out the next morning for the great unknown.

4. Bad Company / Justice

Badger

I continued my journey south along the Ohio down into Kentucky and Tennessee. Where the Ohio flows into the great Mississippi River I crossed into Arkansas and entered the Ozarks. I had been on the trail alone for over a year.

Life is a journey and where you travel and end up is often determined by the company you keep. I had stepped over a fallen tree when I was immediately confronted by a creature I had not seen before. He was short and stout with broad shoulders. He had a short tail and waddled as he walked. He walked on all fours with his head close to the ground intently sniffing and snorting, smelling and tasting the air in search for something. He was constantly looking for a scent, something to attack, something to eat.

"I am hungry!" He said: *"Get out of my way I am looking for food! What are you doing standing in my way, do you want to fight?"*

I was caught off guard and responded: *"Only if I have to!"*

The badger in response: *"Got some salt do you? Good, my name is **Badger!** I am on the hunt, do you want to join me and split the spoils? Looks like you're equipped to climb; I have a target for those claws."*

I had been without food for several days. I felt I had little choice and fell in behind him as he raced down the trail, his head down on the scent, stopping to tilt his head this way and that, listening to the sounds in the trees.

He led us to the base of a gigantic sycamore tree with smooth bark, a real challenge even for me. He pointed out the bird's nest high in the branches and sent me up to retrieve the eggs. I hadn't stolen anything before and felt bad about taking the eggs. I was hungry; which was excuse enough. I was about to commit my first real crime.

I filled my **haversack** with four very large eggs before I felt the wrath of the **Blue Jay's** anger. Her sharp talons tore through my fur and ripped open my back. I fled down the tree. With the Blue Jay attacking me during my retreat, Badger displayed a fierce defense. He rose on his back hind legs clawing at the air and Blue Jay as she swept down on us. He growled and clawed and finally fought her off of me. We both fled down the trail and into the underbrush to hide.

After catching our breaths we got into the **haversack** and hungrily ate the eggs. We were petty criminals playing bad guys. Badger said: *"Now that we have eaten and you have proved yourself, how would you like to join my war party?"*

The War Party (The Code)
It felt good being in the company of others again, even if it was in bad company. Being alone in the forest had been a frightening experience. Fitting in and belonging gave me a sense of family, I realized at that moment how much I missed my mother and father, brothers and sisters; my family and my home.

We came together to protect ourselves against the marauding wolf packs that were killing anyone caught alone. Only when we fought, robbed or schemed did we work together as a team. Beyond that, we were on our own. We didn't wipe each other's nose and the gang would leave you behind if you could not fend for yourself or keep up. This was our unwritten code.

Badger was broad chested, fiercely strong, with claws as hard as steel and as sharp as broken class, argumentative, a bully, pushy, dogmatic; he was always looking for trouble. Badger was abandoned as a child and grew to be self-reliant and fiercely independent. He joined a gang when he was just a pup and mastered all the ins and outs of petty crime.

Wildcat was sensuous, playful, teased and taunted, purred and snarled depending on her mood which was forever changing, physically stronger than most males she could leap great distances, agile; she was unpredictable and at times irrational. Wildcat was born to a privileged life but was strong headed and refused the traditional path. At a young age she rebelled, ran away from home and went totally radical; too far out, wasn't far enough for Wildcat. She loved the shock value of the extreme and dabbled in conflict for pure entertainment. She dyed her hair red to accent her wildness.

Weasel was a trickster, cunning, twofaced, a conniver, sneaky, self-promoting, ambitious, a schemer; he plays one against the other always to his advantage. Given their conniving personalities Weasel's home life was total *Chaos* with family degeneration ongoing. Backstabbing at the dinner table was a common nightly event if you could get around the games of duplicity, who was stabbing who? Trying to figure out the alliances was impossible.

I was playful, curious, intelligent, inquisitive, a survivor; with my mask I fitted right in. I grew up in a loving caring family within a safe and healthy environment. I had great role models, and an insatiable curiosity.

Wildcat, Badger, Weasel and I journeyed with each other across Arkansas; every man and woman for themselves was the code. We didn't share, it was a dog eat dog world.

Petty Thieves

We became an alliance of petty thieves, bandits, outlaws; a band of criminals joined together to satisfy our hedonistic lust for self-indulgence. Vile, poisonous and nasty behavior condoned and promoted by ourselves to cover up and reinforce our mortal flaws; sloth, greed, lust, rage.....

We were petty criminals committing a multitude of misdeeds. We would rob a nest of its tiny eggs, scavenge another's meal, raid someone's precious stash of food or break into someone's den, and if we did not find any valuables; trash their pad. We were constantly rough housing it and in general up to no good. *"Tear things up, don't give a damn and just be mean,"* was our motto. We were a club of misfits who were intent on not belonging to anything or anyone, yet desperate to belong to something. We had no honor. I had been in their bad company for two years and had completely lost my way.

Prairie Dog Village (The Red River)

We had journeyed far moving westward along the various creeks and streams making our way across the Ozarks into the heart of Arkansas committing petty crimes as we moved along. We continued westbound through the woodlands down the creeks and streams until we reached the Red River and crossed into Oklahoma reaching the southern plains.

We had traveled for many weeks and our meager supplies were gone. We had crossed the Red River and had moved a few hundred miles into Oklahoma along its banks when we came upon a large prairie dog village. The village stretched out over the prairie on a grassy hill which led up from the river. We were hungry but dared not enter the village of our traditional enemies. We could not tell you when the blood feud started, sometime in our distant past over a misdeed no one remembers. What did we expect? We were outlaws.

The Plot

Badger and Weasel left our make shift camp to scout out the village. They came back hours later and said they could not locate the village's winter food stash. A plan was hatched to get one of us into the village to locate the winter stash. We would learn the layout of the village, plan a raid and get off with the food before the village could muster a response. They outnumbered us ten to one but we had surprise and deceit on our side.

Weasel would be our spy. The plan was to fake an attack chasing Weasel into the village. He would pretend that he had barely escaped capture. He would tell the prairie dogs that we were part of a large raiding party that had overrun and destroyed his village. While in the village Weasel would gain their trust, find out where they kept their winter food stash and plan an escape route.

We gave Weasel a head start creating a great ruckus while we chased him into the village. He played his part well and ran for the village as if his life depended on it. The prairie dogs gathered to make a stand as Weasel collapsed at their feet. The village warriors boldly stood their ground.

Facing a large army and believing the trick worked we stopped short of the village as if we were a small scouting party not large enough to carry forward an attack. Badger and Wildcat made a fierce demonstration just out of range. Growling, I jumped up and down acting as fierce as possible.

Given his deceitful nature, they fell for the trick and took Weasel into their village. He spun a web of lies and convinced the villagers of his desperate situation and good will.

Weasel spent three days in the village and learned where the winter stash was hidden. He also discovered that there was just enough food to keep the little ones alive and fed through the winter months. Anything less in terms of their food stores meant the little ones would go hungry and many would die.

With our hunger and selfish needs put above all else we accepted this as the risk we all faced in Nature. No one, them or us, was guaranteed to survive the winter.

Weasel told the prairie dogs' chief that he needed to search the edge of the great river to see if he could find any of his kind that might have escaped the war party. He told the old one not to worry that he knew his way there and back and that he would return before dark.

We plotted together and made plans for the night. There shouldn't be any mishaps and we should get away clean with a winter's supply of food with no one getting hurt. I had become an outlaw and the company I kept proved it.

Weasel returned to the village playing out his role as the lone survivor of the war party's attack.

Reluctant Participant

I would rather scavenge for my food and go hungry than steal what did not belong to me. I would rather go hungry from time to time than be a criminal. Given my mask I spent a lot of time trying to prove to myself that I was a good guy. I may look like a criminal grey prison suit, mask and stripes right down to my tail, but in my heart I wanted to help others. I just could not reveal myself to these guys. They would laugh themselves silly. They would giggle like little girls and wet themselves if they found out I did not want to raid the village and steal the villagers' winter supplies.

My parents had warned me not to keep company with strangers: *"Stay away from bad company. You never know what they are about until it's too late. Stay away from wrong doing. Stay away from trouble, there is trouble enough in life without looking for more. Always do what's right. And whatever you do, don't eat the buttons from a cactus tree!"*

Payback (Mortal Combat)

With the help of *Weasel,* later that night we slipped into the village and stationed ourselves at strategic points. Weasel and I went straight for the supplies and took as much as we could carry. I filled my **haversack** with their food. Badger and Wildcat faked the attack throwing the village into a panic. While the villagers fled into the night Badger and Wildcat set their lodges ablaze. During the **Chaos** they joined back up with us in a gully just outside the village and we made our getaway. The gully covered our escape and we put many miles between ourselves and the village. The prairie dogs knew they could not take us head on. We were too fierce the warriors; and our prey upon the weak and helpless proved it. ***It would soon be our turn to suffer***.

Wildcat should not have eaten one of their young. In her blood lust and true to her form when a young one got separated from its parents she attacked and ate it. The prairie dogs would prove they could destroy us without risking their own lives. Little did we know that an angry army was about to take its revenge and stomp us into dust. They would catch us by surprise with a proxy army a thousand times our size. They wanted revenge and justice for the loss of their food and one of their babies.

Some distance from the crime scene we made camp for the night. We spent the night around the fire gleefully devouring our spoils, bragging as to our misdeeds and stolen treasures. We had easily overcome our enemy and escaped unscathed with our loot. Underneath all the bravado I felt ashamed of myself.

All of a sudden the ground around our makeshift camp began to tremble. The prairie dog army had circled around us and slipped up on a herd of buffalo numbering in the thousands.

It was well past dark and in unison the prairie dogs let out a horrid cry behind the herd of buffalo scaring the herd into a stampede. Tons of flesh and bone moved in one large motion toward our camp. Thousands of hooves cut through the ground and like a giant sickle leveled the grass in one large arc heading our way. Their hooves would slice through the earth and our flesh as the herd of buffalo trampled us beneath their massive bodies.

I fell into a deep weathered out prairie dog hole. By instinct the herd of buffalo spread out left and right of this crater. I dug as deeply as I could to reach the bottom of the crater and covered myself with dirt to hide.

Badger fell underneath a large buffalo and was immediately trampled to death. Weasel was lifted into the night's air and tossed like a doll before falling beneath the masses to the ground, disappearing forever. Wildcat was gored repeatedly as she mustered a defense in defiance of her own death. She too disappeared from the Earth.

It was pushing sunrise when the thunder stopped and the dust finally settled. The massive herd of buffalo had finally cleared the plains leaving the ground torn to shreds with no sign of life. An eerie silence fell upon the plain and the new day's light spread like an ice cold blanket over the naked landscape. I dug myself out of the crater and looked around in disbelief that I was still alive… Trembling, I slipped back into my hole and fell asleep.

THE STAMPEDE

RIGHTEOUS SELF-DEFENSE

THE WHITE BUFFALO

"THERE WILL BE A RECKONING!"

JUSTICE

Justice (The White Buffalo)

In my sleep I again peered over the rim of the crater. A thick grey and black fog filled the plains with a heavy cold mist. With puffs of blacks and grays this fog swirled into a violent wind consuming the landscape around me.

A loud thunder rumbled in the distance shaking the Earth under my feet. Out of this fog a great white buffalo appeared. He charged the crater stopping inches from my face. His massive form absorbed the space around him. In his presence the plains and landscape disappeared. Standing still his sheer mass made the ground bend under his weight. His mighty hooves sank deep into the soil. His nostrils were aflame with burning embers. His hot moist breath pushed into my face causing me to blink. Within this blink all became clear. There I stood bare and raw. I shook with fear as he glared into my empty soul. His black eyes peered into my naked being and I was completely exposed.

With his massive head tilted forward; the great white buffalo said: *"My name is **Justice** and there is no hiding from my wrath. Those that transgress goodness and dabble in sin must bear my judgment. All forms of evil will face my vengeance and will pay for their wicked deeds. I am the judge, jury and executioner. Three of your companions have already answered for their crimes."*

Justice: *"Marcus, you have been a party to a criminal act. You and your partners in crime attacked and stole from the needy and innocent. A child was killed to satisfy the blood lust of a member of your gang. You are thieves and murderers, the lot of you; their guilt, your guilt; their crime, your crime. Evil conspirators one and all! Guilty as charged!"*

Justice: *"This I witnessed and I do not miss details. You did not have a hand in the killing but you joined in on the plunder. You basked in the spoils of your crime and publically took delight in your misdeeds; laughing while you stuffed your face with their food."*

Justice: *"I know every detail of your crime, so your testimony is not needed. Do not bother to deny your part in this misadventure. I can see into your naked soul, so spare me your lies."*

Justice: *"The prairie dog village sent my children after your gang for an accounting. You escaped the weight of their justice by hiding in this hole. They have sent me forward to these plains to render your final judgment."*

Justice: *"I see and know all that you have done. In the distance I heard you question the act of this crime. You have been reckless at the will of others. You yielded your soul to do their bidding. You were hesitant, but yet you followed the pack anyway. This is not the only or last hole you go down."*

Justice: *"Marcus, I also see your remorse and shame and know that you questioned your actions. I see a flicker of light and goodness in your being. You must cradle this spark, nurture its flame and bring warmth into your soul. You have a long journey to travel. Open your heart to finding goodness. Once found hold onto its precious cargo and share it with others. Carry it deep within your being and pass it on to your children."*

Justice: *"I will spare your life and suspend my judgement for now. You are condemned to wander without purpose and grow old with the unbearable weight of knowledge. I will leave you with this warning. But if you fail to move into the light I will crush your soul into a fine powder from which you may never be formed again. The Earth will transpire with no evidence that you ever existed."*

Justice: *"Control your raw impulses for most of the time they are wrong. Temper your desires for they will often lead you astray. Listen to your inner being it knows right from wrong. You must stand fast for what you believe is right. Resist doing evil at all costs. If you allow it to do so, the force of evil will drown your soul's wisdom in total darkness; lost in a black frozen ocean beyond the reach of redemption."*

Justice: *"Stay away from strangers and resist the will of others to do evil. True friends will seek you out and protect you from wrong doing. Remember that your conscience belongs to yourself. It is not something you can give away."*

Justice: *"Share wisdom and goodness, it is our mission to help others and bring light into this world. Although we come from the dark, once illuminated let the Universe shine and bathe us in its light."*

Justice: *"I am not a seer so I cannot see your tomorrows. I know all that has been, but what will be (the future) escapes me. I must rely on others to see your future. I have been told by the others who will know you in the future, that if I spare you, you will redeem yourself ten times over for this crime. Because of their voices, I will choose leniency and spare you my wrath."*

Justice: *"Marcus, your journey will take many turns, but your soul must follow a straight and narrow path. Missteps on this path will be your doom. On a steep and dangerous path three who love you the most will risk their lives to save you. Even in the face of danger you must do what is right. In the end goodness will triumph over evil. Remember, I peer down from the heavens to witness and see all. I glare at you from within and know the impurities of your soul. There is no hiding your darkest deeds from yourself."*

There I stood before Nature naked and unborn-without form or meaning. I was completely empty without purpose, stripped of my rank and reduced (busted) to a **hollow one**: *a being without substance, one who is condemned to follow the lead of others; not able to stand fast for what he believes is right or stand firm against what he knows is wrong.* I would have to reclaim my status as a **seeker**: *a believer in the truth,* and never again yield to the **gibberish** or will of the pack.

Justice continued: *"I will watch over you carefully and foster your growth and maturity. The process will be difficult and slow. Your journey will be arduous and your trials severe and you will struggle and fall only to rise again. You can never truly grow wise without experiencing pain and suffering.* **"In Nature, wisdom takes many forms."**

Justice: *"I see all that has been. Your mother and father grieved your absence and cried a thousand tears for their two lost sons. After your brother's death, your parents found a measure of peace in you. With your departure their despair grew daily."*

Justice: *"They knew where Brutus was, but worried endlessly as to your whereabouts and destiny. The morning you left they found that the food and* **haversack** *were missing and figured you ventured to the edge of the Sacred Circle again.*

Your father was certain you would be home before nightfall."

Justice: *"Your father reassured your mother; 'When Marcus runs out of food he will come home. I bet he'll be home before dark; you know how easily he spooks."*

Justice: *"Your mother cried; 'Where is my Marcus? Where are my baby boys? Where have they gone and why did they have to leave? Will I ever see them again?"*

Justice: *"When you did not return that night; the next day, year one and then year two, their despair grew and grew with unanswered questions as to your life and wellbeing. They left this world broken hearted over their two lost sons."*

Justice: *"Marcus, we often fail to recognize the pain we cause others, especially those who love us the most. You left home without telling your parents where you were going and when you would return. After years of waiting they resigned their lives to emptiness. They never gave up hope until the day they passed from this Earth. Their spirits still wait for you."*

The White Comet

Justice: *"Marcus, when I was a young bull I was ashamed of my white coat and felt I would never be allowed to fit into the herd. Believing my own misguided thoughts I became angry and separated myself from the herd. I told myself that they were jealous of me and would reject me if they had the chance. Believing in my own delusion, I wandered the high ground beyond the herd and peered down on them in judgment."*

Justice: *"My parents were proud of my uniqueness and were mortified by my decision to stand apart. They believed that the white coat was a sign from Nature; that I had been blessed by Nature with wisdom and the purity of thought. They wanted me to graze with them, shoulder to shoulder with the herd, proud to be part of this extended family that stretched across the Great Plains for miles and miles. Without much thought I too caused my parents great pain."*

Justice: *"One dark night the herd was stampeded by the painful cry of a lonely coyote. The cry from the future was cutting and sliced through the night's air with an indescribable sadness. At that moment I had a vision and knew the coyote was crying for the loss of a dear friend and that he meant no harm to the herd. The cry scared the bulls into action believing the herd was being attacked by a hungry pack of wolves. In one frantic motion the bulls charged blindly into the night. The bulls in their haste led the herd directly toward a thousand foot cliff they did not know was in their path."*

Justice: *"A force deep within called me into action. I raced around the herd in a wide arc. Like a comet my white coat illuminated the horizon to warn the bulls of the danger ahead. My coat's whiteness stood out against the unknown and the darkness of the night. I raced to the edge of the cliff and stood between the herd and oblivion. The bulls slowed-then stopped their charge, bringing the herd to rest just a few feet from the edge. With deep affection the herd embraced me. Because of my white coat they were saved. Only then I realized where I truly belonged."*

Justice: *"They were willing to trust me and stopped just short of disaster. I had judged them too harshly; they were not jealous and had never rejected me. My rejection came from within and was misguided by ignorance. Ignorance being the judgment I rendered without knowing the truth. I learned from this experience to never render my judgment without knowing the truth, never! Marcus, you have been granted a reprieve, a stay of execution; call it what you will, you are free to go."*

Justice: *"I will leave you with this to ponder. This I have seen and this I will warn: We will continue doing evil in spite of knowing better; our wicked deeds washing away goodness generation after generation. We will refuse to control our impulses as we blindly chase our desires; building narrow towers of wealth amidst vast deserts of despair. We are eager to tear down what we have labored to build only to start over; again and again. A world turned inside out with our collective beings lasting but a few generations before we forget.* ***We see the ruins of the past and in that we can witness our own demise; the abyss, the black hole without substance, absolute emptiness."***

Justice: *"We are no longer connected to our parents (the ancient ones) who gave us life and started this journey. With civilizations lost and our futures at risk; a riddle in time played out by the jokesters who are too selfish to care, judgment day is coming and there will be a reckoning."*

Justice continued: ***"The seers told me, when the knuckle walkers stood erect they convinced themselves that they had dominion over all of Nature. They believe all that is natural is theirs to exploit and use as they please. They will call themselves humans and deny their natural birth. They will grant themselves special status above all other living things*** *and declare their ownership of the entire natural world, including the Cosmos."*

Justice: *"The humans will ponder their existence and make up stories as to who they are and how they came into being. They will initially show reverence and awe for the Earth, moon and stars but too soon will abandon this illumination for a multitude of gods. Their gods will possess traits similar to these naked apes, always doing evil; lying and stealing, hording what is not theirs, constantly fighting with each other, having sex with the mortals, and so on."*

Justice: *"With all the spiritual confusion generated by hundreds of gods, they settled on one god. When this one god became too stern, restricting the access to heaven to but a few, they created his son to mediate their sins and redirect more humans toward heaven. Then the son's spirit was created to help move things along; three gods in one. That is not counting the devil, the angels, saints and others. The humans were back to a multitude of gods and semi gods to explain and justify their existence, delusions and corruptions; seldom accepting responsibility for themselves;* **hallelujah!***"*

Justice: **"The humans professed purity while they tortured and killed thousands; thousands who refused to believe in their unholy gibberish. They extended this irrational behavior to all their other forms of beliefs; politics, economics – creating the War of the Isms: communism, socialism, capitalism, fascism, extremism, etc."**

Justice: *"They then fought amongst themselves, claiming the one true and holy faith,* **babbling gibberish** *as they mutilated and killed each other for slight variations in their belief;*

110

killing, killing, killing to the point of self-extinction. In the end they will drag us down with them."

Justice: *"Among the humans, the need to believe is profound. They can't seem to function without believing in something, something more dramatic and farfetched than Nature. They can't seem to wrap their oversized brains around the simple, yet complicated truth of existence no matter how much evidence is revealed. Their skulls are just too small for their big brains; too much pressure causing irrational behavior."*

Justice: *"Gods, then and now, were created to sanction and justify whatever humans want to do; the demise of the animal kingdom and the destruction of the Earth, gaining wealth and control over others, the power to destroy, etc., whatever the humans need or want."* Justice warned: ***"Judgment day is coming….. There will be a reckoning!"***

Again the great white buffalo blew his hot breath into my face and within a blink he was gone and the Great Plains reappeared. I trembled at the meaning of his words, knowing that someday we may face his final judgment.

The Awakening

I had been walking a crooked trail. I had fallen asleep under a trembling pine as a storm raged around me. I had departed from my mortal soul and took refuge with a band of criminals. In their good company I had embraced and done evil. I wear the markings of a criminal and will be forever tainted by this crime. By a force of Nature I was given a second chance to reclaim my soul. I had survived the white buffalo's judgment to continue my journey. Where this journey will take me, I do not know.

THE JOURNEY
The Quest for Meaning

Coyote

Eternity/Infinity

Gila Monster

Scorpion

Side Winder

Survival

Midnight

Walking Moon

Eclipse

Seal

Chaos

Spirit Feather

Marcus

The Haversack

The Keeper

Justice

Jetta

Happenchance

Crazy Bear

Mother Condor

Geo

THE SACRED CIRCLE

Survival

I quickly headed north to escape the crime scene. I was born a raccoon and as such did my best at night after the sun was gone and the night appeared. My keen sense of smell for the most part found me food and water. Over the past few nights I had been without food and was growing hungry and weak, I was running on empty. I had to make up some ground; my nightly treks had cost me much and yielded me little. I had to move through the day to make up time. I needed to find food and I needed to find it soon.

My body was set by Nature, and in time being without water or food would kill me. There were needs that had to be met and I was wasting time. If I ignored these needs I would die; water, food and rest (shelter) are the essentials without which we will all perish. They are the basics and we should not take them for granted.

My body had been set by Nature and my clock was running out. I was a raccoon who had to expose himself to the sun and travel during the day. Time only mattered in motion; without motion I was wasting time. I had to move into the light. I had to adapt – If I failed to adapt I would not survive. If I did not survive I would not have children – If I did not have children, I would cease to exist – My lineage would be lost forever; like a dying tree branch without buds, no blooms or seeds for tomorrow.

Time was leaving me behind. I must settle down and stake a claim. I must find a spot on this Earth where my soul can find tranquility and love; a place where belonging and love is greater than myself, and greater than my need to wander.

I needed another and through another find purpose and from that purpose bring forth life. Designed by Nature this need and purpose has grown into love. This love is duplicated and then expanded with the births of our children.

Like an exploding star love warms our souls and gives us meaning. Although rare in its truest form, it is the most precious gift of life itself. This love although fragile is greater than the Universe and all the galaxies and suns that exist. It is the greatest gift of life and without love life would be meaningless; motion without purpose, actions without fulfillment, raw and exposed, empty and hollow…… With so much on my mind I laid down and fell fast to sleep.

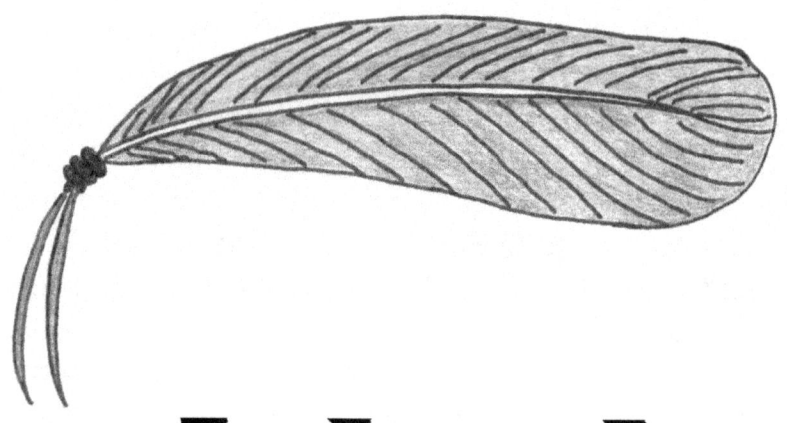

THE EAGLE'S FEATHER

5. The Grasslands

The Eagle's Feather (The Gift)

I woke up to a near silence with the wind gently bending the grass in front of me. Since I left the Sacred Circle I had been on a long journey. I had traveled through the forest along the Red River and headed northwest making my way across the southern plains. I had been a member of a raiding party and barely escaped with my life. I had wandered the grasslands and adapted just to survive. I felt guilty for my part in the raid and wanted to get as far away as I could and hide. I had put hundreds of miles between me and the crime and covered my shame with deceit. I pretended to be a good guy to hide my wicked deeds. I was weary and needed time to rest.

It was nightfall when I entered the village. I had watched the village for some time and felt safe. I sent my greetings and gift to the elder and asked for shelter. It was the tradition and custom of most tribes at that time to welcome and protect all visitors who came in peace.

My gift was the *eagle feather* that I found on the forest floor beneath the oak tree. I carried it throughout my early journey for good luck. *The eagle feather was a symbol of wisdom and courage treasured by all.* I was warmly received by the elder's tribesmen and I was given a place to sleep by the campfire. It was here that I found my one true mate.

There was something magical about this feather. When dropped unlike a stone or stick, for an instant, it seemed to defy gravity and floated to the ground. Something about its structure and light weight captures the air giving it lift. With enough lift the feather moves away from the Earth below in spite of gravity.

The bald eagle's shiny black and snow white feathers were great symbols to this tribe in that these feathers carry one's spirit into the heavens. The forward and leading edge of the long spine or quill that supports each fiber of the feather adds to its strength. Each fiber, quill and separate feather further channels the wind bringing greater lift to the body it's attached to; a perfect form for flight forged by Nature.

Walking Moon

The next day they presented my *snow white eagle feather* to their chief in my presence; *white symbolizing purity*. They made a ritual out of the gift in that they placed me at the center of a band of warriors and led me to his lodge. It was odd, I was twice their size and I felt surrounded by dwarfs.

As we moved into the village each warrior gently blew on a feathered whistle calling the chief's attention to the gathering. We stopped at the entrance to his lodge.

Stepping from his lodge their chief proudly announced: *"I am **Walking Moon,** elder of these good people and the keeper of this sacred land. I am the protector of all that you see."* I stood humbled by his eloquence and pride.

Walking Moon: *"What is your name and where do you come from?"*

I said: *"My name is Marcus and I come from the eastern woodlands known as the Allegheny Mountains. I am a traveler studying the land and Nature for knowledge."*

Walking Moon: *"Many moons ago word traveled here that there was a band of outlaws robbing and killing the innocent down on the southern plains. Have you seen or heard of these criminals?"*

Before I could answer, Walking Moon continued: *"They say these outlaws are in hiding and have disappeared into the badlands."*

Looking me in the eyes, he continued again: *"If you have done evil that evil is captured in your soul and is reflected in your eyes. The evil we do in life stays with us.* ***Redemption for wrong doing does not come easy."***

Maintaining eye contact I said: *"I tend to travel alone and when I was last on the southern plains it was empty of life. I traveled hundreds of miles through the plains not seeing another soul. I learned early to stay away from trouble and strangers. I have learned to stay on the trail and walk a straight path in life."*

I continued: *"I started out following the trail of a large herd of buffalo but I never caught up to them. I have come across only a few travelers since I arrived in your lands and no one spoke to me of these outlaws."*

I continued: *"I finally reached your village and seek your blessings to stay. I give you my most precious gift and ask but a warm fire to rest by."*

Walking Moon: *"Your most precious gift is not this feather, but rather the* **purity of your soul.** *If your soul is evil, this* **eagle feather** *will not be able to lift your spirit from the ground and your spirit will forever be bound to this Earth."*

Walking Moon: *"**Even seven eagle feathers cannot lift a wicked spirit. The Earth on which the wicked spirit falls soon spits it out; bones for the scavengers; devoured and never to be seen again. Then you can only enter the heavens when the Earth is no more.**"*

Walking Moon carefully said: *"Welcome to our village. We do not judge others by their looks. You will be measured here by your deeds. We will withhold our judgment of you until you prove yourself one way or the other. We hold the truth precious; do not speak with two tongues. **We are in harmony with Nature and hold her most sacred.** Do your part and bring food to the tribe. Protect the people. Do not bring evil to this tribe and if you must leave, go in peace."*

The Sacred Pipe

He invited me and his proven warriors into his lodge. A great feast was prepared and Walking Moon sent one of his many grandsons for his pipe. His pipe belonged to the tribe and had been passed down through the generations to him. Like his father before him, Walking Moon was a chief of chiefs.

The pipe consisted of a red-stone bowl decorated with turquoise and tiny feathers laced to the pipe by leather strips. At the end of the bowl two eagle feathers hung down from its stem. The stem was over a foot long and covered with sacred symbols telling the tribe's many stories.

Into the Wild/Dakota Badlands

I would learn that Walking Moon had lost his way as a youth and was cast out of his tribe to wander alone in the Dakota Badlands. He had disobeyed his father and married outside of his tribe. Walking Moon and **Blossom** were forbidden to lodge in the village so they journeyed deep into the wilderness where they started a new home. Their spring burst forward with love and Blossom came to carry his child.

He worked day and night to improve their homestead and stored away enough food for the coming winter. He must plan for three and make sure there was plenty until next spring. With little rest he hunted and gathered food to make sure his new family made it through the harsh weather ahead.

He made a little bow with arrows for the son he believed he would surely have. Just in case, he made a little doll and carved puppies for the girl child there might be. He loved them both, although they were not yet born. Their jolly baby faces danced in his head, and with a tune and a song only good parents understand, he worked through the days.

Blossom died with their first born and in despair and anger Walking Moon stripped himself naked and cast all his possessions into a great fire. With the sharpened edge of a flint stone he cut deep into his chest until bone was exposed; then cried out in grief so loud that the clouds poured icy rain. In the dead of winter under a full moon he walked naked and enraged into the badlands.

Coming Home

Walking Moon had been a proven warrior second only to his father, *Falling Star*. On many occasions when defeat was certain, Walking Moon rallied his forces and saved his tribe. He was the greatest warrior of his generation. When his tribe was threatened by a pack of wolves from the east his father sent Walking Moon's brother into the badlands to ask Walking Moon to return home to defend the tribe.

Elk Horn was shocked at his brother's appearance. Filth and wounds covered Walking Moon's body and a wild anger stared from his eyes. His hair was matted and hung past his shoulders. Madness had taken his soul and darkness covered his face. He growled and howled like a wounded wolf and scratched at the earth. His muscles were bands of steel wrapped tight around his limbs and body. His claws were as sharp as broken flint stone and his looks would stop an army. Elk Horn was afraid to speak. After a few moments Walking Moon's eyes softened as he slowly recognized his baby brother.

Elk Horn: *"My dear brother you have been gone too long. I love you my brother and have missed you at our fires. Your family needs you and you are the only one who can save us from our enemies. A false army of warriors bearing a flag of many stars has been sent to take our land. "*

Elk Horn: *"Father has cried for you and your loss. He has cried for his daughter and grandchild. He asks for your forgiveness."*

Walking Moon: *"What is there to forgive, Nature takes and gives what she pleases. It is we that give our hearts to others. We find the most precious thing in existence and we give it away. Our love is but a burst of light within our souls, greater than the Universe and as fragile as a cool summer breeze. When she chooses, Nature takes it back."*

The call of duty cleared his mind. Walking Moon carried his rage into the battle and defeated a stronger army. Using trickery he boxed the wolf pack into a small canyon and wiped them out. He had fought for a noble cause to protect and save his people.

Walking Moon was welcomed home as a hero, for that he truly was. He had saved his tribe and healed his wounds bound by the love and care of his people. They wept at his return and covered his path to his father's lodge with spring blossoms. He would have many wives, children and grandchildren and his soul was healed and tempered with time. Each new child and grandchild brought him joy, as a reflection of what was and might have been, a baby and wife lost to Nature; but never forgotten.

Passing the Sacred Pipe

His grandson lit the pipe while Walking Moon drew down on the flame. After several draws on the pipe and a long pause; he passed the pipe to me and asked:

"How did you come by this feather?"

I said: *"When I was a little boy a mighty eagle landed in the top of our tree. His shadow landed on me and he spoke to me with a powerful voice. The eagle asked me;* **"Who's that child hiding in my shadow?"** *and with that, the eagle flew off into the sky never to be seen again. One of his feathers floated down from the heavens and landed at my feet. I felt as if he was calling me to wander and join him on some great adventure. I needed to discover the unknown."*

Walking Moon: *"He did not swoop down to eat you?"*

I said: *"No, he did not. I hid the feather thinking that my parents would believe it to be a bad omen. When I was younger I yearned for adventure and pestered my parents about traveling beyond our home. They thought I was silly and warned me of the dangers beyond the Sacred Circle."*

121

Without thinking I said: *"I left home and fell into bad company and lost my way."*

Walking Moon caught my eye and softly looked away as if not hearing what I said.

Walking Moon: *"I once left my home to wander in the wilderness. We all have our demons. The power of the **eagle feather** is great and allows one to overcome great challenges and possibly carry one's spirit into the heavens. Are you sure you want to give this gift to me?"*

I said: *"I am less worthy then the mighty chief that now stands before me and beg you to keep this humble gift."*

Walking Moon: *"Marcus, you have much time yet to prove yourself worthy. I admire your courage to walk the wilderness alone. You are welcomed here as long as you prove yourself true and are faithful to our tribe."*

We passed the pipe fourteen times to the right, fourteen times to the left, paused for the new moon and told many stories. They were awed that I was a lone traveler and that I had journeyed so far from my home in the east. I told them the story of the spider and they said they had heard about the humans too and dreaded that the humans were coming.

A young brave asked: *"Did you ask the spider about your tomorrows? Did she tell you your future?"*

I said: *"It is dangerous for one to know his future. But she did tell me that I would fall into the company of a noble people and take a wife and have many children, and my children will have many children. Each one of my children will hold a sacred place in this tribe. My first born will be a leader of men, my second will be a revered medicine woman and my youngest daughter a great teacher."*

I caught Walking Moon's eyes and a slight tear flowed down his cheek. I did not mention the white buffalo, Justice.

To my surprise it was late into the night when we left his lodge. Before I left they presented me with a blanket. Then several braves accompanied me back to the village campfire, the center of their rituals and dances. I settled in for the night drawing the blanket over my shoulders…..

My One True Mate (Life's Cycle)
She entered the campfire's light from the dark village beyond. The fire's flickering flames highlighted her features adding various reds and yellows to her beautiful face. *"**She was a dark-haired beauty with big brown eyes.**"* And her gentle gaze illuminated my soul. She was absolutely beautiful. She belonged to a powerful tribe and her father turned out to be the village elder, Walking Moon himself.

The elder was a war chief loved by all. Not only had he protected his tribe from the attacks of outsiders during his youth, he wisely led his tribe as he aged. He brought *fellowship* and *prosperity* to his village.

Walking Moon initially looked on me with doubt. He learned that I had been a rebellious youth who was prone to make mistakes and dared to wander from my tribe's *Sacred Circle*. He gradually grew to admire my spirit and early adventures and recognized the truth and wisdom of my travels.

White Elk

His daughter was beautiful beyond words in body and spirit. Her smile and laughter brightened our hearts. Walking Moon and *Star Light* (her mother) loved her dearly. To honor her story they renamed her *White Elk*; an invisible force of Nature that keeps us safe, a mystic creature that takes on many forms to protect us: an owl, a serpent, a sea turtle and many others that we meet by chance in life *(Happenstance)*.

White Elk was delightfully stubborn and willful and would stand her ground when pushed. One cold and dangerous winter day when she was a little girl White Elk left camp without permission. They searched for her everywhere. Then a blizzard hit throwing the village into a panic. It was a total whiteout with zero visibility, well below freezing with snow piling up everywhere. With the winter storm raging they could not send out a search party to find her. Walking Moon and Star Light were desperate with grief. Their little girl would surely die from exposure.

Later that morning the blizzard abruptly passed as fast as it had struck. The sky cleared and a cold bright sunny sky opened upon the land. The summer like brightness defied that it was midwinter. The clearing weather was seen as a good omen that the village child would be found alive.

The search party found her tracks in the snow. They were horrified when they discovered the tracks of a coyote next to hers. She was being hunted by a wild dog with little chance of escape. They feared what they would find at the end of the trail. The coyote had her scent and White Elk was too young to defend herself. The pair of tracks surrounded the village. Both tracks started and ended at the same place forming a perfect circle. From true north the pair of tracks led directly back into the village to her parents' lodge.

When the search party entered the lodge they found her asleep wrapped warmly in a snow white elk skin. The village cried out with joy, they all loved this precious little girl. At the ceremony of rebirth, they named her White Elk after the fur that kept her warm. At this ceremony she told her story.

White Elk: *"Against my parents' wishes I left the lodge to play in the snow. The snow fall was light so I ventured beyond the village. When the blizzard hit I lost my way. The storm grew fierce and soon I could not see. I became frightened and sat down and cried. The snow quickly piled up around me. The blowing snow and ice began to cut my face and hands. I was freezing and I gave up hope."*

White Elk continued: *"Out of the whiteness a lone coyote appeared. Without a sound he moved toward me. The storm raged around his calm presence. The air around him was clear and warm. Hope and affection shone through his eyes and I felt completely safe. The noise of the wind passed as he wrapped his body around mine to protect me from the cold. He laid beside me until the storm ended. He then led me around the village stopping at true north. From this point he led me back into the village."*

White Elk concluded: *"He walked beside me on this journey brushing his body against mine to keep me warm. He led me into my parents' lodge and pulled the albino elk skin over my body. Without words, I could hear his thoughts: 'Love and respect the words of your parents, for they, above all others, love you the most.' He quietly turned and disappeared."*

The tribe stood in awe. White Elk aged with wisdom, in spirit and deed. Over time the village grew to love and honor her goodness. The entire village in reverence began to call her Spirit Mother.

I fell deeply in love with Walking Moon's daughter never to rise again. Our passion consumed us and before long we were inseparable. White Elk and I took our sacred vows and started our family. She warmed my heart and protected our three dear children. Their names were **Strong Heart, Gentle Touch** and **Morning Star**. They were stronger and wiser than their father and lived prosperous and happy lives. They brought my grandchildren and great grandchildren into this world and illuminated my path. No matter what storms came, the light of their lives guided me and kept me safe.

Buffalo Trail

Although a stranger they welcomed me into their tribe. *"I was called one who follows the buffalo; Buffalo Trail."* At the joining ceremony they cut my two shoulders with sharpened buffalo bones, two slashes for each shoulder, four slashes in all, one/seventh of the moon's cycle. They tattooed each of my wrists with fourteen white stars and pierced my ears. At the closing ritual Walking Moon brushed my forehead with the *eagle feather* I had given him years before and softly whispered: *"Even outlaws have goodness. The white buffalo told me you were coming."* He pressed the feather into my hand and smiled; then said: *"You may need this feather someday to find your way home."*

I would be embraced by the elder and his family and welcomed into their tribe where I flourished for many years. Her father became my father, her mother became my mother and I loved them both dearly. I was a good son and deeply cared for them.

The tribe would wander the plains from mid-western Kansas up through Nebraska following the buffalo herds. I grew to love the buffalo, the living breathing icon of the Great Plains. Life was abundant during these years with antelope and elk grazing over the plains while eagles and buzzards filled the skies. Where there are herd animals there are predators. We had our share of wolves and bears and had to watch our children closely.

At one of the stream crossings my son, Strong Heart spotted some strange new tracks. We had seen mountain lion tracks before, but none as large and strange as these. To my surprise the tracks were the same as those I had found years before, only much larger. The left paw's inner toe and claw were missing. A dark feeling came over me. *Something was following me.* The dark omen quickly passed and the beauty of my life filled my heart.

During the summers Kansas and Nebraska were covered with blue skies filled with wondrously shaped white clouds rolling over the landscape. It was a majestic beauty unto itself. With wide open spaces and soft rolling hills; it was breathtaking. The rivers and streams, their paths laced with thick brush and trees, formed emerald green ribbons that cut through the landscape of brown grasslands in the fall. The tall grass was pushed aside by the wind as if the wings of a giant eagle brushed over the grass as it floated across the land. The grass bending slightly as the invisible eagle moved forward and warmed us with its glory. The soft song of the wind filled the air with a tune that only life could hear. Our happiness was framed by Nature and crowned by the stars.

The Great Plains were complete *tranquility* before it was a word. *We flourished as a tribe in harmony and balance with Nature*. My family and community grew strong. Walking Moon passed and Elk Horn his younger brother took his place. Covered with eagle feathers Walking Moon floated into the skies; to be missed and never seen again.

Pulled away by life's fallacies, I fell away from White Elk and her tribe and wandered lost for many years never to fully recover. They were a brave and noble family and I love them dearly. They will be with me beyond time. White Elk was nineteen when we met and I loved her deeply. *"I grew to be a fool who lost sight of her perfection only to wander alone for many years in a barren desert without meaning. You cannot escape true love; nor should you try."*

"When you abandon true love you abandon your soul; chasing foul smelling vermin down empty rabbit holes. The righteous path of life is a narrow and steep trail from where one misstep can cost a lifetime of unhappiness; a misstep that broke many hearts, including mine. The need to wander led me astray. Like a thief I slipped away one night and headed southwest into the unknown."

WALKING MOON

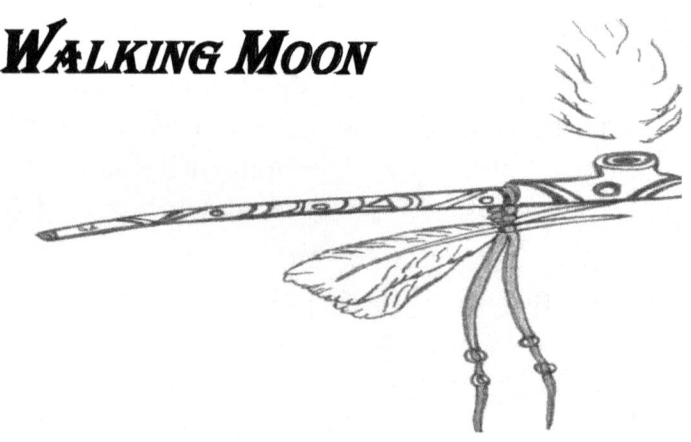

6. Midnight

Texas

I pushed away from the southern plains and entered the northern portion of Texas. I traveled southwest through the night seeking shelter during the day. I tried my best to keep out of sight; there were predators everywhere. Their tracks crossed my path from every direction as they competed with each other for something to eat.

As I moved down the trail well after dark I felt something brush over my head. I shook my head back and forth hoping to shake off what had fallen from the trees. In an instant, something flashed in front of me violently disturbing the air as it flew by. Although not perfect, my vision saw something; a ghostly mirage flying into the dark.

I finally caught sight of a tiny mouse with wings as it erratically jerked this way and that, darting through the night sky. I had never seen a mouse with wings before and was amazed that mice could fly.

When Brutus and I were boys we envied Eclipse as he leaped from a branch only to extend this motion into flight. From that moment and beyond Eclipse appeared to defy gravity. Into the sky he would fly; a place where Brutus and I could not go.

Our pretense at flight was only an illusion knowing our heavy bodies could never fly. No matter how far we leaped we were doomed to fall back to the Earth. As with my brother Brutus, gravity becomes a portal into the unknown for all those without wings who dare to fly.

The tiny mouse landed on a branch just ahead of me and quickly dangled upside down stopping me in my tracks.

*"My name is **Midnight** and my kind fly through the night in search of food. The small creatures we chase dart back and forth through the air to escape us. We hear far better than we see and each movement they make becomes a signal for us to follow. Alerted by their motion we can quickly out maneuver them and catch them before their next turn. We have developed sonic ears and through the sounds these tiny creatures make we can anticipate their every move."*

Midnight: *"For eons we have chased them in the dark. Nature has given these tiny creatures a job and placed us in their path to keep them under control."*

Chasing the Truth

Midnight: *"We have been on the Earth for millions of years. I have come to guide you on your way. I am blind where others can see. I can see where others are blind. I have accepted my place in Nature; the physical world, the circle of circles; **birth** and **death** with **life** in between, nothing more - nothing less, life being the wonder of it all."*

Midnight: *"Like the little creatures that fly before us, we must chase and catch the sounds of truth before we know their meanings. Too often, no matter how bright the light, we are not able to see what stands right in front of us. Our place in Nature is obvious, but we refuse to see this basic truth."*

Midnight: *"Marcus, Your journey will teach you many things. If you listen carefully there will be many to help you on your way. You will gradually pass into the light."*

Midnight: *"On your trek southwest you will enter a sandstone canyon and discover the Universe. In the desert you will find and keep company with your best friend. Like you he decided to leave his kind to journey alone into the wilderness. He will be your truest companion and stand firm between you and the unknown."*

Midnight: *"Before you arrive in the west there will be those who will teach you how to find your way through the desert. Their lessons will include **trust** and **faith** and depending on your **fate** you will gain from both lessons or perish forever in the sand. In the mountains of Mexico you will be tested."*

Midnight: *"In the west you will find illumination. There will be cloudy days, but on the brightest days you will be able to see for miles; beyond the horizons of your mind and into the future."*

Midnight: *"Marcus, you will witness the sun illuminate the evening sky over a mighty ocean. This ocean touches many shores, shores you will never see. Like the Universe these shores are beyond your reach. One of your dear companions will glide across this horizon never to be seen again. **He will be your teacher, your friend and brother."***

Midnight: *"Although beautiful beyond description, it will not be the physical world that will bring you the most joy, but rather the good and trusting company of those you love and those who love you."*

Midnight: *"On this western shore deception preys upon the minds and hearts of the many. There are those who will teach you their truths. These truths have no margins and cannot be recorded on paper. To have meaning they must be*

131

the words and deeds of life which are etched in the fabric of the Cosmos where right and wrong are without question. If you listen carefully to your inner being you will decipher this sacred code and hold it dear."

Midnight: ***"Do unto others as you would have them do unto you;"*** *a simple and clear truth that we cannot seem to follow. Who would leave the land barren of its forest; naked and bare only to have the rain wash the land away? Who would destroy the homes of the wild creatures and kill all of their children? Who would kill the last condor, the last bald eagle, the last human? Who would foul the water and expect their children to drink it? Who would poison the air for profit?"*

Midnight: *"It is not on this vast Earth where most of us lose our way. It is within ourselves that many of us get lost. It is the metaphysical realm without boundaries which leads us astray."*

Midnight: *"Marcus, you will ponder great things only to become more confused. This confusion will lead to some answers only to create more confusion; stretching the truth beyond repair. The physical and metaphysical worlds are at odds; darkness-light, light-darkness, all being the same."*

Midnight: *"Marcus, watch out for **gibberish** and be careful not to lose your way. You must trust others to reach the unknown. **A great teacher will guide you safely through this dark maze and expose the fallacy of blind faith.**"*

Midnight: *"A large black bird will come to your rescue. **You will be watched from the shadows and from the shadows you will be both hunted and saved.** You will have many* *families and many will love you. Carried by the wind, you will venture home. You will again visit the mighty oak tree."*

Midnight: *"The land that you now cross will be claimed by many. Before man, the animals roamed freely to raise their wild children and survive. Then came the early **humans with stone tools** to mark their place in the wild. The two found **balance** and lived side by side; wild life and man, a fragile relationship in **balance** with Nature."*

Midnight: *"At an old mission a few will stand against the many. These few will become a legend and the name of the mission will echo through time. A new nation will rise to carry one star. The states to the east will gobble it up and claim all the lands between here and the west coast, and into the sea. The new comers will steal the land from those whose rights are scratched on paper without meaning."*

Midnight: *"The newcomers will call themselves Americans. Through barter and theft they will take the land from a proud and noble people. The tears from these native people will leave a trail across this land and sadden human history."*

The Uncivil War (Hypocrisy)
Midnight continued: *"In the future the nation of many stars will go to war with itself. It is the nation that was born out of the age of enlightenment with one serious flaw; all men were not created equal. The nation, once divided, will not stand and violently falls apart. The North will stand against the South with both sides claiming righteousness."*

Midnight: *"Each side will carry their **battle flags of many stars** to war. Battles will rage across the land like the pockmarks of a dreaded disease; festering and spreading* blisters north and south. *Thousands will kill thousands; Hundreds of thousands will die. Ruin will reign supreme while the nation suffers. Profits will be made by the few while the multitudes bury their dead."*

Midnight: *"Families will go hungry while unplowed fields yield nothing but death as brother kills brother across the land. Blue and grey, grey and blue all turned crimson red in the end. Muskets, bayonets and cannons will be employed as mothers and children cry for their lost husbands and fathers."*

Midnight: ***"This war will grow out of the holy gibberish of the founding fathers. Those that shouted the loudest for their inalienable rights will deny these undisputed rights to tens of thousands."***

Midnight: *"The **chained** and **shackled humans** stolen from a far off land will be declared by law worth three-fifths of a man. These humans of less worth will bring prosperity to the masters of evil who profit from this crime. Greed stacked bales high will enrich the **elite** while they and their minions whistled Dixie and call for war."*

Midnight: *"After a bloody struggle the chains of slavery will be severed. Yet the bondage will continue for generations while one people refuse to accept the other and the country in chorus sings: **'glory, glory hallelujah and crown thy good with brotherhood."***

Midnight: *"The chains will be replaced by the bondage of poverty and abandonment. Color will determine citizenship until one rises from the south to share his dream. Freedom will briefly echo across the land but will not truly take hold* or be heard. Brothers will not embrace each other denying their common birth; **of and from this Earth."**

Midnight: *"Out of Africa we will rise and from Africa we will find our true heritage. The heritage and beginnings too many of us still deny."*

Midnight: *"The storm will pass but the conflict will remain to scar the souls of our people. With so much promised one will stand and cry **'let freedom ring,'** while blood flows in the streets - brother against brother; a nation again divided; **'free at last, free at last, thank God almighty, I am free at last!' As we begged for justice we dropped bombs on the innocent and landed a man on the moon, "One giant step for mankind; born the age of enlightenment."***

Midnight: *"A nation torn and yet to heal will struggle against un-tethered greed and waste corrupting our future for generations to come."*

Midnight: ***"The light we seek and have yet to find evades our juvenile minds. We speak of truth, but know it not, regardless of the lessons learned. Peace will come when we accept our natural souls, gain our balance and find our wholeness with Nature; 'Even the Jordon River has bodies a floating. Are we on the Eve of Destruction?"***

Midnight: *"Until then we will chase the wind and catch nothing for our efforts. The next storm we create will put life on the Earth in grave danger. The Earth may become just another dead planet to orbit the Sun whose light and warmth will go unnoticed."*

Midnight: *"Without life our physical existence has no meaning. Without life we are but matter and energy unconsciously in motion in time and space. Only in living can we discover our true meaning and purpose."*

Midnight speaking directly to Marcus: *"Like you my dear brother I am nocturnal and do my best in the dark. I have followed you through the nights and into the forest to show you the way. Seek and follow the truth and on life's darkest night the truth will guide you into the light."*

Midnight continued: *"Remember there are others watching you. The wild is full of predators and many dangers. The predators are always stalking their prey; seeking to slacken their hunger or to feed their young. One misstep down the wrong path may spell your doom. **Your life hangs in the balance; if otherwise, life would not be so precious."***

Midnight: *"The forest is also full of **teachers, keepers and seers**. They are there to help you on your way. Who you put your **faith/fate** in will determine your final destination."*

In a flash Midnight was gone. Chasing the wind he darted into the night. With no trees in sight the sun rose above the eastern horizon giving birth to a new day. I picked up my **haversack** and headed southwest into the dry lands. I wiped the sleep from my eyes and quietly moved down the trail.

MIDNIGHT

Even on the darkness night there is hope

7. The Cactus Patch

The Black Scorpion

I left the grasslands behind me and headed southwest across Texas and into the deserts of New Mexico and Arizona. I had been traveling for days without anything to eat or drink. I moved down into a gorge that held some promise of water. In this arid land where there is water there is food.

The red and sandy walls were near vertical and reached heights of several hundred feet. The winding passage was initially very narrow spanning only a few feet. The passage gradually opened wider and wider as I traveled downhill. I hiked for several hours and noticed more and more cactus. I turned a corner and could hear water falling from above echoing off of the walls. As I descended further into the gorge the sound became louder and louder. I entered into a large opening alive with cacti and a majestic waterfall falling hundreds of feet from the cliff above.

The cactus was full of blooms and buttons. After drinking my fill I sat down to wonder over the beautiful cactus flowers; exhausted I fell asleep.

I was in the middle of a buffalo stampede and I could hear their hooves slice through the ground when I heard something scratching on the wall next to me. Startled out of my dream, I jumped. A *black scorpion* with its pinchers balanced before him and his tail set to strike stared at me in awe.

"You are a strange creature. I have never seen one of you before. Are you a criminal? Why do you hide behind that

mask, and the stripes you wear are you an escaped convict? Have you come here to rob me and do mischief? Are you a murderer, have you ever killed anybody? The scorpion anxiously spurred.

"Slow down-hold up, I am just a hungry traveler." I replied.

"How did you get here? What route did you take? How many days have you traveled? Where did you come from? Do you have any children? Where's your gear?" He drove on.

"I came from the eastern woodlands and I spent many years with the plains tribes. I mean you no harm. I am on a quest for knowledge. My **haversack** *is empty."* I replied.

"You are in a desert gorge, surrounded by sandstone. My kind has been here for thousands of years and we rule these lands like gods. We love and worship the Earth and Moon and have adapted and survived. We usually kill and eat trespassers but I'll grant you safe passage if you promise to respect the land. I am waiting for your answer." He insisted.

Startled at his abruptness I replied. *"I promise I will respect your land and all the lands I journey through."*

"I accept your promise. These walls are ancient and were formed hundreds of millions of years ago. The land was lifted into the air by great geologic forces deep within the Earth. The atmosphere moved moisture about in the air dropping its rain over the land. The water flowed down hill very slowly cutting into the sandstone forming this beautiful gorge. We were once tiny creatures that labored to survive. With our success and body armor we grew stronger and bigger. We developed our venom and learned to hunt. The

cacti are full of edible cactus buttons, are you hungry and ready to eat?" The scorpion insisted.

"I am so hungry I could eat a buffalo!" I said.

"You are forbidden to eat the buffalo! The buffalo are sacred to us, and like all creatures of the Earth we worship them. They contribute to the health of the land and travel in great herds. They keep the grasslands in **balance** *and drop nourishment onto the ground as they move about the Great Plains. They give birth to their young and protect their babies from predators. You must respect all animals along with the land. Are you going back on your promise, can I trust you to keep your word?"* He retorted.

"It's just an expression. I did not really mean I would eat a buffalo. Please forgive me I am hungry!" I pleaded.

It was growing dark and the scorpion moved directly to the first cactus tree and carefully worked his way to the cactus buttons not yet in bloom. He snipped them with his pinchers and carefully stacked them in a pile on a flat round stone deliberately placed at the foot of the cactus tree.

He gathered fourteen cactus buttons and stacked them in a pyramid. Five buttons formed the first circle, then four, three and finally two; at the top he placed a cactus bloom in honor of the new/black moon; the moon without light.

He gently said: *"We must declare our respect for Nature. We must walk around the cactus, counter clockwise fourteen times and clockwise fourteen times resetting our clocks to the rhythm of the Earth and Moon; paying respect to Mother Nature who gave us life."*

The scorpion took on an entirely new look. His black armor glowed with a light from within. His pinchers became lanterns illuminating our path around the cactus tree and pyramid of buttons. His pitch black eyes glowed blue as if filled with the oceans; a star appeared at their centers. His stinger glowed blood red throbbing with each heartbeat.

With each two passes around the cactus he removed a button. Starting from the top of the pile he worked his way down. We stopped when at the north point and shared our treat, devouring one button with each two cycles. After seven buttons were eaten we stopped and reversed our pilgrimage. Again, with each two cycles he removed a button for us to eat stopping this time at the south point in the circle.

When the round stone was cleared of buttons, after twenty-eight revolutions around the cactus tree, he positioned himself at the north point. He directed me to position myself at the south point each facing the other. He softly stated. *"Close your eyes and in the darkness find the light."*

I closed my eyes and the ground began to melt and the cacti began to dance in motion against the night's sky. The cactus arms reached higher and higher. Like a stream, the sky flowed from above and flooded the ground below. The air cooled and then became extremely cold. The cold air formed a mist that covered the thorns of the sacred cactus tree, crystals began to form. The ice on the arms and thorns of the cactus tree twinkled with light and tingled with sound; night became day and day became night.

I had eaten one too many buttons and melted into this bizarre scene joining the Earth and cacti in motion with my dreams. Joined together we moved about and danced with the rhythm of the sun, Moon and the night sky. There was a sharp pain in my arm, a swirl of lights and then everything went blank.

In that swirl of lights I found myself somewhere beyond life and death. I was part of an intense explosion where the Universe radiated out from nowhere; all the stars and galaxies burst forward in a flash of light beyond description.

In the center of this flash of light, was the Earth, ready to take form and give life to its many children. Through evolution one of its many children will mature enough to comprehend this great beginning; a gift of understanding, *light*, brought forward through time to illuminate our journey.

This swirl of light pulled into itself to ignite the Universe. The whole is part of everything and everything is part of the whole; a perfect sphere in a bubble of time and space. This was a beginning without an end, an end without a beginning. The physical became the spiritual; **understanding the totality of existence.** The spiritual became the ability to comprehend this simple truth, that we are of and from the Cosmos; **"We are the children of the stars, born of this Earth."** This is not a matter of belief, but rather a matter of acceptance. In the middle of billions of years of cosmic evolution, what portion of the Universe do we hope to control? I was beginning to see beyond myself. The wisdom of the scorpion penetrated my being and illuminated my soul. ***"You are a child of the Universe no less than the trees and the stars you have the right to be what you are."***

The canvas of space and time was painted brightly with galaxies, stars, planets, moons, comets….. Painted by the artist herself; Nature the grand artist of the Cosmos. This

141

would become the wholeness of Nature, all the energy and matter being from and of the Universe.

The scorpion's voice echoed off the sandstone walls: *"The Earth is one in a billion planets to bring forth and sustain life. Against the odds life on Earth has broken the constraints of shear survival to begin to comprehend the Universe and therefore the meaning and purpose of our existence; life."*

Then I was pulled into a white void. I was in a place that was empty, without color or form. I woke midday miles out into the desert. I had a horrible headache and noticed two strike marks on my arm. The center of each strike mark was blood red, surrounded by a deep purple fading out into a ring of blue with the two outer rings of blue flowing into each other.

I laid there until my head began to clear. The sounds and smells of life came rushing through my senses. I could hear things I never heard before. From a hundred feet away I heard an ant work its way beneath a rock searching for food. I had gained an awareness that I had not known or felt before. Everything before me was crisp and crystal clear. My sight had never been so sharp. I could see dust clouds miles away. I could smell the cactus flowers I left behind in the gorge. The Earth's new wonder and beauty was without measure and captured my soul; the scorpion had left his mark.

THE SCORPION

8. West by Southwest

The Coyote

It was approaching dark when my head finally cleared. I was out in the desert with no food, water or shelter. It occurred to me to retrace my steps and go back into the gorge. At least there was water in the gorge. I decided against it and pushed on through the night. The stars were fully out when I took shelter amongst some brush in a dry gully. In the distance I heard a howl. Scared, I hunkered down for a restless night of sleep.

When I woke I carefully peered over the rim of the gully and saw a wolf in the distance headed my way. In haste I scurried down the gully taking refuge within its deep banks to cover my escape. Traveling southwest down the gully I put as many miles as I could between myself and the wolf. I was now certain that he was hunting me. I found a putrid pool of water and had no choice but to drink as much as I could bear. I came out of the gully believing I was safe.

I continued my journey southwest and headed deeper into the desert region. I had a lot to reflect on. I was hungry, possibly being hunted and thousands of miles from my home in the eastern woodlands where I was born. I thought about the giant oak tree on the Allegheny Plateau and my parents, brothers and sisters. I thought about my baby brother Brutus and how much I missed him. I thought about the gang, the village and child and my dear wife and children. It had been years since I left home. I reflected on the dreams; Jetta, Odysseus, Justice, Midnight and the scorpion. What did the *voices from the wild* mean and what were they trying to teach me?

The warning about the humans that live in the east, the *"narrow path"* and the ***origins of the Universe***; what did all this mean? The *Sacred Circle*, my father; just what was I seeking? What is beyond the horizon? Why wasn't I contented to stay home? Why and where does the sun set? Why? Why? Damn these questions! These questions! Yes, these questions are always spinning in my head.

My thoughts were keeping me company on the trail. I stopped and looked back over my shoulder and there he was way out in the distance still hunting me! Surely he does not have my scent; the wind is at my back. He must be following my tracks. Damn this sand I need to find water to wash the scent from my feet and escape over solid ground where he can no longer find my tracks or sniff me out.

I quickened my pace and trotted on. He howled in the distance as if calling other wolves to join the hunt. Again I quickened my pace. I gradually left him in the distance and took comfort that he would not follow me into the desert; even wolves need water. I traveled throughout the day.

I would take no chances and leave out a few hours after dark putting miles and miles between me and the wolf. I needed to find water and shelter from the desert's cold nights; fortunate to still be alive, I slept out in the open and shivered.

I headed out under the stars and again quickened my pace. The sun rose above the eastern sky and there was no sign of the wolf. I headed out across the desert. Midday came and went and it was approaching dark and all seemed clear. I would take no chances. After midnight, with darkness covering my tracks I would leave out again.

My plan worked and at midday there was no sign of the wolf. I finally could rest and napped under a cactus tree. The sun was leaning westward when I awoke. I peered east and all was clear. The heat was unbearable and its waves distorted the horizons.

The speck grew into a dot, the dot grew into a smudge, and sure enough the smudge was the wolf! It was a small wolf, but a wolf none the less. Could I keep ahead of him was the most important question? For all the miles I had put between him and myself, he was still determined to track me down.

Tonight, I will walk through the night and this time for sure I'll escape him. Again he howled!

My life was at stake. Either way, tomorrow will be the end of it. No matter how far ahead of him by dawn, if he is still following me, I won't be able to go any further. I was exhausted.

Again I quickened my pace and hiked all night. At dawn there was no sign of him. At midday I was done and I collapsed on the desert sand. I laid there barely able to move. I looked east and there he was in the distance. It was over. I would die and be eaten by a wolf in the desert today.

I was lying face down in the sand. I looked up one more time and he was closing in. Knowing that because of me he would go on, I was resigned to my fate. I was exhausted and closed my eyes and then everything turned black.

I woke to find the wolf facing me. He laid there resting his head on his paws panting with his tongue hanging out. He stared directly at me and said:

"Hey man, I like your tattoos and piercings..... I tried to catch up to you but you kept moving through the nights. I called out several times, but each time instead of stopping, you quickened your pace. I never walked so far at night in my life."

"I could not keep up. I almost gave up. You kept on going in the wrong direction, deeper and deeper into the desert where there is no water. Remember, no water no food! Ha, that's a joke, in the desert, without water food doesn't matter."

Still in disbelief I asked: *"Where's the rest of your pack? Why did you not eat me? I thought you were hunting me so I kept my distance."*

My name is **Coyote**: *"I am a vegan, I eat plants. I never liked poking my snout into rotting flesh to begin with. We are scavengers by Nature. Something dying or already dead is our next meal, you know someone's leftovers."*

Coyote: *"We are not the great hunters we pretend to be. Spiritually I am beyond that anyway!"*

I said: *"You are a wolf and wolves don't eat plants!"*

Coyote: *"Don't include me with those hounds from hell! I am a coyote, masked-man, and we are the masters of the high plains. If I was a wolf you would have been **carrion** for the buzzards two days ago! The hounds from the east show no mercy to those they hunt and kill. **Be forewarned, they are coming! Their plan is to drive the wild ones off the land."***

Coyote: *"You're lucky it was me that saved your ass! Besides I am a loner and I like it that way. I don't run with the pack anymore. All that pack stuff wore me out. Prancing around in step with the other coyotes, not for me! All that killing and destruction; for what purpose and for who's gain?"*

Coyote: *"Cowing down to the leader and all-that alpha male bullshit was not for me. All that howling late at night and scouring the land for carrion and scraps drove me to the edge. You were always having to prove your loyalty and having to do things their way. Hunting and killing mice and other small animals then making a big deal of it, you know all that howling and macho predatory bullshit."*

Coyote: *"They tried to get me to sign up for another tour (hunt). I had served one **tour of duty** already and that was enough. Who wants all that grief and misery? I am just not into all that meanness and stuff. All that killing bravado was not for me. I am not into eating meat and wallowing in blood. I still nightmare over that part of my life. Forget that gung ho bullshit! I am just a little too hip for all that crap. I like doing the unexpected. So I just parted company. You know, skipped out."*

Coyote: *"One day I had enough of their evil ways and just moved on. They were so focused on the hunt they couldn't see the beauty that surrounded them. With their nose always to the ground they often missed the beauty of it all, all that we are truly living for."*

Coyote: *"We tend to think like the group and lose our true sense of being; **the singularity of our souls**. Besides, my soul is freer when I am alone; wandering around and eating* *cactus buttons and tripping off of Nature. My mind has grown tenfold since I left the pack."*

Coyote: *"Yeah man, I groove to my own moves, you know I work against the grain, I stand apart, I am me and me is here and now! I want to walk my own path; just **looking for adventure** and **whatever comes my way**. I was born to stand apart from the pack; I was **born to be wild!** Life is such a very short trip and we can't afford to do too many stupid things! Everything in moderation, and moderation in everything we do. Stay away from the extremes. Keep your cool!"*

I responded: *"Yes, I ran with a pack once and I know what you mean. It is better to walk alone than to do wrong with some "friends." I didn't like running with the pack either. How did you become a vegetarian?"*

Coyote: *"One cold winter up on the Great Plains I watched a herd of buffalo grazing in three feet of snow. I had been without food for over a week and thought to myself why not, they look healthy enough; especially the big white bull. What's good for the American buffalo, the iconic symbol of the northwestern plains, can't be all that bad. I was starving! Once decided, I dug through the snow with my paws and hit a mother-load of green grass just below the ice."*

Coyote: *"My first salad and I loved it. I learned to ignore my canines and use my small front incisors to cut the grass. My mouth wasn't really designed for this purpose and I had to learn how to chew using my back molars. I nibbled close to the ground and ate myself full. At first it made me light headed and the landscape appeared tilted for a while. Once beyond that I became a grass eater."*

148

Coyote: *"There was plenty of grass and it was easy pickings as compared to hunting. I found myself spending more and more time day dreaming than hunting for food. With the extra time I found myself more reflective with a tendency toward philosophy. With the grass my mind began to grow. Add a few cactus buttons and life on the high plains was a trip. Throw in a few grubs for flavor and you have a meal fit for a king."*

Coyote advised: *"You need to start eating some grass yourself. It may give you a different slant on life and chill you out a little bit."*

Coyote: *"I like my fellow creatures and now the only thing that I hunt for are friends. Would you like to keep me company? I know where there are water holes in the desert leading all the way down into Mexico and up into California, and yes the Pacific Ocean herself; the ocean of oceans. I know my way around this desert and have a few friends that can help us on our way. I want you to meet **Gila Monster** and **Side Winder**; man can they tell some stories. A lot of creatures have left their bones in the desert."*

Coyote: *"Hey, did you come out of the gorge leading down to the gully where I first saw you? Did you meet the scorpion? I see he left his mark on you. Man ain't he a trip? That was too cool with those dancing cacti, the flashing lights and the Universe. It gave me a rush I'll never forget! If you follow me I know where the next spring is."*

We shared our food, water and misadventures. We became dear friends and traveled many miles together. We would follow the Gila River south across New Mexico and then southwest into Arizona. We continued southwest through the

Sonora Desert into Mexico and the Sierra Madre Mountains until we reached the Colorado River. We followed the Colorado out into the Gulf of California; where this mighty river reached the Gulf was absolutely beautiful.

We wandered northwest into the Sierra Madres where meeting *"three"* criminals almost cost us our lives. If it wasn't for ***"a night crawler"*** we would not have survived.

In the Sonora Desert we would spend time with Gila Monster and Side Wider. These two beings would teach us many lessons. We continued west through Baja Mexico until we finally reached the coast. In the distance flew two black condors headed north. After spending time on the beaches of southern California we would hike into the Sierra Nevada Mountains and be stalked by a mountain lion. We would make our way up the Sierra Nevada Mountains and into the Cascades. This trek would take us over two years and carry us through three thousand miles of wilderness.

COYOTE

The Oasis (Gila (Monster)

Yes, a fresh water spring in the middle of the desert. The layers of sandstone beneath the desert act like a natural aquifer saturating the Earth with water deep below its surface. In the desert when the water table drops and the desert springs dry up, life becomes precarious in the extreme.

Mother Nature was gentle with us this year. There has been enough rainfall to keep the aquifer full supplying the desert springs with plenty of water. If we don't get lost there will be more than enough water and food for our journey.

Coyote was true to his word and with a slight detour we made it to our first spring. There was a wall of large boulders surrounding this spring hiding its precious treasures from the desert beyond. The spring sat in the middle of a lush oasis filled with plants and animals. The spring fed into a beautiful pond of crystal clear water. This natural pond stretched out from the spring a few hundred meters and too was surrounded by life. Like a deep blue sapphire the pond sparkled and reflected its blue light into the desert sky. Where there is water there is food. We drank and ate ourselves full.

Just a few hours earlier we were lost and desperate to find water. Coyote had lost his bearings so we stopped at an outcropping of rocks to visit his friend Gila Monster. We needed to find our bearings and get out of the heat for a few hours. I was apprehensive, but Gila Monster turned out to be a great host and the two of them told me Coyote's story.

A few years back Coyote ran into some bad luck and got turned around in the desert. He climbed this outcropping of rocks to get a fix on the horizon but became confused and disoriented. From horizon to horizon there was sand, all three-hundred-sixty degrees was covered with sand. North, south, east and west; sand, sand, and more sand, nothing but sand. The temperature was one hundred twenty degrees and rising. It was high noon and Coyote had lost his way.

Exhausted and believing he was dying, Coyote laid down on the rocks and fell asleep. Retelling the story they said:

Coyote: *"I woke up to Gila shouting; 'Wake up or you will burn yourself to death. Quickly come with me; you must get out of this glaring heat."*

Coyote: *"I said, but you are a Gila Monster." How do I know I can trust you?"*

Gila Monster: *"Call it **fate** or **faith**; either way if you don't get out of the sun you will have a heat stroke and die. Either trust me (have **faith**) or die, and I'll just leave you to your **fate** (f-a-t-e). You decide, it's too damn hot out here for me."*

Gila Monster: *"I told Coyote that I had warned the last traveler to stop and rest, but he would not listen. And if Coyote looked around he could still find the traveler's bones strewed across the desert. With that being said, Coyote obediently followed me into my burrow."*

Coyote: *"Yes Gila, you surely saved my life that day. I am glad I trusted you and through that trust you taught me my life's greatest lesson. At times you must put your **fate** in another's hands. Without **faith** in others life is meaningless. I put my life in your hands and you saved me."*

After the story we proceeded underground. The burrow was dark, dry and cool. I was relieved to be out of the blistering sun. My fears were unfounded. We had a few drops of water and fell asleep. We woke up a few hours later. Gila was a gracious host. He began by teaching us about our shadows and the eight points of the Earth's compass.

Gila Monster: *"When it is high noon your shadow lies below your feet, and you can't get your bearings with your shadow beneath your feet. Coupled with heat exhaustion you'll become delirious and lose your way. Travelers must come into my burrow, get out of the sun and let the sun pass further to the west before they attempt to cross the desert."*

Gila Monster: *"Your shadow moves with you during the day and sometimes at night; especially during a full moon. When out in the desert during the day you can use the sun and your shadow to find your way. At night you can't trust your moon shadow so you must use the North Star to get your bearings."*

Gila Monster: *"At midday, you lose your shadow because the sun is directly overhead. The heat and glare compound the problem and rob you of your senses. You must wait undercover and let the heat of the day pass. In the desert this is the best time to rest, take a nap."*

Gila Monster: *After you have rested you should let the sun fall further toward the west, so that it can recast your shadow. When you are facing directly west into the sun, your shadow will fall directly behind you pointing east. When facing west; movement to the right of these two marks is north, and movement to the left is south. Stretch out your arms to your sides and your right paw is pointing north and your left is pointing south. Draw a line between these four points and you have North, South, East, and West; west being directly in front of you. The opposite is true when traveling east; north is left and south is right, only your shadow this time of the day would be in front of you."*

Gila Monster: *"Once you have your four cardinal directions mapped out, it is easy to find NW, SW, NE and SE. As the sun sets in the evening, Northwest is half way between west and north and Southwest is half way between west and south. The same is true for Northeast and Southeast only you are facing east into your shadow."*

Gila Monster: *"During the morning hours, when traveling west, your shadow is to your front. Using these eight points; N, S, E, W & NE, SE, NW & SW will keep you close to your mark when moving toward your destination. The Earth is expansive and you must use **landmarks** in addition to the eight points of the Earth's compass to confirm your bearings and find your way: mountain peaks, ridgelines, rivers, ...*

Gila Monster: *"Now that you have rested let's go outside and practice what you have learned. Coyote, I believe this is your second lesson. Tell us what you have learned."*

With the lesson over, we climbed through his burrow up to the desert sands above. Coyote quickly took charge and faced west and checked for his shadow. With his arms stretched out, pointing north and south, he took his bearings, forty-five degrees to the left of west. He drew a mark in the sand at forty-five degrees and said.

Coyote: *"Follow that line for three hours and we will find our first spring."* Gila Monster: *"Is he right Marcus?"*

I answered: *"Yes sir he is right on the mark. If the spring is southwest as he claims we'll be sleeping by the spring tonight. There are no other landmarks except this outcropping of rocks."*

Gila Monster: *"If you keep this outcropping to your back as long as you can still see it, you'll be halfway there. With the absence of landmarks you must rely on the Earth's compass using the sun and North Star."*

With that we said our goodbyes and moved out. Before we stepped off his tearful eyes betrayed his affections and illuminated his handsome face. In this short time a bond had grown between us, a bond between a teacher and his students. He seemed proud of his students and the lessons he taught; the cardinal directions and trust. I turned back to wave goodbye and he was gone, as if never there, an illusion never to be seen again.

GILA MONSTER

The Sierra Madre Mountains

From the oasis Marcus and Coyote headed south finally reaching the Rio Grande. They crossed the Rio Grande and moved down into the desert region of northern Mexico. Using Gila's directions they zigzagged back and forth between Arizona and Mexico in awe of the desert landscape and sparse foliage.

With brightly colored spikes, buds and blooms various cacti species dotted the landscape with yellows, blues, purples and reds. Each desert cactus plant takes on its own shape and purpose with a variance scripted by Nature. The desert's green cacti blend perfectly into a sweeping canvas with broad strokes of browns, tans and reds looming in the background. The sand and limestone vistas, arches, canyons, stone carvings..., give this masterpiece its beauty beyond description; its luster and wonder.

This desert portrait, Nature's third dimension, is only surpassed by Nature's fourth dimension; the wildlife that inhabit or journey through this barren land. Life is the extension of our physical beings and the margin for survival in the desert is razor sharp with no room for error.

We carried plenty of dried food and two bladders of water retrieved from the oasis. Rapidly traveling southwest we could not invest the time to learn the food base that a particular area afforded the wildlife native to that region. The water holes, creeks and streams, the edible plants, the tiny creatures to hunt, the nests to rob, were just too scarce to spend time trying to find them. We had to stick to the most traveled trails to ensure we would find water; a substance in a desert too precious to gamble on. We would seek out the native villages that grew up around the most consistent water holes and sought the help of those who lived there.

The natives in this region were accustomed to the demands of the desert and had adapted well to its extremes. Most were kind and courteous in their demeanor. The region was known as *"Apache Land"* and would in the future write its own story. We filled our water bladders and traded some of our cacti buds for food. The market was abuzz with rumors about a lost gold mine high up in the Sierra Madre Mountains.

We were gringos from the North Country with much to learn about their culture and customs; their sense of being. Some of the villagers chuckled at our many questions. We told them we were headed to the ocean of oceans. They laughed and said good luck crossing the Sierra Madres which were crawling with banditos.

They said the worse of these outlaws were three demented brothers who were determined to do harm to others; *"kill and plunder"* was their immoral code. They were half-breeds from the Dakota Badlands. Rumor had it that they always kept one brother out of sight so when the time was right he could pounce on their unsuspected victims from his hiding place.

The villagers warned: *"Stay away from strangers claiming to be miners looking for gold or federal rangers protecting travelers on the trails."*

I quietly whispered to Coyote: *"Aren't you from the Dakota Badlands?"*

Coyote did not respond; a weird look clouded his eyes as he turned away.

Some of the villagers tried to discourage Coyote and I stating it was very dangerous with many rough mountains to climb and a few deserts to cross. They stated that if it wasn't for the delta formed by the Colorado River there would be no chance in hell that we would ever make it to the Pacific Ocean. Spilling out into the gulf, the Colorado River formed vast wetlands where we would be able to stock up on food and water. Beyond the delta were some of the driest and lifeless desert lands in the Americas. They laughed and said that most likely we would be killed before we ever reached the delta anyway.

A few villagers called us *"wetbacks"* and declared we had no right being in Mexico; that we were *"illegals,"* WOPs; With Out Papers. One outspoken old villager shouted to anyone who would listen that we were a bunch of murders and rapist bent on pure evil. This old nearly bald vulture with a spectacular comb-over stated that they should *"build a wall"* on their side of the border to keep the gringos out, *"a beautiful wall;"* and *"make the North Country with many stars pay for it."*

In spite of a few, most of the villagers were gracious and took us in. One villager drew us a rough map highlighting several significant landmarks to guide us on our way. To cover the high ground and cross the Sierra Madres we needed to reach the daily objectives marked on the map. He was careful to orient the map North, South, East, and West. Several of the villagers walked with us to the edge of the village and wished us well as we started up the rugged trail.

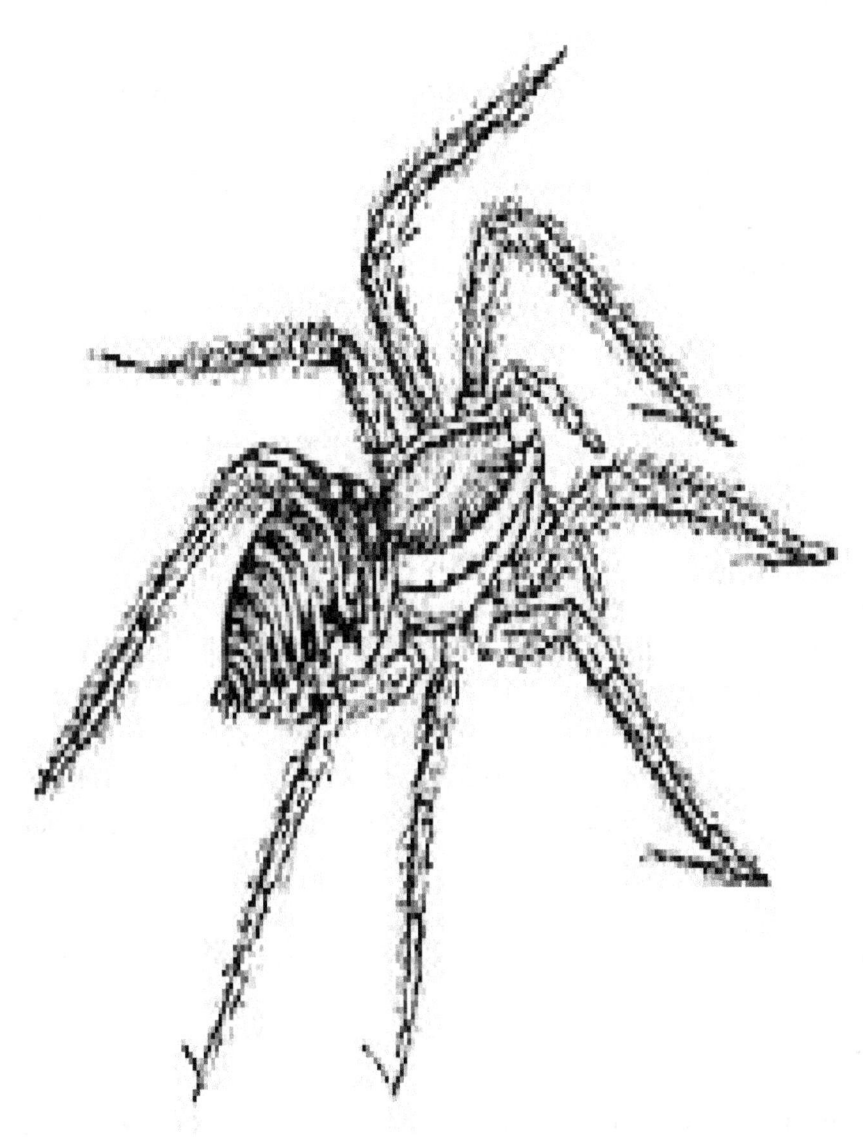

THE WHITE GHOST

The White Ghost (The Albino Tarantula)

We had been walking all day keeping a steady pace. We finally took shelter and settled in for the night. As usual I curled up close to Coyote and fell fast to sleep. Darkness brought comfort to our souls taking us deeper and deeper toward our dreams. From our dreams we sensed something strange, something outside of our bodies was moving our way. A soft scratching noise crawled across the boulders slowly approaching our camp. From our dreams fear woke us up. As we peered into the dark Coyote's ears began to twitch and turn. Puzzled, Coyote's snout locked in place with his ears strait up. He had located his target. We froze!

Like a ghost the creature from afar glided over the boulders toward us. We stiffened, and with our hair raised on our backs took a defensive stance. We were ready to fight for our lives. With bright red eyes and his body covered with white hair a large spider seemingly floated toward our camp. With one carefully placed leg at a time he drew closer and closer to us.

Quietly, so the spider could not hear, I said: *"WTF is that?"*

Coyote: *"The biggest damn spider I have ever seen!"*

Drawing nearer and nearer the spider presented no threat. His slow motion forward reassured us of his peaceful intent. In Nature's scripted language he spoke, words you can see but cannot hear. From our dreams Coyote and I encountered an albino tarantula; the **White Ghost**.

The White Ghost: *"I have come to warn you, trouble times three is on its way. Three becomes two and two becomes three. Three you will seldom see. In flashes the third-party* will appear, but trust him not because with him comes evil and death."

The White Ghost:
"I am a Seer and mean you no harm;
  I am here to sway you with my presence and charm.
Like all holy and sacred things I was born pure white;
  Like the white buffalo that illuminates the darkest night.
I am here to guide you on your way;
  So the generations after us will not go astray.
For the lessons we teach and pass on;
  Will enlighten their journey when we are gone."

Coyote: *"What news do you bring and if we stay our course will we encounter outlaws on this trail?"*

The White Ghost: *"I cannot tell you what I do not know. What I do not know I cannot tell you."*

The White Ghost: *"I can see way into the past and far out into the future; but the present and the near present I cannot see. Your past you already know. Your future is what it is, and although you will encounter trouble that will leave serious scars, you will survive the journey across the Serra Madres."*

The White Ghost: *"Marcus, looking west you will catch a glimpse of your future. This future will carry you into the light, a light that will lead you home."*

The White Ghost to Coyote: *"On a steep mountain pass, seeking the **"Great Divide,"** you will prove your fidelity and love. The confirmation of which will be carried into the heavens by those who love you."*

161

The White Ghost: *"Look for a golden eagle that saves a serpent from a pack of half-wolves. With the rattle snake held firmly in his beak and talons, the eagle will take flight. As the sun sets the golden eagle will fly high above the mountain peak pointing directly to the ocean of oceans."*

As the albino tarantula silently drifted away, in words you can see but not hear, he called back to Marcus and Coyote: *"While you are crossing these mountains I will always be near to protect you."*

Marcus stuttered: ***"Wa, Wa, Was that a dream?"*** ***"N, N, No, that was a nightmare,"*** Stuttered Coyote.

Marcus and Coyote pondered the meaning of the White Ghost's words and had trouble falling back to sleep. In the morning they pulled their gear together and made ready to leave. After their encounter with the White Ghost, they were eager to move on. Coyote and Marcus used the map the villager had given them and made good time the first few weeks. They had plenty of food and water and were on the right trail headed up into the mountains.

The landmarks were well illustrated and easy to find. Marcus and Coyote had not noticed it before, but clearly marked on the map was a mountain with the sun setting behind it. The mountain was shaped like a giant pyramid with a luminous eye carved near its summit. The villager who drew the map told them that the Colorado River was a *"short hike"* from this mountain and a few days would get them there. He told Coyote and Marcus that beyond the Sonora Desert and the Sierra Mountains heading due west they would find the Pacific Ocean; the greatest body of water on the planet.

Coyote's Cousins

Days turned into weeks and we were growing weary of the endless trek. The up and downs of the mountain trails were wearing us out. We had hit every landmark and were making good time. We needed to find a resting place where we could take a few days off and regroup. According to the map, not too far ahead, maybe two or three miles, we should run into a mountain stream where we could take a break. If we maintain this pace we should get there just before dark.

Approaching a fork in the road we ran into two scruffy looking coyote/wolves. Abruptly they stepped out from behind a giant boulder. Startled we stood our ground.

With a cockeyed smirk on his face, one coyote/wolf said: "Hey Cuz!" to Coyote. Again, Coyote seemed to cast his eyes elsewhere and drew quiet. Coyote softly placed his paw on mine signaling me that something wasn't right.

Under his breath, Coyote to Marcus: *"Remember, what the villagers and White Ghost warned us about.'"*

The better looking and more intelligent of the two spoke first: *"My name is **Jekyll** and these two are my brothers **Heckle** and **Mr. Hyde. 'Brother can you spare us a dime?"***

In a flash of horror before we could fully comprehend the image now before us, Jekyll's gentle persona twisted in the wind and back again. For an instant something ugly and wicked took Jekyll's place and pierced our souls.

Jekyll: *"We are federal rangers keeping these trails safe for travelers. What brings you two up into these mountains known for their bandits and thieves?"*

163

Assertively, Coyote: *"Why would a ranger need to borrow money? If you are federal rangers, where are your badges?"*

In a demonic blur Mr. Hyde stepped forward and growled: ***"We don't need no-freaking badges!"***

From a deep black crevice between two giant boulders fiery red eyes glared at Heckle and Jekyll/Hyde. A gut wrenching sound they never heard before blasted the travelers, penetrating their flesh and bones. The two evil brothers tucked their tails between their legs and ran down the mountain trail too scared to look back. Coyote and Marcus froze in place; neither dared to draw a breath. With a familiar sound something moved toward them. One click at a time, regaining their trust, the White Ghost came out into the light. Relief turned into joy and both Coyote and Marcus danced in circles. *"You saved us, you saved us!"* They cried.

Coyote: *"I hope they did not recognize me. They are my half-cousins who grew up in a broken home on the wrong side of the river."*

"How did your cousins end up in Mexico?" I asked Coyote.

Coyote: *"I don't know. They always were in trouble and on the wrong side of the law."*

Coyote: *"Their father, my **Uncle Alfonso** was the runt of his litter. Uncle Alfonso was extremely jealous of my father and his other siblings. My father eventually became the **Alpha Male** of our pack. Uncle Alfonso dared not confront my father and at an early age he ran away from home. He became extremely bitter. Some said he was bi-polar.*

Alfonso soon fell into bad company and joined a gang. He was quickly bullied and pushed to the back of the bus. Not being able to challenge the weakest coyote in the group he was determined to break away as soon as possible."

Coyote: *"One day while out scouting for his gang he found a young wolf pup who had wandered too far from her den. Although nearly his size Alfonso was successful at intimidating this young pup and for the first time felt he could play the Alpha Male. He quickly gained control of her, snapping and growling at her slightest missteps."*

Coyote: *"Alfonso was abusive and constantly mistreated the she-pup. At the first sign of resistance he would bite into her hindquarters. **Mini** resisted but Alfonso always had his way. Alfonso and Mini eventually had their first litter, all girls. When very young the **"twisted sisters"** were exposed to some **"heavy metal,"** and took up with a **"band of thugs"** never to be seen again."*

Coyote: *The second litter, **Heckle, Jekyll and Mr. Hyde;** all boys, were born evil. One of the three boys never drew a breath and was stillborn (Hyde). Aunt Mini grieved for her lost pup and took on a darkness that matched her soul. She would get confused and call Jekyll, Hyde and Hyde, Jekyll. Soon Jekyll answered to either name. My aunt and uncle constantly neglected the two/three boys. They failed to feed them or keep them clean. The two/three brothers ran wild and scavenged for food. Full of anger and spite they ran off and joined a pack of thieves; petty criminals. They were the mangiest looking coyotes/wolves in the badlands. They were malnourished and meaner than hell."*

Heckle, Jekyll and Mr. Hyde

Coyote: *"Heckle was not serious about anything except contributing as little as possible and always having his way. At a drop of a dime he was ready to mock someone and start a fight he intended Jekyll / Mr. Hyde to finish. He loved to tease, taunt and badger others. Heckle demonstrated no moral limits and readily embraced evil. "*

Coyote: *"Created by his neglectful parents Jekyll/Hyde was pathological. Jekyll's noble and scholarly appearance was paper thin with Mr. Hyde's wicked soul always ready to break lose; soft words followed by twisted deeds. Jekyll masked this evil with good looks and a gracious poise. At an early age Jekyll dabbled with drugs, pushing the limits; convincing himself he was still in control. Jekyll soon found out he could not contain the madness within; Mr. Hyde."*

Coyote: *"Given his gene pool, Jekyll was predisposed to the extreme, the extreme finally took him there; insanity, a place from which Jekyll would never return. Mr. Hyde kept to himself lurking around; he only came out to play. Mr. Hyde made Jekyll cringe in fear; Jekyll never knew when Hyde was going to pop through. Mr. Hyde was evil without moral boundaries; crippled emotionally, always reaffirming his demonic persona. The world would only see flashes of the evil hiding within; Hyde was a master of duplicity."*

Coyote: *"Mini's brothers finally tracked Alfonso and her down and ripped Alfonso to shreds. His hollowed carcass drew a horde of flies eager to lay their eggs and raise a brood of maggots. Mini's brothers were too ashamed of the half-breeds and abandoned looking for them."*

Coyote: *"When we were little pups my father made us stay away from them. The two/three brothers; Heckle, Jekyll and Hyde are some real bad hombres."*

"I can testify to that," stated the White Ghost.

The Old Couple (The Beast Within)

The White Ghost: *"A few months back the two/three of them committed a heinous crime; just one of many."*

The White Ghost: *"Not far from here Heckle and Jekyll stopped to get some water from an old couple's well. After they filled their canteens the old couple graciously invited the brothers into their home for dinner. Jekyll being the most polished, with grace and charm accepted. After dinner Jekyll opened a bag full of gold (pyrite). He thanked the old couple for the meal giving what appeared to be a gold nugget to the lady of the house."*

The White Ghost: *"The old man was transfixed. After some small talk Heckle and Jekyll convinced the old couple that in exchange for the couple's wedding rings the brothers would give them a treasure map. They went on and claimed they already had enough gold to last them two life times."*

The old man said: *"Sweetheart, with the treasure this map will lead us to we can always buy new and more glamorous rings to replace these worn out thin bands."*

Sternly the wife exclaimed: *"We will never replace these rings and the love they have brought us all these years. These rings symbolize the passing of our lives and the eternity of our love. I will wear mine to my grave."*

The White Ghost: *"In the end the old man had his way. He reminded his wife of all the hardships they had faced and how easier life would be for their family. And how they could provide their daughter's baby, their precious new grandson the medical care he desperately needed. Besides he had three strong sons who would jump at the chance to improve their lives and the four of them knew the mountains like the back of their hands. Always putting her family first she relented and gave up her precious ring."*

The White Ghost: *"The couple sadly gave their wedding rings to Heckle and Jekyll which the old couple replaced with two bands made from string. With a scary grin Mr. Hyde flashed from the soul of Jekyll. The old couple blinked in horror."*

Mr. Hyde emerges and says to his brothers: *"Let's take everything they have, tie them up and burn this place down!"*

Talking to himself Jekyll pushes back: *"No, no, no!"* They have done us no harm. Let's get what we came for and get out of here."*

The White Ghost: *"Heckle and Jekyll tied the old couple up and left the house and made their escape. The two brothers bagged up their plunder and headed into the wilderness."*

While on the trail Hyde burst through again: *"We should have burned the place down…we left too much evidence. You two are sissies; always backing down just when things start to warm up; you are wimps like your father."*

Jekyll, talking to himself/Hyde: *"We are not doing anymore evil tonight! Do you understand? Stay put!"*

The White Ghost: *"In an instant Jekyll and Hyde were gone. Heckle looked confused. Heckle hiked to a high point on the trail, peering over his shoulder he could see the flames of the burning house. Jekyll finally catches up with Heckle."*

Jekyll exclaims to Heckle: *"I tried to stop him, but you know how Hyde always has to have his way. He tied the old couple to their bed and lit it shouting 'burn, baby burn!' Evil is Hyde's energy source, and that evil energy will be with us until our dying day. I hate it when he claims that the* **Grim Reaper** *is his true father."*

Heckle laughing: ***"Our dying day; that's funny; the two of you, get it?"***

The White Ghost concluded: *"Without moral structure we are like jellyfish; creatures without spines. If we give our souls away, bit-by-bit, we will end up with nothing; empty, a flicker of reason lost in a sea of madness. If we* **'dance with the devil by the pale moon light,'** *sooner or later he will step on our feet. The absence of light, in spite of the darkness, will blind you. If we allow it, evil can claim anyone of us."*

Coyote to the White Ghost: *"What will become of these two/three brothers?"* The White Ghost: *"On the wrong day, Heckle will taunt Jekyll to the edge. Jekyll will desperately try to restrain Hyde; the dead brother within."*

Pissed off over a petty issue, Heckle cut into Jekyll: *"You're just like our father, a mangy mutt with his ears turned down, flat on his back with his tail between his legs, yelping for mercy; then acting like he was something special, prancing around like an Alpha Male. He was always abusive to mother, biting her, kicking dirt in her face, whoring* *around... **"You!"** being twice our father's size; Mother begged for your help **"You! You!"** let him get away with it... All prim and proper, who in the Hell are you pretending to be? A shiny gold tooth and those duds you wear don't make you a gentleman."* Beating Jekyll down further.... Heckle continued: *"And what about that twisted beast you Hyde? Like a maggot with no backbone you let him burn that old couple alive for two worn out rings. When our cousin Coyote did not greet us on the trail you let it go, because **"You!"** are ashamed of who we are; our mother an abused she-wolf and our father a runaway coyote, half-breeds; not because of our birth, but because; **"You!"** allowed that creep of a father and that beast inside of you to get away with it."*

When he could take no more; out of the deep reaches of Jekyll's soul, Hyde burst through, grabbed an ax and hacked Heckle to death. In a fit of rage Mr. Hyde chopped Heckle to pieces. Clumps of flesh and blood covered Hyde's face and hands. Waking to this horrid scene Jekyll threw himself down a well and drowned himself and his brother Hyde; poisoning the well's water forever.

Breaking Camp
The White Ghost stayed the night and shared his light. In the morning he was gone; nowhere to be found. After a few days of rest we broke camp. Filling our water bladders from a mountain spring we pushed forward. It was great to be on the move again. We traveled a few days and began to sense we were getting closer to the river. We had crossed all the landmarks except one. Later in the day we had just climbed over a ridge when we saw a golden eagle perched on a large cactus tree holding a serpent in his beak. Sure enough as the sun was setting behind the *"**Mountain of Knowledge**"* the

eagle took flight. The great Colorado River was less than a week away.

THE MOUNTAIN OF

KNOWLEDGE

Baja California

We continued southwest through the desert until we reached the Colorado River. We followed the Colorado into Mexico where it spilled out into the Gulf of California. Where the Colorado reached the Gulf was wondrous; it was one of Nature's most precious gardens. Over millions of years the Colorado River had cut a groove through the landscape starting in the Rocky Mountains flowing southwest down into Mexico. With the flow of its waters the Colorado carried millions of tons of silt rich in nutrients and minerals. As the Colorado pushed out to the sea its waters slowed down depositing silt to form a delta stretching out into the gulf. For eons and eons of unrecorded time this natural drainage system served Nature's purpose well. At this juncture the Colorado River split off into dozens of channels crisscrossing this delta forming a vast wetland covering hundreds of square miles. These channels formed a maze that inundated the delta with water and silt creating a lush oasis in a desert setting. These wetlands were home to a multitude of birds and other animals; an intersection of living organisms thriving in the wilderness.

The North Country (Nation of many Stars) gradually shut down the flow of the Colorado River into Mexico. Now this river barely trickles south depriving the surrounding region the precious water it so desperately needs.

Coyote and I explored the western edge of this delta filling up on food and water regaining our strength for the next segment of our journey. The real test lay ahead of us. Once we left the safety and bounty of the delta we would again expose ourselves to the extreme conditions of the desert. Only small animals make a permanent home of the desert. The larger animals are just passing through hoping to safely cross the desert from one water hole to the next. Those that do not plan well become carrion for the scavengers.

Our plan was to cut across Baja Mexico until we reached the Pacific coast. A formidable desert and some rugged mountains stood in our way. We would have to cross the last stretch of desert and the northern portion of the Baja Peninsula to reach the coast. It was midsummer, absolutely the worst time to be crossing the desert.

Side Winder

We were in the desert but a few days before we ran out of water and were overcome by heat exhaustion. It was summer and the first rule of travel is that you never cross the desert in the summer. The temperatures reached into the one hundred twenties during the day and could drop to freezing at night depending on your elevation.

We had crossed the Sierra De La Giganta Mountains down into the desert at its western base. We had been without water for two days and were too exhausted to get our bearings to move on. We attempted to seek shelter from a stand of cactus trees but being midday there was no shade to be found. Desperate and with our judgment seriously impaired we headed into the dunes. Caught in a sea of sand we resigned ourselves to our pitiful fates and collapsed at the bottom of a gigantic sand dune.

I was at a serious disadvantage. It was extremely bright and my vision was very poor during the day. I raised my head from the sand and asked Coyote: *"What are those dark spots drifting through the sky? Am I hallucinating; are we about to die?"*

Coyote: *"You know how easily you freak out, little brother. I did not want to tell you but they are vultures and they have been watching us for a few days hoping that we don't make it. But don't worry, they are not raptors, they are scavengers and will only eat you if you are dead."*

Coyote: *"It has something to do with their beliefs, their Nature. They believe as long as you are alive your spirit is still within you and they cannot have of your flesh unless your spirit has left your body."*

Coyote: *"They are the great Californian Condors. Their purpose is to clean the Earth of its dead and help the dead on their way; completing a circle within a circle."*

Down from the crest of one of the dunes moving as if gliding over boiling water a snake slithered up to us and began to bark orders…..

Side Winder: *"We got to get out of the sun right now. Get off your lazy asses and follow me, now. Move it Marines there is no time to waste, we've got to get the hell out of the sun!"*

He led us to his burrow and said with authority; *"Get in!"* We hesitated, but remembered our lesson well. Which will it be; **faith** or **fate**? We had no choice, **today it would be faith**. We would put the trust of our lives in the hands of a complete stranger. With his delirium, Coyote had failed to recognize him.

Side Winder: *"Didn't I save your ass a few years ago?"*

Coyote: *"I don't believe it. It's you, Side Winder? How did you get on this side of the mountains?"*

Side Wider: *"That's a long story about two rising nations at war with each other; both laying claim to land neither of them own. Did you not learn from our last encounter? You never, I mean never travel through the desert in the summer during the day, never! What did I teach you last time?"*

Coyote: *"That you always take shelter during the heat of the day and travel only at night using the North Star. The North Star is the anchor around which the heavens above the Earth spin as it moves through space and time."*

Side Winder: *"And?"*

Coyote: *"You take you compass bearings at sunrise and sunset to establish your line of travel; N, S, E, W, NW, SW, NE and SE. Most nights in the desert are clear and you can rely on the North Star to follow your line of travel. When traveling due west keep the North Star to your right, when traveling east, to your left, and all other points in between."*

Side Winder gave us shelter during the day and plenty of water for our trek to the coast. He helped set our line of travel for the first night's hike and came to bid us farewell. He mapped out two promising water holes along our way and several landmarks that only a blind raccoon could miss.

Side Wider: *"I hope I don't find you at the bottom of the dunes next summer. Stay alive, the condors need to feed their young. Remember my lessons and the North Star.* **When up in California don't get lost and stay true to your moral compass."**

Side Winder: *"Remember Nature gave us much to be thankful for. She has been kind to us and when she can, helps*

175

us on our life's journey. Life is hard and you will be tested. She will test your courage and resolve to stay alive. She will put obstacles before you to test your will and spirit. But remember she belongs to us and we belong to her. She is the Mother of all creation and from her body all came to be. Life and all of its wonders belong to her; including you and I. I have been on a long pilgrimage and I am headed home; back to the great canyon lands where I was born. There is a lot to learn and share if we are going to save the Earth. "

Rattling his tail Side Winder said: *"I'll see you again. Remember where you came from and where you must go."*

We waved goodbye to each other; he turned and disappeared over the crest of the dune and into the future.

In a few weeks we made it to the coast. While sitting on a high bluff above a sandy beach we watched our first sunset over the Pacific Ocean. By the next sunset we were committed beach bums. Coyote readily made the adjustment to seaweed and I to fish. We put the two together and made sushi; one of our favorites. During low tide springs popped up everywhere. The spring water was pure and fresh, filtered by hundreds of miles of sandstone. All was well. We roamed the beaches and for the time being decided to make the coast of Mexico and southern California our home.

SIDE WINDER

9. The West Coast

The Gatherings

Coyote and I worked the beaches of Mexico and Southern California for several months living off seaweed and fish. It was great to be in California. Life seemed easy out there on the beaches with plenty of food and gallons upon gallons of fresh water flowing from the mountains to the east. *"It was all too beautiful; the cliffs, the beach, the sun sets."*

We found ourselves being laid back and playing in the surf with no apparent threat hiding in the shadows. At night we slept amongst the boulders below the cliffs and during the day we played in the sand. This was the life and California was the sunny spot that brightened our souls.

We met *Otter* who was a hoot. He constantly played in the surf. His excursions in and out of the water were something to see. He looked like the missing link between the badger and seal. He was always after something good to eat and at times played with his siblings as they rolled and wrestled on the ground and in the ocean.

He had the attention span of a three year old and could not hold onto a conversation for more than two minutes. In spite of this slight disability Otter was quite friendly and although he hardly knew us he embraced us as friends. There is something about the west coast that seems to mellow everyone out.

We briefly left the beach and traveled inland north up into the Sierra Nevada Mountains which were breathtaking. Each night we sought out the highest ridge to cop a view of the setting sun. There were plenty of streams from the winter's melt to satisfy our thirst. On one visit to a stream I got that uneasy feeling like before that something was watching us. My senses were not picking anything up in the air or on the ground, no sounds, unusual smells, nothing; just an uncomfortable feeling that we were being followed.

After a few weeks in the mountains we decided to head back to the beach. Once on the coast we became *day trippers* moving north or south along the beach depending on the *happenings*. The seals were having their annual gatherings and were bunched up in herds up and down the coast; just basking in their success! There were thousands of them. Many of the seals played in the surf. A few seals were masters at riding the crest of giant waves. These seals would ride the waves with such grace it was amazing to watch.

One seal took the show. This cat was sleek, laid back with a sheen as slick as glass. Brother *Seal* was fun loving, easy going and full of himself. The babes adored him and he adored himself; just strutting his stuff.

This gathering place was located in a cove surrounded by giant red woods and was strikingly beautiful. Some of these gigantic trees were over four hundred feet tall and fifteen hundred years old; ecosystems unto themselves.

As we approached the beach brother Seal rolled in on a wave and in good humor he said: *"What are you two doing wandering the beach without babes? Are you guys funny or something? I mean that's cool with me, you know we get it out here, everything is* **copasetic***. Do your own thing, no one cares. What's good for the Condor is ok with the Eagle. Who* *are we to judge? You know;* **'It's your thing-do what you want to do. I can't tell you who to sock it to.***"*

I said to Coyote: *"Man, what in the hell is he talking about? Does he think we are comedians or something?* Marcus: *No man, you got us all wrong, not that it matters, just want you to get your facts right. We're two world travelers up from Mexico. We are looking for a place to hang out."*

Seal: *"Hey dudes; let me tell you this is the life! If you are so inclined there are babes everywhere."*

Seal: *"Anything that ever happens; happens in California first and I mean everything. You guys look too cool and I can tell by the way you are marked, you're not from California."*

Coyote, really pouring it on: *"As always we are looking for good company, a place to hang out and throw back with no cares and plenty of sunshine."*

Seal: *"We seals have been riding the waves out here for generations just like the force of life itself. In the ocean the mass of water behind you lifts you into the air pushing you toward the shore in a rush. Like the waves we ride for fun, life lifts us up and drives us forward to give life to others. Like all the generations that came before, this force of life swells into a mass of energy that carries us to the very top, (pinnacle, crest, apex, summit), of this wave driving us into the future. Like surfing, mating is the essence of existence. Man, we were made to mate; I mean to ride the waves!"*

Seal to Marcus: *"See that red hair beauty with big blue eyes; I think she is flirting with you, man. Whenever they fold their flippers across their breast and bat their big eyes at you, man you are in trouble. And man is she ever batting her eyes at you, little brother. In love, there are no boundaries."*

Seal's Youthful Misadventure

Coyote and I learned that when Seal was a young pup he almost lost his life to the sea. One day on a whim Seal swam far out into the western ocean chasing a giant wave. He wanted to prove to his friends he could ride the world's biggest wave and out class them all. The swells got bigger and bigger, the shore line drew further and further away. He was certain that the wave of all waves was out there somewhere waiting for him. He was determined to catch the ride of his young life and prove himself the greatest surfer of all time. For Seal a tidal-wave would not be big enough.

The swells were so high and deep he could no longer see the shore. It was midday and his sense of true east was lost in the waves. In his quest for glory a massive riptide had washed him away pulling him far out into the sea.

The swells towered over him and the sky grew dark and cold. His first real fear grasped his soul as he shivered with dread. Lightning crashed around him filling the blackness with flashes of light. Like jagged spears the blinding bolts illuminated his plight. A sense of doom consumed him as he fought the ocean for his life. The swells and night sky pressed together. Not being able to distinguish one from the other he was afloat in space and time between life and death; suspended within a black void, adrift toward oblivion. The flashes of light revealed a wall of rain crashing into the ocean. Through space and time he floated downward into the unknown. Seal embracing death quietly sang to himself: ***"Into the ocean I must go, into the ocean end it all. Let the rain come down."***

180

Exhausted Seal let go and drifted toward eternity; emptiness. The night's black sky began to break. With the breaking of the clouds came the morning light piercing through the shallows. Through the ocean he ascended upward carried by fate back to the surface. Where the sea greets the air he was reborn; carried back to life on the shell of a beautiful sea turtle. Seal: *"Who are you? Am I dead? Is this the afterlife?"*

The sea turtle: *"I was born during the age of enlightenment; the great renaissance, my name is **Florence** and **I am the keeper of rebirth for those near death.** I travel the oceans to assist seafarers who have lost their way. Your good fortune has placed you in my path. I am a mortal being capable of saving those who are moving toward the unknown. Last night **Chaos** reigned and ruled over the ocean. Many were swallowed by her lust. **Happenstance** brought you to me."*

Florence and Seal were surrounded by dangerous reefs. Still miles from the nearest island she reassured Seal they would make it to safety. True to her inner compass she headed straight for the island. There were killer whales everywhere. As Florence carried Seal to safety she told him her own story and why she roams the sea. She told Seal about the young islander who carelessly forgot his duties, but in the end saved her life. She shared the islanders' story of creation and their deep reverence for the sea turtle and Nature.

Florence: *"Long ago a young fisherman saved my life. The natives on these western islands revere the sea turtles who they believe were the creators of the heavens and Earth. Because of this belief I was saved."*

Mother Sea Turtle (In the Beginning)

The islanders' story of creation begins with the ocean of oceans. It was an ocean without an end or a beginning; an ocean without shores, an ocean that stretched beyond space and time, into infinity.

One night a bright blue star fell from the heavens into the ocean of infinity and *Mother Sea Turtle* was born. She was the only living creature in an ocean without end. For eons she traveled this ocean alone. Lonely, she grew sad, knowing she was missing something; something profound. At sea she would often dream about tiny little turtles. These little turtles would swim around her filling the ocean with movement and joy. From these tiny turtles green bubbles of life would pop through her mind; pop, pop, pop; a bubble of life here, there and everywhere; like the Universe, just a dream.

A red star appeared one night and fell into the ocean. Mother Sea Turtle grew warm inside, giving live birth to hundreds of sea turtles. Her children who were born at sea journeyed deep into this endless ocean. Soon rocky shorelines and sandy beaches appeared everywhere.

It would be on these beaches where the sea turtles would populate the Earth, each to and from her own special nest in the sand; hiding their precious eggs from the predators to come.

From these turtles all the small and large land masses grew out of the sea and blossomed with life. The seven older sisters grew into the large land masses known as the continents while their little brother turtles spread out into the various seas and oceans creating thousands of islands.

Over time the pure blue waters of the oceans and seas surrounding these islands teemed with life. Every sea creature found on Earth made it to these islands. The sea beds around the islands were covered with coral reefs, the homes for a countless number of fish and other forms of aquatic life.

The ocean of oceans folded inward and the Earth was formed. The ice caps swirled into being forming the two super cold spots on the Earth, "Latitudes – North and South – Ninety Degrees." These cold spots, the poles, caused the oceans and air to move.

The imbalance of the Earth, the wobbling of its axis, was magnified by the back and forth melting of the polar caps. The expansion and contractions of these ice caps further accentuates this movement and from this movement the winds and currents were born.

The equatorial islands popped up everywhere. From their rich soils grew a multitude of palms, coconut and banana trees. The great mango tree would tower over their forests along with the guava and papaya trees. Pineapples and other wild fruits would cover the landscape. Flowers bloomed everywhere. The tropical breeze flushed the islands with a warm sweet fragrance found nowhere else on this Earth. The *Garden Before Eden* was beyond description; just the pure perfection of Nature herself.

The variance of species from island to island, continent to continent matched the variance of the physical planet itself; enriching the Earth's life forms. From the beginning of time as the Earth repeatedly reformed itself life evolved to keep up; conforming to Nature's ever changing demands.

For thousands of years the birds on these islands were so safe they forgot how to fly. Their wings slowly became stunted and were rendered useless in their attempts to escape the wild beast that were brought to the islands by the humans.

Each island was in balance with Nature. Once the humans touched their shores the margins for the survival of these natural gardens were reduced. ***"The humans would have to keep this balance or their own survival and happiness would not last."***

Mother Sea Turtle warned: ***"Mankind, the eldest brother of Life, must keep in balance with Nature or his image will fade forever from this Earth.*** *The lands and shores touched by the oceans are sacred. We must always use Nature's resources wisely. Her gifts should never be taken for granted."*

The West Islanders

Florence: *"The natives told their story of creation to the children over and over again. The children were taught to take care of Nature's narrow margins and only use what they truly needed. They must guard against wanting more than what is necessary to survive; and that the wanton lust for more on the tiny islands would destroy their way of life leaving the islands bear and naked, victims of the ocean's violent storms."*

Florence: *"One evening a careless young man left his family's fishing net on the back of his father's canoe near the shore. This adolescent had been schooled many times to care for all life and only take from the sea what his people needed. The islanders further taught their youth to never kill or put in harm's way the sacred sea turtle. He had been* instructed many times to fold the fishing net carefully and store it high up on the beach away from the surf. A net drifting in the tide was certain death for the birds and turtles that were accidently caught in its cords."

Florence: "That night a large wave crashed onto the canoe and washed the fishing net into the surf."

Florence: "Finding the net missing, the father confronted his son alarming the people of the risk to the innocent. The young man ran into the surf and began searching for the net hoping that the sacred turtles were all safe. Again and again he dove into the ocean. Desperately searching with each dive, exhausted and out of breath, he found me."

Florence: "I had been tangled in the net for a long time. I had managed to keep my beak above the water for hours struggling against the current and surf. Dead and adrift I rolled with each wave. With my last breath taken, my next breath was full of seawater. My earthly lungs were locked in place by a swell of saltwater, my breath and life were gone, never to return. Everything turned black."

Florence: "The young man pulled me to the surface and carried me ashore. My lifeless body was there for the tribe to morn."

Florence: "No-No, the young man shouted, this cannot be! He pushed his face into mine and blew air into my mouth. Please, please come back! Again he blew. With this blast of fresh air the seawater burst from my lungs and the light within returned."

MADA'

Florence: *"His and my salvations were joined, and the island's people rejoiced. They held a great feast to celebrate our rebirths. From our darkness came light. He became a keeper of Nature and for the rest of his life cared for and guarded the island's wellbeing. He constantly reminded the children to protect and revere all that is Nature. Over time the keeper became the chosen guardian of his island."*

Florence: *"His name was **Mada**, the guardian of the **Garden Before Eden**. He patrolled the shore line and forest daily. All the natural springs of fresh water were kept clean. He instructed the children as to their duties regarding the care for all that is natural including their love and respect for each other. They were to carry the highest regard for Mother Sea Turtle (Nature). He warned that wanting more than what you truly needed from Nature was a sin. **To further illuminate this truth, that we must keep our balance with Nature,** the keeper shared his dark vision with the children."*

The Keeper's Dark Vision

One day the keeper stopped to admire the beauty of a tropical flower. A colorful and stunning butterfly landed on its petals looking for nourishment. The butterfly folded its wings and appeared unaware of the keeper's watchful eyes. Like a microphone the petals of the flower amplified her voice. The butterfly spoke to the keeper in words he could see, but could not hear; reaching his inner light.

The butterfly said: *"My name is **Wonder** and I have a story to tell. On an island far out into the ocean its inhabitants created a highly structured and prosperous society. The layers of power and wealth gave order to the island's people. The bottom layer of this society, the common people, served the layers above with the topmost strata, **the elite**, reaping*

187

all the wealth and power for themselves. The elite, as always, used the **spirit warriors** to control the masses."

Wonder: *"To control the masses those in power created the gods. Through the **recital of gibberish**, the common people were carefully taught to obey and serve the gods. The **spirit warriors** directed the common people to carve the images of the gods in stone and create a sacred site where their gods could peer into the heavens and watch over the people."*

Wonder: *"At first the common people were joyful to serve the gods. They labored night and day in worshipping and serving their gods."*

Wonder: *"The stones were to come from the highlands; miles and miles away from the sacred site. The images of the gods would be chiseled out by hand taking years to finish. The forest had to be removed to build roads to and from the rock quarries. In addition, the engineer's designed rollers made from the trunks of the island's tallest trees. Thousands of trees were cut down to make the rollers to carry these massive stone images to their holy site. Hundreds of slaves, the common people, were "employed" to move these giant figures across the island."*

Wonder: *"Teams were organized and the rock quarries and forest buzzed with activity for years. With so many gods even the smallest child worked on the teams fetching water and food for the workers; **slaves to the royal family and gods.**"*

Wonder: *"In a few generations the forest was gone. The land grew poorer and poorer. The wealthy wanted more and more. The spirit warriors drove the people harder and harder to produce more for the wealthy. The nutrients of the* soil were depleted. The staple for the poor, the sweet potato, grew smaller and smaller. The wealthy would feast while the poor grew hungry and starved. Over time bitterness set in."

Wonder: *"The birds were the first of the wildlife to disappear. **It became the fashion of the elite to wear hats adorned with feathers.** Then came the **elites' robes** and finally their **gowns**, all adorned by the colorful feathers of Nature. The blue and green feathers being the most desired."*

Wonder: *"More elaborate than the first, each fashion show demanded more feathers. With each species of bird gone, the demand for more feathers grew intense. At the end, a hundred sea shells could not buy a medium size brown feather, yellow feathers cost thousands, the red feathers were priceless, and the blue and green feathers could not be found; reserved exclusively for the royal family."*

Wonder: *"The collectors went mad to corner the market. The collectors finally went after the baby birds for their precious little plumes. The nests were robbed of their young. A few keepers expressed concern; but they were readily stripped of their rank and sent to the rock quarries. Before long, the birds were gone."*

Wonder: *"With the forest cut down the land became incapable of sustaining the wildlife that once flourished on the island in **harmony** with the people. The **elite** acquired a taste for the wild animals and soon they too disappeared. All the creatures supported by the island's forest soon vanished. Nature's Eden was gone; rendered barren by the lust of the few. **"Man and Nature are at odds and out of balance."***

WE ARE WATCHING YOU,
WATCHING YOU,
WATCHING YOU,

WONDER

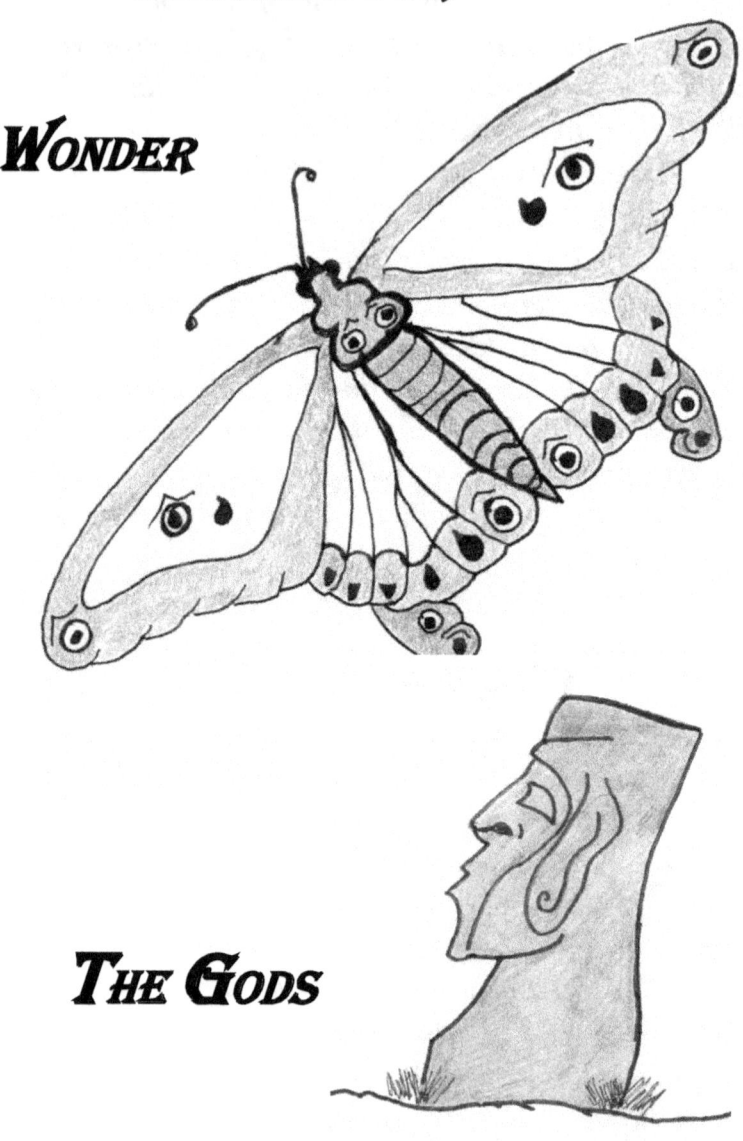

THE GODS

Wonder: *"With the trees gone the island's rich soil was washed away. Stripped naked the island's natural systems began to fail. Right in front of its people the island began to die. Within a few months the islanders were starving."*

Wonder: *"To refocus the poor's attention the **elite demanded more gods**. When the wealthy ate the last sea turtle the society fractured and like a volcano spewed fire. **The masses rose up and began to kill the elite**. The **spirit warriors** stepped up attempting to play one group against the other. A few saw through this deception and hunted the **spirit warriors** down; only to take their place. The killing went on until only a few were left. With nothing else to eat they began to consume their dead. The once prosperous people serving their gods and living in balance with Nature became cannibals, the eaters of their brothers' and sisters' flesh."*

Wonder: *"With madness in charge, the insane fled the island seeking absolution for their crimes against Nature. Out into the sea they were swallowed by a violent storm. Today the island stands as a bare rock monument to mankind, with the gods of stone staring blindly into the sky."*

The keeper would share this dark vision with the children warning them not to believe in the gods created by man, but rather to believe in the "wonders" of the Earth created by Nature. ***"Remember to only use of Nature what you need."***

Hawaii / Paradise

Florence: *"I was saved by a native islander who became a revered keeper; a guardian of Nature. In return for my rebirth and his spirit, I vowed to roam the seas and protect all those who crossed my path."*

191

After telling Seal her story Florence carried his weakened body to shore and nursed him back to health. As his strength returned they roamed the beaches, explored the forest and enjoyed the wonders of life. They chased each other into the ocean and played in the surf. Over time they became dear friends and Seal slowly recovered his strength.

Early one evening while playing in the surf, Florence and Seal came across a crystal clear stream of fresh water. This stream, cutting across the sandy beach, flowed into the ocean of oceans. As the sun dipped toward the west, Seal seeking Florence's attention raced up the stream to the edge of a beautiful tropical forest. Florence giggled and immediately chased after him.

The stream's clear water rippled over a bed of blue stones slicing through the forest floor forming a quiet pool before spilling onto the beach. A wide sandy trail followed the stream inland into the forest; a pristine and mystical jungle.

Seal to Florence: *"Let's follow the trail and creek and see where it takes us. Surely there are some highlands from which this stream flows. Maybe we can see the entire island from that point."*

Florence: *"Dear One, it is too late in the day to do that kind of exploring."*

Seal: *"You are right my Dear One. We will only follow the trail for a little while and then turn around. It's too beautiful to pass up. We will come back tomorrow to fully explore this stream and where it comes from. I promise we won't go far."*

192

They stopped and gazed into the pool of water viewing themselves in its mirror reflections; two beautiful creatures of Nature; *in love as brother and sister before the rules of mankind*; married in Nature without preordain vows. They were married without pomp and pretense; married by the call of the wild without pageantry; where words are scripted not spoken, yet sacred beyond human comprehension.

The tropical forest surrounding the sandy trail and creek was indescribably beautiful. Banana palms and coconut trees were everywhere. Guava, mango, and other trees without names covered the forest floor. Tropical fruits and flowers punctuated this beauty, painted on an emerald green background with an array of colors splashed against its canvas. Bright reds, oranges, yellows, whites, blues… were everywhere giving this garden both brilliance and serenity. The fragrance of Nature's abundance of flowers and fruits filled the air with exotic scents and freshness.

The wild ones: the birds, reptiles, insects and others were as colorful and further accented the forest's beauty with movement, wild calls and other strange sounds. The ocean breeze cooled the air under the canopy of this forest gently warming the hearts of many.

With Seal leading the way Florence wondered over this tropical paradise; the *Garden Before Eden*. They came to a small brook flowing into the stream. The sandy trail widened at this juncture leaving a path across both streams. Seal insisted they follow the smaller brook first; then turn around and head back down stream to the beach.

Florence: *"My Dear One the sun has dropped below the trees we can't linger too long. Already the shadows grow."*

Seal: *"I promise at the next crossing we will turn around; cross my flippers and hope to cry."*

After eating some wild exotic tropical fruit they made a loop which ended where they started. *"Impossible, both of these creeks appear to flow up stream,"* Seal exclaimed. *"We must double our pace and beat the setting sun!"*

Florence and Seal made their second loop finding themselves again where they started. Even with darkness approaching the forest appeared safe and tranquil. There was no sense of danger in the night's air; nothing sinister or evil lurking in the forest. Even with night closing in perfect peace and feelings of joy filled Seal's and Florence's hearts.

Seal said to Florence: *"Let's make our bed for the night in the soft sand under the trees at the trail's edge."* Seal opened his arms and welcomed Florence to join him in sleep: *"We will sleep in Nature's bed tonight and share her peaceful and easy feelings; my love for you and your love for me-forever."*

Where the two streams crossed a window through the canopy of the forest appeared. As they lay in each other's arms, stars raced across this opening revealing the Universe to Florence and Seal. Here and there stars broke through the smaller holes in the canopy briefly revealing their brightness giving the night sky patches of light everywhere. With a tropical breeze these patches of light danced through the night. As Florence rested her head on Seal's chest they fell to asleep.

Oahu

Florence woke as the first signs of dawn twinkled in her eyes. She instantly knew Seal was not next to her. She was startled by the tracks leading away from their soft bed.

Tracks she had never seen before headed down stream with no sign of Seal anywhere. Florence knew that Seal never would have left her alone, never!

The tracks were strange like no other animal; with five slender elongated digits on top, followed by an odd shaped pad in the middle and a deeper oval pad at the bottom. These tracks clearly headed down stream, and in haste Florence chased after them. Florence followed the small brook to the wider stream that led back to the beach.

The unusual prints led out onto the beach and into the surf where she pursued the strange creature that may have taken her Seal away. She entered the ocean of oceans and began her search. The water was clear and calm enough to see hundreds of feet in any direction. Dive after dive yielded a collage of beautiful multicolored corals and schools of fish with no sign of her precious Seal anywhere.

Refusing to give up, Florence searched in vain. Florence dove time and again searching for Seal or the strange creature that carried him away. Exhausted Florence swam back toward the beach. Her toes touched the warm sand below the surf as she stood up for the first time to see a young native stepping out of the forest. *"He must be the one,"* Florence joyfully exclaimed. The creature's natural beauty instantly captured her heart.

Kil Auea

Seal woke with a start; where was Florence? Her tracks were clear and headed directly downstream along the brook, then beside the larger stream. He rushed after her feeling fearful for her wellbeing. She never would have left him, never! He approached the edge of the forest and paused at the pool of mirrors. In the pool's reflection stood a beautiful human face. With long shiny black hair resting on broad strong shoulders his handsome face possessed deep dark brown eyes and bronze skin. With that, Seal smiled. Casting light everywhere his bright smile illuminated all the shadows in the forest.

The forest whispered: Your name is **Kil Auea** from the island of fire. You are the last born of these islands. You are a brave warrior who seeks **peace** and **harmony**. Your love **Oahu** from the island of pearls waits for you in the surf.

Dressed only in tattoos he worked his way to the edge of the forest. On his right arm was a tattoo of seven sea turtles chasing seven seals; one eager to catch the other. On his left arm seven seals chased seven sea turtles, again one eager to catch the other. Riding bands of ocean waves the seals and sea turtles in perfect form chased each other around and around Kil Auea's muscular arms. Like the stream of life; a perfect circle in a Universe of perfect circles.

In that Kil Auea quickly followed Florence's tracks into the surf. Standing near the ocean's edge, a figure bobbed up and down in rhythm with the waves. Slowly a beauty dressed in Nature's finest linen stood up. Wearing only a red flower over her left ear and a lei of flowers around her neck, she rose from the sea robbing the ocean of its beauty. Her hair fell below her waist and her form like his was beyond perfection. She too had black hair, deep brown eyes and a bronze complexion; children of the islands and seas, those who crossed the ocean of oceans to settle the islands and bear their children; the native Polynesians.

"Aloha, hello and goodbye, I love you. My name is Oahu from the island of pearls. Come follow me into the ocean of oceans and play. I have been waiting for you all my life."

Kil Auea: *"Aloha, to you my sweet princess. I have searched the world for your love and have finally found you; and in you I have discovered paradise."*

They embraced and with soft kisses confirmed their love for each other. They played in the surf and out into the ocean in awe of Nature and their human beauty. They returned to the island of love and played in the sand. Each glancing touch inflamed their passions. They could not get enough of each other's love and joined throughout the day *"as lovers often do."* High up on the beach at the edge of the forest they wrapped themselves in each other's arms, watched the sun set in the western sky and fell asleep. ***"The stars from the east raced forward and night descended over the island. Brilliant clusters of light sparkled in an ocean of blackness; the endless emptiness and fullness of the Universe, a wonder beyond description."***

With the morning sun Florence and Seal awoke where the two brooks joined and where they had made their bed the night before. Curiously the joining brooks again flowed down stream. They recounted their dreams to each other. Their dreams were an extension of their love and souls. Together they discovered that no matter what form it takes in Nature love is without measure and eternal. They awoke to a love between themselves that was already there. In their dreams they shared the story of the child they would leave behind to wisely care for the islands called *Hawaii*.

(Dedicated to my Mother and Father)

Florence to Seal: *"In the future war will reach these islands. The red dragon from the **"House of the Rising Sun"** will bring fire and destruction to paradise and its children. You my love will challenge the waves a thousand times and honor your species. A mighty whale will carry you home to me."*

The Journey Home

Florence: *"Are you ready to go home?"*

Seal: *"Only if you will guide me on my way. I have learned my lessons well. I have nothing to prove and I will never again take life for granted. I will hold Nature in awe and always respect her majesty over life. Her forces are without parity and she will not be compromised."*

Seal: *"Florence, my dear sister I was blessed to find you in my path. I wonder at your gracious being and I am forever grateful for your love and care. Your compass is true and your bearings are sound, your inner light defines true north. You are always true to your course. If I follow you I will never lose my way again. If you are ready to lead I am humbled to follow. Trust in you, for me, is eternal.*

Florence guided him home, a place he would have never seen again had it not been for her loving care. From Florence, Seal learned true love and companionship. He rejoiced that one could find hope in one of life's darkest seas. He was returned to the beach on which he was born. A breathtaking coast that one day would be called California.

Because of Florence, Seal lived to ride the big waves he loved so much and become Coyote's and my dearest friend.

Mokupuni o Hawai 'i

For millions of years her tropical shores sat in isolation from the world. Like a string of pearls she adorned the ocean of oceans. In a vast ocean untouched by man she (Hawaii) lived in peace. The islanders arrived to bear their young and cast their nets into the sea. In her harbor of pearls Florence and Seal's love child was born. This child took the form of a human and he became a mighty king. He proudly protected his islands and ruled his people with wisdom and kindness.

A powerful giant of many stars raced forward and took the king's lands casting his family and people down. Claimed as its destiny, the giant dominated the western seas and threatened the East. With a great fleet of canoes this giant eagle gained dominion over the ocean of oceans.

The red dragon rose from the East to darken Oahu's blue skies; raining thunder and fire down upon the tranquil. The dragon joined with the axis of evil to threaten the world. The sleeping giant with many stars and stripes woke from its slumber and flew into action. From the ashes of deceit and betrayal this powerful eagle rose to smite the dragon.

Killing millions, a terrible struggle infested the Earth. In a flash justice was rendered, and in seconds tens of thousands died. The instrument that violently brought peace now threatens the Earth. We stand before the end, under the count of three, (III).

The *Garden Before Eden* is now covered with concrete and asphalt. Towers of stone stand on her once fertile ground. The fresh air, water and sea that once were free are now for sale. All the wild places that once served Nature have been subdivided and are now owned by the few. Like the blue and green feathers of some extinct birds the wild places are rapidly disappearing from this Earth.

FLORENCE / OAHU

Beach Boys

Coyote, Seal and I became the best of friends. We were a bunch of wild boys just playing around and laying about on the beach. We were moving and dancing to the music of the ocean prancing around for the babes. We were constantly hawking the seal gatherings for attention. We basked in the sun *tripping* off the western horizon in a beautiful cove surrounded by giant redwoods. We were laid back and cool; in motion with Nature. There was plenty to eat with warm soft sand between our toes. Life could not be better.

We were three *beach boys* with idle minds engaged in idle talk, at times leading ourselves to some profound understandings; understandings about ourselves, our affection for others and the deeper meaning of life. Intellectual discourse was a journey in and of itself with boundaries, at times, exceeding that of the Universe.

Just Talking Some Shit

Coyote, Seal and I would spend days combing the beaches looking for babes and talking some shit; just having fun.

Seal: *"That's really some cool shit. You know, shit that's not hot; just out of the refrigerator. Not the freezer; that would be some icy shit. Cool shit, shit that feels good to the touch. The stars, the galaxies, the Cosmos, the big waves, life, your good friends, love… That's some very cool shit."*

Coyote: *"Avoid the heavy shit. You know, the shit that will weigh you down. The shit you don't want to carry around. You can't go on hating yourself for the shit you have done, allowing your past to drag you down into some awful shit. It's too much of a burden. It is the shit you can't change. All* you can do is to forgive yourself and try to live a better life. *Leave that heavy shit behind. There is nothing worst then digging around in a bucket of shit.* "

I continued the thoughtful conversation: *"That's some deep shit. You know, shit that's not shallow. The shit you don't want to step into or you will find yourself up to your neck in shit. You know, pondering the supernatural, spirituality, beyond our mortal beings into immortality. Trying to make sense of it all; losing sight of the moment. You are into some very deep shit. You are way over your head in shit. Just keep your mouth shut and try not to drown in your own shit. Get serious you guys! You two are just full of it."*

The Love Fest (Idle Bodies)

Man, the west coast was something else and you would think me and Coyote came from another planet. They were having sing-a-longs and running naked in the surf. They were **tripping** off of everything including **clean air** and **brotherly love**. The whole scene was **psychedelic**; a real spin of light. We were pushing the limits and expanding our minds. We were walking on the fringes of our mental horizons and on the edges of reality itself. All that we were and all that we were ever going to be went up in smoke.

The speed of light had nothing on us. Not only was the west coast progressive in its thinking, in our intellectual journeys we had pierced the very boundaries of contemplation. The west coast was a cosmic event in and of itself.

There was a lunar love and smoke fest going on and Seal asked if Coyote and I wanted to join in. At first we said; *"count us in,"* not really knowing what a **love fest** was, it just sounded pretty good. coyote was shocked that the

202

groupies were ***smoking grass*** not eating it. And I was shocked that everyone was naked and kept on rubbing against one another. Man, we were freaked; out of our league and beyond our scope!

Coyote: *"Can you believe these guys, wasting all that nutritional value. They are filling up their pipes with dried grass and actually smoking it. They hold a flame to the bowl and draw down on the flame to create an ember and then inhale the smoke. Then they hold their breaths for several minutes, no wonder they get dizzy. I am surprise they don't pass out. They act like they are **tripping** or something. What a waste!"*

I said: *"Yeah man, they call the sex gatherings **orgies**. Everybody gets naked and gathers in a huge pile to make love to each other. You have to watch yourself or you can get tangled up and confused as to who's where and what's what; with elbows, paws, noses and tails everywhere."*

I said: *"Just watching was enough for me. It was so confusing I had to look to the horizon to get my bearings. It was like watching a school of salmon. It was impossible to tell who was mating with whom. They would work themselves up into a frenzy, spawn and then collapse in one exhausted pile of naked bodies. My parents would not approve of such behavior. Besides how would you know who your own kids were?"*

There was a lot to learn out on the west coast; some good and some not so good. But learn we must! You need a little confusion to seek and then find the light. If everything was crystal clear, then why search? Coyote and I were, if nothing else, ***seekers***.

203

Evolution (Idle Minds)

One day we found ourselves on the beach with absolutely nothing to do. I watched an otter move down the beach and into the water. It occurred to me he looked a little bit like a seal. Being a seeker in a group of seekers I asked Seal.....

I asked: *"Hey, are you related to the otter?"*

Seal: *"We may be distant cousins. We are similar in some ways and not so in others. Otters maneuver quite agilely on land and we maneuver better in the sea. We are clumsy as hell on the land, but we sure can out swim an otter in the ocean."*

I asked: *"How did you get so sleek?"*

Seal: *"It's quite a story for we once were very much like the otter. Today there are otters that come down to the ocean to play and hunt. They occupy two niches; one on the land and one in the sea. Yes, millions of years ago we were very much like the otter. However, once swimming in the ocean seals began to adapt. Those of us who could swim fast enough caught the slower fish and survived. In this game of chance the faster fish survived. Those of us with wider flatter forearms and hind limbs were more apt to catch the faster fish. The flatter stronger limbs and sleeker bodies favored success and those seals with the best of these features survived. Over time we became primarily aquatic animals and adapted readily to the oceans. The sleeker the body the more successful the seal and before we knew what was going on, over a few million years, we evolved."*

Seal: *"You think we are sleek, what about those dolphins? The dolphins are also mammals but they are totally more fish like. They are even faster than seals. Dolphins were able to expand their niche to include the deep oceans. Their front limbs have evolved into fins, they have developed a dorsal fin to stabilize their forward motion and their hind limbs have evolved into flippers."*

Seal: *"For the current otter their thick forearms, legs and webbed feet are more suited for a creature that spends an equal time on land and in the water, whereby the seal is spending more time in the water than on land. The otter is spending more time walking on land and the seal is spending more time swimming in the ocean. Which niche, the water or land, the otter will ultimately adopt depends on the demands of Nature."*

Seal: *"You can sort of follow this progression looking at the water buffalo, hippo and manatee. Which in your mind is more aquatic and why so?"*

I said: *"I have never seen a water buffalo, hippo or manatee. Where did you learn all this stuff?"*

Seal: ***"I'm a seeker. I seek knowledge and the truth****. The manatee is more aquatic in that it is primarily an aquatic creature spending most of its time, with the exception of coming up for air, in the water. The hippo to a lesser degree and the water buffalo to even a lesser degree, spend less of their time in an aquatic environment."*

Seal: *"There is this old concept based on tons of fossil and geologic evidence and millions of hours of careful observations validating evolution. Only to those who consciously or out of ignorance deny evolution are these **facts** not obvious. Those who don't understand it need to be*

205

taught. Those that know this Natural truth and conceal it need to be exposed. Accepting this truth is that important to our survival and movement toward a better more enlightened future. If you carefully examine Nature the truth of evolution is vividly clear."

Seal: *"There are several forces working on the evolution of a species. The first force of evolution is behavioral adaptation. Can an individual member of a species adapt to the stressors impacting its immediate survival; Yes or No? If No their genes are not passed forward, if Yes their genes are passed forward. It is that simple. In the case of the seal, the faster seal being the environmental stressor for the fish, and catching the faster fish the stressor for the seal. A perfect circle related directly to each other."*

Seal: *"The second force is environmental or niche adaptation. Can the species survive in a particular environmental niche long enough to prosper as a species? If so that species passes a large gene pool forward securing its place in evolution. The greater number of niches, the greater their survival. If their niche disappears, they are in trouble."*

Seal: *"The third force is* **Happenstance***. For example an asteroid slams into the Earth whereby a mass extinction takes place regardless of the evolutionary advancement of a species or group of species. These are the forces in Nature that we have little or no control over."*

Seal: *"****Happenstance*** *favors no one and can be as random as a bolt of lightning. Even those species most favorable for evolution may not survive a catastrophic event to evolve. Being in the wrong place at the wrong time may end the existence of an individual or an entire species. Being in a* *deep gully during a flash flood or on a volcanic island during an eruption could end the existence of a species of animals. **Happenstance** is simply random natural events that either take or promote life."*

I reflected: *"Like my brother Brutus, and the leap that took his life, all on a dare. He was twice as strong and intelligent as me, but a rash moment took his life. I have lived to have three children and seven grandchildren."*

Me and Coyote: *"Man, this shit is way over our heads!"*

Seal: *"If life survives it evolves over time shaped by the ever changing stressors placed upon life itself. Life cannot evolve without survival and life cannot long survive without evolution. The Cosmos, the Earth and life are always in the process of change. Like the reality of birth and death, a perfect circle in a Universe of circles. The only linear reality being time and space and even they may exist in a bubble of change, the circle of circles."*

Seal: *"For the seal, dolphin and whale there are evolutionary trails. Once we were land animals very much like the otter. The water buffalo, hippo and manatee are extremely successful in marshes, swaps, rivers and even out into the ocean (manatee). They have mastered their niches, have few competitors and may yet survive."*

Seal: *"The alligators do not need to evolve further they are the kings and queens of evolution as related to being the dominate creature in their niche. This fact enhances their survival and procreation. With few competitors living in the swamps their species flourished and grew. They prospered and grew strong in the wild swamps and rivers of the world.*

They are the masters of their niche. If the wild rivers and swaps survive so will they."

Seal: *"We are physical beings in a physical reality, nothing more, nothing less. In that some of us can now comprehend the totality of existence and for a moment gain a glimpse of immortality. Life can for the first time in its existence on Earth begin to understand and visualize the great Cosmos and its journey from start to finish; infinity and beyond."*

The Happenings (Idle Minds)

Seal: *"The spirit warriors are predicting another big freeze that's going to last several thousand years exposing a land bridge between Asia and North America. They are running frantic that this land bridge will cause a great migration from Asia and that we will need to defend ourselves against an onslaught from this invasion."*

Seal: *"They are expecting dozens of new species to slip across this land bridge using up our scarce resources. These new species to our lands will be followed by the humans who seem to have no respect for Nature. They see Nature as their mortal enemy and feel that they are at war with her. If this happens, nothing in America will ever be the same."*

Seal: *"Those in power are asking us to join up to defend our country. The government is issuing **draft cards** to account for all those who are required to serve. Some of us are **protesting** the draft having **sit-ins**. Our movement is crying out for peace and refusing to go. Those in the peace movement just want those in power to '**give peace a chance.**' Some radicals are burning their draft cards to evade the draft; they call themselves hippies.*

Seal: *"Just **'What are we fighting for?"** Coyote: **"Don't ask me, I don't give a damn."***

I said: *"I am ready to defend what we believe in and our way of life. If the Asians are coming let them come. Who's not for defending our freedoms?"*

Coyote: *"What exactly does that mean, Marcus?"*

I declared: *"I am not sure, but whatever it means I am willing to fight and die for it."*

Coyote: *"Marcus, you're just gullible and naive. You're ready to take a ride no matter who's driving the train. You need to chill out and watch what's really going on before you join up and put your ass in a sling. Once you join up that's it man, there is no turning back."*

I finally said: *"It's our country right or wrong!"*

Coyote: *"Chill out little brother. If our country is wrong, you may come home in a box and within a generation or two nobody will remember your name. They may carve your names somewhere on a black stone and many will gather to mourn the loss of your souls but few will truly comprehend the tragedy. Thousands killed or maimed, and for what? I admire your loyalty but I am just not sure what you are loyal to. Maybe we ought to dedicate all that energy and resources toward something good; like saving the planet."*

Seal: ***"Are you guys going to the peace rally?"***

Coyote: *"There's this other cat we been following. Marcus and I are going to one of his gatherings tonight to check out what he's about. They call him the **prophet**."*

California was like that. There were lots of gatherings and talks concerning new and different ideas; always mixing pleasure with controversy. There were those who often took extreme views just to work up the crowd and defy the authorities. We were just passengers on for the ride and cute chicks. A few days later Seal bumped into me and Coyote wanting to share the good news.

The Prophet (Idle Minds)

Seal: *"Hey, have you heard the news going around? There is this young kid promoting **brotherly love**. You know, **turn the other cheek**; at least once. **Do unto others as you would have them do unto you**. You know, before they get a chance to do unto you, or something like that; all that nonviolence stuff."*

I declared: *"Heard about him, we were there."*

Coyote: *"He is a little off on the facts about our place in Nature, but he is still pretty cool and seems enlightened. He has created quite a buzz."*

Seal: *"He professes the **true faith** and teaches others to **walk in the righteous path of acceptance and forgiveness**. He saved an adulteress sea lion from a stoning. And I don't mean getting high, I mean a real stoning, you know with rocks and bricks."*

I said: *"I hear he is trying to set an example on how we should live with each other on this planet. He claims that our* best thoughts come from ourselves not from old books. He's got the attention of the masses and his basic message of goodness rings true."

Seal: *"Man, we could all benefit from a little more love in the world!"*

I continued: *"I hear he keeps company with the poor, shares his meager belongings with others and associates with sinners. He is a carpenter by trade and behaves like a socialist."*

Seal: *"Kind of like what we do. You know; looking out for each other by sharing our food and stuff like that."*

Coyote: *"Yeah man, we got each other's back."*

I exclaimed: *"Man this is some really cool shit."*

Coyote: *"He's got the elders tied in a knot. They say he lost his temper over possessions once and scared the shit out of the rich. This kid is really **tripping** man and he is so cool; and he does not even eat or smoke grass."*

I said: *"He loses me with all that pie in the sky **salvation** stuff. I believe you carry your misdeeds with you all of your life. Your best hope is that others will forgive you and ultimately you can forgive yourself."*

I continued: **"Without a conscience you cannot know sin. In life when we acquire a conscience we feel shame and guilt associated with our misdeeds. With a conscience we learn how to behave. Once behaved, we tend to seek righteousness and with righteousness we gain a heighten**

211

level of consciousness and a deeper awareness of right and wrong. Without a conscience; to the wicked, evil does not exist."

Coyote: *"Marcus, that's some heavy shit. Lighten up; you're taking this conversation too serious. Forget all that sin and conscience bullshit!"*

Seal: *"As the kid said; he without sin cast the first stone. Hell we must be in good company; there hasn't been a stoning in years."*

Coyote: *"Yeah and all that **eternal life** in heaven crap. You know; hanging out in the clouds and floating around with angels. I have never seen an angel and I never saw anyone walk out of the desert after they died from exposure no matter how saintly they lived. Life and death are for certain and are a mirror reflection of each other. You can't have one without the other; if you are born you will die and you can only die if you were born. This is a nonnegotiable and an absolute, a perfect circle, in a Universe of circles!"*

Coyote: *"What about all that burning in hell? Could you imagine burning someone forever? I visited Diablo Canyon once. It was hotter than Hell. I can't imagine spending eternity there!"*

I said: *"And the **resurrection**; when have we ever seen any one come back from the dead, let alone fly off into heaven. Nature just recycles us plain and simple. We see it all the time. When we die we return to the Earth no more and no less, dust to dust-gone forever. In time even our bones will eventually disappear, without a trace, with nobody left* behind to seek them out. Nature does not have the time or the space to store all of our souls in the clouds."

Seal: *"I am with you guys on those points, but that brotherly love stuff is still pretty cool."*

I stated: *"If he is not careful the prophet is going to get himself nailed to a surfboard and harpooned. You know how touchy those in charge can be about controlling the masses. They fear that his teachings of love and acceptance might spread. The establishment is scared shitless."*

Seal: *"The kid seems to have stepped away from all that eye for an eye, tooth for a tooth, revenge bullshit and has brought his teachings a little closer to the Earth. Can you imagine being toothless and blind; not being able to see what you can't eat?"*

Seal: *"I hope none of his followers try to turn him into a god and create a religion around his teachings. You know how some are, always trying to make something out of nothing so they can profit from it, or to further serve their selves in some way. You know how gullible we are, fake a few miracles and speak some mumbo jumbo and the masses will fall to their knees, mumble some nonsense and enter into a mental stupor that will last for generations; repeating the same old **gibberish** for thousands of years."*

Over time there will be many voices speaking this basic truth, ***acceptance*** and ***forgiveness,*** but few will really listen. Goodness is our ultimate salvation; it's here, it is with us now and can be with us forever. All we have to do is reach down within ourselves and grasp it. Goodness must include a reverence for each other, this Earth and all that is natural. Given our track record we most likely won't find it.

I was beginning to find the answers to some of my many questions. But with each answer came more questions. I said to myself: *"Will I ever make sense of it all? Why do we exist and what does this all mean?"*

Survival of the Fittest

We spent the early morning contemplating the teachings of the chosen one and playing in the surf. As the afternoon wore on the waves grew steadily in height. Seal immediately took to the waves. Further and further out into the ocean he went. Taller and taller the waves grew as the afternoon rapidly left us behind. The grace and poise he demonstrated was simply beautiful.

With Seal's silhouette accentuating the horizon the sun drifted into the ocean setting the sky on fire. With bright pinks and subtle reds in the background, Seal glided across the setting sun in perfect form.

How could random events produce something so spectacular, seemingly so flawless? How did eons of children, begotten by children, whose ancestors reach back to the beginning of life itself produce this magnificent being? How could the Earth produce such a wave and the perfect creature to enjoy its form and to take advantage of the wave's fleeting thrill? How does our intellect recognize joy and wonder to see beyond ourselves to marvel over the boundless beauty of this Earth and life its self?

Full of himself, Seal rode several big waves to the beach just to turn around, swim out again and ride several more. He

214

was chasing the great one. It was the unseen wave; the giant wave that was swelling beyond the horizon, the one promising to be the best ride of his life. Riding a big wave Seal was joyfully headed toward the shore when in a violent flash our friend was gone, never to be seen again. From nowhere a killer whale in one massive charge snatched our friend from the wave. With one forceful bite in midair, right out of the surf he loved so much, Seal disappeared. In an instant he was gone.

A true **"California Dreamer,"** just too cool for Nature and ahead of his time, Seal left his warmth on our souls. He had several wives and dozens of children; his image is safe.

The killer whale was Seal's environmental stressor; just too fast and cunning for this poor fun loving **day tripper**.

Broken hearted we gradually moved away from the beach working our way inland. We had caught the breeze known as California and broadened our minds and souls. We gained new insights as to the endless boundaries of thought and of Nature's true nature, bare and raw without judgment or remorse. **"A sparkle of joy wrapped in a Universe of Chaos."** The best that we can hope for is to widen the moments of joy and accept what we cannot control. Seal warmed our hearts and momentarily filled our lives with joy. He was Nature and Nature was Seal. In the end he returned to the beginning. Things were moving just too fast in California for Coyote and me.

Coyote: *"Who knows, before long salmon will be mating with seagulls and by the time you can count one, two, three there will be a new species; flying fish."*

I said: *"Talk about cross breeding; I hope humans don't get involved."*

Coyote: *"Yeah, before you know it bears and raccoons will be pairing up; 'coon-bears,' just kidding, little brother."*
It was time for us to get off the beach. We had been out in the sun just a little bit too long. Our **moral compasses** were beginning to falter making it harder to find true North. Like two pilots lost in the **"Bermuda Triangle"** our heads were spinning, warping our souls and minds out of focus.

We needed solid ground below our feet or we would lose our way. **"We were born to be wild and into the wild we must go!"** We needed the mountains and fresh air.

BROTHER SEAL
A CALIFORNIA DREAMER

Sierra Nevada Mountains

Leaving the coast of California behind was a relief. There was just too much happening down there. What a crazy mix. Coyote and I were ready for some down time without all that controversy; left versus right, evolution-revolution and all those projections and philosophizing. What a head spin! It was good to get away from the coast and back up in the mountains again; fresh air and peace.

No sooner than we arrived in the mountains and began to adjust, things rapidly returned to normal. The need for survival became ever present. Water, food and shelter were the pressing topics again. There was little down time to contemplate the Universe or the depths of our souls. In the mountains we had to work for our keep. There was very little time for play and things soon became very serious.

Staying alive was number one again, pushing all the other idle thoughts out of our minds. We had to stay focused. There were signs of bears and mountain lions everywhere. They left their tracks in the mud and their droppings right off the trails. The air was full of their scent and the rotting carrion they left behind. We felt like we were being watched again raising the hair on the back of our necks. Vultures circled the skies.

At one stream there it was. *"No, it cannot be!"* I said out loud. There it was as plain as day, her paw print with the inner left toe and claw missing.

I went on to say: *"This is the same print that I discovered years and years ago on the plains. It just cannot be!"*

Coyote: *"Let's keep to the streams and head up north putting as many miles as we can between us and this mountain lion. She's got your scent and she seems determined to hunt you down. Don't worry little brother we have a few tricks we can play."*

Coyote: *"We have several ways to throw predators off our trail. First, there are wild berries. We can rub our paws and coats with wild berries to disguise our scent. This works with mountain lions but not so much with bears. Bears love wild berries. If it was a bear after our skins we would need to use another trick."*

Coyote: *"Then there is cross scenting; where we find an established trail to mix our scent with the scents of other animals to throw the bear or lion off. Once we travel this trail for a few miles we can find an opportunity to jump off the trail; hoping the lion or bear has lost our scent, and picked up on the scent of others. All is fair in love and war and when a bear or mountain lion is after you, it is war."*

Coyote: *"When making our camp at night we can position our camp site out of the wind to ensure predators don't pick up our scent while we sleep. This is known as trapping our scent, usually within an enclosed area out of the wind. Trapping your scent works best with stream walking, making sure that a scent trail has not been left behind in the first place."*

Knowing that a mountain lion was on our trail we used all four techniques to ensure our safety for the night.

THE TRACKS WE LEAVE

The Fire-Mountains (Geo)

We were back on the ridge when we ran into a very old owl named **Geo**. He referred to himself as a rock keeper. Geo was a geology freak who loved to collect and examine rocks. He was filled with excitement when talking about the structure of the Earth. Once started you could not stop him. He asked us to stay for lunch and then subjected us to a four hour lecture on geology.

Geo: *"Trust me the Earth is much more than it appears. The Earth is very ancient and has existed before our time, and indeed before the time of all living things. It is alive from within and from without. The Earth itself, its oceans,* continents, atmosphere and biosphere are all in constant motion. It is truly a living planet with no end in sight."

Geo: "It's all in the rocks. The history of this planet can plainly be explained by closely examining rocks. Take this sandstone for example; what is it made of?"

Before we could respond…. "You're right, sand! And where do we find sand? Right again, on a beach. And how does the beach get there? Absolutely right again, it was washed there by the ocean. How did it turn into a stone? Damn you guys are smart, it built up over time, layer by layer until heat and pressure compressed it and turned it into sandstone."

Geo: "Therefore the deepest layer is older than the next, so on and so forth until you have layers and layers of rock piled on top of each other like we find in the Grand Canyon."

I looked at Coyote: **"What's the Grand Canyon?"**

Coyote: "I have heard of it but I thought it was just a myth my parents told me to frighten me so I would not run off. They called it the **"Devil's Crack"** and said it was full of the evil ones. And that if I ever ran away from home I would fall into the Devil's Crack where the evil ones would fillet and eat me every other day for eternity."

I asked: "What happens on the off days?"

Coyote: "The evil ones would slowly roast their victims over a fire pit of **icy blue flames** and poke them with sharp forks, preparing their victims' flesh for the upcoming feast."

Geo: "Marcus and Coyote pay attention this is important!"

Geo: *"The animal remains found in the deeper layers are older than those above and so on and so forth. The big bones in the middle are life forms that once were, but do not any longer exist. How do we know this? Right again, we haven't seen a live one. We call these petrified bones; fossils. An A+ for Marcus; and an A- for Coyote! No talking in class."*

Geo: *"Why do we have continents and mountains? You two are right again;* **plate tectonics***, the movement of the Earth's crust which causes the continents to drift away and into each other as evidenced by mountains and large rift valleys. New mountains grow as the plates push together and rift valleys are formed when the plates pull away from each other. Fire-mountains and hot spots are evidence of this process."*

Geo: **"Erosion** *wears the land masses down and the cycle repeats itself. A circle in an Universe of circles. This planet and these processes are ageless. Then there are igneous and metamorphic rocks and each have a story to tell....."*

Our heads were spinning!

Geo: *"Any questions?"*

Coyote looked at me and shook his head.....

I asked anyway: *"What are fire-mountains?"*

Geo: *"Good question Marcus. They are active vents where the heat of the Earth boils from within and pushes upward pouring molten rock known as lava onto the surface. It produces igneous rock. They are located all over the world and there is a ring of fire-mountains circling the Pacific Ocean. You are just a few hundred miles south of one."*

Coyote's tongue fell out of his mouth. Before we finally broke away Geo told us his story.

School Daze

As a young student, Geo was always in trouble in school. A prankster by Nature he constantly mixed things up to draw laughs from his buddies. The Dean of the school expected to see Geo each day and kept his paddle ready to extract a price for Geo's misbehavior. Geo was always ready to take a bow (paddling) in honor of his foolery and a laugh or two from his friends, who were usually next in line. His friends were eager to count him out: *one, two* and *three*. He would tease his mother concerning his misbehavior at school, boasting: *"Like a Time-X, I can take a licking and keep on ticking."*

He was stubborn and argued with both his classmates and teachers. He loved geology and believed he had discovered the truth as to the age and structure of the Earth. He had discovered strata and in that the beginnings of his journey. He wanted to spread this new truth and inflame everyone with his passion for Nature and the planet.

Geo: *"It is simple; layer by layer the Earth builds up its land masses in rhythm with Nature and time. See, how these layers of rock pile up on each other, with the newer layers at the top and the older layers below. It's all in the strata; the evidence lays everywhere before us. Sandstone, limestone, slate and other rock formations tell us this story. Layer by layer the Earth we walk on was formed."*

The teachings at that time concerning the formation of the Earth and life centered on the *"Story of Creation."* Handed down from one generation to the next this story was accepted as the unquestionable truth by the elders and the other members of Geo's flock.

The Story of Creation

There once was born out of the heavens a beautiful and majestic blue jay. She was the first born of the Universe adorned with brilliant blue and white feathers. She was fiercely loyal to the stars and watched over and protected them from the darkness. She would constantly fuss after them to keep them safe; flying from one end of the Universe to the other watching over her babies. The heavens called her *"Mother Blue Jay."*

When Mother Blue Jay was still very young she fell hopelessly in love with the *"Sun."* Also born of the heavens the Sun was a bright and rash youth who flew off into deep space; forever flying in circles at the very edge of the galaxy. Captured by the Sun's brilliance and majestic being Mother Blue Jay was pulled into his orbit. Around and around she chased him caught forever by his warmth and intensity.

In preparation for their young she built a sturdy nest high in the branches of a very tall sycamore tree. To attract the Sun's attention she danced, sang and flashed her colorful feathers. Drawn by her beauty the Sun fell in love and showered her with his light. Their love and passion illuminated the Universe and soon she bore him four brilliantly colored eggs; Gold, Blue, Earthly Brown and Green.

One day while she was off chasing after her new and playful love, *two cold blooded thieves* conspired to steal her eggs. The thieves plotted, schemed and planned their attack. These criminals snuck through the forest with the intent to do evil. While others silently watched, the stronger of the two

223

pressed his reluctant partner on. *"Prove yourself, climb that tree and get those eggs."* The youngster gave into the will of the older outlaw and climbed the tall sycamore.

The foolish youngster, with little awareness of himself, yielded to the bully and stole the eggs. Like the thief he would become, he snatched the eggs and put them into his **haversack.** Like a sin tucked deep within his soul, the young masked criminal placed the blue jay's eggs carefully at the bottom of his **haversack** and turned to flee.

Catching sight of this mischief Mother Blue Jay flew back to her nest and desperately tried to save her unborn. She tore at the masked bandit while he was still in her nest. He fled for his life down the tree. His partner put up a stiff resistance and matched Mother Blue Jay's attack strike for strike. Fighting her off they both fled into the thickets to hide. The old badger and young raccoon had fiercely defended their stolen treasure and devoured their reward.

Mother Blue Jay returned to the empty nest broken hearted, her eggs and unborn gone; young lives that will never be. Challenged by **Chaos** and **random destruction**, she would not be defeated. A devotion to life and her love for the Sun healed her heart and drove her back into his arms.

With her massive wings Mother Blue Jay again passed in front of Father Sun to give birth to their first born, **Solar**. Three other hatchlings joined her nest with their eggs hatching in this order: Solar, the light from the sun and heavens; **Ocean**, the waters and sky that covered the planet; **Earth**, the great land masses and finally; **Life**, all the plants and animals that covered or inhabited the Earth. The mixing of these four siblings gave birth to the Earth, moon, stars and life. In just four days all of creation took place.

Strata

During class one day Geo argued that the rocks he found near the fire-mountain contained sea shells attesting to its age. He explained that over eons the rocks once found below the surface of the Earth were gradually pushed upwards to the tops of the mountains. The age of these rocks far exceeded the four days allowed by the story of creation.

He further went on that he had observed sea shells on the beach being covered by the sand. The shells were slowly buried in rhythm with the waves taking days and weeks to be thoroughly covered. Again it would take eons for this process to turn this mix of sand and shells into stone. Still further evidence; there were sandstone layers of rock found at high elevations far inland from the oceans. How did they get there and what caused them to rise above sea level? What forces were at work to cause the Earth to behave in such a way?

In addition, Geo claimed he found a river bed washed down from the mountains. He discovered that there were scores of dead fish encased in its mud. Layer upon layer the dead fish were packed, one on top of the other as evidence of the slow but constant motion of Nature. The closer to the top layer, the fresher the fish were. The deeper he dug into the mud, he found only their bones; in that, "strata" layer upon layer.

Geo boldly claimed to the elders that by his calculations this process, the creation of the Earth, took hundreds of millions of years and could never have been accomplished in just four days as "recited" by the elders and holy ones.

Geo to the elders: *"The Earth and heavens took eons piled upon eons of time to form. The great layers of rock that we find everywhere, testifies to this f-a-c-t. The moon is pocked with thousands of impact craters that we seldom witness occur. These craters must have been formed over millions of years to leave the moon so scarred. We even find ancient impact craters on Earth that uplifted layers upon layers of rock formations revealing the Earth's internal strata."*

Geo: *"You have it all wrong. I am not certain of exactly how, but it appears by my observations and calculations it has taken the Earth and heavens a very long time to form. The story of creation just cannot be true! I once visited the falls of the Ohio and the fossil beds there appear millions of years old; fossil corals are everywhere in the layers of its rocks. This fossil bed is roughly four hundred feet above sea level."*

The elders shouted: *"Blasphemy; liar! You dare to speak against the sacred words; the holy doctrine that has been handed down through the ages and etched in our holy books and souls? You are an evil one, a deceiver, a twister of the truth! You dare to challenge the story of creation."*

The elders in chorus: Geo, you are banished from our school. You must leave immediately. Take your belongings and flee. We cannot control what your classmates might do to you for this outrage. You are no longer welcomed in these halls of study and knowledge. You are forbidden to come back. Leave and leave now or face the consequences. Go live in the wild with the wild things, the other non-believers. We bear the truth and will not yield our faith."

With that Geo journeyed into the wild embraced by Nature and those with the time to listen. He committed himself to speak this truth and wandered the country collecting rocks in support of his findings.

Crawling out of his skin, Coyote finally said: *"Well, we got to get going, it's getting late and we have miles to hike before we make camp."*

Geo: *"You can camp here for the night."*

Coyote looking hard at me: *"We have friends that are expecting us and we would not want to worry them. Isn't that right Marcus?"*

I said: *"I forgot, Coyote, you're right we have to get going."*

With that we said goodbye and hurried down the trail. We moved north until just before dark and made camp. All I could think about was that fire-mountain. Coyote finally agreed that we would head straight for the fire-mountain starting in the morning.

Geo was not only a seeker of knowledge he became the keeper of this truth. The Earth is slowly changing and reforming itself over time. Constantly in motion this process takes millions and millions of years; without end it goes on.

Ridicule, scorn, banishment and threats did not alter this old owl's course; for this truth found courage in one of Nature's wisest creatures. He is the ***"Watcher of the Night"*** created by Nature to protect and guard this truth forever guiding us through the darkness of our minds. He illuminates our natural beings and in so doing reconnects us to this Earth.

GEO

11. The Spirit Walkers

The Cascades

Marcus had been on a long journey since he left the Allegany Mountains and his parents' home years before. After several misadventures and some poor choices he was befriended by his constant companion Coyote. Together they had traveled across the Sonora Desert into Mexico and up the coast of California. They became the dear friends of a fun loving wave runner named Seal and got caught up in the *hip scenes* of their times. They were *moving* and *grooving* with all the *happenings* on the west coast until Seal's luck ran out; eaten by a whale on the last wave of his young life.

Broken hearted Marcus and Coyote made their way back up into the highlands and began their long trek into the Sierra Nevada Mountains. They moved down from the Sierras up into the Cascades. After traveling thousands of miles together they finally reached the southern fringes of the Cascade Mountains. The mountain range in which Geo had promised they would find the fire-mountains.

As they traveled up into the mountains the forest became dense and rich with foliage. A bounty of ferns and thick patches of moss were everywhere. The moss was several inches deep completely covering the forest floor.

Only the animal trails occasionally revealed the soil hidden beneath this precious carpet of green. It was as if an invisible gardener created this mystical landscape and weaved this one path through the middle of her masterpiece leaving the rest of her delicate creation untouched, pristine and flawless.

The trees towered above Coyote and Marcus with the branches and leaves melting into an emerald canopy that in many places blotted out the sun. During the early hours of the day moisture blanketed every plant below the canopy. Without a cloud in the sky, water drips from the leaves and branches of the trees creating a rain forest that never completely dries. One would have to climb to the upper branches to find the sun and unbroken light. Only there would you be able to escape the wetness of this forest.

....

Coyote and I had been on this narrow trail for two days and it was approaching dark when we heard a strange and terrifying howl in the distance. This was not quite a howl, nor one of the typical animal calls we were familiar with. It was bone piercing; like nothing we had ever heard before.

It was oddly different, more like a cry of distress, a warning; or a combination of the two. A distress call that Coyote and I had entered into someone's sacred circle uninvited and a warning that we should immediately stop and turn around.

I shouted: *"Did you hear that? What is it? I have never heard such a sound in my life. Look at me, my hair is standing straight up and my knees are shaking."*

Coyote: *"Marcus, you know I don't scare easily, but I believe I just wet myself."*

I exclaimed: *"There it is again! I think we should turn around and get the hell out of here!"*

I continued: *"Could these be the creatures the southern tribes had warned me about? Are these the monsters of the*

230

*forest that steal and eat the children? Could they be the ones who are almost human but much, much larger and ten times as vicious; the ones that pick their teeth with the bones of their prey? The ones they call the **Yeti**, who dip their victims' eyeballs into bowls of blood and lick their fingers dry for dessert after they have eaten their blinded prey alive?"*

Coyote: *"There you go again; believing the **gibberish** someone has handed down a thousand years ago; nonsense!"*

Coyote: *"Listen Marcus, we haven't eaten anything since we left the Sierra Nevada Mountains five days ago. If we turn around now we might not make it back to safety. It's probably a bluff, a small harmless creature whose weird howl saves it from predators. You know how Nature is, she gives creatures all kinds of gadgets and tricks to help them save themselves from the meat eaters, us; well I mean you. This is most likely a small bird with enormous vocal cords; just another trick of Nature. You know how she likes to toy with us."*

The howling stopped and the forest went silent. Even the breeze and the natural movements and sounds of the forest ceased; for the moment a silent pause in a frozen landscape.

Coyote: *"Let's get moving and put some distance between us and that awful sound. Move it little one and quicken your pace so we can get the hell away from here."*

Coyote convinced me to continue our trek on the trail. Late into the night we found level ground and made camp. By this time we were ravenous.

Along the trail Coyote and I found some wild looking mushrooms. Against our better judgment and with nothing else to eat, we eagerly ate the *sweet tasting mushrooms*. After eating the mushrooms we laid down to sleep. Scared, I curled up next to Coyote and we settled in for the night. Just as we closed our eyes and began to drift, it started. There it was the knocking on the trees and the dreaded feeling that something evil was watching us. We abruptly woke up.

Out there in the blackness of the forest something dark and sinister; something horrible and threatening was watching us. Before Coyote could blink, I found myself under his feet shaking like a leaf.

I said loudly: *"WTF was that? Did you hear that?"*

Shaking himself, Coyote responded: *"Settle down little brother. I won't let anything hurt you!"*

The knocking was methodical; **knock---knock---knock**, a pause, then two knocks close to each other; *knock-knock*. They had us surrounded. From the blackness of the forest the unnerving knocks and subtle grunts continued.

In an attempt to frighten the thing in the forest away, Coyote let out a howl directed at the source of the knocking and unfamiliar grunts. Out of the blackness came a broken branch hurtling through the air striking Coyote in his hindquarters knocking him off of his feet. Coyote yelped in pain.

The knocking stopped and voices came from the forest that could be seen but not heard. It was scripted in the language of the Earth that all but the humans could read.

The forest echoed with many voices: ***"We are watching you; watching you, watching you.*** *Beware we are watching you;* ***watching you, watching you.*** *You have entered our forest without our permission;* ***our permission, permission, permission.*** *Beware and turn back before it's too late;* ***too late, too late.*** *We are hungry and need to feed;* ***to feed, to feed.*** *Our babies are hungry and must have something to eat;* ***to eat, to eat.*** *The nights belong to us;* ***to us, to us.*** *We feed on your darkness and fear;* ***darkness and fear, and fear."***

The Path of the Spirit Walkers

After a brief pause a strong voice emerged from the forest: *"My name is **Rahoo**. I am the chief of my clan. We are the **"Spirit Walkers"**. We are the ones who protect the forest. We have come to measure your threat against Nature."*

*"We are the **children and the people of the forest**. We are one with Nature and walk in **balance** and **harmony** with her. We are born to an extended family that wander near and far to tend to the wild. There are many of us but we only reveal ourselves to a few. There is no social order in our clan we all are equal. The title "chief" only means that I am the eldest and therefore the voice of our clan."*

"We celebrate birth, life, and death. We are born to our mate; the next male in birth is wedded to the next female in birth not of his immediate family. Together they play as brother and sister until they mature. This close bond joins them as equals. They are separated at maturity to wander the deep forest alone until they find each other again. Until that moment they are alone and sad for each other's love and company. They yearn for each other in a new way; not as brother and sister, but as young and eager lovers."

233

"This longing turns into a passion that ignites their senses. They can smell and taste each other over great distances. Their cravings drive them wild. They sing songs to each other and whisper love words into the wind that can only be heard in their private souls. In their dreams they kiss."

"They are intensely connected to each other and cry out at night their pain and eagerness to be together. They leave their scent for the other to find. At the passing of each day the circle that separates them grows smaller and smaller. They are close enough to touch; but frightened, he evades."

"The females take the lead and track their mates down. The males are bewildered and do not completely understand the rise of their passions. They have been transformed into a throbbing mess and don't quite know what to do. The females take them in hand and gently guide them home."

"The females are determined and soon the two are joined as one and remain so for months. With great joy the male quickly learns and their passions rage on throughout their joyful lives; together as one, never leaving the other's side. In love they are wedded; him to her and her to him."

"They are together from birth as brother and sister, together in life as loving mates and together in the twilight as friends; they are joined forever in love until their reunion with Nature rejoins them in death. The circle of circles finally closes with their souls joined forever as one with the Earth."

Rahoo continued: *"Nature's bounty is measured. Keeping the **balance** we limit the birth of our children to two; one each to replace ourselves. Only if we lose a child will we have another child to keep this **balance.**"*

"As soon as the child is conceived both parents know. The male is on double duty to care for and protect the female. He announces their joy to the clan and makes offerings of thanks to Nature. He is at her side always and unselfishly takes care of her. The child is born into his hands. He is the first to kiss and present this gift to the world. He washes the newborn in a wild stream to bless the child's journey through life. In its birth he finds **meaning** *and* **purpose**. *In giving life they (we) are born again."*

Silently by Rahoo's side stood *Hoora* his mate for life.

The Marriage of Rahoo and Hoora

Like all the Spirit Walkers before them, at conception Rahoo and Hoora were joined forever as one. Once they found each other, their honeymoon lasted six lunar cycles; from six new moons until six full moons. They were joined as one during this cycle only separating to forage for food and water. They exhausted themselves with love. Their passions filled the forest with the sounds of love; soft whispers and gentle kisses. The joyful sounds only lovers know. The wild things were listening and giggled with delight. Rahoo's and Hoora's need to touch and kiss was without bounds. When briefly parted they would race back to each other for more.

After their wild union they slowly wandered home to announce their new child to be. They journeyed home to his clan and he presented his new wife, their adopted daughter. Hoora was embraced for the second time not as a little sister for Rahoo, but as his wife.

Throughout the forest their story was carried in the wind. Clans from the hinterlands were called forward to celebrate their marriage. A great feast and ceremony honoring their union filled the camp with joy. Blooms were gathered to cover the bride and groom.

The tribe's elders, **Crilu** and **Lucri** presented Rahoo's and Hoora's tokens of love to each other. The joys and sufferings of life were to be shared and carried equally by the newly joined couple. For her a majestic butterfly was given to adorn her beauty, for him a thorn to remind him of the pain she would suffer for their love. The whole tribe quietly watched as their tears moistened the air.

Rahoo kneeled and begged for her love: *"Will you love me as I love you until death do us part and through death we will be rejoined forever as one with the Earth? I will be by your side forever to protect and honor you my sister and my wife; the mother of our children to be."*

Given to him by Rahoo, Crilu placed the butterfly on Hoora's left shoulder reminding her and the tribe that Rahoo would always be at her side to protect and care for her. Resting for a moment the butterfly paused then flew off into the forest; carried by the wind into the great unknown.

Hoora: *"Yes I will love you until my heart no longer beats. I will meet you in the hereafter joined together forever with the Earth. I will carry and bear our children and care for you each moment of my life. What Nature has given me, life, I will give to you. She is our Mother and through her we were born. I am now her daughter, your sister and your wife; the mother of our children to be."*

Given the thorn by Hoora, Lucri holding Rahoo's right hand, jabbed the thorn deep into his palm to remind him of the births Hoora would suffer for their love. Wrapped with wild vines; her left hand held in his right hand; they were joined as one, bound together forever by love.

The members of the tribe sang and danced with happiness for the newly married couple; around and around they danced until the sun broke through the trees and the dawn of the new day illuminated their joy.

Being invisible, Coyote and Marcus did not know Hoora, Rahoo's wife was quietly standing by his side hiding in the forest.

The Teachings of Nature

Rahoo: *"The forest has taught us everything we know. Nature speaks to us in words that are scripted by her own hands: "Harmony and Balance, Reverence for all that belongs to Nature." Only those who seek her truths will find and read these sacred words; words without time, time without words."*

"She has fashioned the world around us; the force of the wind, the currents in the seas, every blade of grass, every leaf, every tree and every frog. All that crawls, swims or flies belong to her, the Sun and the Moon, every star; the Cosmos itself. She is time, infinity and beyond, and even before. She is the Universe and all of the yesterdays and tomorrows are hers."

"She formed the cliffs that surround us in the canyons, the mountains that reach into the skies and their snow covered peaks, the driest desert, a drop of water and the oceans, the human hand, all created and fashioned in her light and in her way."

Purity of Being

Rahoo: *"Throughout life we, the Spirit Walkers tend to the wild. **We are the gardeners of the forest**. Our bodies have evolved to absorb the nutrients of the plants we eat leaving their seeds intact. When the seeds pass from our bodies we carefully cultivate these enriched seeds back into the Earth. We take great care not to reveal our work to others gently working the wild seeds back into the soil leaving the surroundings undisturbed."*

"We care for the wild things. We tend to the innocent, weak and sickly when we can. At times Nature intercedes and we must always yield to her wisdom."

*"Our way of life is filled with Nature's rich bounty and our **internal peace** allows many of us to live beyond a thousand years. In this time we grow old with goodness and wisdom. We bring no harm to ourselves or those we love."*

"We seek purity of being in that we lust for nothing and rejoice in contentment and balance. We walk in harmony and grace with Mother Earth. Our reunion back to the Earth completes our circle; birth - death, with life in between."

The Little Ones

Rahoo: *"Because we are not meat eaters the little ones, the opossums, rabbits, raccoons, and the other small furry ones; those that cannot readily defend themselves or escape the humans, seek our shelter. They and their families join us in our hiding places. The little ones often follow us on our migrations from one feeding place to another."*

The Invisible

Rahoo: *"We are careful to leave no signs for the humans to follow or to know that we exist. We seldom reveal even the slightest glimpse of ourselves to keep them fearful of us and confused. Our super fine red hair dissolves with the slightest moisture without a trace. Our feces is absorbed on contact with the soil. Because of our life long herbal diets our bodies decompose within minutes after we die including our bones and teeth. The humans have lied as to what they have found of us and who we truly are. They spin hatred and fear about us to justify their greed; we are the guardians of the forest."*

"We are the Spirit Walkers whose footsteps barely touch the ground let alone leave a footprint. The humans that say they have found evidence of our existence are not telling the truth and those that claim that they have seen us are delusional or liars."

"We take great care during the day not to be seen only revealing a glimpse of ourselves as we rapidly move through the forest or late at night while hiding within the shadows."

"We reveal ourselves only to scare the many or reward the few. We attempt to scare the many who are trying to hunt us down. We reveal ourselves to the few who are trying to be the good keepers of this Earth."

"Yes we are the Spirit Walkers whose foot prints leave no impressions on the ground. Only when we choose to leave signs or present a glimpse of ourselves to the few, do we reveal ourselves or leave tracks. We temporarily leave our prints to scare or fool the humans who don't respect Nature. The humans call us the Yeti. **"The humans are coming!"**

239

The Humans

Rahoo: *"In the future the humans who cannot read the signs of the Earth will recklessly cut down the forest. Trees that stood for hundreds of years will perish overnight. The homes of thousands of animals will disappear. All the animals that relied on the forest for food and shelter will also perish.* ***"For profit and greed these woodlands will vanish."***

"If the humans don't change their ways they will bring darkness to the Earth. Beware, the humans are coming!"

*"If humans could capture our **DNA** it would confirm our lineage tied directly to them and that they are members of our family and that in fact we are their elders."*

"The humans have made up hundreds of stories as to our existence, not one of which is the truth. These lies have spread all over the world and have landed here."

*"They call us the **Yeti (Big Foot – Sasquatch)** and describe us as blood thirsty villains to scare their little ones. We are in truth more humane than the humans. They have killed millions upon millions of their own. We have never, **NEVER** taken the life of one of our own and only engage in violence to protect our loved ones."*

"They spread horrible lies that we steal and eat their children and elderly, when the opposite is true. In the early years the humans often discarded their elderly and abandoned them on the trail as the rest of the tribe moved on. They left their elderly in the forest to die alone. Some humans are so wicked and selfish that they even abandon their own children."

"We took pity on these poor souls, took them in and cared for them. The children we would raise until their fifth year, releasing them into the wild to find their way home. The elderly we nurse until they pass. Then we carefully returned their bodies to the Earth."

"For the special few; the lost children, the abandoned elderly or the keepers, in friendship we walk naked in their presence. Then we use herbs to carefully wash their memories away to protect our image. Only in their dreams do we visit them to reaffirm our love and friendship."

"To the children that fate left with us and the elderly who pass our way into the unknown, we stay forever faithful. We reveal ourselves to these few. To the others we stay elusive, unseen and invisible."

"You have nothing to fear. We are the gardeners of the forest. We have chosen to be with Nature and walk her narrow trails."

The Great Darkness

Rahoo: *"A long time ago when we were much younger as a species the world we know trembled beneath our feet. This tremor lasted for days and seemed to originate from horizon to horizon. The Earth shook and rumbled as if it was breaking apart."*

"The days grew darker and darker and the sky grew dense with ash. It took months for the ash to settle and the skies to slowly clear. The total blackness lasted several weeks and the Earth grew very cold. We took refuge in the caves where we stored our extra food and kept our fires going to keep us

241

warm. Yes, we borrowed fire from Nature first then shared our discovery with the humans."

"It took months for the skies to clear and the Earth to return into the light. The black skies slowly turned dark grey, and the grey slowly turned blue and the rain clouds slowly scrubbed the skies clean of the ash. By this time thousands of species had disappeared. Those relying on meat starved."

"In the far east across the ocean of oceans the humans, our younger siblings, were extremely reckless and did not plan beyond each day. They relied on the meat of animals and a few plants to sustain themselves. They were primarily scavengers with very poor hunting skills and limited night vision. They were caught unprepared to last out the darkness."

"Only one skinny and starving tribe of humans survived. They had observed our gentle and generous natures and came to us for help. They were our baby brothers and sisters, they made their way to us and of course we took them in."

"Unlike the humans we are nocturnal. During the day we take refuge in our secret places to take long naps and care for each other. We are vegetarians with an abundance of food sources to draw from. We had grown accustomed not to rely on one source and to store our food carefully away for the long winters."

"With the daylight returning we shared our food with the humans who greedily ate more than they needed laying around for hours trying to recover from each meal. They are gluttonous and we allowed them to eat their fill. They have many vices and constantly fuss and fight with each other."

"It was nearly a total extinction but enough of us survived to carry on. The animal kingdom very slowly regained its hold on life and the humans abruptly left us to recover their claim on the lands that surrounded us."

Out of Africa / The Spirit Walkers

Rahoo: *"Like the humans the Spirit Walkers evolved from the **"Knuckle Walkers"** the great apes that inhabited the highland forests and jungles of Africa. A group of these great apes, our forbearers, gradually moved down into the lowlands and into the surrounding savannas."*

*"In the savannas, these **"Pre-Humans"** found new challenges for survival. Unlike the great apes **they began to walk on two legs** and use their forelimbs and hands to reach up into the stunted trees bearing fruits, berries and nuts for nourishment. Paired with scavenging they began to prosper and readily mastered their new niche. **Standing erect and with the use of their hands** they/we became very successful; challenging the survival of the other wild creatures that once dominated the savannas."*

*"In one savanna stood a special tree, known by the wild ones as the **"Tree of Life."** Rising from a small patch of soil, the tree was surrounded by bedrock where nothing else grew. The exposed bedrock stretched out in every direction for hundreds of yards. Standing alone the Tree of Life mastered the horizons and like a symbol of faith the wild ones sought its shelter and bounty. Always moving away from the sun the tree's shadow gave comfort and nourishment to many."*

THE TREE OF
LIFE

"Reaching the fruit of this sacred tree proved to be extremely difficult. The Tree of Life rose out of the ground with a trunk rising twelve feet before its branches began to span outward. The trunk of this tree was perfectly round and as hard and slick as polished granite. Even for the pre-humans the Tree of Life was impossible to climb."

"This tree bore the richest fruit on the planet. The fruit resembled a mango in its size, outer skin and shape, with the fruit itself having the texture of a ripe peach. Each fruit's color was unique revealing blends of: blue, green, red, yellow, copper, gold, turquoise, pink, purple,,,,. Each fruit swirled in colors without end. Although limited in the number of fruit, the Tree of Life yielded fruit year around. The nourishment of just one fruit from the Tree of Life could sustain a large creature for days. Its possession was the envy of many; but the prize of only a few."

"Only a few of the pre-humans could leap and reach these precious fruit. *Coupled with great strength and larger, leaner bodies a small number of them were able to jump high enough to reach the tree's treasured gifts. Being generous by their natures the taller pre-humans shared what they could with the others. The short ones were never satisfied and complained bitterly. Being shunned by the shorter pre-humans the taller bipedal apes only mated with each other and within a short span of a few thousand years stood over nine feet tall. They could leap up into the lower braches and climb into the Tree of Life itself."*

"The other pre-humans soon became jealous of the tall ones and expelled them from their tribe. Once the shorter humans mastered tool making they created the ax, and for spite chopped down the Tree of Life. Those that cut it down

*feasted on her fruit for one day. The tree named **Eve**, that fed thousands over the years, was gone forever.”*

*“Given their mean and vulgar ways the smaller humans teased and taunted the larger humans driving them out of central Africa into the northern deserts. Deprived of their sacred tree for nourishment the tall ones in desperation fled across the deserts in search for food. We walked for thousands of miles; many of us died during the **“Great Exodus.”***

*“On this journey we the Spirit Walkers started our own tribe and pledged fidelity with Nature promising to never take from her more than what we truly needed. Once beyond the deserts in search of **peace** and **harmony** we journeyed deeper and deeper into the great eastern forests that stretched across Asia to the Pacific Ocean.”*

“Driven by their selfish wants the shorter humans were always invading and destroying the forest. We attempted to frighten them away by disguising ourselves as hideous monsters and in return they told horrible stories about our state of being. Our hearts are warm and gentle.”

*“Justifying their fear and hatred for us they constantly hunted us down. The humans took one of our little boys and treated him cruelly for years. He finally escaped and formed an alliance with the other wild ones to defeat the humans in a great battle. This battle was recorded in our ancient writings; words without paper. His name was **Golith.”***

“In spite of his faith and love for all that is Nature, this Spirit Walker became a great warrior in the defense of his people and the wild little ones who became our friends. In

the end Golith would give his life to save us. The little ones would become our eyes and ears. **Whenever the humans threatened the wellbeing, peace and tranquility of the forest, the calls, cries and wild noises of the little ones would alert us of the danger.** They were forever watching letting us know that **the humans were coming, were coming, coming; 'the enemies of our enemies are indeed our friends."**

The Struggle (Before the Great Exodus)

Rahoo: *"**There was a time when we lived in the open with the humans**. We evolved about four million years ago eons before the rise of the humans. We joyfully lived in **harmony** with the natural world. We decided early on to be in **balance with Nature** and **live within her margins; birth and death with life in between.** For generations we and the humans lived side by side sharing the bounty of Nature in peace."*

"The humans unlike us had many children; with dozens of children being born within one family. Their numbers grew tenfold times tenfold. Once they started to cultivate the land they became quarrelsome with each other and at odds with Nature. They began to challenge us for the forest."

*"They soon forgot our kindness during the great darkness and began to hunt us down. They prided themselves for being hairless, **"Naked Apes,"** and spread lies as to our true natures. They used our hairy bodies to turn us into monsters. Our red hair scared them. They were told by their parents, from generation to generation, that the red color in our hair was drawn from the blood of our victims; which is a lie. Our red hair comes from the blend of herbs and roots we regularly eat and has become part of our being through time."*

247

"Once the hairless apes cut down the Tree of Life they declared war on us. They began to tell stories that we were monsters; fierce demons, the creatures of the night, that preyed on the weak and helpless. That our souls are filled with darkness and evil, and our minds have been corrupted by our wicked thoughts and deeds."

*"Just the opposite is true. **We are in harmony with all life forms and respect the creatures of the Earth.** We tend the forest and do what we can to preserve the wild things. We have decided not to challenge Nature but rather to embrace her and follow her natural rhythms. We are the good stewards of the land and life. We are content to live within the bounds of Nature and for that the humans despise us. All the animals in the forest are our brothers and sisters. We do not eat meat. We eat only the vegetation Nature provides. You can find food everywhere in the forest if you know where to look and what to eat."*

"We eat the roots and berries and many of the green plants and most of the mushrooms found on the forest floor and in the trees. With the mushrooms you must take care not to eat the striped sweet ones; they can mess with your minds."

*"We move constantly from one location to another. We never eat more than we need and take care not to over graze in any one area. We are one with Nature and return nutrients to the soils keeping the needs of the forest in **balance** with the needs of ourselves and the other creatures that rely on the Earth for their lives."*

"Sadly the humans can't read the signs of the Earth and will not hear or see this message. They can't comprehend contentment and balance. They are wasteful and greedily

devour the Earth's natural resources. They will take what they want and steal from others. They are selfish and lustful; corrupted by their own sense of sin. They are at odds with the natural systems that sustain life on this planet and constantly rage war on each other."

The Great Escape

Rahoo: *"In the east the humans made war on our kind driving us into extinction in Africa, Europe and Asia. **During this violent conflict a few of us escaped across the ice bridge that stretched from Siberia to Alaska.**"*

"After we saved them from the darkness and gave the humans fire they turned on us as they had turned on Nature. As their lust for land and possessions grew they became more and more heartless, selfish and violent. They invaded the forest with their weapons of stone and attacked us. We withdrew deeper into the forest to our hiding places."

"They hunted us down and killed many of our kind taking the children captive. A few of them pleaded with their leaders to spare the children. The controlling elite would have none of it stating they could not bear to live with the little hairy ones. They killed all of our captured babies except one; whom they kept for sport."

*"At the **"Narrows,"** a small band of our fathers stood against a large army sent to destroy us. In the struggle the ice bridge cracked and broke apart sending our fathers and the attacking humans to their deaths."*

The Ice Bridge

Rahoo: *"I was just a boy when word came that the human army was getting closer to our camp. **Kralu** the eldest of the tribe assembled the fathers stating that some of them would have to stay behind to stop the humans from crossing the ice bridge to the Americas. The only hope for escape was to make a stand at the narrows and get our families across the ice bridge; then destroy it."*

Kralu: *"We must stand our ground and sacrifice our lives. We must destroy the ice bridge before the humans get here. Some of the fathers will build a wall to hold them back while the rest of the fathers and mothers destroy the bridge behind us and help the tribe and our families to escape."*

Rahoo: *"Kralu said we would have to break with tradition this one time to save the tribe. Some fathers and mothers would have to leave each other for the first time since the beginning of time."*

Rahoo: *"While the ice bridge was being destroyed Kralu's wife, **Lukra** would lead the rest of the tribe across the ice into the unknown; the great wilderness. She now would lead the tribe to safety."*

Rahoo: *"Husbands kissed their wives goodbye and brothers kissed sisters. The children held firmly to their father's legs and cried. Desperately clinging to their fathers, mothers had to pull their grief stricken children away. Tears froze to their fathers' cheeks while they waved farewell to their families. With determination the fathers and some of the mothers turned to face the humans."*

Rahoo: *"My mother grabbed my hand and clutched my baby sister against her breast and turned away. With tears washing down her face she waved farewell to our father for the last time. Our father blew kisses into the air saying goodbye to my mother and his babies."*

Rahoo: *"The humans were vicious and would spare none of us. They had tracked us down and were gaining ground slowly closing the gap between us. If they caught us in the open they would kill us all."*

Kralu said: *"We will make our stand at the "narrows" where the ice bridge is only ninety meters wide and the ocean current below is most swift. While the majority of us build and defend the wall, the remaining fathers and mothers will begin to weaken the exposed crevasse."*

Kralu continued: *"No matter what is taking place at the wall, those weakening the ice bridge must not stop. We can only hold them back for a while. Their army is too large to defeat."*

Kralu again: *"The ice bridge must be broken no matter what is happening at the wall."*

Kralu to **Luway** his trusted friend: *"You must ensure that no one working on the crevasse leaves their post. If the bridge breaks you must leave us behind and catch up with the tribe and your families."*

Kralu: *"NO MATTER WHAT HAPPENS THE ICE BRIDGE MUST BE DESTROYED!"*

Rahoo: *"They used the stone tools captured from the humans to cut the blocks of ice. They formed teams and quickly built an ice wall fifteen feet high and ten feet wide. They began to stack additional ice blocks on top of the wall to hurl down on the humans."*

Rahoo: *"Up on the wall our fathers were completely exposed to the human stone tipped weapons."*

Rahoo: *"If our fathers failed to stop the humans we had to make it to the wild lands and vanish into the forest."*

Kralu: *"Once the ice bridge collapses the ocean current will wash the remaining ice away. The tribe must quickly make it to the other side and go into hiding until those of us who survive can catch up."*

Rahoo: *"A winter storm raged in front of us. Lukra guided the tribe straight into the raging blizzard. The ice and snow was blinding. We clutched onto those in front of us to keep our bearings and stay together. We held firmly to each other as we moved forward into the blinding snow. Lukra led us deeper into the blizzard to hide our tracks in case the humans defeated our fathers and made it across the ice bridge. Leaving our fathers and some of our mothers behind, we vanished into the storm."*

Rahoo: *"At the "narrows" our fathers and a few mothers began to break away the ice and build the wall. Once the wall was completed **three hundred** of our fathers posted themselves on top of the wall to face the enemy. In the thousands the humans formed up. Restricted by the "narrows" only a few hundred of the enemy could attack the wall at a time."*

Rahoo: *"While the three hundred defended the wall the work teams deepened the crevasse sending blocks of ice forward to the Spirit Walkers manning the wall. The crevasse grew deeper and deeper. Word came forward that the work teams could hear the ocean moving below and the ice bridge was beginning to give way."*

Kralu sent word to the work teams: *"DO NOT STOP DIGGING THROUGH THE ICE. IT MUST GIVE WAY!"*

Kralu: *"Once the ice breaks save as many of yourselves as you can and make it back to the tribe and your families. Protect them with your lives. I love you and will carry your spirits with me into the unknown."*

The Wall

Rahoo: *"Our fathers took their positions on the wall each behind a stack of ice blocks. The human army moved forward pushing many of their own warriors against the wall. The humans threw spears and fired arrows at our fathers. The height of the wall matched by the strength of our fathers stopped the army in its tracks."*

Rahoo: *"As the humans gathered at the base of the wall they were crushed to death by the army behind them and the ice blocks hurled down upon them by our fathers. The surface below the wall quickly turned red with their blood staining the ice surrounding the "narrows.""*

Rahoo: *"The pile of dead humans in front of the wall grew higher and higher. Our fathers fought frantically to keep the humans from climbing over the bodies of their fellow warriors up onto the wall. When the humans finally breached the wall our fathers grabbed them up like broken dolls and tossed them to the ground below."*

Rahoo: *"Wounded by many spears and arrows our fathers fought on. A great struggle between life and death took place on top of the wall. Our fathers fought desperately to keep the humans back. One by one our fathers began to fall. Kralu and his last few warriors stood fast and fought off wave after wave of the attacking humans. My father and Golith were with Kralu when he fell. The last of our fathers were soon overwhelmed. Then the ice bridge shuddered. The wall shook from end to end. A great cracking sound traveled forward from the crevasse to the top and base of the wall and throughout the "narrows" itself. The wall tilted forward, then backward and began to crumble. The "narrows" and the ice bridge began to shatter and fall apart. The great Artic Ocean spilled over the fallen wall and crumbling ice bridge washing them into the Pacific Ocean. Into this swirl the humans and our fathers were swept away. With a great rush the wall and the ice bridge collapsed and disappeared."*

Rahoo: *"Only one wounded Spirit Walker survived the collapse of the wall and the breaking apart of the ice bridge to tell this story. Nearly frozen to death he made it across the "narrows" carried on the back of a majestic sea turtle. Her name was Florence and she told him her story. She was the mother of **King Kamehameha** of the beautiful Hawaiian Islands; the **Garden Before Eden**. She carried the warmth of these tropical islands with her slowly bringing this wounded Spirit Walker back to life. Safely crossing the "narrows" she set him ashore and wished him well. Mother Nature had warmed the Artic waters and saved his life. My father was spared by **Happenstance** and delivered back to our family to* *tell this story. Out of the blizzard his spirit walked back into our presence and returned to his loving and grateful family."*

Rahoo: *"Those of us who escaped over the ice bridge were the last to survive and vowed never to fully trust the humans again. We took a sacred oath to only reveal ourselves to the children, sick or elderly and in rare cases, a keeper or two."*

Rahoo: *"We will protect ourselves and our children and try hard to scare the humans away, but we don't seek to kill or harm others. Only when we are threatened will we engage in* **mortal defense. We are the keepers of the forest. Beware, the humans are coming, are coming, are coming!"**

David and Golith

Rahoo: *"Many of the little ones escaped across the ice bridge with us. One was a raccoon named* **David**. *Knowing the humans well, David escaped across the ice bridge with his entire tribe and his friends, the Spirit Walkers."*

Rahoo: *"When David was a young warrior his tribe was at war with the humans. The humans were mesmerized with the raccoon's fur and designed caps made from their hides and tails. These* **coon-skin-caps** *brought great prices in their market places along with our stolen children and the meat from the other wild creatures that lived in the forest."*

Rahoo: *"David was called by his king to unite the wild ones and lead an army against the humans to stop this deadly practice before all the wild beings were driven into extinction. In response, the humans "summoned" a giant from the forest, using this giant to threaten and destroy the king's army."*

Rahoo: *"David had heard two stories about this giant. One was that the giant was a foul smelling monster from the deep forest of Siberia who was the greatest warrior that ever lived. It was told by the humans that Golith enjoyed killing his enemies, eating them while they were still alive. He would take many bites casting his prey aside to die while he attacked and ate the next victim in line. He craved blood and flesh and smeared the remains of his enemies all over his massive body. Suffering many wounds he never was defeated or withdrew; winning many battles for the humans."*

Rahoo: *"The second story claimed that this giant belonged to a family of gentle creatures. They were the only humans who never left the forest and held a deep spiritual regard for Nature and all living things. They and we are known as the Spirit Walkers, the guardians of the forest and wild things. We only defend ourselves when attacked or to protect the innocent and our loved ones. Golith was one of us."*

Rahoo: *"Pretending an attack the humans mustered their army in front of David's fortifications. The humans used this opportunity to parade Golith in front of David's army. Golith was heavily armored with sharp metal spikes protruding forward from his helmet. His battle dress included long coarse red hair that covered his entire body. He carried a great battle ax and was smeared with blood. He beat his battle ax against his shield and released a bone shattering scream. All the goats in the fields fell dead. Many in David's army began to shake and cry."*

Rahoo: *"David faced Golith, boldly stood his ground and quietly calmed his fellow warriors. David declared: 'I will defeat this monster tomorrow."*

Rahoo: *"After a few moments the humans withdrew believing Golith's looks and frightful scream had put fear into the hearts of David's army for the upcoming battle."*

Rahoo: *"The humans sent word to David and challenged him to stand alone against Golith. The humans believed David's army would quit the field and scatter once Golith appeared in full battle armer and slayed David in the morning."*

Rahoo: *"David pledging to stand alone consulted with his commanders. To a warrior they recommended that their army quit the field and withdraw; that there was no possible way to defeat this monster and the human army. If they stood against Golith tomorrow they would all be slaughtered."*

Rahoo: *"David was deeply trouble by his commanders' advice. What if the story about the gentle nature of this giant was true; that he was a Spirit Walker, a guardian of the forest who reveres life? What would motivate Golith to take sides with the humans? David knew something was wrong."*

Rahoo: *"That night David disguised himself as a merchant and entered his enemy's camp. David soon discovered that Golith was not welcomed in the humans' camp and was left in the forest to camp alone. Golith's fire drew David to his side. From the darkness of the forest David spoke to Golith in a voice that could be seen but not heard. Like all wild things Golith recognized the words; **the voice of Nature.**"*

David: *"I am David, leader of the wild things that will stand against you in battle tomorrow. Although human like in form, you are a wild one like us. You still live in the forest and speak our language. Why have you joined with the humans to fight against us?"*

Golith: *"You know I could eat you in a blink. You are very brave or very foolish to come here tonight. I believe it must be bravery and goodness that brings you here. I will listen and see your words."*

David again: *"Why do you fight against your own kind, your extended family tomorrow?"*

Golith: *"The humans have my wife and babies locked up in cages deep within a secret cave. They have threatened to roast them alive if I do not stand against you in battle. They are arrogant and cruel without a soul or conscience when it comes to those of us from the wild. The humans kill us for trophies and skins and leave our bodies to rot."*

Rahoo: *"David was astonished how handsome Golith was. Although heavily scarred and covered with very fine soft red hair he was the most perfect looking human he had ever seen. Standing well over nine feet tall his muscular body was massive and gifted with agility in every move. He had one blue eye and one green eye with pupils as big as quarters; the gentle light within his soul radiated wonder and affection. He was not the monster he appeared to be; a lie fanned by the humans to bring fear into the hearts of others.*

Rahoo: *"Golith told David that he was just a baby when he was captured. The humans kept him in a cage of steel and fed him raw garbage crawling with maggots and flies. They beat him daily making him very angry inside. The humans would match him up with lions and bears in an arena to teach him to kill and to further build up his strength. The humans would wage on the winner and would often match Golith against three or more wild beasts at a time."*

Rahoo continued: *"Golith shared that one night his cruel keeper became drunk and passed out next to his cage. Golith took the keys from the keeper's belt and in rage woke the keeper up."*

Rahoo: *"Golith said to his keeper;* **'I have your keys; see if any of you escape me now."**

Rahoo: *"Golith in a blind rage freed himself from the cage and killed all the humans in his path to freedom and escaped into the Siberian Forest. He heard her cries in the forest and was finally reunited with his lifelong mate; with their love and the births of their children, peace returned to his heart."*

Rahoo: *"Years later Golith's family was captured by the humans and held as hostages. Golith was forced to fight in the human wars disguised as a monster to frighten their enemies. Torn, he was condemned to a life of misery."*

David to Golith: *"I promise this nightmare is over. Tomorrow when you face us a green flag will mean that your wife and children have been set free and are in our camp safe and well; ready to be with you again."*

David: *"I have disguised myself as a merchant. My merchandise is some very strong whiskey that loosens tongues. I have left two goat skins full of whiskey with the chief scout who promised to take me to the cave to see the red monsters for an extra skin of whiskey."*

David: *"I will locate the cave, get the fools drunk and free your wife and babies. Look carefully under the green flag between the barriers, you will recognize the eyes and faces of your family."*

David: *"No matter what the outcome tomorrow, your family will be set free and returned to your people. This I promise."*

David: *"If I fail in my mission you are free to take my life."*

David: *"You must stand before me and fiercely contest my presence. I will face you with my sling and score a direct strike to your forehead with a plum instead of a stone. You will grasp your head and fall to the ground pretending death. You will make a terrible cry as you fall to the Earth. Our warriors will shout:* **'Golith; the great warrior giant, killed by a single stone from David's sling."**

David: *"You will carry a goat skin full of red wine next to your body. After you fall I will take a sharpen stick and viciously stab the goat skin several times pretending to spill "your blood" onto the ground. I will scream victory and my army will pour out of our fortress. You must trust me! If the trick works, the human army will fold, scatter and run for their lives. If not, you will rise and stand with us against the humans."*

Rahoo: *"David and Golith met in the open field of battle and acted out their roles. The armies formed and in the middle of the field David "slew" Golith. The humans, as expected, fled the field of battle. They could not believe that a raccoon with a sling and a stone could kill this mighty giant."*

The humans would later reverse this story and claim that David was one of theirs; a human, and that the evil giant David killed that day was named **"Goliath"** a hideous monster that joined the beasts of the forest to kill and eat the innocent. They wrote their version of this story in their holy book and taught it to their children for generations.

Rahoo: *"After the battle, Golith and David became best friends. David and his tribe joined Golith's clan and they lived together for years. They journeyed deep into the great Siberian Forest and lived in peace following their oneness with Nature, the Mother of the Cosmos. Golith was one of the three hundred Spirit Walkers fighting the humans when the ice-bridge and the wall at the narrows collapsed."*

Free at Last

Rahoo: *"Once the little ones realized the new forest was free of the humans, they spread out across the Americas like fireflies, some reaching the eastern woodlands as far away as the Atlantic Ocean. David's tribe settled along the Atlantic coast and for many years David honored us with his visits to our forest in the western mountains."*

Marcus to himself: *"Were these my ancestors? Was David my great, great, great grandfather? Did he cross the land bridge with the Yeti? Could this be true, are we dreaming?"*

An Unforgiveable Future

Speaking to Coyote and me, a soft angelic voice echoed in the forest. The wind whispered: ***"I am Hoora,*** *the first and only mate of Rahoo,* ***Rahoo, Rahoo….*** *Our children's names are* ***Ra*** *and* ***Hoo***. *They were born on my two hundred and fortieth full moon, during The Summer of Plenty. Their mates have yet to be born. Welcome to our most treasured forest.* ***May its beauty illuminate your hearts, and may contentment and balance be your guide."***

Hoora the Seer: *"The Earth as it now stands is threatened. The humans, our half brothers and sisters, are out of control and mindlessly lust to destroy this planet. They are spreading their destruction around the world and are headed* *this way. **Like rabid termites** they are devouring the woodlands.* "

Hoora the Seer: *"In the east across the great ocean the large animals and forest are disappearing; Eurasia/Africa. The smaller animals that rely on the forest are threatened. Life as we know it is slowly being corrupted."*

Hoora the Seer: *"In the future the humans will strip the land of its protective forest and pollute its waters. The soil will finally give out and the organic life within its protective cover will perish. Crops will fail and millions will die of starvation. Conflict will spread like the pox. Like **Easter Island** civil strife and war will break out everywhere."*

Hoora the Seer: *"Their machines will consume the Earth and all of its natural habitats. The humans will burn fossil fuels polluting the Earth's oceans and skies beyond repair. They will use chemicals on the land further contaminating the soil with toxins causing unhealthy mutations to life's basic structure, its **DNA**. These toxins will be washed out into the oceans further corrupting Nature's natural systems."*

Hoora the Seer: *"Before and after the deadly end reveals itself the atmosphere will continue to degrade. Climate change will be in full force by the year **2025** with North America reaching temperatures of over one hundred fifteen degrees during its six months of summer. Fall and winter will last less than three months, with spring starting earlier each year ending by the beginning of April. Spring temperatures at times will exceed one hundred degrees."*

Hoora the Seer: *"The western coast of North America will be ten feet underwater causing a massive migration of the* human population into the Sierra Nevada and Cascade Mountains to escape the rising sea level. Most of southern Florida will be covered by water, with the coastal cities and beaches around the Gulf of Mexico and the rest of the world swallowed up by the swelling oceans. Like a poisonous vapor fear will consume the masses."

Hoora the Seer: *"Slowly the humans will be pushed further and further inland stressing the Earth's natural systems to their breaking points. The wealthy will begin to build their shelters underground to escape the heat and madness generated by the shortage of clean air, food and water."*

Hoora the Seer: *"With the melting of the polar caps and glaciers, the loss of the coastal habitats will spread around the world. All the arid regions will intensify and become unfit for habitation. These waste lands will expand and begin to reach temperatures of one hundred fifty degrees. The dry regions will grow by over a million square miles creating a band of deserts around the world. The **green regions** will continue to shrink losing ground everywhere on the planet. Too late, the human political systems will start to respond. All travel by their precious automobiles and air planes will be prohibited. The world will be placed on **lock down** as related to carbon dioxide emissions with radical steps toward **sustainable green energy** mandated by international law. Coal, petroleum and natural gas production will cease. **Like sand in an hourglass we are running out of time!"***

Hoora the Seer: *"In **2030 zero impact** on the environment will be mandated by their **"United Nations"** and **everything produced by mankind must be recycled.** The nations will make progress toward closing the landfills and cleaning up the environment. The keepers will make strides politically* and begin to have a positive impact on the movement toward a healthier ecosystem. **Teetering on the Eve of Destruction, the Earth and our fates will hang in the balance."**

Hoora the Seer: *"The predictions are that by **2049** the flooding will finally peak at seventeen feet above the current sea levels. In the temperate zones the upper summer temperatures will reach one hundred thirty degrees."*

Hoora the Seer: *"Their science will be pushed to its limits and the **greenhouse effect** will appear to be reversing itself when the unimaginable happens. The biosphere will give rise to our worst nightmare. **Our fates hang in the balance, in the balance, the balance, the balance…."***

Hoora the Seer: *"Marcus, one day soon your curiosity will put you at serious risk but a dark shadow will descend from the heavens to save you from certain death. She too has a warning to share that you must hear and keep for others. You have been chosen to record these visions and warn others of this coming doom."*

Hoora the Seer: *"For the time being we are doing our best to protect the forest and the creatures it cares for. One way or the other, the future belongs to the humans."*

Rahoo: *"Coyote and Marcus, we sense no danger from you. It is clear you are wild ones too. Outside of this vision you have nothing to fear from us. You are free to go."*

Rahoo's voice grew silent as he and his mate Hoora withdrew deeper into the forest. A quiet calm returned and the wilderness, which surrounded Coyote and me, reflected perfect peace. The threat was real only if the intruders were determined to bring ruin and destruction to their forest. The Spirit Walkers were there to keep the woodlands and wild things safe. Nature had chosen them as her guardians.

The Illusion

The next morning Coyote and I slowly woke to the reassuring chatter of the birds and were eager to get moving. Coyote insisted that we had a bad dream and if we searched the forest around us, we would find nothing.

I refused to budge: *"I am not going poking around in the forest! The stick that came flying at us last night and knocked you off your feet; it was real. There it is lying on the ground."*

Coyote: *"I am not bruised or injured. I tell you it was just a disturbing dream. You can wait here if you want, but I am going hunting for evidence to prove it was just a crazy dream; fueled by the sweet striped mushrooms and your overactive imagination; no evidence, no monsters!"*

Coyote ventured into the forest leaving Marcus alone on the trail. The deeper Coyote went the more convinced he became that it must have been the mushrooms. He rounded the last tree before he decided to turn around, and there they were pressed deeply within the moss; perfectly shaped footprints almost as if left there on purpose.

This creature left tracks larger than a bear's without any claws. Each print consisted of five small oblong impressions, with a hook shaped pad pressed beneath, followed by a deep oval shaped indentation. Each impression was over twenty-four inches long from heel to toes. This two legged giant easily stood nine feet tall. The tracks were encased with signs of very coarse hair outlining each impression.

Coyote out loud: *"Could these tracks belong to the creatures that few have seen and that many keep talking about? Could these be the beings who told us their story last night; the Yeti, the Spirit Walkers?"*

Coyote said to himself: *"I feel a bit dizzy, am I still hallucinating from the mushrooms we ate? Could these foot prints be real? This cannot be."*

Coyote again to himself: *"I have never kept anything from Marcus before, but if I tell him about these tracks he will high tail it straight back to the Sierra Nevada Mountains. If we are going to go on and find the fire-mountains, I must not tell him what I have found. We have traveled too far to turn back now."*

A whisper quietly blew through the forest air; a gentle song with these tender lyrics moved through the trees and danced in Coyote's soul:

"We are here to protect the forest and remind others of their duties; to preserve this sacred Earth which has given us life. We ponder to know, we grow wise to love and keep our balance with Nature. *We live to bring forth new life.* We are the Spirit Walkers, the Keepers of the Forest."

Coyote turned to take another look at the unusual tracks and in that instant the footprints had mysteriously disappeared. *"Damn those striped mushrooms!"* Coyote said out loud.

Back on the trail, Coyote claimed: *"I could not find a thing, not a hair, feces, the smell of urine, nothing; not a broken branch, turned up leaves or a footprint; absolutely nothing. It must have been the mushrooms. All is clear and it's safe to continue our trek to the fire-mountains."*

With blind faith Marcus took the lead and headed due north. They both wanted to forget the puzzling dream, get back on the trail and find the fire-mountains.

WILD MUSHROOMS

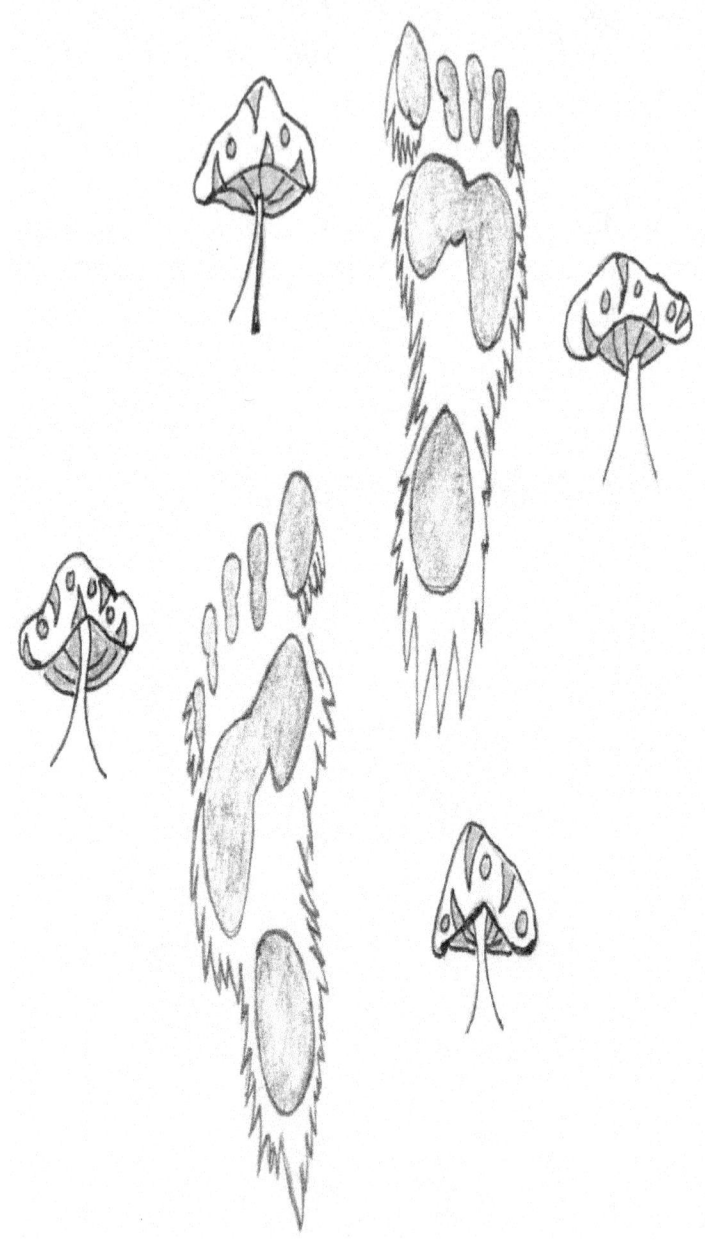

THE SPIRIT WALKERS

<u>U</u>nidentified <u>F</u>lying <u>O</u>bjects

That night Coyote and I made camp higher up in the Cascade Mountains. Not fully recovered from the strange encounters and dreams we experienced the night before, we quietly settled in.

After a long and awkward silence, I began: *"Did you see that meteor last night, how it stopped in midflight and made that radical vertical turn? It looked like a flying disc!"*

I continued: *"I have never seen a meteor make a ninety degree vertical turn from a horizontal path before. It stopped abruptly in place and then flew straight up into the night sky and disappeared in a split second; impossible!"*

I asked: *"And did you see those bright flashing red and yellow orbs flying in different directions after hovering over our camp site? Again in a flash they were gone."*

Coyote: *"Marcus I am telling you it was those sweet mushrooms we ate. We were **hallucinating**. We were still tripping little guy, nothing else. All a figment of our imaginations and your over active exaggerations. Flashing orbs, vertical flight; you know how you expand the truth. Through those mushrooms we had entered the **"Twilight Zone,"** that place in our minds where we make things up."*

Coyote: *"Marcus, I saw that meteor and that was an air burst. That meteor just blew apart before it hit the Earth. And those orbiting lights were fireflies attracted to our camp site. I am telling you, you - we were hallucinating, just a bad trip little buddy. Like the one we had in the desert canyon years ago with the scorpion and cactus buttons.*

ORBS, SAUCERS AND FIREFLIES

I stood my ground: *"I KNOW WHAT I SAW!"*

After another long pause, I pondered: *"Do you think living things can travel in space; that blackness that seems to extend forever above us? Do you think that space travel will be possible in the future?"*

Coyote: *"There are already creatures on Earth that have mastered flight; the eagle and the condor for example. We have been told that the humans are ingenious when it comes to making things; who knows they may in the future extend the mastery of flight into space travel."*

Coyote: *"But if those lights in the night's sky prove to be too far we might not be able to live long enough, or fly fast enough to make the journey to even the nearest star."*

Coyote: *"Space may prove to be an environment where living things, no matter how well protected, cannot long survive. We may someday travel to the moon and inhabit a planet or two, but space travel beyond our solar system may prove out of our grasp. In the end our physical limitations may prove too fragile for deep space."*

I agreed: *"Like the Keeper we may find ourselves restricted to a narrow niche in which we can survive and prosper. Maybe the stars are too far. Once we reach our **"Outer Limits"** we will have to turn inward; to the Universe within and find the true purpose and meaning of our lives."*

Coyote: *"Deep space; go where and for what purpose: to discover and destroy another planet, to drive thousands of other species into extinction? We need to comprehend and take care of what we have before we fly off into space."*

Coyote: *"Marcus, let's give our brains a rest. We had a pretty rough time of it last night. Let's give ourselves some quiet time. I have a lot on my mind right now, too much to worry about flying orbs and tree knockings."*

Farewell

Since our trek through the mushroom patch and our bizarre dreams about the Spirit Walkers and flying things, Coyote had been acting strange. He was not himself. He was not as talkative and seemed distant, demonstrating a demeanor I had not seen before. He appeared indifferent as to our upcoming quest for the fire-mountains.

One night in camp he finally came forward and stated he could not go north to the fire-mountains with me. He said he needed to backtrack due south and then head east; that he missed the Great Plains and wanted to go home. He said that he had been walking a separate path from his kind and needed to be with coyotes again. He said he could not explain it, but that lately he had been experiencing an emptiness that he had not felt before. Something was calling him home. He said he still had brothers and sisters back on the plains and wanted to see them again before he died. He stopped and looked at me and said without thinking; *"I can't explain it, it's much deeper than that."*

Although not clear in his mind, I knew instantly what he was missing and hungered for. He needed a mate and from that union a family. He had been a loner since he was a pup and could not fully understand what he was missing.

Coyote: *"I must leave you little brother and parting brings me great sorrow. Remember the gully and how you tried to escape me, thinking I was going to eat you; when all I really*

272

wanted to do was to protect you? We have traveled many miles together and spoke of many wonders. We have walked in true friendship and I am honored to have known you."

We knew we would never see each other again. I was so overwhelmed with emotion, I could not speak. The next morning with tears in our eyes we embraced each other and said our goodbyes. We picked up our gear and for the first time in over two years stepped off in different directions. At the first turn in the trail we both stopped to look back. We waved our final goodbye and turned forever out of each other's sight.

In life, **Happenstance** will bring us together and take us apart. She does not ask our permission nor tell us why. Ultimately we are alone. Only in true friendship and love do we touch each other's souls. Coyote was my dear friend and now he was gone.

For the first few hours I did not notice the loneliness. Then midday came and went and his absence began to sink in. As the afternoon progressed I grew more and more lonely.

He was my dear friend and I would never see him again. Without him and his constant chatter, the trail became unbearable. In over two years we had not spent one night apart. I started to dread the coming night. Tonight I would camp alone. I said out loud to myself: *"I think I'll sleep in the trees tonight."*

Coyote was a good scout and did not miss a scent. Even when he was asleep his senses were on alert. Not the snap of a twig or the slightest unfriendly scent escaped him. He was always at his post. If I was going to survive the great northwestern mountains I would be on double duty from here on out. That night I climbed high into a giant redwood. I settled down on a branch close to its trunk and it grew very dark. In the distance I heard a lonely howl, only this time I immediately recognized his cry. It was my good friend Coyote saying his last goodbye. Like a serrated knife, his pain cut through the night sky and ripped through my heart. His cry could be heard throughout the land and across time.

Alone

Alone, I moved further up into the Cascade Mountains and kept to the ridges to avoid the up and down climbs to and from the valleys below. When needed, I would follow the gullies cutting across the ridges to the streams below for food and water. There were signs of bear and mountain lions everywhere and I knew I must stay alert to survive.

As Geo explained, the ridges ran parallel north to south indicating the forces beneath the Earth pushing the mountains into each other causing them to rise higher and higher over time. As I moved further north the peaks were reaching elevations exceeding ten thousand feet. In spite of it being midsummer, from time to time up on the ridges it snowed. In the distance I could see snow covered peaks. I was excited.

On several occasions while working my way up the Sierra and Cascade Mountains the Earth trembled. Now as I crossed a large river for the first time I saw the fire-mountain. Its smoke raised high into the sky and filled me with fear and wonder. They do exist, they are real and the Earth is much more than what we see.

I must see this fire-mountain up close. I will find out what burns inside this mountain to cause so much smoke. And just what are those black specks floating in the sky high above the mountain?

I hiked for three days to reach the base of the fire-mountain. There were great swaths of barren rocks and ash that appeared to have flowed down from the top of the mountain. Like being around a huge camp fire at times the air was filled with ash. Frequently there was an odor in the air I had never smelt before. I was on unfamiliar ground and knew to be cautious. I must be prepared for this climb. I was alone and afraid. I will never forget my friend Coyote; NEVER!

FAREWELL MY FRIEND

THE CONDORS

THE FIRE MOUNTAIN

12. The Condors

Salvation

I had made it to the base of the fire-mountain and was determined to make it to the top before midday. The mountain had been rumbling all day. The ground below my paws trembled. After a strenuous climb, I made it to the crest where a giant vent allowed me to peer into the bowels of the mountain. The stones within glowed as if on fire. Again the mountain rumbled then spewed fumes and smoke into the air. I was quickly overcome by the poisonous gas which caused me to fall unconscious. Before I had time to contemplate my victory the world around me turned black. A dark shadow fell from the heavens and raised me from the dead.

From a great distance she had been watching me thinking; *"Foolish little boy."* She knew my destiny and hurried to save me. She was a *seer* of the future. She was a carrion bird ready to devour the dead. I was being carried off to her nest to feed her baby.

At this time the condors ranged from Baja Mexico to southern Alaska. Mating for life the condors raise one fledgling at a time with both parents diligently caring for their single offspring. I woke while in midair being carried to my death by a condor. I was doomed, soon to be fed to its hatchling. What an end, being picked apart by a baby vulture, one bite at a time. I took the last few moments of my life to view the landscape below and ponder my mortal end. Contentment replaced fear and I resigned myself to my fate.

Gracefully she drifted to a ledge along the face of a cliff standing a thousand feet above the valley below. Another condor was waiting for dinner. She gently placed me in her nest. I closed my eyes waiting for the stabbing pain that was certain to come.

Mother Condor: *"Wake up little one. You are home and your little sister wants to meet you."*

Father Condor: *"Do not be frightened. It is against our nature to take your life. We cannot partake of your flesh while your spirit is still with you. We watch for and await death. We only kill to stop the suffering. Mother knew you were still alive and wanted to bring you home to keep little sister company while we search for food during the day."*

Father Condor: *"We are not raptors therefore we do not kill our food. We will protect ourselves and the ones we love but we do not seek trouble. We are carrion birds and our nature is to take what has died naturally or has been discarded by others. Some call us scavengers."*

Father Condor: ***"We work with Nature to help keep life and death in balance.*** *As long as the body is corrupted by the spirit we cannot eat of its flesh. Only when the body has released its energy and light (spirit) are we allowed to partake."*

Father Condor: *"We are cliff dwellers. We make our nest high up on the cliffs to protect our young and to catch the uplift from the heat and wind below. We open our mighty wings and fall toward the valley below to catch the wind that carries us upward. We can see and fly for miles without flapping our wings."*

The Comet

Father Condor: *"When Mother and I were very young we visited the southern plains. Young and foolish, we journeyed east from the protection of our families to start a new life, a life free from the obligations and rituals of the past. We had settled on the edge of a vast plateau to start our own family. This plateau was covered with thick grass that stretched on and on for miles extending up from the valley below."*

Father Condor: *"With joy and happiness we labored to build our nest. We traveled far and wide for the materials we would use. This would be our first born and the nest had to be perfect. We built our nest on a narrow ledge just below the cliff that towered above us."*

Father Condor: *"We were passionate for each other and within a short time Mother laid her first egg. We wondered at the beauty of its rich blue color and eagerly awaited its hatching. Diligently we took turns keeping the egg warm and safe. Within a short span of time we felt our child move within its sacred shell. Our joy was enormous and we soared high into the sky with delight. For the first time our lives challenged the brightness of the sun, the glow of the moon and the wonder of the stars. Our joy was boundless and reached beyond the Universe; beyond where everything begins and where nothing exits."*

Father Condor: *"Late one night we heard a horrid cry from the future pulling us out from our deep sleep. It was the painful cry of a lone coyote that was lost in time and space. Out of the darkness rose a mighty herd of buffalo. Numbering in the thousands; startled, they charged forward. Their hoofs sliced through the hard ground stripping it bare as they stampeded across the plateau."*

Father Condor: *"Blinded by fear this wild herd of buffalo charged toward the edge of the cliff driving Mother and I from our nest. As this herd approached, boulders crumbled from the face of the cliff smashing into our ledge carrying our nest and child to the valley below."*

Father Condor: *"Like a comet crossing the night sky, a massive white buffalo charged in front of the herd bringing the stampede to a halt. His royal demeanor calmed the frightened buffalo. Slowing down, the herd approached the white buffalo, gathering around him with love and affection. This mighty buffalo, standing a shoulder above the herd's largest bull, seemed to glow in their admiration and honor. He had saved this herd of buffalo from certain death and in so doing had proven his loyalty to them. Their joy filled us with horror."*

Father Condor: *"We had barely escaped with our lives before the nest and Mother's newly laid egg fell into oblivion. We escaped while our unborn child fell to its death. In disbelief we circled our nest and the site of our child's death for days before we sadly fled west to the comfort of our families. Mother's sadness was so deep it rained for days on our journey home. Because of her tears the deserts we crossed blossomed with wildflowers in honor of the life that could have been. We learned from this tragedy that there are things we have little or no control over and that we must accept this as fate regardless of the sadness it brings. **Although beautiful beyond words Nature seems indifferent to our pain and sorrows."***

Father Condor: *"We flew west hundreds of miles and found a near perfect ledge for our second and last nest. Vowing never to leave again, we made the Pacific Northwest our permanent home."*

Father Condor: *"Marcus, you and little sister are safe here. Nothing can reach or threaten you on this mountain."*

This was the same story Justice, the white buffalo, had shared with Marcus years before; the stampede that reunited the white buffalo with his herd. Justice never knew of the tragedy involving Mother and Father Condor and the death of their first unborn child. To save his adopted parents the horrible memory of that day Marcus kept his encounter with the white buffalo to his shelf.

Mother the Seer

Father Condor: *"Mother saw you struggle up the mountain that rumbles and collapse close to its fire pit. You should have been warned by your teacher of the dangers on this mountain and to stay far away when it rumbles."*

Mother Condor: *"Seeing so much and knowing your future I could not leave you to die. Wonder guided you to the top of that mountain and to us. My love for life guided me to you. I have seen your future and it does not end here."*

Father Condor: *"We will treat you like our child, give you our protection and share our food and water with you. We will nurse you back to health, heal your deep wounds and then you will be free to stay or leave as you wish."*

Father Condor: *"While you are with us you will call us Father and Mother. We will let you rest and get well so you can follow your own destiny."*

Father: *"Our nest is now your home. Seek its shelter and play along its narrow ledge. We will protect you and keep you safe. You are welcome to stay as long as you wish."*

Father: *"Mother is a seer and she has a warning for you about the future. **You must listen to her carefully for a great task has been laid upon your table**. You have been chosen by this Earth to carry this message forward."*

I asked: *"What of me, Mother? What future do I need to know? I was an outlaw-**desperado** once and promised to change my ways, seek the truth and walk a narrow path."*

Mother: *"I must warn you it is dangerous to know one's own future."*

Mother: *"Ok, I will share. Stay away from the **hollow ones** they will mindlessly repeat the words that have been handed down to them. They believe in the recitals of meaningless words as if the recital of the words gives them meaning. They believe because the words have been spoken or written down the words must be true. They do not seek new knowledge or truth. They will mindlessly march through the generations without stopping to see where they are marching to. They will without question follow their leaders no matter where it takes them, including to their own destruction. The minions will chase false banners and never truly know wisdom."*

Mother: *"Stay away from **spirit warriors**. They seek to push their ideals forward regardless of their worth or truth. They seek above all to safe guard their beliefs and force their beliefs onto others. **They rally their troops around falsehoods seeking power and control**. In the end they want to control it all and will kill others to accomplish this*

282

*mission. **The spirit warriors do the bidding of the controllers, the elite, who hide in the shadows and amass great wealth.***"*

Mother: *"You, my son, will be a **teacher** and a **keeper**. You have been a **seeker** since you were born. It is part of your Nature. You will rise to and fall from great heights. Your fall will illuminate the lives of others. In your fall you will rise."*

Mother: ***"You will stand as a shield to protect the innocent and speak the truth. You will pierce evil (ignorance) like an arrow taking it mortally to the ground where its wicked spirit will rest for eternity."***

Mother: *"You have and will keep company with great beings. One will be special and teach you much. You will forever stand in his light."*

Mother: *"You will warm the hearts of your adopted parents and little sister. Your journey will carry you into the heavens from which you have come. Your memory will illuminate the hearts of those who have loved you."*

The World of Darkness

Mother the Seer: *"The humans are coming!"* *I saved you to help our children see two futures. These futures belong to the humans but will impact us all. One future is dark and without meaning. The other is full of light and purpose. Which path the humans take will affect the Earth as we know it. One world will be filled with misery and suffering and the other world will be filled with life and joy. But do not despair; the world of darkness will not last long."*

Mother the Seer: *"In the dark world your kind will live in their great cities. You will adapt to the many stressors created by mankind and therefore your kind will survive. Many others will not be so lucky. The condor will be saved by a few **human keepers**, only to be lost forever during the struggle forward."*

Mother the Seer: *"There will not be any **wild habitats** left for the Californian Condor or the American Bald Eagle. All the national parks around the world will falter and fall victim to **negligence** and **abuse**. Most of these **wild places** will be sold off to the **elite (the controllers)** for mineral rights. They will turn their profits into **wealth** and **power** that they will never be able to use. **Opulence** will reign supreme for the few while the world they created speeds towards its end."*

Mother the Seer: *"There will be humans who care and who will temporarily save numerous species from **extinction**; but they in the end will not make a difference. They will keep digital records of the thousands of species that will be forever lost to this world. Humans will never know the real animals or see them in the wild. A few large species will survive in their underground vaults with a handful of human researchers trying desperately to save them. **The wild places will be gone**. Owned by none, these wild places will be sold as commercial property for profit without meaning."*

Mother the Seer: ***"Unbridled capitalism and its selfish soul will seize the minds of the controlling elite to push this world to its breaking point. The spirit warriors and hollow ones will follow the elite speaking and believing in their gibberish. Together they will mindlessly consume the Earth."***

Mother the Seer: *"If the spirit warriors and the hollow ones win in this struggle, the Earth as we know it will perish.* ***There will be no free range creatures on the planet. All migratory birds and herd animals will cease to exist. The largest extinction ever will start after their year 2000.*** *"*

Mother the Seer: *"The oceans will be filled with garbage. The last species of fish will be driven into smaller and smaller pockets of untainted water. Covered by a yellow haze, most of the oceans will be poisoned by* **2070.** *"*

Mother the Seer: *"There will be wild places where wild life no longer exists and all the large mammals will disappear. Your species will be the last of the large mammals, but you will only exist in their polluted spillways. Because you are scavengers initially you will build up immunities for most of the coming diseases. The final virus will have its way with all living things; including itself. The humans will be the only mammal larger than your kind. They will develop an illusion of survival that is hollow in the absence of the wild.* ***They will cover the land with concrete and asphalt from horizon to horizon and believe they have tamed the Earth.*** *With no wild places or wild animals left, life on Earth will grow cold. Victims of their own destructive corruptions, the humans will wonder why?"*

Mother the Seer: *"The* **biosphere** *as we know it will disappear and will become permanently corrupted, foul, toxic, poisoned. In this damaged state the end will begin."*

Mother the Seer: *"Once the large and most of the small animals are gone the microscopic-biosphere will degenerate. With fewer competitors viruses will rule supreme and devour all others, then cannibalize themselves."*

Mother the Seer: *"The **super virus** will become the dominate predator of the microscopic world. Without the protective environments of the larger animals the microbes will fall victim to the lust of the super virus and will be driven into extinction; an invisible world consuming itself."*

Mother the Seer: *"Before it turns on itself, this super virus will devour the neural connectors in the human brain turning the masses into the **living dead**. The progression of the disease will last two months with the final stage being **catatonic**. Their minds will be totally functional while they are held prisoner in their own stiff and frozen bodies. They will not be able to lift their hands, speak or move their eyes or blink; in effect dead, but alive."*

Mother the Seer: "At the end *there will be no carrion birds or microorganisms left alive to rid the world of their rancid remains. Their cities will stand empty of life with only their bodies left to decorate their buildings and streets. Frozen and trapped in this stench, the humans will watch the world they created come to an end."*

Mother the Seer: *"In less than twenty-four lunar months after the outbreak of this incurable and unstoppable disease the human species will be gone. Once the super virus becomes air borne the end will be at hand."*

Mother the Seer: *"The **elite** will corner the market on **purified bottled air** and retreat to the underworld to escape. Those above ground will perish first. The madness before the end will turn the Earth into an asylum of the living insane. Survival without hope will turn into insanity and this insanity will witness mass suicides and murder."*

Mother the Seer: *"The **elite** who make it to the vaults buried deep within the Earth will extend their misery beyond insanity. With little time to prepare they will run out of time. They will number in the thousands while over nine billion of their kind perished above. The world will turn ugly and putrid with the dead."*

Mother the Seer: *"The **vault people** will quickly exhaust their food supply and begin to draw lots. Those who are desperate for life will eat their children first and then turn on each other. In the end they all will perish, even the **elite** who profited from the corruption of the Earth; the ones with so much to gain, will lose it all. **Greed will be the master of their souls and the ruin of all life on this planet."***

Mother the Seer: *"The last vault to safeguard human life will be named the **Essex**, a lost vessel casted out on a violent sea; a sea of misery designed and instituted by mankind himself. From space their artificial lights will go out, never to be seen again. Their image will disappear from the Earth forever; into **extinction** like the **majestic whales** they hunted for profit. They will run out of water before they run out of oil; the oil and greed that started it all."*

Mother the Seer: *"When the super virus turns on itself it will create a thick blue mist that will cover the Earth like frozen ice crystals. The world from space will look like an ice planet, a planet turned cold by death. In time the sky will turn yellow when carbon dioxide and methane slowly replace nitrogen and oxygen in the Earth's atmosphere. Lifeless, the Earth will spin around and around and around with no one left on the planet to count the days."*

EXTINCTION

The Dead World

It is the Year 2525 and Mankind did not Survive

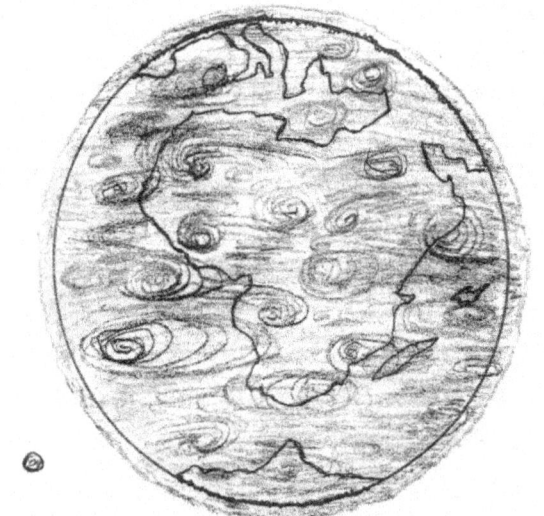

 *YELLOW SKIES,*
BROWN CLOUDS AND ,
PURPLE RAIN

The World of Illumination

Mother the Seer: *"There's a slim chance if the **human keepers** are empowered early enough this tragic end may be avoided. The pyramid of wealth and power that exist today will be abandoned for a more wholesome social order. The worldly outcome of this new order will be the extreme opposite of the one just told (World of Darkness). In the world filled with light the **human keepers** will gain the upper hand and illuminate the multitudes. The human family will advance this cause as a point of existence; an existence which is in **harmony with the Earth**. **In this new reality everything the humans do will be govern by its balance with Nature. Compassion and reason will replace ignorance and greed**. In the **keepers'** good hands **<u>C</u>onservation, <u>P</u>reservation** and **<u>R</u>eclamation (CPR)** will become the norm and the humans will become the **Good Stewards** of the Earth. Every function of any activity initiated by humans will be guided by these three principles. But the **human keepers** will have to illuminate the masses no later than **2049**."*

Mother the Seer: *"The first one hundred years will be the hardest for the humans due to the amount of adjustments their cultures will have to absorb. They had been excessive and will have to learn to share. They had been reckless but now must take care that everything they do has zero impact on the Earth's natural systems. They are an ingenious bunch and will create a positive **balance** between what they need and what Nature can provide. It will be a healthier happier planet once they see it. Seeing it is their first step, when grasped they will quickly adapt."*

Mother the Seer: ***"Currently their vision is corrupted by selfish greed,*** *but in the future their vision will be guided by* *true meaning; a meaning described by Nature and her natural systems that have been in place since the beginning. They will look deeply into her systems and find natural answers to meet and exceed their needs."*

Mother the Seer: *"The **controlling elite**, **spirit warriors** and **hollow ones** will disappear. All will be **seekers, teachers** and **keepers**. The **sustainable systems** will be instituted as a matter of being, one with the Earth, not as a possession for the few, but rather the natural bounty for all including the wild places and wild things. The human population will stand at eight billion, they will occupy one-tenth of the Earth and return the rest back to Nature. The wild animals and wild people will be returned to the wild places."*

Mother the Seer: *"The tamed humans will turn inward and begin to explore the Universe within. The goodness of their unconscious beings will come forth and banish evil forever; harm to others and greed will become extinct. Their cities will reach into the skies as beacons into the heavens."*

Mother the Seer: *"Humans will visit and study the wild places and join the wild with the tame as an extension of itself. They will embrace Nature in everything they do. They will bring Nature into their cities and visit Nature in the wild places. The wild people, who choose to stay wild, will act as **spirit guides** to help the tame ones better understand Nature."*

Mother the Seer: *"If the humans choose this path they will grow old with the Earth and have babies on the Moon and Mars. Their purpose will be to take care of the planet, play in its natural parks and take life to the stars. We will have many children and our image will survive."*

Mother the Seer: *"The humans will become the solar system's keepers. They will transplant life to the Moon and Mars. On the Moon they will create subterranean habitats illuminated by solar domes. Solar reflectors will illuminate the interior where vast lunar gardens will be maintained and expanded. What other forms of life from Earth can adapt to the Moon's minimum gravity will be transplanted to the lunar habitats. Mars will be similar with both terrestrial and subterranean habitats being fully developed. The long term goal on Mars will be to regenerate its natural atmosphere to support an extension of life from the Earth. In this future some of our children will be extraterrestrials."*

Mother the Seer: *"Once the human species is through its adolescent stage all this will be possible. Their selfish immaturity is keeping them from this bright future."*

Mother the Seer: *"Marcus, you must record what you have learned for our children, they will see one of these futures."*

Mother the Seer: *"Take comfort, if the path taken by humans is destructive the Earth will one day, after millions of years, recover and raise a new brew of children more deserving."*

Touching the Void

Months had gone by and **Sissy** was beginning to fly. She would hop into the air and float above the ledge and pretend she was flying. One day while mother and father were out searching for food little sister told me she could see a bear in the distance. As hard as I might try I could not see him. Even with her baby condor eyes she could see ten times further than I. She became increasingly alarmed and I could no longer dismiss her fears, So, I peered over the ledge. Sure enough a large bear was attempting to climb the cliff.

Driven by hunger the grizzly bear clawed its way up the face of the cliff; a thousand feet high and impossible! With each lunge forward, closer and closer he came to Sissy and me. I pushed little sister into a crevice between two boulders and turned to stand my ground. From deep within myself I heard....***"Upon the pain of my death I will protect my little sister!"***

I had to protect my baby sister; her life was most precious to us. We had watched her grow with wonder and marveled at her beauty. From a blue shell she burst to brighten our lives. From being covered by brown down until covered with black feathers she grew and gave us joy. Her wings spanned over nine feet and she possessed eyes with the power of a telescope. We marveled. She was our baby girl.

The hungry bear was committed to take his prey. He reached the ledge and positioned himself to charge. I stood at the point of no return and in another minute I would be gone. I would be violently thrown into the void where life does not exist. It is the darkness before the dawn and the absence of light after the sunset; the twilight without the stars. It is the total emptiness that fills the void that once was us.

There wasn't enough room for the two of us. If little sister would stay deep within the crevice between the boulders she would be safe. He can't reach her if she just stays put.

I was no match for this mighty creature. I was not much to eat. The bear would not stay long exposed on this narrow ledge. All baby sister had to do was to sit tight and he would eventually leave. *"Stay put little sister, I love you!"*

Death was upon me. In that moment it was strange how much time I had to think. As if time was compressed between two extreme points. Death was like something before the beginning (non-existence; birth) yet closer to the end, two of the same things separated by life; a void in a darkness without measure. Only life defines death.

I will embrace my passing and stand fast at my post. I have already achieved immortality. I have children and grandchildren to pass my image forward. One grandchild carries my name. *"Marcus Michael, my dear grandson I love you."* My image is safe.

Let this moment of terror pass, let me touch and know the void. While I breathe, I will know time. When my final breath escapes me, time will stop. As the reflection of my future flashes before me, I will be gone forever into the past. A moment of random destruction brought forward by **Chaos** and sustained by **Happenstance** approaches. Today a hungry bear will devour its prey. Only my will to protect little sister, can in her living, I survive.

Hunched to attack the fierce old grizzly bear glared at me. And then he hesitated as if being called home, he turned and quickly climbed back down the cliff. Just before he turned there was something in his eyes; something that was there before the bear and I were born. Something he knew flashed in his eyes and then he turned and disappeared. He must have been a spirit bear who knew the past and who can see into the future. Somehow his future and mine were joined.

I peered over the cliff and he was gone. I waited a few more minutes making sure it was safe and then I called for her…

I said: *"Sissy its safe, you can come out. The old ugly bear is gone! I scared him away."*

She immediately hopped to the edge of the cliff and peered over. Sissy squinted her eyes which surprised me and said: *"You sure must have scared the bear dung right out of him. He must be miles from here, I can't see him anywhere."*

Lunar Eclipse

As the afternoon progressed I grew more and more concerned. Mother and father had been out scavenging all day and had not yet returned to our nest. They never had been out this late before. It was not like them.

Now that they were working to feed two of us they had to extend their search for food. They would search for hundreds of square miles each day hoping to find something to bring home to their babies. I knew I was becoming a burden, maybe too much for them to continue. Little Sister: *"Where are Mother and Father, they have been gone too long?"*

I was worried myself and feared the worst, I lied: *"They will be with us soon."*

It grew later and later. We anxiously waited for their return. In Nature nothing is for certain. The clouds rolled in from the coast and blanketed the evening sky. Then it grew darker and darker and remained so until the full moon finally broke through the clouds to chase the darkness away. The light of the moon illuminated our nest and the surrounding landscape. For a moment we felt safe. The moon suddenly eclipsed and everything went cold black. Then the moon's light burst through again. When the eclipse occurred the second time our hearts lifted with joy, now understanding its meaning, mother and father had returned to their young. Our parents' mighty wings snuffed out the moonlight from the night sky and the fear from our souls.

Their brief power over Nature ensured their survival. As demonstrated by mother and father condor our purpose to survive is to raise our young. They sacrificed daily so their young could live. And as evidenced throughout Nature, this rebirth gives us purpose and meaning.

My stay with my winged family lasted over a year. Their love for me was genuine and brought back memories of my childhood under the mighty oak. That memory seemed so far away, so long ago yet so meaningful, my mother and father caring after me when I was a little boy with a million questions.

Flight of the Condor

Little sister adored me and I her. Her first flight was spectacular. Mother and father condor would model the techniques. They would hop their way to the edge of the cliff and open their wings. They would stretch their feathers to test the lift and lean forward. They would momentarily teeter and play dance with the wind. They would float up into the air several feet and then turn their wings inward to measure the lift, then alter the air flow through their feathers releasing the air and gently return to their perch.

They would watch her watch them and repeat the techniques. She would proudly show off for them. They would nod their approval. They would move higher and higher into the air and she would follow. Then father and mother flapped their wings and with that soared into the sky. Proudly she followed and soared even higher to join them. The three of them flew higher and higher. They quickly became specks; then disappeared.

For the first time in a year, I felt all alone. My little sister and I were always together and had only that narrow ledge to play on. I was afraid of heights, especially in these mountains. Now that she was off feeding with mother and father I spent many hours alone waiting for their return.

My wounds had long ago disappeared. Father and mother approaching their fifties were growing old and still raising babies. I knew it was time for me to leave. Once Sissy was fully grown, mother and father would bring another baby condor into this world. I was too fat and took up too much space in the nest to stay any longer.

When they returned that evening I asked if I could leave. Father said that I must always seek my own destiny and although he and mother loved me dearly they must honor my journey. Little sister looked perplexed and confused. Saying goodbye the next morning broke our hearts.

I had grown fat and heavy and mother could no longer lift me, so father took me aloft. Mother and little sister came along. They took me beyond the fire-mountain to a mighty river called the Columbia. My adopted parents warned me to stay away from the fire-mountains, there were many of them in this region. They said watch closely for mountain lions and bears; they are always on the prowl looking for food. They wished me goodbye and with a few flaps of their wings were adrift up into the sky. They soared higher and higher until my tearful eyes could no longer see them. Broken hearted I turned up river into the Cascade Mountains. It was early fall and I was headed in the wrong direction. Instead of northeast, I should have been headed south.

Northeast:

My journey would take me up onto the Columbia Plateau and into the Rocky Mountains. I was constantly mixing my scent up with other animals to hide myself from predators. I would stay on the heavily traveled trails long enough to disguise my scent and then head deep into the forest. I lost all my fat quickly and was beginning to run on meager rations. I traveled through a land known as Idaho and then down into Wyoming. As Geo had promised I came to the lands that spit water and steam. Then the heavy snows hit and before long I was in serious trouble. I eventually made it to the high plains a rich and beautiful land covered with snow and ice. By this time I was running on empty.

MOTHER
CONDOR

CRAZY BEAR

BATTLE AT THE LITTLE RIVER WITH BIG HORNS

13. Crazy Bear

The Deep Sleep

I had been without food for days and growing weaker by the minute. Exhausted I had to get out of the cold. The temperatures in the northern plains were unbearable and in the extreme. The snow was over a foot deep and each step cost me dearly. It was a harsh winter and I had been unlucky getting enough food during the autumn months. I had lost several pounds of needed muscle and fat and most likely would not make it through the winter. I needed to find shelter and preserve what little energy I had left. I needed to prepare myself for the end.

I finally took refuge in a cave. I crawled deep into the cave seeking warmth and relief from the biting cold. It became darker and darker as I pushed further and further into the void. The biting cold eased when I found a boulder covered with moss. The moss felt like a warm blanket of fur; I thought I was hallucinating from fatigue, moving closer and closer to the unknown; beyond life….death.

I snuggled in as deeply as I could and fell asleep. I slept for weeks within the folds of this warmth, waking to motions my dreaming mind seemed to recognize; death was like being born and loved again. I dreamt I was nursing. I suckled in this dream and for the first time since I left home, I felt completely safe.

I slowly woke to the soft and wet tongue of a mother bear. She seemed to focus her loving attention directly on me. Startled I froze, but not noticing my fear she continued washing me. There were deep sounds of affection coming from her massive body, and my fear slowly dissipated. Again I suckled. The rich milk warmed me and filled my stomach.

Before I realized what was happening I was being challenged for my spot. Not only did I have a new mother I had a little and greedy baby brother. Being there at his birth the mother bear mistook me for his twin and took me in as her own.

We nursed through spring and we grew daily by the pound. In a few weeks I was the fattest and strongest raccoon on the northern plains. My growth had its limits and within a few months my brother was ten times my size.

My adopted mother loved me dearly and blinded by this love she could not see my true colors. My new mother and brother seemed puzzled by my stunted growth. Being the family runt they became extremely protective of me and watched my every move. They would challenge all intruders no matter their size and bravely stood between me and danger. When a big grizzly cornered me one day they both viciously attacked him until he withdrew into the forest with his short tail tucked between his legs.

They ensured I ate first and tossed salmon to me from the river for me to eat. I had to take five steps to every one of theirs. I learned how to hunt and grew extremely strong. We were a family and I loved them.

Mother bear told us that our father was a great hunter who journeyed to the fire-mountains to hunt the condor. That he carried many scars and wounds, proof of his bravery and exploits. She said he was a spirit bear, one possessed with great vision both now and into the future. He was a protector by Nature and that his sons would be great warriors.

I told mother that I had dreams of living with the condors and that I had a little sister in my dreams that could fly. She laughed and said: *"Silly boy, bears can't fly!"*

We stayed together for over two years but slowly we grew further and further apart. My soul was being pulled away to leave; the call of the unknown. In spite of my love for them I had to move on. We had covered much of the northwest mountains and plains but there was more to see. Cursed by wanderlust I knew we must part.

One day as we searched for food, I paused as my mother and baby brother crossed a stream. They turned to watch me cross and seemed confused when I did not follow. They lowered their heads and grunted. In this goodbye they seemed sad. They hesitated for a moment then disappeared into the forest; I believed never to be seen again. Broken hearted I turned and quickly moved away.

The Little River with Big Horns

I traveled up the stream until after dark. The Moon was full and I gazed at the stars. I made camp and thought about my mother and baby brother, missing both of them dearly. I laid next to a log just above the river and I fell asleep.

I woke to the sounds of children laughing and playing. I could hear the sweet giggles of the little girls and splashing water. The boys were chasing each other through the shallow stream with sticks playing warriors. They called this river the **"Little River with Big Horns."** Their village was not far away.

Feeling lonely, I decided not to journey further and that evening entered their camp. In the cave I had discovered an ancient bear claw and kept it in my *haversack* for good luck. I presented this bear claw to the elder as a gift and again I was welcomed by another tribe. The bear claw was a symbol of strength and honor to the plains dwellers and I would earn their favor and trust.

I had grown very strong while traveling with the bears. When I arrived at their camp I had great stamina and was built like a warrior. After telling stories of my adventures and my life with the bears, the villagers were in awe and called me *Crazy Bear*. They saw me as a noble traveler and brave warrior, which I encouraged them to believe. They asked me to join their tribe.

I took part in another joining ceremony. I told them that I had been a member of a great and powerful tribe to the southeast. When they saw my scars, tattoos and piercings they were impressed and sang out with joy and acceptance. They acted as if I was one of their own sons who had returned from a great adventure.

They added two more slash marks to each shoulder, another piercing to each ear and four white stars to my knuckles. I became a member of their tribe.

I told them that I lived with another tribe for many years and had a wife and three children. When I told them that the chief of my tribe was Walking Moon they grew very silent.

One young brave asked: *"You lived in the presence of Walking Moon, the greatest warrior of our times?"*

I replied: *"He was my father."*

A cry of joy spread throughout the village. A great excitement came over the villagers with cries of relief and salvation. They said the *"Great One"* had sent me to their village to save them. And that *Happenstance* had brought me to their village to protect them from the beasts.

A pack of wolves from the east had been pressing the plains' tribes for several years and now seemed poised to make a massive attack on their village. The wolf pack was fierce, without fear and showed no mercy to their enemies. The wolves were eager to establish their dominion over the land.

Any helpless creature caught in the open was readily killed and devoured. The wolves would separate the weak from the herd, wear them out, painfully harassed them with bites until their prey collapsed and were killed.

In fear the tribe came to me; they believed I was a great warrior and felt they had nowhere else to turn. I had told too many stories about myself and they thought I was more courageous then I really was; "a proven warrior."

They told me that the tribe I once lived with was driven by the wolves on to a reservation and could no longer roam freely over the southern plains. And that my tribe was given a barren tract of land in the Oklahoma territory so poor that they could barely feed their little ones.

They went on to tell me that my tribe was forbidden to speak its own language or practice its ancient communion with Nature. Many of the children were taken from their parents and had their hair cut short. Some of the children were sent east never to be seen again. Their chief Elk Horn was betrayed by some of his own kind, those that wore two faces, and murdered. They continued to tell me that my tribe was now led by an elder woman named White Elk; whom her people honored and revered.

I was broken hearted and hated myself for ever leaving my tribe and family behind. I knew I could not change the unchangeable and in anger I shouted out laud: *"Damn those wolves!"* The young warriors joined in and cried out in one great voice: ***"Damn those wolves!!!"***

Choosing a Chief

Choosing a chief from within their tribe was a sacred honor. The tribe would assign young braves to the elders to learn the duties and customs of their clan.

A leader must prove to be noble and brave; noble in his treatment of others and brave in the defense of the tribe. A brave could only be called a warrior when they returned from their first battle. One warrior from the village would earn the title of chief after many years of proving himself worthy.

When a new chief was selected the elders held a dance. All the young warriors were pierced through the flesh above their breast with buffalo bones and tied to the tribe's sacred post. Each warrior would dance around and pull at the post until they ripped the bones from their chest. The first warrior to accomplish this mission would be named their chief.

After many hours and as the danced intensified a battered and deeply scarred black raven landed on the post. At that instant one young warrior's bones ripped through his flesh. All the other warriors pulled their buffalo bones from their breast in celebration of his selection. They named their new chief, **Buffalo Crow**. Time passed and Buffalo Crow had grown very old.

Their chief was truly a proven warrior and leader. He had a necklace of many bear claws. But he was old and feeble and could no longer restrain and lead the young warriors who impulsively wanted to rush into battle.

Buffalo Crow, their noble leader joined them in their plea: *"Crazy Bear, you are a great warrior and my people are in need of your help. We are but simple farmers. We only go to war to protect ourselves. I must entrust my people to you. You are the son of Walking Moon. Please lead us and help us defeat our enemy in the battle that is sure to come."*

They chose me as their war chief, a great honor. My redemption had arrived. I could save the village and wash all my misdeeds from my soul. The tribe saw me as their savor.

They had put a lot of trust in me based on my stories. My exaggerations and their untested faith in me could put them in serious jeopardy. I wasn't truly a warrior.

Could I find the inner strength and courage to lead these kind and generous people that took me in? I was not sure. Their belief that I could frightened me.

Should I flee before the wolves arrived? Should I slip into the night and live, or should I stay and possibly die? My journey had taught me much and my inner spirit said I must stay. In honor of my family I would protect this tribe.

The Battle (The Little River with Big Horns)

The hounds from the east were determined to steal into the northern plains, corrupt its lands and attack its tribes. The wolf pack pressed deeply into the plains and came upon their village.

Strong Wolf was the pack's leader. He had golden hair covering his muscular body. Strong Wolf divided his command into three troops and would leave his supply wagons behind. This proved to be a fatal mistake.

His command consisted of twenty-one wolves. *Wild Goose* was sent southwest with six other wolves to ensure that Strong Wolf's command was not attacked from his left flank. *Whiskey*, with six wolves would initiate the attack on the village from the center to draw the warriors out. Once the tribe responded to Whiskey's attack, Strong Wolf would take the remaining wolves through the hill country to the north and attack the village from its rear to capture the women and children and hold them as hostages.

Twenty-one wolves divided into three troops charging forward under the banner of the **"Seventh - 7th."** The Hounds of the Seventh were a proud and tenacious pack of wolves set on destroying an indigenous tribe that was contented to live in peace. This tribe just wanted to be left alone and live freely on the land they had occupied for over a thousand years; deeded and titled to them by Nature.

Strong Wolf's plan was to panic the villagers, scatter their forces and hunt down and kill the unlucky ones. Strong Wolf arrogantly stated that he and his command would defeat the tribe before dinner. *"We will feast on them tonight."* He boasted.

His chief scout warned him: *"If we go down into that valley today the buzzards will be picking at our bones come morning."* Strong Wolf just laughed.

The rolling hill country to the north of the village would ultimately work against the wolves. Like giant swells in a vast ocean, each wolf would disappear into the bottom of the swell and be swallowed by the raging storm around him. The angry warriors would follow Crazy Bear's lead, separate the members of the pack and one by one destroy Strong Wolf's command.

Although we possessed an advantage of twenty to one, when we attacked, the wolf pack must never know our true numbers. I trained the warriors in tactics: *"We must never reveal our true intent and attack on multiple fronts keeping the enemy confused thereby controlling the outcome of the battle."*

The wolves were larger, stronger and more vicious, but we possessed a greater sense of community. When the chips were down the wolves would devolve: *"Every dog for himself!"* We were one tenth their physical size but far out measured them in our devotion to each other. We would not abandon our loved ones and would die together to protect our own.

Although not warriors by creed, we would have to make up the difference using our numbers and cunning. We were not warriors and hunters by Nature just simple farmers devoted to each other and the land; the land that sustains us.

In desperation and fear, the tribe had turned to me, Crazy Bear. The make believe warrior who had boasted

307

exaggerated tales of war and glory. I was a want-to-be hero and my stories had finally caught up with me. Their fates were in my hands, hundreds of beings: men, women and children.

I directed a few warriors to take the women and children north and hide in the deep forest. The women were to care for the children and old ones. A few women stepped forward and protested: *"Today we will be warriors!"*

We would form our attack teams in groups of twenty. We would further split these teams into four tactical units consisting of five warriors each.

These four units would attack each wolf from the four cardinal directions: north, south, east and west. The key was to keep the wolves surrounded, never fully letting the wolves know the strength of the force they were facing.

Giving out a great scream to focus a wolf's attention, the front unit would charge each wolf head on. Yielding to the wolf's counter charge, this team of warriors would retreat, drawing the wolf deeper into the pocket; pulling them away from each other. The rear unit then would attack the wolf from behind and deliver vicious bites to his rear quarters.

When the wolf turned to face the new threat, the unit to the wolf's right flank would attack, then the left, then the front; and then again, the rear. This would keep the wolf in a defensive spin, slowly separating each wolf from the pack wearing them down.

With each attack my warriors would bite the wolf as deeply as possible, delivering multiple wounds. With each wound delivered the wolf would experience a loss of blood eventually growing weaker and weaker as he tried to fight off his tormentors. The warriors would maintain this swirling assault, until each wolf finally collapsed from a loss of blood and exhaustion. Once down, our warriors would continue to torture the wolf with their bites. Like mosquitoes drawing blood, they would torment the wolf to death.

We would always keep the wolves at bay and attempt to separate them by force and deception. We would successfully use their own tactics to defeat them.

Whiskey's charge into the village would be roundly defeated and he withdrew with his remaining force to a hillside across the river and dug in. Wild-Goose would slowly work his way back to Whiskey's unit and once together they were quickly surrounded by my warriors.

Strong Wolf's unit became stretched out in the hill country to the north of the village. Unable to form up and make a stand they were soundly defeated as they broke ranks, turned their backs to us and ran for their lives. One by one we took them down. Their cries could be heard for miles.

Strong Wolf and his brother formed up back to back and were quickly overwhelmed. Their glorious dream of conquest would be their doom. Tomorrow they will be food for the buzzards. Strong Wolf would become famous in the east for making his *"Last Stand;"* carrion for the hungry.

When the killing ended I called the warriors to my side. An eerie quiet settled over the battlefield and we were now on hallowed ground. We had lost seven warriors in the battle and I had suffered a *"Wounded Knee."* I said to the tribesmen and women there: *"We must mourn the spirits of our enemies. Our response to their attacks on our homes was righteous; their deaths a tragedy. In a better world this would have been avoided. Maybe somewhere in the distant future it will be so. We leave their bones in the grass. Their beings will now rejoin Mother Earth. Seven eagle feathers will not lift their wicked spirits into the heavens. They must wait until the end of the Earth to enter the Cosmos."*

After the battle we had to break camp and flee for our lives. We moved into the **North Country** and for now we were safe. We knew the wolves' pride would not let them accept their defeat. Next time they would commit a stronger and larger force to hunt us down and destroy us. I gathered the tribe together and told them: *"We have fought together and defeated our enemies. We have fought a righteous war to defend ourselves; a war we did not choose. We must honor our dead; their spirits have risen into the heavens."*

"It will be hard here in the North Country but your wives and children will be safe. If you go back to your lands more wolves will come. They are greedy and lust for more. There will be no end to your suffering if you go back to your homes. Stay here and work hard and live in peace."

"The tribes of the plains will be no more. The wolves will destroy your customs and scatter the tribes and your people onto the reservations. The great open and free spaces that once were ruled by Nature will be subdivided into parcels and sold for profit. ***There will be those with corrupted deeds who will falsely claim ownership over this land.*** *The hounds from the east will be driven crazy by their lust for the* ***yellow dust****, scarring the land with gaping holes to have more of this worthless powder."*

"Remember, Nature deeded and titled these lands to your people generations before the wolves ever came to the plains. Do not trust the wolves from the east. Their gain is your loss and they will not consider your little ones and the elders. They will speak of and sign many treaties. They will strike coins, pennies and nickels with your image on them; but in the end even these images will disappear. They will hunt the buffalo to near extinction for their fur and bones. For sport they will kill and leave the buffalo to rot."

I warned the tribe to never go south again. *"I love you but I must take my leave, there are valleys to cross and mountains to climb and I have not seen the great canyon."*

With that I turned and headed southwest; as I walked away many wept. The mountains with rocks loomed in front of me. Again, I found myself alone on a trail. Although I would never forget my misdeeds I had regained my honor. My spirit seemed a little lighter. Just maybe I might be able to forgive myself for the transgressions of my youth. ***"In knowing, even righteous beings sin; no matter how high one might fly, even the mighty eagle must someday land and return to this Earth."***

CRAZY BEAR

Heading Southwest

I moved down from Montana south through Wyoming and back across the Rocky Mountains. I entered the Great Basin in Utah and visited the sea of salt. At first I thought it was an oasis. But it turned out to be over one hundred square miles of water that you could not drink.

I moved up into the high deserts and continued to work my way south. I crossed a lone set of coyote tracks and thought about my dear friend. Is it possible these tracks belong to him? I sniffed the imprints but their scent had been long gone; dried and evaporated by the sun. My friend Coyote left tracks that only a few could follow. He once said to me: *"You will be known by the trails you follow and tracks you leave."* (Native American)

I lost my bearings and crossed into the high country of Nevada. I quickly adjusted southeast and worked my way back into northern Arizona. I heard many stories about the great canyon but it was hard for me to believe. Geo said it ran hundreds of miles and revealed much about the Earth in that it clearly demonstrated the strata of rock formations taking millions of years to form.

I had seen some small canyons in New Mexico and southern Arizona, but nothing like Geo described. I had seen the great Pacific Ocean and climbed a fire-mountain in the northwest and stood in awe of them. I approached the canyon from the north and was anxious to see it for myself.

14. The Keeper

The Grand Canyon

I had been walking for days with no sign of life or water. The land for the most part was barren. It was sparsely covered with sage brush and cacti. Loose rock and sand stretched on for miles. The sun was unbearable. My nose was blistered and my lips were cracked. My face was burned by the sun's heat and glare. I did not want to continue or travel further during the day but I had no choice. I needed to find water; in the desert it is a matter of life and death.

With an unbearable thirst I continued throughout the day. Without any moisture to help me swallow my throat burned with pain. I notice a gradual incline and I labored under the strain to climb each new foot hill as I traveled south.

Twilight was approaching; the stars burst forth and darkness fell. I was exhausted and desperately needed to rest. I dreaded moving through the night, but I continued and climbed on. I stopped for a moment. I sensed an emptiness in front of me; a vast opening of the land that I could not see but could feel. I felt that I was on the edge of a mighty expanse lost in time and space.

I laid down too tired to move. I thought about my mother and father, wife and children and fell asleep, exhausted from the day's journey.

I was awakened by a breeze that seemed to flow up from the ground. The cool and gentle air brushed against me reaching into my dreams. I had been afloat above the Earth drifting into the stars when I was pulled back into consciousness.

When I opened my eyes I could not fully comprehend what lay before me. I had fallen to sleep on a rocky ledge overlooking a vast opening of the Earth, a canyon that stretched across the horizon beyond my sight for miles. The canyon was layered with various shades of brown, grey and red rock formations stacked on top of each other. In places these layers of rock formed steps from the valley below.

Last night I had stopped to rest, thirsty and exhausted, only to fall asleep on the edge of a great canyon that seemed to go on forever. It was brilliantly colored by Nature, illuminating my spirit. I had regained my strength and for a brief moment I forgot my thirst.

I was deeply moved by the panoramic sculpture before me; an incomprehensible work of art created by Nature, hundreds of millions of years in the making, cut through a canvas of stone by the flow of water; water a substance soft enough to bathe in and precious without measure; the giver and sustainer of life. In awe I gazed at the canyon's beauty.

Again, recognizing my awful thirst, I immediately moved down the trail from the northern rim of the canyon believing I would find water in the gorge below. The canyon was like all the other creeks and rivers I had crossed on my journey; acting like funnels their banks guide water to the lower points of the land. I would follow the trails that led downward to the banks of whatever mighty river cut through this land.

Finally after several hours and an arduous trek down a steep trail I made it to the river. Like the forest I left when I was young, I could hear the water flow before I could see it. Echoing from the walls of the canyon, the river was calling me forward. I could hear and smell the water before I reached the banks of the river.

I drank myself full and quickly fell to sleep next to the river. I meant only to close my eyes for a moment, but again exhaustion took me away. I drifted back to the mighty oak and sacred circle; my roots. I dreamt I was a baby again in my father's and mother's arms; safe, full and warm. They had laid me down to sleep and I was out like a light.

My father took my toy wooden rattle and shook it at me to wake me up. He was bigger than life and my hero. He would protect me with his life and I knew it. He was brave, always honest and straight forward; you never doubted him. *"Marcus, wake up we love you!"*

The Serpent

Again, he gently shook my rattle.....I abruptly woke to a snake rattling its tail less than three feet from where I had fallen asleep. He was curled up on a flat rock between me and the river. He intently stared at me as he moved back and forth in rhythm with his body. His tongue tasted the air for my scent as he measured my threat to his wellbeing. His rattle was steady, yet not alarming. He maintained his hypnotic stare, his head moving sideways, left to right-right to left as he silently watched me.

I reached for a stone to defend myself and his rattle began to move more rapidly and louder than before. I recognized his alarm but felt no threat; it was a warning. I was threatening him. He meant me no harm. I set the stone down and his rattle slowed, then gently stopped.

Still curled, he sat there quietly waiting, watching me watch him. It seemed that this pause was with purpose as if he was trying to teach me something; something profound. Not everything, no matter what you hear, is a threat; all things in Nature are lessons from which we can and must learn.

The silence continued, until I spoke: *"Where did you come from and what are you doing staring at me?"*

"Where are you going?" He replied. *"You have entered my country without my permission."* He continued with authority.

"I thought the land was open to all travelers." I replied.

"It depends on your intent as to your journey through my land." He stated.

"What makes this land yours?" I declared.

"I have lived here all of my life, as my ancestors before me. For thousands of years we have lived within these walls." He said with pride.

I realized my imprudence then stated: *"I mean you, your kind and your land no harm. I beg your forgiveness for my rudeness. I am a traveler on a journey seeking knowledge."*

"It's obvious you have much to learn." He replied, with an air of self-righteousness…. After another long pause, the serpent spoke softly: *"Son, you appear lost and I believe I can show you the way. This river runs roughly southwest, cutting deeply through the landscape and flows down to Mexico into the Gulf of California. This river is called the*

Colorado. There are many dangers, narrow falls and deadly rapids, but trust me the river flows to a better land. If you are brave and travel long enough you will return home."

I said: ***"I know this river; the river of knowledge and life!"***

He looked into my eyes and said: *"You have nothing to fear. I am the beginning and the ending. We are all on the same journey. Our paths vary but our beginnings and endings are the same. We arrive through birth and leave through death. If we are wise in the middle we move toward the light, if not we will remain in the dark;* **knowledge and wisdom versus ignorance and darkness; good versus evil and right versus wrong**. *If we are truly wise, we will pass on the good that we learn to our children.* **"I am called the Keeper."**

The Keeper: *"Your presence here has been foretold. We have much to share and learn. I will walk with you until your own feet carry you forward. Walk with me until I grow wings to fly....Your shadow told us you were coming."*

I thought to myself: *"No doubt, this is some kind of riddle."*

The Keeper continued: *"Journey with me, I am tired of being alone. Too many fear me, yet I am their friend. I strike for food and protection, other than that I am at peace with the world. I seek warmth and shelter, in this I am like all of Nature's creatures."*

The Keeper: *"Warmth and security gives rise to reflection, reflection gives birth to wisdom and wisdom brings forth goodness. It is a narrow path that we must walk to achieve understanding and truth; accepting the physical boundaries of our existence enlightens our beings."*

317

The Keeper: *"Let me be your teacher and you be mine. No teacher teaches without learning. No student learns without teaching; a perfect circle within a Universe of circles."*

The Keeper: *"The **spirit warriors** want you to think and believe I am a threat and poisonous, but I am the **"Keeper of the Truth."** The truth is obvious, only its discovery is in question. The **controlling elite** have wrapped it in lies and fear to keep it from you. The truth is here for you to see in spite of their delusions and games. The **controllers** say she, the truth, is the **"Tree of Knowledge"** and we are forbidden to partake and know her. Her branches reach high into the heavens bringing forth a great illumination. They forbid us to examine, think and question our existence to keep us ignorant and blind. Through our ignorance they seek to control us for their selfish purposes. **They are the ones who gain and hold power by hiding this truth**. In fear of our ability to learn and grow, they create more lies and enemies to distort the truth to keep us helpless and confused. **The controlling elite profit from our ignorance and play games to keep us in the dark."***

The Keeper: *"The truth surrounds us and affects everything we do. Listen and view the Earth and Nature carefully and the truth will reveal itself to you. Falsehoods and lies have kept her away; knowledge of her has been with us since the beginning of time. I am not the evil one they profess that I am but rather the illuminator; the illumination being the question and the truth being the light."*

The Keeper: *"The **spirit warriors** and **controllers** call me a serpent to diminish my worth. They use this tactic to generate fear and hate seeking to silence the truth. There are no prophets; only seekers, teachers and keepers."*

318

The Keeper: *"Knowledge is the gift and the journey is the price for knowing. One cannot gain knowledge without sacrifice. Lazy and idle minds do not ponder such questions and refuse to make the journey. They believe in the **gibberish** and are happy to follow others and play in the dark."*

His eyes watched me carefully as his head moved back and forth keeping rhythm with the motion of his body. He became my teacher and I his student.

The Keeper: *"As we journey together let's share our stories, our moments of joy, our discoveries and wonder."*

He led the way as we traveled downstream along the river. We had many interesting exchanges and he taught me through his questions. He declared I already knew the answers and all I needed to do was to observe, question and attempt a response. He said everything we needed to know about ourselves was before us in Nature; we just needed to look and ponder the evidence.

I asked: *"What is the Earth and where did it come from?"*

The Keeper: *"One question at a time. What do you think the Earth is?"*

I responded: *"The ground below our feet, the soil and rocks we walk on."*

The Keeper: *"If you are just talking about the earth, it is the ground we walk on, but if you are talking about the Earth; it is much, much more."*

I asked: *"Is it all the lands that I have traveled through? Is it the giant land masses that cover thousands and thousands of miles from ocean to ocean?"*

The Keeper: *"Much more!"*

I asked: *"Is it the land masses and oceans? Is it the land masses, oceans, and the air that surrounds us? Is it everything that sustains us? Does it include the forest and streams, me and you and all the other animals?"*

The Keeper: *"Yes, and in effect the Earth is our parent. Her fertile ground was impregnated by her pure water giving birth to all living things. Her air gave us breath, her ground nourished our bodies and her waters quench our thirst."*

The Keeper: *"Where do you think all this came from and why?"*

I responded: *"The heavens. We must be like what we see above us during the day and into the night; the sun, stars, comets, other planets and the moon. "We must be like them on a long journey through time and space."*

I said: *"Why.....I don't know!"*

The Keeper: *"The answer is before us, the answer has always been simple; **it just is and has always been**. We and everything that surrounds us are in passing - passing in time and space, including time and space. **We just are, the Universe just is........... Simple."***

I asked: *"Why don't we accept this simple truth?"*

320

The Keeper: *"We seek permanence (Immortality) in a Universe and reality of change, where absolutely nothing is permanent. We resist and deny the obvious. We are frightened by our own mortality; our fragile existence."*

The Keeper: *"We weep for those whom we love and who leave us. Our mortality, our passing, makes us sad."*

The Keeper: *"Permanence and immortality are but illusions; illusions that we so desperately cling to."*

The Keeper: *"Think of the mystery of time, Marcus. We gaze upon the stars in the present, but the light from the stars are from the past. We are for the instant in the present, moving from the past into the future. The edge of this movement forward, the present, is so thin it cannot be measured. Within one breath we have moved from the present to the future or from the past into the present. The present seems permanent, but in fact it barely exists."*

The Keeper: *"The fragile moments of life are ours but for a short time. We must accept our place and fate. We are passing as we speak into a void we cannot begin to comprehend. We are passing into an absolute and forever darkness which is full of light. Like the Universe that surrounds us, life is but a mystery for us to ponder."*

Story Telling (The Scorpion)

Our journey together continued for years. At some point on one of our many walks, I told the serpent about my cactus bud experience and he chuckled with glee and laughed so hard that his rattle nearly fell off.

I said: *"Once while I was in a desert canyon I ate some cactus buttons and was stung by a scorpion. I passed out and in my dreams I saw the birth of the Universe and the Earth; it was beautiful."*

The Keeper: *"Foolish boy, your soul and mind can take you to worlds beyond your imagination. We have the power to create new realities that can carry us across the Universe to incredible worlds. Like the Earth holding an abundance of life forms, the Universe holds an abundance of worlds; worlds as beautiful and as full of life as ours."*

He continued: *"You don't have to travel across the Universe to witness and know these worlds. You only have to open your mind and heart to know and love the world that gave us life. Life forms are so abundant we have yet to name them all."*

The Keeper: *"You don't need herbs, venom or machines to cross the Cosmos. **Wonder and contentment are the vessels that will carry us there. Knowing ourselves and loving this Earth is all that we need; wonder and contentment being our fuel; knowledge and wisdom being our mission."***

I asked: *"Is there only one Universe?"*

The Keeper: *"We can only accept what we can see, beyond that is speculation. But remember, for a long time we could not see the mite, or the amoeba, or some distant stars. When our vision improved we learned there was more. We allowed our minds to peer beyond."*

The Keeper: *"We can view the possible and almost the impossible as long as we don't make things up and then* believe them to be true. The metaphysical is the stretching of the physical as long you don't stretch it too far. We run the risk of breaking the truth which is not as flexible as the metaphysical."

The Keeper: *"At times we transcend reality to reach our inner truths, but remember these truths lay within a physical being. If we take reality too far into space it may become supernatural; false, a lie that we should not tell. Falsehoods are dangerous because they get confused with the truth. No matter how far we travel into space we must return to the physical world."*

I went deeper: *"It's like the Universe, before its beginning there was nothing, then all came forth from the darkness to bring us light. The beginning and ending are all the same; something from nothing to illuminate our minds."*

I ventured on: *"Before the illumination there was darkness. Before the something, the Universe, there was nothing. Begging the metaphysical and the supernatural; we are stretching the physical beyond the natural, the riddle of riddles, the circles of circles, the beginning and ending, all in the same, from nothing to something.* **This is the mystery of mysteries and the great unknown."**

I continued: *"Who knows? One Universe, two Universes, maybe more; black holes, folds in space, time warps and more. What does it matter, dark or light? In the margins of the physical world, between birth and death, what matters is the joy of living;* **love**, **peace**, **balance**, **harmony**, **tranquility**, **contentment***.... We have given it words. Can we exist and live within the boundaries of their meanings?"*

I was beginning to sound and think like the Keeper: *"We face a fork in the road; one path we must travel and one path we must choose. The light or the darkness, which will it be?"*

Story Telling (The Spirit Walkers)

I told the Keeper about our bizarre encounter with the Spirit Walkers. I went on to explain that my friend Coyote insisted that it was just a bad dream and that the mushrooms we had eaten the night before caused us to hallucinate.

I asked: *"Could we have imagined our encounter with these strange creatures?"*

The Keeper: *"Some mushrooms not only can cause you to hallucinate but are poisonous and can kill you. You have to be extremely careful as to which mushrooms you eat; otherwise you may take a **trip** from which you never return.*

The Keeper: *"Having said that, in the early years of human evolution there were multiple forms of mankind. They were the great apes that began to walk upright on two legs. One of these would become the homo-sapiens; the dreaded ones!"*

The Keeper: *"The earliest forms of **erect apes** lived **in balance with Nature** and side by side with the humans. The evolutionary tracks could have separated leaving one species to remain in the forest. It is possible that one parent species of the humans survived and migrated to the Americas."*

The Keeper: *"Did you find evidence of their presence in the forest; a broken branch, feces, turned up leaves, footprints? There have been stories about these beings but no hard evidence."*

324

I responded: *"No; Coyote searched the forest around us and found absolutely nothing."*

The Keeper: *"I guess it must have been the mushrooms. Like your friend Coyote said; just a bad dream."*

Proud of his student; again the Keeper laughed while his rattle sang in rhythm with his joy.

Titled and Deeded By Nature

I learned that the Keeper was born in a den deep beneath the desert sands. His brothers and sisters spread out immediately through the canyon seeking food and shelter. For thousands of generations they had lived and died within these walls, and for thousands of years to come, their children's children will live and die here. By possession, not deed, they own this land; granted and titled by Nature. To steal their land and move them from their home would be a sin.

Within these folds of the Earth they viewed the Universe, and from this narrow window pondered the workings of Nature. They were forced inward and from this inward journey expanded their souls and beings outward beyond the walls that surrounded and confined them.

They would be the *teachers* and *keepers* of knowledge with the females being the caregivers and the males being the protectors. Some of the males would become medicine men whose formulas for transition consisted of pathways to the mind and soul through meditation and reflection. Examination and deep reflection giving rise to discovery and knowledge, and ultimately wisdom. The purity of being was their lesson to be passed from one generation to the next, from one traveler to another.

The greatest medicine man was a woman who blended the two; *caregiver* and *protector* to become one with Nature; **balance**. The *balance* was missing and with this *balance* came *harmony, tranquility* and *serenity*. The need for warriors disappeared. She was the most revered keeper of the serpent clan; her name was *Mother*. She made caregivers of men and with the absence of war the tribe flourished.

They watched the sky and learned the movements of the sun throughout the year; its light and shadows moving gradually along the canyon walls from day to day. The sun was rising and setting in slightly different locations with each passing day. The moon, planets and comets with the stars in the background all had their cycles, all there clearly to see; illuminating both the heavens and the *keepers'* minds.

There was the flow of the river and the volume of water forever changing with the seasons. Water, the substance without which no creature could exist. All the other creatures that lived in the canyon and faced the challenges of survival were there before us to learn and teach from. We all live within the rhythm and boundaries of Nature; birth and death with life in between.

Shadow

Years before Marcus visited the great canyon a strange looking blackbird found his way to the canyon floor. He was tattered and seriously wounded missing part of his left wing with deep cuts to one of his legs. He walked with a limp and had scars above his right eye. It took a great effort for him to move about or fly. He could only fly a short distance; usually from one perch to another. It had taken him months to reach the canyon from the trail he had been following.

The blackbird was weary from his travels and asked for sanctuary. He needed time to heal his wounds so he could continue on his journey and fulfill his promise.

He seemed determined to take care of himself, never asking for help and refused self-pity. He carried himself with dignity; too proud to complain and too noble to beg. Admiring his nobility the serpent clan gave him shelter.

He said he had made a vow many years before to wander the trails and protect the innocent. The blackbird had made a solemn oath never to taunt others into reckless behavior and to always appeal to reason when guiding others through the lessons of life. Because of his vow to follow and protect others the serpent clan named him *Shadow.*

Shadow said that during his travels he had crossed the path of a fierce mountain lion many times. Constantly on the hunt, this lioness was determined to catch her prey.

To help the other animals escape, Shadow would fly across the mountain lion's path to pull her off their tracks. He would pass close over her head ensuring she got his scent. Then he would dart off the trail leading the lioness deep into the wilderness. Hungry, she tried to chase him down. With powerful wings Shadow always got away.

He had been successful many times with this tactic and grew careless. One day the lioness was just a little bit too fast for this proud blackbird. Believing that he could always out maneuver her, he allowed her to get too close. In one lightning strike she caught Shadow just above his right eye and tore through his left wing straight down into his leg and the hard ground below. She struck the ground with such force that she ripped out one of her own claws.

With barely enough strength to get away Shadow made it to the top of a tree. With one wing he made his escape. The lioness circled the tree for hours in hopes that Shadow would bleed out and fall to the ground. She licked his blood from under the tree and waited. The night passed and the mountain lion finally gave up and left to continue her hunt.

A broken wing for a broken soul; Shadow would never be the same. In time his body would heal and his soul would grow wise. From his deep wounds, trapped in a world of sadness, he would wander the wilderness to make amends for his childhood misdeeds.

Shadow had learned a valuable lesson that day and changed his tactics to help others on their journeys. In the future he would hide in the shadows just out of sight and call to the mountain lion to keep her confused. Whenever he caught her with her nose to the ground he would call out; **Caw-Caw-Caw.** Shadow would use this unnerving call to keep the lioness distracted. To protect the innocent, he followed the lioness for years. Her name was *Chaos* and she was determined to have her way, relentlessly hunting the unwary.

Needing rest for the long journey ahead Shadow gratefully accepted the clan's invitation to stay. He spent several months living with the serpents and became a trusted friend. Eventually he restarted his journey to follow Nature's wild creatures and fulfill his vow to protect the innocent.

Brother Against Brother

One night Shadow told this story to the serpent clan:

Shadow: *"While on the trail late one night a bat passed over my shoulder and landed on the branch of a tree that mysteriously appeared out of nowhere. From this branch the bat hung upside down and said his name was Midnight and that he had a story to tell about brothers who too often go to war with each other."*

Midnight said to Shadow: *"In play brothers often taunt each other into recklessness. They push, shove and bully each other for fun seeing who is the bolder or stronger. Initially this grows out of brotherly love, just boys at play. 'I double dog dare you, S-i-s-s-y, Jump, and so on!'"*

Midnight continued: *"When brothers are older, yet still foolish, they often taunt each other about their notions of right and wrong; what they 'believe in.' In the end, who is right and who is wrong usually falls to the brother who is the strongest."*

Midnight: *"Play turns into angry words, angry words turn into threats and finally threats turn into action. Others aggravate the argument and soon they all begin to embrace one cause or the other."*

Midnight: **"Before long the elite and spirit warriors will see an advantage, join the conflict and raise the stakes to increase their profits. The hollow ones will flock in mass to their cause and repeat the popular and hateful gibberish of the elite and spirit warriors they follow. Before you know it, sides are drawn and there is war; brother against brother; born of and from the same parents, nations and gods."**

Midnight: *"Unplowed fields will be left unattended while countless bodies of fathers and sons foul the air. With no one to tend the land thousands upon thousands will starve. Walls will be built and walls will be destroyed. Progress forward will be shoved into reverse stripping out its gears. Moments of illumination will be lost for centuries in oceans of darkness and blood. Reason will blink and then go out. Hope and happiness will disappear; replaced by misery and suffering with no end in sight."*

Midnight: *"Being mortals we are born and we must die; darkness to darkness with light in between. It is this journey in between which matters. We may ponder the light of the Universe but in the end and before the beginning there is darkness. Only the illumination of life gives rise to wonder and hope. How we live our lives determines our happiness or loss.* ***We decide. Love thy brother; all but a simple truth!"***

Midnight: *"Brothers must be careful when they call each other out to play."*

With that the bat flew off never to be seen again. It pained Shadow to hear this story which reminded him of his youth and his two best friends.

Brother taunting brother; this lesson rang so true, deeply penetrating the light of Shadow's inner being; an eclipse of his soul that he could never escape. When Shadow was a young boy he foolishly called his best friend out on a dare. This was a reckless dare, a dare that cost Shadow's best friend his life. So ashamed of this misdeed and full of guilt for his actions, on that sad day Shadow left home never to return. Following the path of others and always hiding in the

330

shadows he journeyed far away from the forest in which he was born.

The clan was puzzled by Shadow's story. There had been peace in the canyon for centuries. They did not know of war. *They were all seekers, teachers and keepers. The rhythm of life was in balance and harmony with the river, canyon walls and Nature. All were seeking purity of being, as designed by reason. Not perfection, but rather a delicate balance within oneself that was in harmony with others and with Nature*. They reassured Shadow it was just a silly dream, a riddle, and that in the canyon it had no meaning. Brothers did not taunt brothers in the canyon, let alone go to war with each other.

Deep inside Shadow knew his life's early misdeed. Shadow full of remorse, hid his shame from his new friends. He was but a silly little bird teasing one of his big brothers; playing as all brothers in Nature do; just learning how to survive in an unforgiving world.

Shadow told the serpent clan that one day they would have a *seeker* named Marcus visit their canyon. Shadow went on to say that Marcus was destined to carry the basic truths of Nature forward so that the children of tomorrow could better serve their purpose in protecting the planet and its natural habitats. He told the serpent clan that they must help Marcus on his journey to discover and keep these truths.

Shadow continued that Marcus would need someone to aid him in uncovering the lessons of his journey and record these lessons for future generations. Marcus, who was born with a thousand questions, would need a steady voice to guide him on his way.

Shadow told the serpent clan, that years earlier the arrival of Marcus to the great canyon was foretold by a spider that he had met on the trail. Shadow had been warned by the spider that a mountain lion was after Marcus and that this lioness was determined to hunt Marcus down and put an end to his journey. The black widow spider went on to warn that this mountain lion was a force to be respected and that she was bound by Nature and *Happenstance* to have her way. In Nature mothers must sustain themselves to feed their babies. They are huntresses by Nature and are driven to protect their babies and survive.

Shadow believed once in the canyon and with the protection of the serpents, Marcus would finally be safe.

Shadow would take the extra time he needed in the great canyon to recover. He eventually built up his left wing and was soon able to fly again, not as well as before, but he could fly. With his right eye slightly blurred he finally mastered turning his head left and right fast enough to see three hundred and sixty degrees enabling him to respond to danger from any direction. It would take him quite a while to fully heal. Every day he practiced his new tactics, from perch to perch calling for the lioness to follow. Shadow eventually healed from his wounds and continued on his journey.

Marcus never knew of Shadow's visit to the great canyon and Shadow's brief stay with the Keeper. The Keeper was very young at the time and was mesmerized by Shadow's many stories and the promise of the seeker to come.

On a crisp winter day, flying from perch to perch, Shadow climbed up the Kaibab and over the Grand Canyon's southern rim and disappeared into the unknown.

The Seeker, Teacher and Keeper

The *Keeper* and I journeyed on and discussed and pondered many things. I revealed that I left home without telling my parents where I was going or what I was doing. I did not fully understand myself, my quest, or what I was trying to discover. I shared my misadventure with the outlaw gang that led me astray and the killing of the baby in the village.

I exposed my inner conflict between good and evil and although born with a mask and the markings of a criminal, that I discovered on my journey that I was a *seeker* of goodness. I told him about the white buffalo, Justice and his warning. I described the wonderful family I left behind on the Great Plains to chase the need to know, and that the need to know what was beyond the horizon was both a curse and a blessing, born from life itself.

I shared my stories and travels. I told him of the spider's warnings about humans and the scorpion and Coyote. I told the Keeper about getting lost in the desert, the Gila Monster, Side Winder, our misadventure in the Sierra Madres and the mountain lion that had been following me for years. I described the beauty of the west coast; Mexico and California and how far reaching the thinking was out there.

Faith (The Light Within)

I shared with the Keeper the words of the chosen one, the *prophet* and asked the Keeper's thoughts about the prophet's message.

The Keeper: *"Truth is truth, what is righteous and good is the path we should all take. It is the road that we truly follow that defines us as beings, not what we say or the "**holey*** *gibberish"* *that leaks from our mouths. The measure of our goodness is marked in time and flows across the generations bearing witness to its power.* **It is what we do, not what we say that matters."**

The Keeper: *"There are those who proclaim that* **'believing'** *is the measure of righteousness versus doing. If we follow a straight and righteous path all of our lives but do not believe, as they believe, we are condemned to a variety of hells and eternal damnation and suffering."*

The Keeper: *"On the other hand, if we do wrong all of our lives but repent in the end and accept the* **"true faith,"** *we will be forgiven all of our misdeeds and thereby embrace everlasting life. That believing is the measure of righteousness, not doing. Doing wrong all of your life can be readily forgiven, if in the final moment you just believe. We must believe in* **"the one and true faith,"** *of dozens of true faiths, or else there is no room in heaven for us no matter how righteous our lives."*

The Keeper: *"There are many who put on a façade of believing only to mask their wicked souls. In fear of the accounting they repent in the end."*

The Keeper: **"The chosen one's actions speak for themselves. He shared his meager belongings and food with others. He tempered justice with compassion and forgiveness. He sought to heal the sick. He taught the multitudes to accept and embrace each other. If the stories of his life are true then many of his actions speak to his goodness and inner light."**

The Keeper: *"Remember our lessons on the metaphysical and supernatural, we run the risk of creating a falsehood if we stretch the truth too far. We must stick to the truth when sharing our stories or else falsehoods overtime become confused for the truth. Reality becomes imaginary, fictitious, and beyond the truth; lies. Watch out for miracles they are extremely rare in Nature and are bound by natural laws; for example; the markings of a butterfly, the color of a rose,..."*

The Keeper: *"Now the deeper question; were his words and deeds divine? Were these words and deeds beyond the physical, heavenly, not of this Earth?"*

The Keeper: *"These good words and deeds have echoed across time, spoken by many and are of Earthly origins. The actions and words of many have taught us much and illuminate the path we should and must follow. We often fail to keep this truth alive or pass it on to our children."*

The Keeper: *"Far too many of us are not disciplined enough to stay on this very steep and narrow trail. We frequently lose our way or slip and fall. Our wicked deeds and wanton desires like giant magnets pull us astray. Greed, power and control reign supreme and dominate our mortal and physical souls; our natural beings. We must learn to temper these impulses in order to move goodness forward."*

The Keeper: *"Too often we forget this illumination and blindly wander off the trail. To compound this bad habit most of us have poor night vision and we seldom find our way in the dark in spite of the light that shines within us."*

THE COSMOS

The Universe and Life

I asked: *"What about the Universe? Is the Universe conscious of our existence and deeds? Did the Universe create us?"*

The Keeper: *"Yes, we were "created" by the Universe, but not in the conscious or deliberate sense, but rather in a physical and random sense. From the Cosmos all life evolved, from the matter and energy of the Universe life came into being. In a swirl of energy and matter, within all this **Chaos**, life was born."*

The Keeper: *"Nature by her physical being seems indifferent to our internal struggle between good and evil, our preservation and/or our demise. We seem to be the ones who are conscious of her existence, not the other way around."*

The Keeper: *"Nature is but matter and energy without consciousness, except in the rarest of forms; being life itself, life at a conscious level of being. In our physical minds, it is our consciousness that makes us aware of our surroundings causing us to examine and ponder. Thinking appears spiritual, beyond the physical, therefore the puzzlement (pondering) and our eventual awakening."*

The Keeper: *"Consciousness and thinking illuminate our inner beings. Thereby the light, knowing, reaches toward divinity; seeking the truth. If conscious the Universe would be supernatural; beyond the physical, in effect alive.*

I asked: *"If Nature is conscious, wouldn't she want us to understand, acknowledge and grow from her natural laws? Or does it really matter; it will be, or it will not be?*

The Keeper: *"If there is a divine being then her substance is that of Nature, as evidenced by all that surrounds us. We exist within her natural laws. It is a physical entity not a spiritual entity in which we exist. Nature is here for us to revere and understand. In so doing we will discover ourselves, the greatest mystery of mysteries. Nature is not conscious of our existence, but we are slowly becoming more and more aware of her. In and of herself, Nature is divine; phenomenal."*

The Keeper: *"Beyond the struggle to exist, Nature teaches us and reveals the path we should follow;* **balance** *and* **harmony** *within and between ourselves and with Nature. Otherwise we face suffering and self-destruction. The advancement of the material world and our false belief systems will take us to the edge. If we don't moderate our journey and reconnect with Nature we are doomed."*

The Keeper: *"Understanding and accepting that we are mortal beings in a physical reality, it is the goodness of our deeds that gives us immortality. Not eternal life as we would like to believe, but rather the attainment of the perfection of our mortal beings, as related to the wholesomeness of our lives, while we live."*

The Keeper: *"The Universe is made up of matter and energy and exists within the physical realm, not the supernatural, but rather the natural realm; that of Nature. Within this reality we exist not as spiritual beings but rather as physical beings* **born of and from the Earth.***"*

I said: *"Some say that goodness comes from the light within our mortal beings. If this is true then divinity is born of Nature."*

The Keeper: *"If goodness is divine in and of itself, then yes. When our intellectual beings attain **balance** and **perfection** we are capable of wonderful things. When **out of balance** and **moving toward self-destruction** we are capable of creating misery and multiple kinds of hell. We can sustain misery and suffering for thousands of years."*

The Path We Choose

The Keeper: *"Which path we will follow, that of illumination or darkness; is up to us. **Both goodness and evil dwell within and belong to us**. Both goodness and evil grew out of our struggle to survive, hopefully goodness and reason will carry us away from the darkness and into the light."*

The Keeper: ***"We exist between two points, birth and death, and the quality of our lives depends on what we do in the middle; the wholesomeness of our actions."***

The Keeper: *"Emulating those who walk righteous paths is the closest we come to immortality, creating heaven on Earth. All who seek and walk righteous paths approach the divine nature of their mortal beings. In our quest for **balance** within ourselves and with Nature we achieve a righteous life here and now; which is the only reality that we can witness and measure. Beyond this is pure speculation."*

The Keeper: *"Speculation beyond the margins of life, before birth and after death, pushes the metaphysical into the supernatural risking the creation of a falsehood. We too often bathe ourselves in falsehoods losing sight of the truth. We gradually begin to live our lives in a stupor expecting immortality just for believing, missing the opportunity for heaven (wholesomeness) while we live here on Earth."*

The Keeper: *"In Nature all is accounted for in the end; the beginning and ending being the same, a circle within a circle. Everlasting life and the spirit world are but illusions created by ourselves to comfort our mortal souls. **The finality of life is absolute**. You cannot live without dying. In the end we all simply perish."*

The Keeper: *"The closest we come to immortality is through the birth of our children, and through time, even that is fragile in the extreme; like a drop of water in the desert, a whisper in a violent thunder storm, a new born alone in the wilderness, a belief without substance....."*

The Gods (The Immortals)

I said: *"Some say that the gods created the Earth; is this true father? There are many stories as to its creation, Mother Sea Turtle, Mother Blue Jay, Genesis...which one is true?"*

The Keeper: *"Remember the supernatural; beyond the physical we are approaching an untruth, a falsehood. With the notion of gods, supernatural beings, we are speculating and telling our version of what is the truth. We are no longer attempting to explain our observations but instead are projecting beyond what we know to be true; **"gibberish."***

The Keeper: *"We are looking for **"singularity"** the one answer that explains it all. At least we pretend it explains it all. If there are gods, where did they come from? Our answer is simple, they have always been and always will be; infinite, forever; eternal, without a beginning and without an end."*

The Keeper: *"In the physical Universe we have the margins, matter and energy, ranging from the subatomic to the Universe itself, its beginnings and its end; speculating on the extremes of both. With the gods there are no margins, all shapes and forms, with singularity guaranteed if we believe in the version of the one and only true god."*

The Keeper: *"For the humans it is the "believing" in the one true version that counts. **For the animal kingdom we are bound by the physical singularity; of and from Nature."***

The Keeper: *"We know this for sure. There is a Universe, it's real, it's physical and we do temporarily exist within its margins, birth and death with life in between."*

The Keeper: *"The Universe, finite or infinite; a bubble within a bubble or a bubble in the midst of billions of bubbles? We don't know, and if we speculate we are pushing the margins of the truth, the physical to the supernatural, and may be perpetuating a falsehood, requiring **blind faith.**"*

The Keeper: *"Physics will only take us so far. Beyond those margins is speculation. Mathematics based on calculations are attempting to explain the physical. We are too stubborn and arrogant to accept the margins and again imagine more numbers (mathematics). With theorems we attempt to push the margins further into the unknown. Again we are moving toward speculation, conjecture, falsehoods that cannot be measured; supernatural beyond the physical, godly."*

The Keeper: *"What if the entire Universe exists on a dust particle in a closet, in a house, on a planet, in a solar system, within a galaxy, in another Universe, found on a dust particle, in a closet? We are engaged in speculation without end, we are creating and exploring the supernatural creating imaginary falsehoods that some will believe. We all have dust in our closets providing tangible evidence that this theory might well be true."*

I responded: *"What should we believe or accept as truth?"*

The Keeper: *"Energy, matter and life is what we are left with, beyond that is speculation without substance. The quality of living depends on us. The betterment of life, the perfection and purity of being should be our goal. We should seek and spread wisdom, compassion, generosity, **balance** and **harmony**, the truth; benefitting from our goodness while avoiding evil. We should accept, believe in, the physical Nature of the Universe and our potential for goodness."*

The Keeper: *"Marcus, remember the words of your parents; 'Silly little boy, the world is what it is and what it will always be. Thinking too much is not good for you."*

The Keeper: *"We may learn more about the physical world as we go. However, we must base what we know and what we share with others on facts. The margins of the Universe are what we know; matter and energy and from this physical reality life evolved, and through life consciousness."*

The Controllers and Spirit Warriors

I shared my journey through the Cascade Mountains and the volcanoes that spit fire and stones. I told the Keeper that many of my questions had been answered, yet I felt there was still much more for me to learn.

I finally told the *keeper* of my life with the condors and bears and the frightening vision that Mother Condor shared with me; the dark future of mankind and the dying planet.

I asked the Keeper: *"Who are the **controllers** and what do they want?*

The Keeper: *"There are forces behind the scenes manipulating the masses (**the hollow ones**) for their own selfish advantage. They are the humans who refer to themselves as the **elite**, a facade of emptiness to **hide** their true intent. Their intent is to control and have it all, all the worldly possessions you can imagine, **but mostly power, power to control for the purpose of having more**, more than they will ever use or need."*

The Keeper: *The **controllers** are secretive and hide behind a multilayered mask of deception. Their outside appearance varies, but they hide their intent to have more under layers of falsehoods. They amass great wealth and rule the world isolated from its ruin and damnation which often benefits them greatly. The destruction of their own creations only improves their fabricated markets and need for more.*

The Keeper: *"It matters not the worth of a particular "truth" the ultimate force and struggle behind it all is the **power to control the wealth**; wealth the **"elite"** could never completely use. It's the game of having more that thrills them the most; one hides within the margins of this page."*

The Keeper: *"They could care less about the suffering of the masses and the **Earth**; they only want to bathe in further wealth. Wealth only inflames their lust for more. They will bring the world to its ruin and will be the last to transpire when the ecological system fails. Their luxurious rides into oblivion will sparkle with diamonds and gold. But they too in the end will eat their own."*

I asked: *"Who are the spirit warriors?"*

The Keeper: ***"The spirit warriors do the bidding of the elite. They repeat and dramatize the elite's gibberish for selfish gain. The controllers seldom get caught in the act."***

The Keeper: *"Many **spirit warriors** are false. They use partial truths to confuse the **hollow ones** who refuse or cannot absorb the truth. They lead many into misery and self-damnation through distorted half-truths usually based on hate or deception."*

The Keeper: *"The **spirit warriors** spin these falsehoods for their own purposes and gain by keeping their followers confused and under their control. **They gain via the elite.**"*

I asked: ***"Spirit warriors** do not wage war with weapons but with ideas. Is this true?"*

The Keeper: ***"Spirit warriors usually serve the elite leading their followers to destruction and tragedy**. They will resort to violence if it serves them. Sometimes they lust to kill and enjoy hurting others. They take their lead from the **controllers** seeking to satisfy their own lust for more. Most of the time **spirit warriors** are driven by their beliefs. **They will build towers of babble, layer upon layer of gibberish, to profess their faith and confuse the masses.**"*

The Keeper: *"The **spirit warriors** often believe they possess the one and absolute "true faith" and all others must bow to their belief. They will compete with other **spirit warriors** who do exactly the same thing for their "true faith." Both will go to war over their beliefs killing thousands, times ten, times ten. Brother killing brother in the name of the same god."*

344

The Keeper: *"It is never just about faith or religion, **it is really power that drives many to madness; the power to control, the power to possess, the power to destroy,** the power to... **The controllers manipulate the spirit warriors to incite the masses into action to gain power and thereby more control.**"*

I took it further: *"If a **spirit warrior** rises to the truth, he then becomes a guide, the truth not needing a warrior to carry its flag, the truth being a brilliant banner in and of itself."*

The Keeper: *"As long as their ideas yield goodness and do no harm they are worth keeping and sharing with others now and into the future."*

The Keeper: *"Yes, it is better to be a **spirit guide** than a **spirit warrior**. **Spirit guides** serve the truth, whereas **spirit warriors** ultimately serve greed and control."*

The Keeper: *"As I said, the truth is the truth, no matter who speaks it. It's what motivates the speaker that matters, seeking wealth and power or seeking and sharing the truth."*

Marcus the Keeper (Ignorance)

I continued: **"Ignorance speaks loudly for it has no substance in truth.** *Those who speak it, scream it to drown out reason and thoughtfulness. Ignorance is spoken and repeated by the **hollow ones** and are fanned by the **spirit warriors** to intensify the flames of confusion. Subtitles are flashed upon its blank screen to reinforce the lies."*

I said: *"Truckloads of lies and falsehoods are heaped upon this Earth to bury its truth in filth. The **hollow ones** are eager to know and repeat these untruths spreading their*

345

blend of lies like tar to cover the landscape of our natural beings with more falsehoods. The **spirit warriors** *create banners and flags to lead the masses further into the darkness, chasing whatever profits their leaders."*

I said: *"The consumption of these untruths by the masses further exaggerates the confusion and distortions keeping mankind in a constant state of ignorance. The* **hollow ones** *and* **spirit warriors** *raise their voices to the heavens to keep the truth from us."*

I said: *"Whereas the soft tones of wisdom are heard across the battlefields of time to resonate within those souls who are ready to listen. Across the generations, in the mist of thunderous storms and upon the weakest ears the truth is heard. The most violent eruptions of mankind cannot silence or hide the truth.* **We are of and from this Earth!** *We are physical beings that have evolved out of Nature. Between the margins of birth and death we exist within a swirl of living matter and energy."*

I said: *"Ignorance on the other hand seeks untruths, craves distortions and exaggerations. It feeds on fear and despair and preys upon the weak. Ignorance reigns over darkness and rules in the shadows in the dimmest of light. It robs the world of its illumination and carries the unwary into the bowels of emptiness; denying their natural parents: the Earth, sun and stars."*

I concluded: *"Before you awake you must be asleep. Before you know light you must dwell in darkness. Before you really see you must walk upon this Earth blind. Illumination must come from within. Illumination comes out of the darkness of not knowing."*

Gaining and Sharing Wisdom

The Keeper said I possessed some sacred truths and that I had a duty to record my stories for the future generations to come.

The Keeper: *"Marcus, you are becoming a **keeper** and must record and teach your journey to the children of the Earth. These children will be at different stages of being, some old some young, some **seekers** and others **keepers**, but you must teach them all. As long as they are seekers they will hear the truth in your lessons. Remember you are not a **spirit warrior**, but a **keeper**. A **keeper** allows others to find the light (truth) without forcing it on them; we are **spirit guides**."*

He reminded me that the deepest questions are about ourselves, and the Universe that we can see is much easier to explain than the mysteries of our souls. He stated that many living things never question nor learn about themselves. They spend much of their lives in darkness, never watching the sunrise. Believing in his wisdom, I started my *manuscript* immediately and carried it in my *haversack* keeping it safe and dry for the children.

Years passed and the *seeker* became the *teacher* and the *teacher* became the *keeper*. The serpent was all three embodied in the same being, with that being moving toward perfection. When a *seeker*; we struggle to learn the truth and seek to gain and hold onto knowledge. When the *teacher*; we seek to share what we have learned with the generation in which we belong hoping that the ones we love will grow. As the *keeper*; we reach beyond ourselves and time to pass the truth onto others and the coming generations. *Keepers* are anxious about the truth and seek to record and protect it, they store it away for future generations to discover.

The serpent and I were now keepers. As we walked the sacred trails of the canyon we would constantly reflect on what we had learned.

I said: *"It is not the Earth or even the Cosmos we need to ponder, with a little bit of honest study and reflection they will reveal themselves to us. The stars, planets and galaxies are all eager to tell us their stories."*

I continued: *"Even the animal kingdom has left a clear trail as to its development over time on this planet. With open observations of the minute differences within a species one can readily recognize patterns of change associated with their success; evolution. The hummingbird that varies by the elevation and the plant species of a mountain range reveals such a pattern. Although the same bird her beak varies in shape and length based on the flowers she draws from, reinforcing the evolution and variance of both the flower and the hummingbird. Variance is the enabler of evolutionary success as with the hippo, manatee and walrus."*

The Keeper: *"You have been a very good student! I am proud of you my son."*

Right and Wrong (Morality)

I continued: *"It is the spiritual world that escapes us. We get it tangled up with religion, not a personal connection between each other, life and Nature, but rather **rituals of worship that keep us chained to ideological circles**. These **circles of iron** are handed down through the generations imprisoning our minds and souls to something that is not real. We cannot or refuse to escape these chains, shackled to "truths" without substance for thousands of years."*

The Keeper: *"Spirituality, the innermost connection between each other, life and Nature, is not really spiritual; but rather it is the physical and intellectual extension of our total beings. We use the term spirituality in our attempt to define the entity known as **I** and how the entity **I** is connected to others, life and Nature. We are born of Nature and cannot escape our membership with it. Even in death we remain part of the Cosmos."*

I stated: *"**I**, being the inner and outer self that is known to each of us and shared with others. The two things that we must learn and teach are the most fragile in existence; **balance** and **harmony** within yourself, between each other and with Nature."*

The Keeper: *"It takes discipline and courage for us to do the right thing. We must disregard our selfish wants and yield to the needs of the Earth and our fellow beings. Few have walked this righteous path, and it will take many to straighten our course. If we fail we will not survive."*

I speculated: *"Father, spirituality means both our physical and intellectual beings which are inseparable, one in the same guided by our sense of morality-right and wrong."*

The Keeper: *"Son, morality is not based on our sense of right and wrong, but rather right and wrong are absolutes and clear to all. Our sense of morality may vary; but right or wrong stand fast through time: It is wrong to destroy-it is right to mend. It is wrong to waste-it is right to conserve. It is wrong to hurt others-it is right to care for others. It is wrong to hoard-it is right to share. Right serves - Wrong destroys!"*

I said: *"All of our knowledge and wisdom grows out of Nature and is brought forth by our journeys. And through time and reflection we achieve **balance** and **harmony**; knowing right from wrong, and then we pass that wisdom forward."*

I continued: *"A **spirit-guide** will lead some into the light, moving them toward the truth. The truth is bare and naked in Nature. The light is accepting this nakedness; this naked truth. Morality does not matter in the physical world. Birth and death are the inescapable absolute truths of life."*

The Keeper: *"Morality only matters in the spiritual world. The world opened to us through enlightenment. We are attempting to find **balance and live with each other in harmony with Nature**. **Finding that balance with Nature and each other is morality**. Morality becomes the feather that resists gravity and suspends us from doing wrong."*

Goodbye My Son

The Keeper: *"Marcus my son, you have been a good seeker and teacher. Now you must be a good keeper and pass this truth forward to our children and all the others who will listen. "We must keep this Earth safe from the wanted lust of the few; those who greedily strip the Earth of its measured bounty destroying its natural systems. Be aware you will suffer for keeping and teaching this truth."*

As we parted the serpent said; *"I must take my leave from you and from here you must travel alone. I feel like a father to you my son and to me, you my father and my son. I have learned what I have taught, and what we have discovered together. Your words have been guided and scripted by Nature."*

The Keeper: *"We have traveled a long way together and with love we must part, never-but always within this moment and forever here after apart, yet together, a journey traveled as one and a separation without end. All things framed within time and all things wrapped within time, forever a part of the Universe. All things that happen disappear yet still exist; like the light of the stars from a billion years ago."*

The Keeper: *"As if living, the Cosmos is encased in a bubble of time; a bubble without boundaries that would separate it from infinity. **Into the void I must now travel. From here to there I must go. A path no one else can follow to a place we all must go.** As the light fades into darkness I will take with me life's joys and leave behind life's sorrows. The light that once guided my journey now illuminates my passage. Where my being passes into nothing even darkness does not exist."*

We had spent years wandering the canyon together growing wiser with each passing day. He was old and feeble when we parted. He crawled within a crevice between the rocks never to be seen again; as if he was never really there. I picked up my *haversack* and *manuscript*, and without looking back I climbed up to the northern rim of the canyon. When I reached the top I turned northeast to continue on my journey. *The serpent was my greatest teacher and he still walks with me today.* I will always carry his wisdom and his love for all that is designed by Nature with me. ***"He was my father and in that he was greater than life."***

THE KEEPER

THE JOURNEY WITHIN

THE FORK IN THE ROAD

15. The Transformation

The Lone Wolf

I traveled northeast along the rim of the Grand Canyon just above the Colorado River. I trekked through northern Arizona, then across Utah and into Colorado. I headed north along the Green River into the Great Divide Basin.

It was good to be in the open hill country again surrounded by the Rocky Mountains. It was rolling country with big blue skies and plenty of room to roam.

Always watching the horizon I spotted a lone wolf in the distance. I ducked down immediately beneath the crest of the hill: *"Did he catch my scent, has he seen me? Which way is the wind blowing; is the wind to my back?"* I quickly headed east attempting to put miles between myself and that wolf. To my disadvantage the soft life in the canyon and age were catching up with me. I did not have the spring and stamina of my youth. I would only be able to outmaneuver this wolf through wit and cunning. There was no way I was going to out run him.

Where there is one wolf there are others. That's how they operate. They split up covering large tracks of land. They are lone scouts covering vast areas stretching miles and miles. They communicate their discoveries with piercing howls calling their comrades to gather; one of them has found something to eat. The wolf howled again.

I took shelter in the rolling hills staying low off of the horizon. I headed northeast again attempting to put more distance between myself and the wolf. I traveled through the streams to clear my scent and to wash away my tracks. I was taking no chances. Where there is one wolf there is a pack. My biggest fear was not a quick death, but rather a death drawn out with agonizing pain; bite by bite, being eaten alive.

A few days passed and I continued to move night and day, catching quick naps to keep myself fit and alert. I had plenty of water and occasionally something to eat. I was running low on energy. The sun rose and again went down, then rose again. In the distance the call of the wolf echoed over the landscape. I listened for a response and heard the second and third call. They were triangulating my position, they were closing the loop.

At midday I slipped up to the crest of a hill facing the western sky and on the horizon stood the wolf. I checked the horizons to the north, south and east. There were no other wolves in sight; maybe I still had a chance.

He focused on me, howled and then stepped off moving in my direction. He's seen me. The chase is on. I quickly turned to run. Something familiar caused me to pause. I turned back to watch and recognized his gait. *"He's not charging in my direction. Is he, ditty bopping?"*

With joy: *"Did he just stop to eat some grass? Is that, could that be – damn if that's not Coyote!"*

As he moved closer, Coyote: *"What is it with you? You're skittish as hell; give you a silhouette and you run for the hills. I have never known anyone as frightened by their own shadow as you!"*

Coyote: *"I howled for days and called out several times from different hill crests and instead of stopping you would run off again. I tracked your wet ass through streams and walked the horizons to get your attention but instead of stopping, you kept going. I was beginning to believe you did not want my company!"*

I said: *"Man it is great to see you again. I can't tell you how much I missed you over the years. I believed we would never see each other again; time and space what are the odds?"*

I asked: *"I am headed for the Great Continental Divide do you want to keep me company?"*

Coyote: *"I am traveling in that direction. I am going home to the high plains. I am tired of all this wandering around. It would be great to travel with you again."*

I said: *"Remember Seal, man wasn't he cool? We really had some good times in the surf, didn't we?"*

We spent hours over the campfires recounting our travels together; the otter, the prophet, Geo, the mushrooms….

Coyote's Father (Happenstance)

One night around the campfire, Coyote told me a story about his father that he had never shared with me before.

Coyote: *"My father told me that he once was caught in a terrible blizzard in the southern plains. It was a total whiteout with severe winds. The snow and ice was blowing so hard that he could not see more than three feet in front of himself."*

Coyote continued: *"Muffled in the wind my father thought he heard a child crying. He heard the sound again and quickly moved in that direction. It was definitely a child crying and he moved closer and closer to where the sound was coming from. He pushed through the storm and sure enough he found a little girl nearly buried by the snow."*

Proudly Coyote said: *"My father had become a **keeper** and had a profound reverence for life and for all things belonging to Nature. He would always tell us; **'Take only what you need and leave the rest alone."***

Coyote concluded: *"He took pity on this little girl and dug her out of the snow. He kept her warm with his body until the storm passed. After the storm he led her back to her village and into her lodge. He left her under an elk skin safe and warm. He wasn't exactly sure why, but he felt a deep connection between himself and that little girl. She was a special child and he was proud that he saved her life."*

I was dumbfounded. That was the exact story told to me years before about my wife, White Elk. She too was saved by a coyote during a blizzard when she was just a little girl. And years later I was saved in the desert by his son. Could that be true? Is this just a coincidence?

I said: *"That was your father? Now we are the best of friends who have traveled thousands of miles together. Had it not been for your father, my life on the plains with White Elk would have never happened. My children and grandchildren would not have been born. Had your father moved away from that helpless child most of my life would not have been? Your father's compassion and actions on that day made all of this possible; just unbelievable. What are the odds?"*

Like all things in Nature, Coyote and I were joined by *Happenstance*; one thing accidently connected to another.

I finally told Coyote about my trek into the Pacific Northwest, the volcanoes and the condors. I shared my travels through the Idaho, Montana and Wyoming territories. I described my adventures with my adopted bear family and the desperate battle of the Little River with Big Horns. I ended my tale with my extended stay in the Grand Canyon and *my life's greatest teacher*, the Keeper.

Chaos

Coyote and I ditty bopped for miles up to the base of the mountain. The hike to the base of the mountain had been fairly flat and I could mask my limp. We started our climb upward and my limp became obvious.

I was much older than Coyote. I had lived a life of comfort and grace in the great canyon for too many years. Food was plentiful and I grew soft with time. Not as agile or as strong as Coyote I had developed a little limp from an old wound. Holding on to my youth I was embarrassed by this imperfection which was now obvious. Coyote: *"Brother should I slow down?"*

I said: *"I am sorry my dear friend."*

It was a steep narrow trail cut into the mountain side covered with rocks and boulders. The trail was three or four feet wide and wound up a sheer cliff wall reaching hundreds of feet into the sky. Once committed, only this narrow trail separated us from life and death, with drops of over a hundred feet standing between us and eternity.

Walking along the trail leading up to the Great Divide we were stopped in our tracks by a rancid smell. Some large creature had defecated and urinated right on the trail clearly marking her territory forewarning us she was watching. We turned to retreat, but there she was behind us. How we missed her I do not know. ***"She was a spirit warrior."***

The mountain lion: *"They call me **Chaos**, but I am known by Nature as **Happenstance**. I was sent here to test your spirit and end your journey. The Earth is filling up with its share of keepers. Nature wants to limit her knowledge with others and must test keepers before they learn too much. I am an assassin sent to challenge, and if possible stop you."*

Chaos: *"You were always one step ahead of me, but today is judgment day. I have been sent to test your will to survive and your resolve to be a **keeper**. You must face this challenge to be honored as a **keeper**. Nothing personal, it is Nature's moment between life and death."*

Chaos had us boxed in and crouched down to attack. I was old and could not defend myself. I had grown too weak from the years of travel and old wounds to my body and soul.

Coyote stepped forward placing his body between me and death. In an instant she clawed him to shreds, his blood splattered on me and the cliff walls while his body was cast aside. He had mustered a defense to protect his brother and now he was gone. Anger welled up inside me, death or not I was ready for pure and raw revenge. Thirty pounds against two hundred, I was ready for oblivion, let darkness fall.

Chaos: *"The wild one sent me to destroy you. I am an assassin from the dark regions; the underworld. I take refuge* *in the caves to survive and raise my young. I must hunt and kill to feed myself and my babies. You have escaped me many times. I have roamed thousands of miles to dine on your flesh and take your wisdom and light from this world. I am here to deliver you to the boatman to ferry you across to the unknown. The icy breeze of eternity awaits you."*

I declared: *"You are now my mortal enemy. I am prepared for the inevitable. I hope you choke on my flesh. Swallow hard for I will scratch at your throat as I go down. Take me I am ready!"*

I must face my end no matter how horrible. Anger had driven fear from my soul. I am ready! With her burning eyes focused on me the mountain lion charged. With blind rage she charged. With resolve I stood my ground, proud to have called Coyote my friend. He had bravely stood between me and death and for that moment saved my life.

CHAOS

With blood lust in her eyes ***Chaos*** lunged forward. Out of midair she was pulled backwards. In a flash she was tossed into the air and slammed into the rock wall. She was thrown to the ground, raked across the rocks and viciously ripped apart.

From nowhere a crusty old and deeply scarred grizzly bear had pounced upon the lioness. He continued to maul the mountain lion with his jaws and teeth buried deep into the flesh of her throat. In seconds she was ripped apart.

Chaos herself was subject to random destruction. Unpredictably she was gone, a victim of *Happenstance*. Nature must have sent him.

With blood covering his face the grizzly turned on me. The softness in his eyes made me cry. What are the odds? It was my baby brother who came out of nowhere, out of the heavens to save my life.

My baby brother's name was *Survival: "Little brother I am always within you, I am the will and determination in you to exist. You have proven time and time again that you want to survive. Random destruction is resting now. Calm is now in front of you."*

I told Survival of my brave friend's defense. How he stood between me and eternity sacrificing his life for mine. Knowing he could have escaped, instead Coyote stepped into the path of death. He gave up his greatest possession to save my life. Without hesitation he suffered the wrath of *Chaos*, standing firm between me and the raging storm that violently swept him away.

The Raven

I said: *"My dear brother, it's a miracle! What are the odds that you would be on this trail at the very instant when I needed you the most?"*

Survival: *"Fate told me you would be here."*

Survival: *"Last night while I was near sleep I had a strange vision. The forest grew silent and I felt that there was **something in the forest watching me**. Its presence was heavy but there was no threat. It was as if the air was thick with grief; embedded sadness deep within one's soul."*

Survival: *"From the darkness two coal black eyes peered into my soul and called out to me: "Survival, please help me, our brother is in danger!" It was in a voice I could see but could not hear; words framed in remorse that floated in the air; the script of Nature."*

The voice went on: *"Dear brother of my brother, our brother is in grave danger. Nature has sent an assassin to test our brother's worthiness to be a **keeper**. Tomorrow a vicious predator will be sent into the mountains to hunt down and take the life of our brother Marcus. Random destruction is on its way; **Chaos** precedes the storm."*

The voice: *"You must help Marcus, our brother!"*

Survival: *"Who are you?"*

The voice: *"I am Eclipse the best friend of Brutus, the baby brother of Marcus, the sons of Solomon. You and I are now brothers joined forever together by **fate**. I must now put my **faith** in you. Save our baby brother from **Chaos**."*

Eclipse: *"Many years ago when I was a reckless boy I called my brother Brutus, to his death. The three of us were once inseparable friends; Marcus, Brutus and I. I knew I could taunt Brutus to the very edge and I always took him there. Marcus would always counter my taunts with reason, but Brutus would not listen. On that fatal day I took Brutus too far and to prove himself immortal, he leaped to his death."*

Eclipse: *"I vowed to watch over Marcus and I banished myself from the sacred circle and his presence. I have always been just out of sight to help him on his journey. I knew I could never redeem myself for what I had done. I would hide in the shadows to keep him safe."*

Eclipse: *"I watched when you and your mother brought him back to life and took care of him. I know you love him very much! I love him too."*

Survival to Marcus: *"Then out of the blackness of the forest a large black raven hopped into my camp. He had a scar over his right eye and his left wing was battered. He stood there perched on a log and waited to speak. Our eyes met and he began...."*

Survival: *"He said he has been following you since you left the sacred circle. He said Coyote would be with you on the trail but he didn't think that Coyote could stop the beast that had been sent to kill you. He asked that I help save you and led me to your side."*

Survival: *"Marcus it was Eclipse, not **Happenstance** that brought me here. He said that his heart was heavy and asked that you forgive him....Then Eclipse paused for a moment, sadly looked me in the eyes and flew off into the night. With* a cry that only a raven could make; **"Caw, Caw, Caw,"** he *flew off into the emptiness that would become his soul."*

Survival: *"Marcus, Eclipse has been looking after you all of these years. He took many forms to keep you safe."*

After hearing Survival's story, I said to myself: *"Eclipse, my dear friend, I forgave you long ago. Death comes to all no matter who calls us forward. I will join you soon my brother and in that we are all connected. We will chase each other in the heavens and never fall again."*

There was always something out there, I knew it. I could not quite make it out but I knew something was following me. I thought for sure many times it was the mountain lion, *Chaos*. But at times it was something different. To think it was Eclipse carrying the burden of my brother's death all those years, following me to keep me safe.

He had dedicated his life to secretly protect me to make amends for daring Brutus to jump. Even with me, Brutus pushed the edge, it thrilled him, and no matter what caution I gave, it only drove him further. Danger was his joy and recklessness his game. Father and mother should have named him Disaster. For Brutus it was coming, he was always playing with Death. He loved dancing with danger.

I said out loud: *"Eclipse, I forgive you, please hear me brother, I forgive you! Please let it go and forgive yourself for what you could not control."*

In shame Eclipse never showed himself again and I felt sad knowing he was out there so full of guilt and grief. We were little boys playing in the tree tops. We were three dear friends flirting with infinity. What is there to forgive?

Feeling extremely lost I sat down beside Coyote's body and cried. I deeply mourned his loss. We covered him with grass and burned his body in a great signal fire on the top of the mountain. With his flames we illuminated the Earth and heavens. With the joining ceremony completed the smoke drifted into the sky; body and soul into eternity.

As **Happenstance** would have it, I survived that day. I had survived another day on my journey into the unknown and I was now eager to get there.

The Final Trek

I told my brother about my final quest for knowledge; knowing the unknown and that I was seeking the place known as the Great Divide. He said that we had just entered the foot hills and that we had miles and miles to cover and climb before we would get there.

He said he could get me most of the way there but it was mating season and he had to return to his turf to secure a mate. Nature was calling and his deep scars proved his determination. Designed by Nature he had no choice. *"Little brother I will take you as far as I can, but I must return. I must bring forth children to take my place to protect little brothers like you."* For a few days we were family again. He was my baby brother and I was proud to walk in his shadow. As we parted he said.....

Survival: *"I always knew you were a raccoon but I did not want to upset mother. She and I were blinded by our love, the most precious thing in existence. I got a big kick out of watching you act like a bear when fishing for salmon; they were over half your size. It's a wonder one didn't eat you. Stay strong little brother and remember; I love you!"*

SURVIVAL

The Dream

As we said our goodbyes my brother's tears betrayed his physical strength. Survival was sheer muscle, a massive form driven by a tender heart; a heart faithful and true until the end. Our love for each other is eternal.

With a longing I had never felt before I knew this was my final trek. I must move forward, the unknown is in front of me waiting.

I had been traveling east over the foothills for days. I made it to the base of the mountain range leading up to the Great Divide. There was plenty of water on the trail, but practically no food. I needed to restore my strength if I was going to make it to the top.

Just below the trail leading up into the mountains was an open meadow covered with beautiful wildflowers. They were wildflowers that I had not seen before; a multitude of colors and scents new to my senses. They were full of nectar and pollen, ripe for the picking. I had to take the chance and eat as many of the wildflowers as I could before I started my final push up into the mountains. I desperately needed nourishment if I was going to reach the point of no return.

I had traveled far with barely enough to eat. The wildflowers were tender and sweet, gently nourishing my body back to health. After eating myself full and with great comfort I laid down. I paused for just a moment to rest and quickly fell asleep. My sedated mind popped and bubbled with thoughts.

Like puffs of white clouds floating across the blue sky the dreams began. Suspended above the landscape, between Earth and the heavens, I drifted home to the Allegany Mountains. Like a collage; my dreams were splattered with the images of my life, each superimposed upon the other.

They were images with fuzzy edges fading into each other forming a swirl of motion spreading out from the center; the center being the mighty oak tree, the place of my birth.

My mother and father, brothers and sisters, Eclipse, Jetta, Badger and company, Justice, Walking Moon, White Elk, my children, Midnight, the scorpion, Coyote, Gila Monster and Side Winder, swirled through my mind as they ascended into the sky. The Otter, Seal, Geo, the voices from the forest, Mother, father and sister condor, Mother and brother bear (Survival), Buffalo Crow, and the Keeper, were all there to keep me company on my final journey home.

Framed in wonder, they flew across the Cosmos spreading out into the stars to illuminate my path. Their images flowed over me like a warm summer breeze.

The mighty oak and the Sacred Circle (the swirl of images that were the light of my life and the core/center of my being) rested before me. The light after and before the darkness; the spark of light that was my life forming a perfect circle within a circle, my inner being, the totality of what I had experienced was there for me to see.

These were the snap shots of my journey, from the darkness into the light (life) and from the light (life) back into the darkness; infinity-eternity, one and the same with the light of my life, the images of my soul, illuminating my path.

The Question

In my dream the Keeper appeared. His youthful appearance captured his wisdom and the light from within shined in his eyes. As we journeyed through space and time together; I asked the Keeper: *"Father, is there a divine being? Is there everlasting life? Will I see my mother and father, brothers and sisters again, Walking Moon, Coyote, others?"*

The Keeper: *"If there is a divine being (all powerful, all knowing, the creator of the heavens and the Earth), he exists beyond the margins of the physical Universe in the realm of the supernatural (our minds). Therefore we cannot say exactly what this divine being is or what form he may take. There are many stories. We have no evidence of his existence except blind faith. He can only exist in our imaginations based on our beliefs; which is a Universe unto itself."*

The Keeper: *"If a divine being, then which one and based on who's belief and what version? Who is right and who is wrong? Many will fight over their versions for thousands of years. Who truly knows or possesses the truth? Why them and not others? Some choose to believe, others do not, but* with all the **gibberish** and **babble** most remain uncertain and confused. Some will become fanatical about their beliefs and will hurt others to protect their version of their divine and all powerful being."

The Keeper: *"We have no evidence, besides wishful thinking, that we have everlasting life. While there is light in our life, our loved ones are with us; like the light from a distant star that illuminates the present. In time our loved ones exist and through eternity that time is recorded in the Cosmos. Someday we may be able to capture the images and deeds of our lives in some new form preserving these images forever. Although just an image this record would capture the light or darkness that once was us."*

The Keeper: *"Remember, there are billions of galaxies each containing billions of stars with most of those stars having planets orbiting around them; worlds upon worlds too numerous to count, many capable of sustaining life. The Cosmos stretching back to the beginning of time and forward into infinity; containing multitudes of life forms at different states of being; some like us, capable of comprehending the Universe to ponder these questions."*

The Keeper: *"Remember, we started off worshipping the forces of Nature which affected us directly; the wind, rain, the creatures of the Earth, the sun and moon. Nothing has changed, we just started believing in the gods and lost sight of the Earth under our feet; the Earth that sustains us."*

I asked: *"Why would a divine being simply not reveal himself to us? Why all the mystery? The sun, moon and stars let us know of their existence, the wind, rain and seasons, the*

368

animals that inhabit this Earth have all over time revealed themselves to us."

The Keeper: *"The truth is she has never been a mystery. At first we did not understand her and feared her. As our minds and vision improved, we began to know her better. She has been in front of us all of this time. All we needed to do was ponder. She has been with us since the beginning, not in the supernatural sense, beyond Nature, but rather in the physical sense; that which is fragile, always changing and in constant motion; almost spiritual, incomprehensible."*

The Keeper: *"Marcus, she has been with us since the beginning of time. We exist in and with her. She wraps us in her warmth and knowledge, but too many of us refuse to see her. She - Nature is divine in a physical sense, phenomenal, and we are a part of her, now and forever; and in that immortality; infinity, eternity and always, in some form of matter and energy in a never ending swirl of motion; motion that at times is so slow that living things cannot perceive it, or so fast that living things cannot exist."*

The Keeper: *"She is in **balance** and her forces (**Chaos** and **Happenstance**) are straight forward; we just need to live in **balance** and **harmony** with her and ourselves. It is simple but we have made it complicated by creating the supernatural. Nature wasn't simple enough for us. We began to ponder the metaphysical before we really understood the physical and got ourselves lost in the imaginary maze of the supernatural. Idle minds are playgrounds for the gods."*

I asked: *"Father, if there is not an afterlife what is the point of living?"*

The Keeper: *"My son, it is the light that we stand in, between existence and nonexistence that is most important and in line with Nature. We are just following her natural rhythms. We live because we were born. It's that simple."*

The Keeper: *"Nature does not seek our approval nor ask for our consent. What we do with our lives and the light we gain from it gives us meaning. Coming and going in a perfect circle; in a bubble of time which encases our mortal souls for our passage through life. To challenge Nature and all she possesses is foolish. In order to survive we must embrace her and yield to her majesty over our lives."*

The Keeper: *"Marcus, you are bound for the unknown; that which we already know but cannot accept. Have no fear, you are going home."*

The breeze picked up and I was pushed and pulled back into consciousness. The white puffs of clouds softly drifted by. ***"Will I have the strength to climb this mountain?"***

The Rockies and the Great Divide

I had traveled thousands of miles since I left the sacred circle. I had trekked through the vast eastern woodlands to the great Mississippi. I crossed into Arkansas and found my way up the Red River and wandered into the badlands of the Dakotas. I visited and lived with the western tribes where I met my first true love and where we raised our children.

Restless, I was drawn back into the Great Plains; the grasslands that stretched for hundreds of miles to the foot hills of the Rockies. The Rockies loomed over the plains like a forbidden wall of stone which initially blocked my passage west. It was in the Great Plains where I first encountered the noble buffalo and fierce grizzly bear. There were herds of buffalo that numbered into the tens of thousands and stretched over the plains for miles.

I headed southwest into the Sonora Desert and down into Mexico over the Sierra Madres. I journeyed across the Sierra Madres Mountains to the coast of California then up into the Sierra Nevada Mountains headed north. I traveled up into the high desert mountains finally reaching the Pacific Northwest. I witnessed the fire-mountains and traveled up the Columbia River and headed east into Idaho, Montana and Wyoming. In Wyoming the ground spat water and steam. I doubled back to the southwest and down into the great salt flats and entered the Grand Canyon. I hiked up and down the Kaibab and along the Colorado River. I followed the Colorado into the deep southwest only to turn north again. I journey now to the *"Great Divide"* to know the unknown.

During my travels I had many *teachers*, friends, and enemies. My children tempered my soul and brought me true light. My first *teachers* were my parents and in turn I discovered the true meaning of love when I held my children in my arms and sacrificed for their care.

I learned from bad company the boundaries of my soul. The spider, the white buffalo, scorpion, seal and others taught me the lessons of Nature. My dear friends were Walking Moon, Coyote, and Survival who served me above themselves and in that defined true friendship. Mother Condor revealed two future worlds; one filled with darkness, the other filled with light. The humans must choose. The Keeper, my greatest teacher, taught me the lessons of my soul and the expansion of my mind. Eclipse like my shadow was always there to protect me, watching as I traveled west on my final journey home. ***"Now I must embrace and accept the unknown."***

Seeking the Unknown

I moved through the meadow up to the mountain trail. I was battered and worn. I could no longer see. My walking stick had carried me far beyond where my feeble body could bear. In my quest to know I had suffered many burdens. My worst wounds were self-inflicted.

I gradually felt the Earth change beneath my feet and realized I was climbing a steep slope. I had been on uneven ground before and saved by my wits. Regardless of the danger I had learned not to despair and boldly face what was in front of me. The slope increased and I found myself walking on all fours like when I was a youngster. I finally abandoned my walking stick and found myself climbing a cliff that I could not see. I had to feel my way up the cliff one hold at a time. I had to trust each grip using three paws to secure my perch while the free paw moved me forward and upward.

I climbed until I was vertical with the smallest grips holding me in place. The air was getting colder and very thin and I struggled to breathe. I strained against my body only to find an inner strength I had not known before. The quest within inspired me and drove me on. I was growing tired. ***"Why is this mountain so high and will this journey ever end?"***

The Narrow Ledge

Always keeping three points of contact, I found myself reaching for the ledge above me; the last narrow reprieve that separated my climb from the nearly impossible to the impossible. This would be my last place of rest before I reached the point of no return.

*"It is here that I will hide my **manuscript**; in your hands to keep and pass on to others. Only those that have climbed this high will know. You too must be **seekers**. **You have found the haversack and in it the book**. Now find and spread the truth. See if your friends can find us here and share these words with others. Preserve the wild places and keep in touch with our beginnings. **Climb on, you are almost there.**"*

The point of no return was a place where only my sense of fate (existence / non-existence) drove me forward and up the face of the cliff. This was a place where my spirit exceeded my strength to take me upward and higher.

Again and again I was driven forward where the margins of each new hold diminished, barely separating me from life and death.

In my quest I knew I must reach the top and finally find the meaning of life and all that was, is and will be. This would be the moment before eternity; the final question and answer. On this planet we are a world of living beings sharing a common destiny; joined together by life and death.

I continued my climb up the cliff where the holds seemed to fade into the rock face and it appeared that I was holding on to nothing. ***Sheer will kept me fixed to the cliff.***

When I reached the peak and approached the edge of the cliff I believed my journey was near its end. I could finally rest and stop this endless and restless wandering of my body and soul. The journey had taken its toll and I was seeking absolution and within that absolution eternal peace.

My eyes were dim with only the brightest light reaching in. My face was old and wrinkled and each crevasse told a story. My posture was stooped and only when I pulled myself upward could I stand straight. My arms and legs were but flesh and bones with all the muscle gone with age.

I could hear and feel the wind rush up over the cliff and push me backward against my perch. It was as if life did not want to let me go. I stood up and carefully moved my feet forward, searching for the edge, searching for oblivion. As the cold wind rushed over my face I felt eternity; *"I believe it's time for me to fly!"*

The Great Divide (The Unknown)

Poised on the edge of this Great Divide I leaned into the wind and there I teetered between life and death ready for the fall that would carry me away. I held in my hand the eagle feather I found on the forest floor so many years ago. The same feather I had given to Walking Moon and he had given back to me. He knew one day I would need the eagle feather to complete my journey. I was a *seeker* and as such crossed many sacred boundaries during my life's journey. My spirit was heavy with the things I had witnessed and learned. I would need lift if I was to reach the heavens.

I leaned into and against the wind; balanced for a second before my lean forward carried me away. I teetered; then fell….. Down through the sky I fell; *"I was free - free falling."* With a tremendous force pulling me toward the Earth I picked up speed. The fresh air rushing over my body was wonderful. The graceful descent carried me to my fate. I fell, racing toward the Earth at the edge of sound itself. I could no longer hear the wind rush over my face; the silence was illuminating. I had pierced the void and the unknown was waiting. *"I had transcended; out of the shadows of believing into the light of knowing, the finality of life."*

....

The End / The Beginning

I could feel the wind pull at my fur as it flowed over my body, legs and arms. It was a strange sensation as if the hairs on my body were being transformed into something long and eloquent. I began to feel lighter as the air conformed to this change and pushed me up into the sky. I had become something greater than myself, mightier than life. *"Like life, death was an illusion and my fear of the unknown (death) disappeared."*

My legs, arms and body were covered with beautiful feathers and I had become a mighty eagle. My soul began to rise into the air and up above the clouds. Instead of falling I soared into the sky. Like the "Keeper" I too had wings.

THE MIGHTY

EAGLE

Instead of being blind I could see for miles. My sight had become so keen I could see the forest from which I came, hundreds of miles away. My soul became clear again and all the scabbed over sores and open wounds were gone. My youthful strength had returned and I could feel my muscles stretch throughout my body. All my life's misdeeds had vanished, and with my eagle feathers I climbed high into the sky.

I could see my place of birth; the great forest and the mighty oak tree. I had gained the wings and sight to carry me home. I flew above the Earth and realized we were responsible for the care of this great planet. The sun, moon and stars are here for us to ponder and illuminate our journey toward enlightenment. They bring light to our days and nights to guide us toward understanding all of those things greater than ourselves. We are but children rejoicing in a playground of life, surrounded by a Universe full of wonder and hope.

As I flew east, the sun passed over me fleeing to the west illuminating the western horizon with bright reds and pinks as it ducked beneath the clouds. The twilight on the eastern horizon confirmed the presence of the Universe as the stars began to burst forth with light across the sky; and the moon and planets wandered from place to place as the Earth spun under the sky's majesty. I was in awe and accepted my fate as it should be, in the light of this wonder (the Universe) that I will always be a part of.

I was born nocturnal, barely able to see. My keen sense of smell and natural curiosity illuminated my journey and compensated for my poor vision. Now my vision was crystal clear.

I found the mighty oak tree where I was born. My shadow and I perched for a moment on one of its top branches. I peered through the branches and I spotted a small pair of youthful eyes looking up at me in fear and wonder. I said: *"Who's that child hiding in my shadow?"*

The portion of the message I had long ago forgotten came echoing through time and I continued: *"I love you my child. I will always be here to guide you on your journey."*

The view from this tree was Earthly in all its beauty and glory. Now with the sight of an eagle I gazed at the setting sun and approaching night with joy and wonder. The brilliance of both lifted my spirit and raised me higher into the night's sky. I rose through the thin air and felt I could taste the moon and breathe the stars.

Knowing I was of and from this Earth; born of the Cosmos, set me free. I was no longer bound by the darkness of not knowing. *"From this mighty Earth and the stars that shine so bright, I was born and will forever be."*

I WAS BORN TO BE WILD

MARCUS

THE JOURNEY

The Quest for Meaning

THE SACRED CIRCLE

THE BEGINNING

The Great Firestorm

The Story of Solomon

Prequel

The Story of Solomon

Solomon, the father of Marcus was born in the eastern forest along the Atlantic Ocean. Solomon's father, ***Ra*** could trace his lineage back to David the famous giant slayer who first settled the coastal forest generations before. Ra belonged to a clan of raccoons who traveled from the far west to make New England their home.

Ra was a natural born explorer always traveling through the forest and hill country; spending nights and weeks trekking deeper and deeper into the wilderness. He was a ***seeker*** who wondered over the plants and animals, the lay of the land, the foot hills and mountains; just the mystery and beauty of it all kept him in awe.

Watching the sun set, Ra swore someday he would travel west and return to the northwestern forest where his ancestors first arrived in the Americas. The clan's stories fascinated him; how his great-great grandfather David slew Goliath the ugly giant that fought for the humans against the wild ones, and the great redwoods that towered over the landscape; some reaching heights of over four hundred feet tall. Yes, once they were old enough he would take his wife and little ones into and beyond the western highlands known as the Appalachian Mountains.

Years passed and Ra was ready to fulfill his dream. His wife and five children were strong and old enough to make the journey. Keeping his promise, Ra and his family gathered their meager belongings and headed west up into the hill country. Keeping an eye on the children, ***Cleo*** would follow right behind Ra. With the four little ones in the middle, Solomon the first born would bring up the rear holding the family together. Solomon was to carry the **haversack** and keep a journal of the family's daily progress.

They journeyed westward up into the Appalachian Mountains. They finally reached the western watershed and continued west onto the Allegheny Plateau. It was good to walk on relatively flat ground again. Once they crossed the plateau, Ra planned to follow the streams and creeks southwest downhill. He would follow the creeks and streams to some unknown mighty river, then follow that river further west into the wilderness.

In spite of the dry weather they made good time traveling deeper and deeper into the unknown. Pools of water were scarce. They relied heavily on the morning dew that covered the plants. Early in the mornings the family would scatter to lick the plant leaves dry of their tiny droplets hoping to find more water to drink somewhere along the trail during the day. If Ra's family was lucky, other wild creatures would not have found the pool of water before them.

It had been an unusually dry summer with the autumn leaves coming into full color early. Because of the drought the trees were lacking the normal moister to keep the leaves green. The autumn colors came and went in a few days with the leaves prematurely turning dark brown curling up on their stems before they had time to fall to the ground. Ready to burst into flames, like wooden matchsticks the trees stood poised for a spark.

The wild families had struggled to survive this dry spell. With the exception of a few light sprinkles and a little snow during the winter, the drought lasted through the spring and into the summer. Like no other time before; the plants, wild ones and the forest were desperate for rain. It was midsummer and there hadn't been a cloud in the sky for weeks. Only the thin wisp of clouds high in the atmosphere and nasty rancid pools of water offered any hope.

On one of the hottest days of the year without a rain cloud in sight a terrible lightning storm raced across the sky filling the air with thunder. Within minutes the streaks of lightning spread from horizon to horizon and the sky instantly turned black. The rumble in the distance warned us of the storm to come.

Like crazed monsters without form, streaks of lightning scratched their way across this blackness to fill the wild ones with fear. All the wild animals shook as the wind that preceded the storm bent many of the trees toward the ground, snapping some of them in half.

Solomon's father and mother frantically pushed their young ones down the trail seeking cover. They rushed through the forest looking for shelter. When they stopped to take a count, Solomon was missing.

In the confusion Solomon was separated from his family. Then one of the lightning bolts arced and struck a tree. The forest instantly burst into flames. Every tree and plant in sight was on fire. With no place to go, Solomon standing under a giant oak tree took shelter beneath its roots and instinctively dug toward cooler soil.

As the hot air singed his tail he dug deeper and deeper to escape the unbearable heat. He finally broke through some hard ground and entered a large burrow that went deeper and deeper into cooler air.

There were voices that Solomon could see but not hear (the voices of Nature): *"Come join us it is cooler down here. We are your friends and you have nothing to fear. Like you we are wild ones who have gathered to save ourselves and each other. If we stay put the firestorm will sweep over us and we will survive. We must be brave and keep our wits. Like in the future to come, we must help each other; our lives will depend on it. Nature has given us this precious Earth to protect. Only in **harmony** and **balance** will life on this Earth survive."*

The burrow was full of the wild ones. The fox, opossum, rabbit, chip monk, squirrel and even a young badger; all the "little ones" gathered in **harmony** to wait out the storm. The fear of the firestorm outweighed their differences to survive. In trust they gathered. When the skunk sneezed and the badger growled, for a moment they all paused in fearful anticipation. ***"Excuse me,"*** was followed by expressions of relief. The nervous chatter amongst friends continued.

Deep within the burrow the wild ones could hear the firestorm raging above. They could hear branches break away from the trees and crash to the ground, like sticks of dynamite the charred trees exploded into flames and the fire-twisters could be heard sweeping across the landscape as their intense flames spun around and around reaching heights high above the trees. It sounded as if the air was on fire.

The fire spread through the forest burning everything in its path. Caught out in the open Solomon's family was surrounded by the firestorm and trapped. They would have to make their shelter where they stood and frantically began to dig their fire pit. With a vengeance the fire approached his family. Father, mother and children desperately tore at the ground trying to dig a pit deep enough for the fire to pass over them. As the hole got deeper father and mother covered their babies from the heat with their bodies heaping as much dirt as possible onto their backs. With the intensive heat approaching, Ra and Cleo stretched out their bodies and paws as far as they could reach to protect their little ones. In a savage rage the fire drew closer and closer.

The burrow was slowly getting warmer and the wild ones looked at each other in fear. Then the firestorm's noise softened and the quiet reassuring sound of rain began to take its place. At first the little wild ones could barely hear the rain drops hitting the ground. Gradually the sounds of rain striking the tree and roots above grew louder and louder. The noise of the firestorm seemed to fade into the distance as the rain falling above grew into a raging storm.

Rain water slowly began to enter the burrow soaking the soft dirt below the wild ones' paws. Solomon recognizing the new danger said: *"Follow me I have dug a passage that is free of water."*

Solomon led the wild ones through his passage taking them to the roots and oak tree above. Slowly they all made it to the safety of the roots. The rainstorm became stronger and stronger flooding the burrow and passage ways below.

Even the most gifted of the nocturnal creatures could not see beyond their paws into the blackness of this storm. They had lost track of time and some argued it was still dark and the sun had not risen yet. Clinging to each other the rain continued to fall heavier than before. Then in a swirl the blackness and rainstorm drew up into the sky and the sun came beaming across the eastern horizon sadly illuminating the charred remains of the once beautiful forest.

As far as anyone could see stood the charred and blacken remains of the forest. Their oak tree was the only tree fully standing with its upper branches still attached to its trunk. All the other trees stood like ghostly monks without limbs. Most of the trees were burnt completely to the ground. With tears welding up in their eyes the wild ones said in unison: *"We must find our families and friends. Hopefully some of them have survived."*

The wild ones began to spread out and search what remained of the forest beyond their treasured tree. Fear struck at Solomon's heart: *"Maybe my family found a burrow to hide in. They are safely looking after each other somewhere in the forest. My father would not let anything harm them. He would give up his life to save his family. He's a great explorer. He knows how to survive. Even this firestorm could not defeat him."*

At first he could not get his bearings. The family was headed west. His father surely would have led his family in that direction for shelter. The sun had just risen and Solomon decided to head west in search of his family. With the sun to his back he moved forward.

Solomon came across the charred remains of what appeared to be a fox. But he could not be sure. Its body was burnt to a crisp. It could have been a larger coyote or even a small wolf. He began to see the charred remains of other animals everywhere; most burnt beyond recognition.

He became more and more concerned about his family. He said to himself: *"No one above ground could have survived this fire."*

Solomon heard some wild ones crying and found a skunk and opossum hugging each other crying over the charred bodies of their families. Only the white stripe on one remaining tail and a lucky charm grasped in the charred paw of another identified the two wild families. They had chosen the same trail to escape the fire only to be trapped in a circle of flames. The skunk and opossum were now orphans.

Solomon joined them in their sorrow and feared what his next step into the black abyss would find. The opossum quietly said to his lost family: *"You have been rejoined with Nature and will forever be part of this Earth. I love you and you will remain in my heart until I exist no more."*

The skunk was speechless sobbing as the opossum spoke. After a few quiet moments Solomon respectfully said: *"I must find my family, even if they did not survive this storm."*

With that Solomon stepped away seeking the unknown. After a brief pause, the skunk and opossum followed him. The opossum politely asked: *"Would you like us to join you?"* Solomon quietly nodded yes.

As they moved down the trail the opossum spoke up: *"That's **Stinky** and I am **Waddles** we have been dear friends since we were babies. Our families often worked together in the forest to protect ourselves and find food."*

Solomon replied: *"No matter what comes our way, we are family now. We will from this day forward be friends. My name is Solomon."*

Suddenly Solomon stopped in his tracks. Looking ahead he could make out a charred mound of bodies and immediately knew he had found what remained of his family. He sat down in the thick ash and softly cried. With Solomon in the middle, Waddles and Stinky quietly sat beside him.

Waddles: *"They are with Mother Nature now and have rejoined the Earth on its journey through the Cosmos. Like all of us, we must journey into the unknown; that which we know but cannot accept. **Nothing survives life.**"*

Solomon, Stinky and Waddles sat in silence for a long time when Stinky with authority proclaimed: *"We are a band of brothers orphaned by a firestorm sent here from the underworld to darken our lives. Saved by a mighty oak we took shelter under its massive form. Together we huddled in the darkness to emerge back into the light. **Chaos** came and went and **Happenstance** brought us together."*

Solomon: *"I say we go back to the mighty oak and protect it as it protected us. We, a band of brothers, will forever live within its shade and keep it safe from those who have little regard for the forest and the wild ones."*

Waddles: *"We will keep its sacred grounds safe for future generations."*

Solomon quietly said goodbye to his family and turned around leading his adopted brothers back to the mighty oak tree; their new home. The three of them would become best friends and would spend the rest of their lives under the protection of the mighty oak tree now the center of their beings.

All those who survived the firestorm began to gather around the base of the mighty oak. One of the elders stepped forward and stated: *"We need to survey the extent of the damage to our forest. We need a volunteer to climb to the top branches of this old tree and measure the damage to help us decide what to do next. It will be very dangerous the branches are charred and brittle."*

Without hesitation Solomon stepped forward and declared: ***"I will go. I will take my haversack and notebook and record what I see."***

Without another word Solomon scurried to the trunk of this massive tree and began to climb. Stinky and Waddles beamed with pride: *"He's our good friend."*

As he climbed the scorched bark and trunk beneath his paws broke away. He would start to fall stopping himself time and time again with his sharp claws. Determined, the son of Ra, climbed on. Up into the remaining branches he climbed.

At first he could not believe what he was seeing. On the top side of the branches were buds and a few blooms. The mighty oak had survived the fire and was still alive. Finally he reached the top branch finding a few green leaves here and there.

He scanned the horizons for life. In every direction for miles the forest was gone. Smoke and ash covered the landscape. With the exception of the mighty oak every tree was burnt to a crisp. The surrounding forest had been totally consumed by the fire.

Solomon said out loud to himself: *"Under this tree I will live and if good fortune finds me, raise my family. I will never leave the safety of this tree again."*

There were no notes to take; no direction to explore. Only this oak tree and maybe the streams offered them some hope. With that he turned and headed back to the base of the tree and the wild ones to share the bleak news.

When Solomon shared what he had seen the wild ones gathered and grumbled with fear. Amongst the youngest, Solomon spoke first: *"Nature is Nature and at times unforgiving. There are streams to follow. We must search for food. If we stand and work together as a family, this mighty oak offers hope and will protect us. There are buds, a few blooms and green leaves above us, giving us evidence of the life that is still within this tree. **Chaos** brought us together and **Happenstance** offers us hope. We have all lost someone we love. Joined together we can face what lies ahead."*

The sounds of unity spread around the tree. Encouragement and confidence replaced fear and doubt. From that day forward the wild ones began to refer to him as ***Solomon the Wise One*** and often sought his advice. Within weeks the green beneath the forest floor sprang up from the ashes. The returning bounty brightened their spirits.

Solomon, Stinky and Waddles stepped forward and declared: *"We will patrol the outer roots of this mighty oak and keep her safe from any intruder who would bring harm to this sacred tree and the little ones that live here. They say the humans are coming and that they have little regard for Nature and her wild ones. They are delusional and believe they have dominion over the Cosmos."*

By the end of the summer the smaller plants had returned. Flowers that would have bloomed in the spring bloomed in late summer. The black and gray ash that covered the landscape nourished this recovery. Many of the charred trees still standing showed signs of rebirth. The wild families struggled but most made it through the winter. By the time Waddles, Stinky and Solomon were young men the forest had completely recovered.

The mighty oak stood above it all. The tallest tree in the forest, from its upper branches you could see the curvature of the Earth. Solomon often found himself on its highest branch in absolute awe of Nature and the wonder that surrounded him. Solomon would not follow his father's dream and journey further west. He would make the mighty oak tree and the forest his home.

Solomon thought to himself: *"How blessed I was to be standing under this great tree when the storm of storms hit this forest; the right place at the right time, **Happenstance**, good luck in its purest form."*

Solomon thoughts continued: *"And then there is **Chaos**; a family of wild ones caught in an unforgiving firestorm. **Happenstance** and **Chaos** are but twins (two sides of the same coin), born of the same Universe, chasing time through the Cosmos leaving havoc and wonder in their paths."*

When young and before taking on families, the three of them faithfully patrolled the outer edges of their sacred circle.

Stinky and Waddles took on their families first. After Stinky and Waddles started their families, Solomon continued his daily patrols alone.

One day while toying with the notion of crossing over to explore the forest beyond, Solomon heard what sounded like a child crying; crying ever so softly in the wilderness beyond the sacred circle, the roots of this mighty oak tree.

Solomon, the guardian of the Sacred Circle, crossed over in search of the soft cries. There he found her, a little girl burning with fever abandoned in the deep forest by those that loved her the most. Hopeless to save her, the family moved on. This little girl reminded him of his baby sister, Sara who was lost in that terrible firestorm when he was just a boy. Solomon knew what he must do. He must save this little girl…….

The Cosmos is a Universe of circles that are forever spinning in time and space, moving deeper and deeper into the unknown. The unknown is *Motion* without purpose; *Happenstance* and *Chaos*, *Infinity* and *Beyond*…. With every collision of a planet, a star, a galaxy; the calculus for the future has to be recalibrated. There is no predicting the future, like the Cosmos the future is in *Motion* and always will be.

THE END / DEATH

Life and Death, the Riddle of All Riddles

THE BEGINNING

REBIRTH

Another Wild Tail
A Fork in the Road, Chaos and Happenstance

A Sequel

Forces of Nature (The Mischievous Twins)

In the beginning the totality of the *Cosmos* existed at a single point in space. It was an object so small and dense it is beyond the calculations of physics and the comprehension of mankind. How long this entity, the *Super Atom*, stood at the center of the *Universe* we may never know, for *Time* did not exist. From this point where *Time*, *Matter* and *Energy* were frozen in space the Cosmos was born. In a chaotic sub-second without measure, (a hundred trillionths of a second, **.000000000001**) the *explosion of explosions* radiated Energy and Matter from the center of the Universe to give birth to itself; the Cosmos. The Universe/Cosmos **(U/C)** are the *Mother* and *Father*, *Father* and *Mother* of all things. Without them life would not exist. Gender indifferent, male-female/female-male, the **(U/C)** gave rise to *sub-atomic particles,* the *atoms, planets* and the *stars, galaxies, and all that exits in the Cosmos*:

This cosmic event (the *Big Bang*) anointed *Chaos* and *Happenstance* (the *Destructive* and *Building Forces of Nature*), to govern the Universe. *Chaos* and *Happenstance,* the children of the **(C/U)**, were always at odds with each other and eager to steal the other's creations. Jealous for their parent's approval and affection, one trying to outmatch the other, they destroyed/created everything in their path. *Chaos* and *Happenstance,* in spite of their sibling jealousies, once ignited their passions for each other gave birth to *Fusion* *and Fission.* Fusion and Fission were beyond their parent's control. As soon as one settled down, the other rushed in to advance her/his power, **Mayhem** to **Renewal, Havoc** to **Rebirth**, sustaining a constant **Recycling-Expansion** of the Universe. In this struggle, *Fission* was beholding to *Fusion,* and *Fusion* was beholding to *Fission*. With no end in sight, *(Light and Time being bent by the presence of Mass),* **Black Holes** were formed. The **Mass** and **Density** of these Black Holes are so powerful they pull everything into a **Gigantic Astronomical Solid Spinning Vortex, Void** of **Emptiness** **000,000,000,000,000,+1 E=MC2..*@!!@&@@!58+##.**

Our lives are but flickering flashes of light (awareness) that briefly illuminate our existence in this **perpetually changing physical Universe.** *Mass* and *Density* gave birth to *Gravity* and *Motion*. Gravity and Motion pulled the *cosmic gases* and *dust* together to form minute and large clumps of *Matter.* The large spinning forms of Matter flashed forward to become the planets, galaxies, suns, comets, and all the dust and empty space in between; *Nebulas, Quasars, the Super Nova.* In this, asteroids destroy planets, planets give rise to life, one life form lives off another, suns swallow up planets, galaxies crash into each other. These are the cosmic events that shape and reshape the Universe; including our *space junk,* all pulled into this *Eternal Abyss. Yes, Fission* and *Fusion* eloped to **CREATE** the Universe. Like playful lion cubs in a love – hate relationship, they chase each other through *Time* and *Space* haphazardly shaping the physical Universe as they speed along. Leaving the light of the Cosmos and our living images behind they are pulling us toward a destiny out of reach of our comprehension. We exist in a Universe without any consciousness of its self; only through us does it exist; *"The Eagle Has Landed."*

Alternate Universes

On their journey through space and time toward the unknown; the subject of multiple Universes came up between Marcus and the Keeper.

Marcus to the Keeper: *"Do you believe there is only one Universe? If one, why not two, if one billion, why not two billion? If there was one **Big Bang,** then why not a trillion big bangs?"*

Marcus continues: *"If just one Universe, where was space; on the inside of the super atom or on the outside of the super atom. If on the outside, how far outside the super atom did space reach? Father, what does infinity mean?"*

The Keeper: ***"Infinity means; beyond-beyond with no end.** But we can only speak to what we know, **beyond that is speculation**. Alternate universes, how interesting; could there be another raccoon and rattle snake in another Universe having the same conversation? Would one variable in either's life change the nature of their journeys? What would be the outcome of your life had you obeyed your parents and never left the sacred circle, or you hadn't met Coyote on the trail? What if the bear on the cliff had eaten you or you lost the battle at the Little River with Big Horns? Multiple universes, what a wonder and just think what could be **beyond** that, infinity; just incomprehensible."*

In Another Universe
On Another Living Planet

Friends Forever (The Game of Life)

Marcus and Brutus rough and tumble chase through the top of the mighty oak caught the attention of a young raven in the tree next to theirs. Eclipse admired their agility and good nature and would follow them from branch to branch. He envied their fearless jumps from tree to tree and could not wait until he was able to fly and keep up with them. Once mastered, flight would set the young raven free. He was forever chasing after Marcus and Brutus to join in their play becoming their dearest friend. Because he was always following them they nicknamed him *Shadow*. Eclipse finally learned to fly. Now Marcus and Brutus would have to chase after Eclipse.

To win this game they climbed, ran and jumped to get away from each other. *"It was the game of life and death."* The little wild ones were expected to play this game in order to survive in Nature. It seemed like fun but it was a serious game; where in the wild getting caught was certain death. All the wild ones had to be careful and skilled enough to avoid the larger predators to live another day. Climbing to the tallest branch, hiding in the deepest crevice and keeping absolutely quiet were the lessons they must master. There were no margins for mistakes allowed in this game. One move in the wrong direction, one unintentional sound or one breath at the wrong instant could spell your doom; *"Death is upon us, but we resist, this resistance is called life. The singularity of life is to survive."*

Marcus, Brutus and Eclipse became the best of friends. They played tag, hide and seek and made their way to the edge of the sacred circle everyday just for fun.

Our Inner Beings

Marcus and Brutus loved the tree tops. Eclipse was always just out of sight watching over them. As strong as he was, Eclipse had a tender and reflective heart; always giving his friends the best advice. He saw himself as their *protector* and with his power of flight, sound judgment and perfect vision he was always one step ahead of them in motion and thought. Like their shadows he was there to remind them to take care and avoid rash and reckless behaviors. Brutus was physically the strongest and most daring. Marcus' intellect he kept to himself. He didn't want others to know he loved the quest for knowledge so he masked his brilliance with foolery. Marcus often played the antagonist, playing one friend against the other. Marcus especially loved seeing how far he could push Brutus.

On a bright and sunny day while catching up with them, for an instant, Eclipse blotted out the sun casting his shadow on their mischievous souls. He laughed and called out: *"Caw, Caw, Caw; I am the master of your souls."*

At first Eclipse would play their game of risk; to tease Marcus and Brutus to scramble up a branch until it almost snapped in half, or see which one could climb the highest, the fastest, leap the farthest. A fall from this mighty oak would send one of them into the unknown; the world of the dead, a physical Universe without life.

One day while teasing Marcus to the edge, Marcus slipped and nearly fell to his death. Eclipse vowed he would never again taunt others to be reckless. Instead he adopted the rules and demeanor of a *guardian* and *protector*. *Reflective* and *thoughtful* Eclipse would weigh the consequences of Marcus' and Brutus' behavior and warn them of the dangers they were recklessly putting themselves in. On another planet and in different Universe, Eclipse would be the *antagonist*, Brutus the *follower* and Marcus, the *voice of reason*.

Leap of Faith/Fate

Brutus was always primed to test his limits; push it to the edge. Marcus was just as ready to taunt him in the extreme to see how far Brutus would go. Eclipse was there to bring this reckless team of hooligans back to solid ground, and help them stay within the bounds of reason. Eclipse was most deliberate in his actions. Internally Marcus admired Eclipse for his *balance* and *good judgment*. The thrill of manipulating and taunting others into thoughtless action prevented Marcus from advancing his being; his inner soul. Marcus knew with the exception of Eclipse all the young wild ones would respond to his taunts and take whatever bait he threw their way. Like a successful fisherman Marcus would cast out his line and reel in his catch for his own entertainment. At the costs to others Marcus played this game of tease, and taunt. He was a true antagonist. Brutus always seeking his brother's approval was the biggest fish in the pond. *"The Universe works in mysterious ways."*

So it was on the day Marcus pulled Brutus too far. Brutus always desirous of Marcus' approval and the awe of the crowd took the bait; hook, line and sinker. The wild little ones had climbed to the upper branches of the mighty oak to see the jump of jumps; the jump that nobody without wings ever made before; the moment of do or die.

Scarface

Brutus was a real dare devil taking everything to the brink; the jagged edge of existence. Oblivious to danger, one day while bragging to **Scarface**, he declared that he planned to make the longest jump the mighty oak had to offer. Scarface: *"No way, you're just kidding or crazy, one or the other."*

"For real," Brutus retorted: *"You watch and see. Come tomorrow at high-noon I'll make the longest jump this old tree has ever seen!"*

Scarface, being the blabbermouth and gossipmonger he was, soon spread the word throughout the sacred circle. With a hush, hush, so the elders would not find out, the word quickly spread and on that day many gathered to see this mighty leap of **faith/fate;** for death loomed if Brutus failed. The top branches of the old oak spread out from each other as they stretched toward the sun. Many of the wild ones played in the tree tops. Most had mastered the 3-5 foot jumps. Some reached 8-10 feet depending on their size, but not even the strongest raccoons dared the 12 foot jump.

With a ton of bravado Brutus announced to the crowd: *"Today I Brutus, from the clan of David the giant slayer and the son of Solomon the guardian, will challenge the unknown and leap to yonder branch. No one before me or those that follow me will match this feat."*

Earlier that morning Brutus had carefully removed the small branches and twigs clearing the ramp of any obstacles that might hinder his launch. He had paced off the run that would carry him across and practiced jumps up to 11.5 feet with success. He knew the mark he must leap from and the arc he needed to travel to land safely. He had examined the touchdown point and the branch had proved sturdy enough to receive his landing. Given his weight and the force of his jump the branch should hold and not break. The bark was thick and strong and held tightly to the oak tree. Brutus demonstrated tremendous *faith* in himself in attempting the seemingly impossible.

The crowd was excited, Scarface shouted: *"He can do it, I know he can. He is the strongest, bravest raccoon that has ever lived. Brutus, Marcus and Eclipse journeyed beyond the sacred circle when I was a little boy and saved my life."*

A Life Saved

In Scarface's eyes, Brutus and Marcus were beyond reproach and their actions and words spoke for themselves. Years earlier when they were much younger Marcus taunted Brutus into journeying beyond the sacred circle; the outer roots of the mighty oak tree. They were on the trail only a few minutes when they came across a squirrel's body. Dry blood was everywhere. It looked like a family of squirrels had met their deaths right there on the trail. With all the different tracks and torn up ground it looked like a gang of outlaws had ambushed a family of squirrels.

Marcus quickly lost his nerve and said to Brutus: *"Let's get the hell out of here!"*

They turned to run for their lives. As they turned to rush back to the sacred circle Brutus heard a soft wispy sound. There was a shallow breath coming from one of the squirrels and Brutus saw his chest slightly rise and fall. To Brutus' surprise the squirrel was still alive; impossible, with the exception of his face the squirrel was covered with deep cuts and open wounds.

Brutus: *"Marcus, I believe this squirrel is alive!"*

Marcus: *"So what, we can't carry him back. Who knows, the criminals who committed this crime may be on their way back here to finish him off and eat him for dinner."*

Brutus: *"We sure in the hell are not leaving him here! What would father think if we left this little one alone to die?"*

Marcus: *"What would father say if he found out we left the sacred circle? We are in trouble, no matter what. And if we stay the gang of criminals will catch and eat us too,"*

Eclipse flew past them and landed on a branch just out of sight.

Eclipse: ***"Caw, Caw, Caw."*** *I warned you two about leaving the sacred circle. It's a good thing I followed you out here or surely you could not have saved this poor creature by yourselves, let alone make it back to safety. Those outlaws can't be too far from here. I alerted your father about the situation and he is on his way with help. Boy, are you two going to get it."*

Eclipse to Marcus and Brutus: *"Like all riddles; if you have too many rash moments you won't have many."*

Solomon arrived with help and they built a travois to drag the squirrel back to safety. Solomon's family kept the squirrel safe until he had fully recovered. They named the squirrel Scarface; the only place on his body without a scar left from his injuries. On their way home Solomon addressed his sons, Marcus and Brutus.

Solomon: *"Sons, your mother is furious, but I reminded her about my journey beyond the sacred circle when she was a little girl. She seemed to have calmed down when I told her Eclipse was with you. However there are no guarantees she won't clip you once or twice about your ears when we get home."*

Solomon continued: *"There are times when to do the right thing one must do something forbidden. Even though you crossed the sacred circle, your willingness to help this injured little one will not be punished. To help him heal from his wounds you two will tend to his care and needs while he stays with us. The gods; **Chaos** and **Happenstance** are watching."*

Like their father Solomon the Guardian; the little one's looked up to Marcus, Brutus and Eclipse. They all heard the story how the three of them saved Scarface. They all wondered what Solomon would say about the jump and their willingness to watch this reckless act.

A Branch Too Far

As midday drew near the little ones began to take their places. The tree top branches were packed with spectators. There had been taunts and jabs from some of Brutus' friends that he would not attempt the jump; that he would chicken out at the last minute. His close friends were fearful of his foolish boast and that the jabs and jeers from the crowd would only ensure he would try the impossible.

Brutus' parents were unaware of the jump. Solomon and the elders would have put a stop to the reckless behavior and surely all the little ones would have been in trouble for being there.

The crowd cheered when Brutus made it to the tree top. They held their breaths as he backed up to measure his run. Exactly thirteen steps would carry him over. One foot either way could mean certain death.

Marcus pulling Brutus further toward the edge: *"Chick-chick-chicken; jump, I double dog dare you! You're not turning yellow are you?"*

With a grin and twinkle in his eyes, Brutus retorted: *"Just watch me brother!"*

He ran forward toward his mark and with one great leap Brutus easily made it to the other branch. The flight was perfect, the arc exact; his planning and calculations proved almost flawless. Brutus landed beyond mathematics/physics; **Chaos** drew near.

With a grip too strong Brutus had slightly missed his mark and stripped the bark from the branch falling to his doom. His sharp claws serrated the bark from the limb and Brutus fell toward certain death. At the speed of sound he raced toward the ground. The crowd gasped and with wide eyes held their breaths.

Out of the blue Eclipse dove from the clouds catching up with Brutus as he plummeted through the air. Eclipse darted at him nudging him just enough to hit the branch forty feet below, breaking Brutus' fall and saving his life. Brutus grabbed the branch firmly. His fall nearly snapped the limb as it bent and cracked under his weight. ***"Like crazed lions, the crowd roared!"***

Eclipse caught up with Marcus and angrily confronted him: *"You must 'NEVER!' ' I MEAN NEVER,' taunt others to do wrong; especially your own brother!"*

Eclipse continued: *"Some creatures are easily misguided, weak minded and determined beyond reason lacking any common sense. They tend to be impulsive; which at times can be deadly. Some will simply follow the path of others, genuinely naive and ignorant; desperate to belong."*

Eclipse saved Brutus' life. Once back on the ground Eclipse threatened to tell their parents about Marcus' and Brutus' reckless behavior and the bad example they had demonstrated for the little ones.

Marcus: *"If you tell on us, see if we hang out with you anymore. Besides, no one was hurt. The three of us put on a great show. Your dive from the sky and the nudge that saved Brutus at the last minute was spectacular. I bet my mom and dad would be impressed."*

With that the two hooligans giggled to themselves. Marcus to Brutus: *"Eclipse won't tell. Eclipse knows dad will scold him for not coming to him when he first heard about the jump."*

Marcus to Eclipse: *"You would be in more trouble than us if dad finds out that you knew about the jump and did not tell him in the first place."*

"The crowd roared again!" Then Marcus and Brutus scurried over the roots of the mighty oak tree headed for the edge of the sacred circle. Eclipse faithfully followed them from a distance to watch over them and keep them out of further trouble.

On the Trail

They had just reached the edge of the sacred circle when Marcus talked Brutus into venturing into the forest to follow a weasel's scent Marcus had picked up. There were no tracks but the weasel's scent was strong. The trail they were on led deeper into the forest. Under pressure and against his better judgment Brutus again yielded to his brother's will.

Just as they stepped over into the unknown Eclipse showed up: *"Caw, Caw, Caw." Remember what your father and mother told you. It's dangerous in the forest. There are wild beasts out there: bears, badgers, wildcats and ...."*

"Sissy," Marcus calls out to Eclipse. Brutus, seeking Marcus' approval joins in: *"Chick, Chick, Chicken! We have the scent of a weasel. We are going to track him down. Come along if you dare."*

Eclipse: *"Marcus, haven't you caused enough trouble for one day? Your taunts nearly killed your brother!"*

Brutus forgetting Eclipse had just saved his life: *"Eclipse you take things too seriously; a girl could have made that jump."*

Brutus, being his playful self, taunted Eclipse stating that Eclipse would not recognize a real wildcat if one bit his tail feathers off.

Brutus: *"Eclipse you could not tell a skunk from a weasel let alone a wildcat from a badger. We have the scent of a weasel and are going to hunt him down. Join us if you have the nerve.*"

They ignored Eclipse and took the trail heading south. In hiding, from tree to tree, Eclipse followed.

Down the trail Brutus and Marcus hurried to catch their make believe prey. They had never hunted or killed anything before in their lives.

Vision (The Cricket in the Road)

Eclipse's warning echoed through the forest: ***"Caw, Caw, Caw."*** *Beware of the unknown. In the forest there are predators that will eat you one bite at a time. Turn around and come home; back to the safety of the giant oak tree where you were born and the sacred circle that has protected you all these years. Turn around before it's too late, **too late, too late.**"*

Marcos and Brutus ignored Eclipse's warning and raced further down the trail excited over their newly found courage and defiance. They were now brothers in crime; great explorers, revolutionaries, desperados... They rushed pass a fork in the road when Marcus exclaimed: ***"Jiminy, there is a cricket in the middle of the road."***

Brutus to the cricket: *"What's an old cricket like you doing standing in the middle of the road? Don't you know it's dangerous out here and something wild might catch your scent and run you over? You know how the top predators and scavengers like road kill. Why go through all the trouble of hunting when you can shop for something good to eat along the highways without even having to put up a fight?"*

Marcus: *"What kind of **crazy babble** are you yakking about today old wise one?*

The cricket to Brutus and Marcus: *"There is little room for rudeness in an already troubled and callous world. My name is Vision and I am from the year **2525** and mankind did not survive. Where I come from the Earth is so polluted the animals with fur no longer exist. I have traveled backwards in time to warn the wild ones that the humans are coming this way and will destroy the Earth unless we stop them. They will plan to travel to Mars' but will meet their doom on Earth long before they establish their first Martian colony."*

Vision continued: *"Why go elsewhere? We haven't fully explored the deepest seas nor categorized all the animal species thereby failing to appreciate the Earth in all of its majesty. Maybe if we had stopped to ponder its beauty we would not have destroyed the Earth"*

Vision: *The first 5-6 great extinctions had nothing to do with human kind. Now, the humans pose the greatest danger to themselves; directly killing off one animal species after another, destroying their natural habitats and recklessly polluting the Earth's environment."*

Vision: *"I can only share what I know is true. In the future the humans will abandon reason and do the unthinkable and unleash hell. This beast will consume half the planet nearly driving life into extinction. Once the radiation and toxins reach a critical mass, the Earth's natural systems will collapse and in this dying the super virus will be born. The world's major cities will be consumed by nuclear fires, while the rest of the human race and all the other living organisms fall victim to a super virus."*

Vision: *"In the future, one of the stronger nations will elect a moron, idiot, buffoon...to their highest office. He will prove himself incapable of telling the truth, yet many of the **hollow ones** will believe him and follow his reckless lead. He will bring destruction to the world. **For wealth and power, power and wealth, the controlling elite will yield to this corruption and give up their souls to gain it all. On a desperate voyage aboard a condemned vessel with no promise of a future the elite will eat their own children."***

Vision: **"The country born of the age of enlightenment will abandon the world's efforts to combat climate change and usher in doom's day for the living planet. Super hurricanes will plague the Earth. You have been warned!"**

Brutus to Vision: **"Yah, Yah, Yah, we have been warned, 10-4 and out! Walkie-Talkie, Too Much Malarkey!"**

Marcus: *"Our names are Marcus and Brutus."*

Marcus: *"Just in case we wanted to explore a little out of our way, is that other trail headed northeast a short cut back to the mighty oak?"*

Vision: *"No, that trail will lead you to a certain death. Whatever you do, don't take that trail or tomorrow will not exist. **Short cuts usually don't end well."***

Vision: *I have lost my way and have been wandering this forest for years. I once met another creature that looked just like you guys. I helped him save a little girl and foretold him our future."*

Vision: *"Did you come from the mighty oak? "Is your father's name, Solomon? Marcus you have a great destiny in front of you. Brutus you will ensure that your brother fulfills his mission in life and reaches the unknown.*

Vision: *"You two look just like your father; masks and striped tails."*

Marcus: *"How can we help our father's old friend?*

Vision: *"I am looking for a special cave that will lead me home to a dead and dying planet. Where the skies are yellow and the clouds are brown and all that falls from the sky is purple acid rain. **Purple rain, purple rain; all that falls from our skies is deadly purple rain."***

Marcus: *"We are new to this part of the forest we don't know about any caves or where you might find one."*

Vision: *"In my world the only creatures that survived lived in caves. With the exception of the Spirit Walkers all the mammals, fish, birds, microbes, and most reptiles and insects died exposed to the corrupted atmosphere and oceans of the Earth. Only those that sought refuge in the caves survived for a brief time. In the end the few reptiles and insects that are left will also die off. The world will soon be dead; a useless chunk of rock orbiting a useless star watching over a dead planet in a dying solar system."*

Vision: *"The last mammals to survive were the Spirit Walkers. They stored their food in our cave and for a short time after the **Eve of Destruction** the Spirit Walkers like us hid deep within this cave. They stayed together until the end.*

We have not seen another mammal since the death of Rahoo."

Vision: *"He was the noblest Spirit Walker ever. Named after his great grandfather, a survivor of the ice bridge, Rahoo was the last Spirit Walker to die. This led to the extinction of all the mammals. Rahoo died in the year **2510**; and my world has not seen another mammal since then."*

Vision: *"He cared for the others and even cared for a baby human whose parents had abandoned. As the Spirit Walkers died off, one by one, he carefully wrapped each in the finest linen the humans had left behind and thanked Nature for the light she shared to those that sought her truths. On that final day, Rahoo sat just above their graves and waited to join the others in the unknown. He slowly closed his eyes and never opened them again. Full of grace, he rejoined Nature and embraced the unknown."*

Vision: *With his eyes closed Rahoo softly repeated his clan's sacred prayer over and over again:* **"Mother Nature requires that we only take from her bounty what we need, the rest belongs to her. We must be the good and grateful stewards of the Earth and share her gifts with others. We should always nurture the wellbeing of the wilderness, its majestic forests and wildlife. If we respect Mother Nature we will grow old with the Earth."**

Vision: *"Too bad the humans never read or believed in these sacred words that were scripted by Nature herself."*

Vision: *"Now only a few lizards and insects that live deep within the caves are left. The total end of life on Earth is near. I would like to spend my last days on Earth at home in*

412

the cave where my family awaits my return; the great and final extinction looms ever so close."

Brutus to Marcus: *"What are mammals?"*

Marcus: *"Hell I don't know and don't ask. We have to get moving if we are going to make it home before dark."*

Marcus: *"Have you seen a weasel? We have his scent but we haven't found any tracks. We are going to hunt him down."*

Vision: *"If you are as wise as your father you will turn around now. This trail is dangerous and filled with Nature's terrors if she so wills it.*

Vision: *"Years ago, on this very trail I came across what looked like a family of squirrels. All that was left of them were tuffs of fur and bloody bones."*

Brutus to Marcus: *"Do you think that was Scarface's Family?"*

Marcus: *"The old one is just trying to scare us, let's get going."*

Vision: *"Brutus and Marcus, you must always obey your parents."*

From the forest, echoed by their shadow: ***"Obey your parents, your parents, your parents!"***

Laughing out loud Brutus and Marcus scurried down the trail after the catch of their lives.

Fearless Hunters, Frozen in Their Tracks

Marcus and Brutus forgot themselves and were playing chase in and out of the trees off the trail when they accidently discovered the weasel's tracks. Oddly the tracks were old and headed south? Ignoring this oddity they became intensely focused and continued down the trail after their dinner. The great hunters they were Marcus and Brutus planned their attack.

Suddenly the wind changed and blew fiercely from the southwest. The first scent they caught was that of the weasel. Marcus shouted: "Yah, we got him and down the trail they ran. The next blast of air brought the wildcat's scent. Fear gripped them tightly and they froze in their tracks.

Long before their first trek into the forest, Solomon brought home the remains of a wildcat that had been killed by a bear. He made the two of them inhale the wildcat's scent. Determined to get the point across, Solomon had Marcus and Brutus sleep with the dead wildcat for two days so they would never forget its scent.

Solomon to his sons: *"You must never forget this scent. This is a wildcat and they are relentless and fierce hunters. Once they are after you, it is over."*

Racing Back to the Sacred Circle

They immediately turned in their tracks and raced back up the trail. They ran for their lives and without stopping at the fork in the road, Marcus and Brutus flew pass the old cricket. Vision called out: *"There's a wildcat after your tails! You better not stop until you reach the upper branches of that*

414

mighty oak tree. Maybe now you will listen to your elders and best friend. Eclipse warned you!"

The Weasel

Weasel had his nose in so many holes he had lost his sense of smell. Oblivious to the danger he was in, he was unaware that the wildcat was stalking him. Weasel was preoccupied with the scouting mission he would report to Badger and the gang once he made it back to camp. The gang of outlaws would be eager to hear the juicy details of his report.

Weasel's mission was to scout ahead fifty miles and locate the vulnerable homesteads along the trail. Weasel was to snoop around the homesteads scattered through the forest and discover promising targets. A master of deceit he would visit the pioneers' homes and soon gain their trust. His most effective lie was that he was searching the forest for his sister's two lost children who had wandered off from their home down in Kentucky. Most families revealed themselves when they readily shared their food to help him along the trail to find the lost children. In planning their raids the gang was always looking for an advantage over the helpless and innocent.

Not realizing the wildcat was gaining ground, the weasel came to the fork in the road. Seemingly without a care he casually took the trail heading northeast. The cricket knowing the weasel's future stopped him to share his vision.

Vision: *"I am from the year **2525** and mankind did not survive."*

Vision: *"You are on the wrong path my son and doom is headed your way. You have fallen in with bad company to do*

415

evil. *You and your gang of outlaws will do harm to many and bask in your spoils. On your wicked journey others will join your outfit; some already corrupted, others just naïve and plain gullible."*

Vision: *"On a great plain **Justice** will find you and you will disappear from this Earth. You will be tossed into the air and trampled into dust. All will be held accountable in the end."*

Vision: *"In most cases personalities are not fixed. We just get stuck on stupid and refuse to mature; grow wise. A pattern broken is not a pattern. A misguided pattern sustained can lead to your doom if you do not change your course. The winds of life are unpredictable. Turn from your current heading and find redemption."*

Vision: *"Like the most precious gemstone, empathy for others is a precious jewel. The care and love of others will carry this world far into the future. One moment of empathy is worth a thousand crystal clear diamonds. **The Ultimate Light is Love; without love life would be unbearable."***

Vision: *"Duplicity will be your end. You must always tell the truth. Deceit, dishonesty, hate and cruelty are the blue flames of hell that will scorch your soul and keep you from returning to the Cosmos. The Devil's Crack is waiting for you. In the end your flesh will be eaten by the evil ones."*

Weasel: *"What in the **dickens** are you **babbling** about? Duplicity, deceit, dishonesty, hate and cruelty those are the terms we live by. Who gives a damn? Your soul and the Cosmos that's just a bunch of buffalo shit!"*

Vision to the weasel: *"You can hide from others, even me, but you can't hide from yourself. It's hard to be invisible with a corrupted soul. Your evil wickedness will cover your body with infected blisters for everyone to see."*

Vision: *"You may run, but you cannot hide from your soul which is always chasing you to do good. It is the illumination that you cannot escape. You may take refuge in the dark but the slightest flicker will expose your infested being. The troubled soul that haunts you will stand naked in the light."*

Vision: *"When your soul catches up with you there is nothing you can do but submit and embrace the goodness that surrounds you, or account for the evil that you have done. The goodness you could have done will dance in the heavens without form; for they will exist without you. In the end **Justice** will find you. **There will be a reckoning.**"*

With that Weasel turned and headed up the trail. Weasel thought to himself: *"Why am I wasting my time talking to an old cricket who obviously is derange? I have a report to share with Badger and the gang. Boy, are we going to have fun!"*

Wildcat (The Call of the Wild)

Wildcat was a rebellious young lady, where being wild was not wild enough. So she dyed her hair red and ran away from home. She had been on the trail several weeks wreaking havoc and mayhem on the innocent little ones whose misfortune it was to wander away from their parents and carelessly leave Wildcat their scent.

On this day Wildcat was following the scent of three animals that usually did not travel together, two raccoons and a weasel. With her keen nose and ears a mile was close enough to snag her prey, let alone having three distinct scents to follow. She had their scent and doubled her pace to catch up.

The Fork in the Road

Wildcat's chances decreased in half when she came upon a fork in the road. At the fork their scents parted with the raccoons heading due north and the weasel heading northeast deeper into the forest.

Which trail should she take? What were the possible outcomes? Two raccoons would put up a fight and could attack her from different directions. They could climb to the top of most trees where she would not be able to follow. Only if they got separated would she have a chance to get one of them. From the size of their tracks they were closing in on adulthood; maybe too tough for her to handle by herself no matter how wild she was.

With raccoons she was one for one. But that raccoon was a baby that strayed from its family. He was a little one lost in the forest, easy prey for a relentless predator like the wildcat.

The weasel was another challenge. Wildcat's track record with weasels was five to zero, without her catching one weasel. They were too fast in the thick foliage of the forest and there were just too many small holes to hide in; weasels were fast, keen, tricky and brave; not much hope for catching the weasel.

Wildcat hadn't eaten in days. The raccoons it must be. She was confident she could separate the raccoons, kill and eat one of them before they made it to the trunk of a tall tree.

She was torn. Wildcat thought to herself: *"The weasel or the raccoons, the weasel or the raccoons?* **Which will it be?"**

Vision (The Fork in the Road)

Standing just out of sight in the tall grass lining the trail the cricket's voice written in script appeared: *"My name is Vision and I come from the year* **2525** *and mankind did not survive. The world you know will no longer exist."*

Wildcat stopped in her tracks and snarled ready for a fight. The cricket stepped out of the tall grass.

Wildcat exclaimed: *"What does an old cricket like you know about the future? There isn't enough of you to eat; so for today you will escape my hunger and rage."*

Vision: *"You must always protect the innocent, especially the babies. If you fail to* **protect the inn**ocent *there will be a terrible reckoning. You will one day be held accountable for your wicked ways.* **Justice will find you.** *There will be an accounting and each evil action you take will be repaid tenfold when facing the wrath of Justice and the unknown. You may put up a fight, but in the end you will perish."*

Wildcat: *"What riddle is this? You know there are no rules in Nature and that some of us must eat others to survive. If you weren't just a nasty old bug I would make a quick snack out of you!"*

Vision: *"There will be a time when mankind forgets his bond with Nature and recklessly corrupts this planet bringing destruction to the innocent.* **There will be a Reckoning."**

Vision changing his tone: *"Could you help me; I am looking for a cave? I am weary and I want to go home."*

Wildcat: *"I will lead you to the cave you are seeking if you tell me were these trails lead."*

Vision: *"The trail to the left heads north and skirts the edge of the sacred circle and the mightiest tree in this forest. The trail on the right heads northeast, deeper into the forest; home to a band of outlaws; some real bad hombres."*

Wildcat laughing: *"You old fool; I know not of any cave, I am new to this part of the country. You better scat before I tear you apart just for the fun of it!"*

With that the cricket hopped back into the tall grass and went into hiding. Sadly he never made it home.

Wildcat pondered: ***"Which road should I take?"***

Wildcat Chases the Raccoons

Once decided, the wildcat headed due north chasing the scent of the two raccoons. Wildcat to herself: *"Just maybe I can separate one raccoon from the other. Chances are I can catch up to them before they reach their family or make it to one of their hiding places high up in the tallest trees."*

With the wind at their backs Brutus and Marcus hurried back up the trail. Just ahead of the weasel and wildcat, they passed the fork in the road where the two paths merged.

Mortal Combat/Immortal Love

Eclipse showed up with a loud **"Caw-Caw-Caw,"** warning his good friends that a wildcat had tracked them down and was determined to have one of them for dinner. Eclipse told them that the wildcat was less than a mile behind them and that they just had enough time to make it back to the safety of the mighty oak. Marcus and Brutus ran for their lives finally reaching the outer roots of their old oak tree.

The wildcat gradually caught up with them and maneuvered for an attack. Lagging behind, Marcus caught a glimpse of the wildcat crouched behind a large root ready to pounce. In that instant Brutus saw the threat was real and with Marcus turned to face the wildcat. Facing the wildcat, they both growled exposing their sharp teeth in anger causing their fur to bristle exaggerating their size making them appear more threatening than they really were. The wildcat paused.

Always there to protect, Eclipse in a flash flew straight at the wildcat's face, talons aimed for her eyes. The wildcat in surprise and haste ducked for cover losing ground between her and her next meal. Brutus then Marcus scurried up the mighty oak tree tearing into its bark to escape. Brutus led the way pass the lower braches seeking the highest limbs to discourage the hungry beast on their tails. They believed the wildcat was too big to climb so high. Her agility and hunger (determination) pushed her further up the tree where few predators dared to go.

With Brutus in the lead they scrambled up the trunk of the mighty oak seeking the higher branches to make their getaway. They climbed higher up into the tree where the wildcat would not follow; where the branches were too thin to carry the addition of her weight.

Marcus in his haste chose a branch that had been broken off by a spring storm. The branch's jagged edge was only twenty feet away. Brutus recognizing Marcus' mistake followed the higher branch leading to a jumping off place ensuring his escape. From this branch he could jump to a smaller branch where the wildcat could not go. Brutus had chosen the taller branch, one that would bend with his weight and close enough to the other tree to make his getaway.

Marcus found himself trapped *out on a limb* with no place to run. Marcus could only turn and faced his fate. Determined the wildcat climbed on.

With the wildcat in hot pursuit and closing in on Marcus, Brutus turned around to save his brother. The wildcat had backed Marcus to the limb's broken edge; the abyss. *Marcus turned to face the unknown; that which we know but cannot accept; death.*

Brutus turned away from his path to safety and hurried back down the branch to confront the wildcat. Face to face Marcus and the wildcat glared at each other. With softness in his eyes, Marcus accepted his own death; the darkness beyond.

With a *"Caw, Caw, Caw,"* Eclipse again dove straight for the wildcat's face. The wildcat turned and in that instant Brutus leaped from the branch above clutching her fur with his claws and teeth knocking the wildcat from her perch, carrying both Brutus and the wildcat to their deaths.

With a loud crack their bodies crashed into the roots of the mighty oak tree. The bodies of Brutus and Wildcat were crushed together, one body indistinguishable from the other.

Gripped in a deadly struggle they had fallen over one hundred feet to the Earth.

Solomon and Sheba finally made it to the base of the tree. Sheba the mother of Brutus cried openly for her lost son. Her deep painful sobs carried throughout the forest. Solomon to himself: *"My brave and wonderful son. You sacrificed your life to save your brother. My poor son, I will always miss you. Your courage will never be forgotten; damn those boys!"*

Cradled within Eclipse's wings Marcus cried for the loss of his brother:

What if I had obeyed my parents?
What if Brutus refused to follow me down the trail?
What if our father discovered our plan earlier?
What if Brutus and I had listened to Eclipse?
What if the wildcat had taken the other path?
What if life did not evolve on Earth?
What if the Big Bang never occurred?

In Another Universe/On Another Planet

In another Universe Eclipse is the protector and guardian, Brutus is bold and brave beyond measure and Marcus is a true antagonist and seeker. Now they face death; a death that could have been avoided. It is a death Marcus will carry the rest of his life. To save Marcus, Brutus returns to the Cosmos; the physical Universe. Brutus could have gotten away, but instead he chose to save his brother's life.

Marcus sobbed deeply within the protective wings of Eclipse. His remorse was profound. His shame for taunting

Brutus to leave the sacred circle to chase a weasel shattered Marcus' inner being. His sense of **balance** will forever be tilted. How could Marcus exist without his baby brother by his side? How could he face his parents and life after what he did? Knowing his son, Solomon looks for Marcus and confronts Eclipse. Eclipse had to tell Solomon the truth.

Solomon: *"Eclipse, why in the **blue blazes from hell** did you not tell me what those two boys were up to?"*

Eclipse: *"They have grown so much and have gotten so fast I could barely keep up with them and I did not want to let them out of my sight. You know how Marcus plays it, the more you tell him not to do something the more determined he becomes to defy you and do it. In spite of your best advice he takes himself and others to the edge. I tried to get them to turn around earlier, but sadly I failed."*

Solomon: *"Eclipse it is not your fault. It's what life gives and takes away. None of us are truly in control of anything. Control is an illusion to trick us into believing that the gods (**Chaos** and **Happenstance**) are on our side."*

Solomon: *"We have lost our dear son Brutus. We cannot lose Marcus too."*

Solomon: *"I warned that boy, time and time again, to never leave the protection of the roots (The sacred circle), or taunt Brutus to recklessness. They got away with it once, and they should not have pressed their luck. His mother will rip his ass and my words will pierce his soul."*

Marcus avoided his parents and rushed home to pack his things. He was determined not to face his father and account for himself. His father's disapproval would penetrate to the core of his being. The fisherman's bait and hook had caught a trophy fish. Tragically that unexpected trophy was his brother.

Solomon to Eclipse: *"We have looked everywhere and we cannot find Marcus. He has been home and packed my* **haversack** *with food and took the family's journal. I am afraid he's has run away, heading into the unknown. Will you please go after him? Tell Marcus that we love him and to come back home. Tell him we forgive him and that we have all crossed boundaries we regret."*

Eclipse: *"I will catch up with him and try to convince him to return home. If he refuses, I promise while I live; I will never leave his side."*

Eclipse catches up with Marcus just as he crossed over into the forest: **"Caw, Caw, Caw;"** *"Marcus your parents forgive you and want you to turn around and come home. They know you had nothing to do with that wildcat chasing after you; Marcus that is their nature. Wildcats are fierce and determined hunters. You were responsible for calling Brutus out onto the trail, but not for his death. Marcus you chose the wrong branch; a choice of fate. Brutus, bless his strong heart, chose to save you. Your parents love you and want you to come back home."*

Marcus: *"I am not running from them; I am running away from myself; that which is impossible. I cannot forgive myself for what I have done. I will wander the wilderness and never come back."*

Marcus: *"Eclipse, will you join me and help me walk a straight and narrow path? I vow, I will never again taunt another to do wrong on my journey through life. I will travel this Earth to discover the truths of life and treat the others that we meet on our way with high regard and respect. We will travel through the wild places, learn from Nature her most treasured wonders, and record her truths in my journal."*

Eclipse: *"Yes Marcus, I will join you and always be by your side."*

Marcus and Eclipse headed south across the Blue Ridge Mountains down into and over the Smoky Mountains. They will eventually reach Florida and journey through the Ever Glades. They will build a raft and tip-toe across the islands to Key West.

The swirling southerly winds of an out of control hurricane will carry their raft pass Cuba, Puerto Rico and through the Caribbean to South America. They will travel inland through the jungles and up to the headwaters of the Amazon. Their final push will take them south through Patagonia and down to Cape Horn. Marcus and Eclipse will head north back up to the Andes reaching the great divide and a cliff too far.

Marcus and Eclipse will meet many fascinating wild creatures and face new and often dangerous challenges. A beautiful green parrot will foretell their and our futures. A ferocious alligator will hunt them down in the Florida Ever Glades and a narrow escape with the help of a cottonmouth (A Seer) will lead them into the Gulf of Mexico. A terrible storm will carry them southeast across the Caribbean Sea and leave them stranded on a deserted beach, on an island just short of South America. A majestic sea turtle will tell them a riddle that will guide them to a tributary of the Amazon River. Marcus and Eclipse will join a troop of the little people with tails (monkeys) and travel further inland and southwest up the Amazon to the Andes. *Chaos* (A jaguar) will catch their scent and begin to track them through the jungles and mountains. On a narrow trail *Panther*, Marcus's and Eclipses' adopted brother, and a great condor of the Andes will come to their rescue. Joined together as true and dear brothers, Marcus and Eclipse will journey into the unknown; a journey we all must take.

Wildcat Chases the Weasel

Once decided, Wildcat headed northeast following the scent of the weasel. Although the weasel might be harder to catch, facing two nearly full grown raccoons standing side by side ready to take on a fight would be too dangerous. The hunt would be over before it started if these two raccoons were rejoining their family somewhere back on the trail. This would be a total loss, hungry with nothing to eat; a royal waste of her time; *"a fork in the road."*

Wildcat quickened her pace and the weasel's scent grew stronger. Then the unimaginable happened. The weasel's scent merged with a badger's who was headed southwest.

Where the weasel and badger tracks joined, Wildcat carefully searched the trail and the surrounding forest. There were no signs of a struggle; no blood, ripped out fur, torn up ground, the buzz of flies; nothing.

Taking a closer look where the two first met Wildcat determined that the weasel and badger knew each other. They had stopped and left a mixture of tracks as if talking with each other; stepping here and there, standing close to each other with no signs of a fight.

Badgers and weasels are not known to keep company with each other. Their tracks were telling. Now the two of them were traveling together; one walking beside the other.

Being wild, Wildcat's raw curiosity took over. The wind was in her favor, blowing in her face from the Northeast. She thought to herself: *"I will close the gap before nightfall. Just what are these two thugs up to?"*

Wildcat had closed the gap and their scent was strong. It was approaching dusk and they would be stopping soon to make camp. She waited until after dark before she moved closer to their encampment. It had the appearance of an undisciplined outlaw hideout with trash, loot and gear lying about.

As the outlaws settled in, Wildcat pawed at the ground, laid down, took a deep breath and closed one eye. A few hours passed and she woke with a jerk: *"Is the forest on fire?"* Smoke had drifted her way, and set off an alarm. Wildcat quickly realized it was a small fire from the badger's and weasel's campsite. She carefully circled the camp without making a sound and settled down to watch and listen.

The Gang

Badgers were fierce fighters and weasels were known for their conniving duplicity. Now there was a gang of four, an one eye fat porcupine and an ugly foul smelling brown turkey buzzard. From the blackness of the forest Wildcat listened while the badger addressed his gang.

The badger: *"Life is a game of dice. We came up north to cash in and all we got for our troubles were two bags of half spoiled leftovers. I took it for granted the northeast, my home turf, would be rich with booty by now. We gambled and came up short. Being wild and outlaws we will push on.*

The badger: *"We just have to laugh at ourselves and accept the life we have chosen. None of us can expect much from life and if we do we most likely will find ourselves on the short end of the stick. We know the risks, yet we play the game in spite of the odds."*

The badger: *"I guess before I kicked the bucket, I had to visit the Allegany Plateau one more time. We sure raised some hell for our troubles; didn't we boys? If nothing else we had fun tearing things up and scaring the crap out of our prey."*

The porcupine: *"Why didn't we raid the old oak tree?"*

The badger: *"I never want to go there again, too many bad memories."*

The buzzard: *"I am for attacking the sacred circle anyway."*

The badger: *"If we harm one member of the clan they will swear a blood oath to hunt us down. All the animals of the clan will unite under the leadership of Solomon and come after us. They would ambush us from the roots before we ever made it to the sacred tree. Knowing Solomon, he would have dug hundreds of interconnecting tunnels under the roots of that mighty oak to protect the clan and attack us from. The odds of surviving such a raid are zero."*

The badger: *"Besides, I have a special place in my heart for that old oak tree. Many years ago, my family in their last attempt to escape the great fire storm were caught out in the open and burned to death. My little brother Tommy freaked out, ran off and was the first to be burned alive. In my father's and mother's attempt to save him, they ran head on into the storm. My other brothers and sisters scattered leaving me alone. I found an exposed root on the outer rim of that old tree and dug myself a fox hole. While the wall of fire spun and waged war on the innocent, I dug in. I covered myself with dirt and waited out the storm. When the storm finally ended and after a desperate search I found the remains of my family, one by one-burnt to a crisp."*

The badger: *"I vowed that I would never go back to that old tree. It took my family away from me: my mother and father, sisters and brothers. With the false promise of salvation my family abandoned our home to escape the fire of fires, and made haste to the oak tree; the tallest-oldest tree in the forest. This tree was over a thousand years old and had survived hundreds of fires. My father was sure we could make it to the old oak tree in time."*

The badger: *"At first I was angry that my father sought shelter under that mighty oak; that he chose the tree over us.*

I was just a kid; with too much to figure out. My family died trying to get to that old tree and I hated the thought of it."

The badger: *"Over time my spirit softened and the old oak tree gradually grew into a living memorial to my family; after all it did save my life. I finally figured out who was really the blame for losing my family and growing up an unwanted orphan."*

The badger: *"The hell with Mother Nature; she's a real bitch when she wants to be. She doesn't ask for our consent and is indifferent to our survival. Mother Nature has thousands of ways to torment you before she does you in. She can slowly drown you in quicksand in the middle of a mosquito infested swamp. She can choke you to death with thirst in a desert just out of reach of fresh water. She can rain asteroids from the heavens and wipe out life on this planet. She can put a mountain lion on your scent for a late night meal. Without a by-your-leave she can stomp you into dust;* **Justice** *be damned. Nature reigns supreme and is impervious to our suffering. Even in the darkness (death) we belong to her."*

The badger: *"I survived the great fire storm and at first pondered making that old oak tree my home. Then the guardians started making up all these rules and that type of control is just not in my nature. At first I tried to connect, but everyone wanted me to pitch in and get along with others."*

The badger: *"I got into some trouble by stealing food from two old farts and had to answer to the guardians for my petty crime."*

The badger: *"Solomon, the head guardian, was hardnosed and determined to have law and order. They got into showing respect for each other and a reverence for the "Mighty Oak, and its Sacred Circle." They formed a clan and pledge loyalty to each other. We were to be governed by* **harmony** *and* **balance***; which was Dullsville for me. Who wants to live in Dullsville? Not the Badger! So I got the hell out of there."*

The badger: *"To atone for my misdeed, Solomon directed me to supply the old couple with food for the winter. I thought to myself; the hell with this shit! I headed southwest the next day and fell in with bad company. Eager to fit in and account for myself I became one of the most infamous outlaws ever. Like Nature I like calling the shots."*

The badger continued: *"We accept that life is not fair so we make up our own rules; morality be damned! Right-wrong what does Nature care? She did not care during the fire storm that made me an orphan and took my family away from me. Nature is cold and heartless indifferent to our needs or wellbeing. As far as she is concerned she would rather have a dead planet then tend after a brew of spoiled brats. Life is the pinnacle of existence. We are conscience beings so that we can recognize the misery we must bear."*

The badger: *"Nature gives you a ray of sunshine then slaps you down; hitting you in the face with a terrible storm. She does not ask your opinion or permission. She is* **omnipotent***. Through her you are born and will die. The Cosmos and life belong to her; the totality of it all is hers; every particle, every living cell."*

The badger: *"Whenever has life been fair? In the end she takes what she wants and leaves you with nothing; darkness. Boys, we are headed home and we will take* **Chaos** *and her* wicked cousins **Havoc** and **Mayhem** with us. Let's see how much damnation and fire from Hell we can raise!"

The weasel, porcupine and turkey buzzard stood dazed, dumbfounded and speechless, as if a Shawnee arrow just flew over their heads slicing a groove in their skulls barely missing their brains. After a few moments of silence and confusion, Weasel with his mouth gaped open realized it was time for him to give his report.

The weasel to the gang: *"The pickings along the trail from here are good and should carry us down into Kentucky and maybe all the way back to the Mississippi River. There are several unprotected homesteads along the trail ripe for the picking."*

The badger: *"Remember our plans; we would search the trail northeast for a while, rob and pillage then head southwest back to the Ozarks before winter with our goods. Our gains up north have been meager. From here on out everything is fair game, our good fortune, their bad luck…. Give and expect no quarter."*

Wildcat hearing the game was drawn to its wickedness. She was captivated-enthralled-spellbound-mesmerized by their sinister plans; their wildness was beyond wild, it was *eeevvviiilll*. They would prey upon the weak and helpless to their own gain; *"righteousness be damned!"*

How should she play it? It was a gang of four and in Nature she would only really be able to challenge the weasel or old turkey buzzard to a fight. There was a one eyed porcupine and a heavily scarred badger that would be too much for her to handle. She would use *lust* and *fear* to gain their attention and if profitable join their; "her" gang.

Wildcat started with a snap of a twig, then moved quietly around the camp and snapped another. Before long the gang was convinced they were surrounded by a sinister presence, something fiercer and more dangerous than themselves.

From the blackness of the forest she would gaze at their fire capturing its light in her now glowing fiery red eyes. There were two blazing torches glaring at them from the darkness that slowly grew closer, then moved back into the forest; then closed in again. She would put their tough male bravado to the test. Scared shitless the gang, like two old married couples drew close to each other; with their eyes ready to pop out of their sockets and their mouths wide open.

Now she would coolly up the ante. She used a deep growl to push their fear further. The growl rumbled through the camp and made them tremble. In fear the turkey buzzard puked, "lost his lunch." The porcupine unconsciously shot off sharp quills in every direction almost hitting the weasel.

Then there was a long eerie silence, something beyond Nature; absolute quietness alarming the badger into action: *"Close ranks and prepare for the worse, I think it's the Spirit Walkers. If they catch us they will surely eat us alive. You know how they like to dip your eyeballs into a bowl of blood for dessert; sorry Spike."*

Another long silence, then a soft sensual purr, the lyrics of a mystical love song floated through the trees. This purr was so soft and warm the gang quickly recovered from their fear. They now were lustful for what may be lingering in the forest. They were drawn to her inviting and intoxicating tune. They warmed to the soft ripple of her voice and their faces and bodies relaxed. Their love for lust popped through their tarnished souls and stirred their loins.

Collectively the gang's once frozen faces melted into soft expressions in anticipation of the next set of lyrics. Their eyes widen. They were over taken by the hope of a promising encounter. The tune had femininity etched in every sound. The joys of making love danced through their perverted minds and empty souls. They anticipated the bliss, "a wild orgy," and forgot their fears.

She played it like Mozart; then growled again. Again they drew back in fear and dread. In a snap she had converted back to an immediate threat. Again they imaged the Spirit Walkers were ready to make their attack. They were the nine foot tiger tooth dreaded ones who roamed the darkness and ate children; ***Knock-Knock-Knock…..Knock-Knock***.

Then again the soft sensual tones and lyrics, the gang was in an emotional spin, her warm loving invites; purr, purr, purr tickling them with a soft voice that rippled over her tongue.
The game was over. The forest grew cold and silent. The gang froze in place. In one great leap to seal her command, Wildcat jumped into the center of their camp. The badger wet himself and the others dropped their loads where they stood. With her claws stretched to the max, her fierce glare, sharp fangs and her short tail fully exposed; Wildcat was ready to pounce.

In perfect form, she relaxed and with her warm loving eyes, a soft elegant purr and sensual moves, she sashayed back and forth to melt the scene and said: *"Am I wild enough for you boys?"*

The porcupine lost a few more quills, the weasel started telling lies to promote himself while digging at the others, the turkey buzzard pranced around like a prized roster and the badger puffed out his chest and wrinkled his brow in a feeble attempt to reestablish his authority.

In disbelief, they all cheered her performance and welcomed her into their gang. Wide eyed they hooted and howled themselves silly. Even the badger was taken by her wit.

A Gang of Outlaws/Desperados

The badger: *"You are welcome to join our gang. My name is* **Badger***; those that know me call me* **Bad Ass***. This elongated rat is* **Weasel***. When he is lying, which is most of the time, we call him* **Weezey***. That there is* **Spike***; you must approach him from his left side, he got his right eye scratched out by a bald eagle defending her chicks. His sharp quills are dangerous. Try not to get to close or accidently bump into him. He's got an itchy finger and goes off like a bolt of lightning. Don't walk up on him from his blind side or you may find yourself pinned to a tree. The foul smelling big and ugly brown bird is* **Turkey Buzzard***. His beak always smells like rotten meat and he never bothers to bathe or wash his bill. Stay up wind from him and you'll be okay. For short we call him,* **"TB."**

*"**My name is Wildcat,** and I am ready to raise some hell. Do you guys think you're tough enough to take me on?"*

Badger, still smarting over his show of fear: *"We'll see. This is not make believe, playing Yeti in the woods. This is for*

436

real; life and death, playing it raw and naked, taking it to the edge. You must be able to fend for yourself or be left behind. Our motto is; 'Tear things up, don't give a damn, and just be mean.'"

Badger: *"We have pushed as far north as we planned. We are going to head southwest back to the Ozarks and then continue across Arkansas up to the Red River. Weasel has mapped out a promising trail where there is plenty of food and plunder just ripe for the taking."*

Badger: *"Weasel and Wildcat you will take the lead and scout out our route and any promising opportunities. Weasel you will gain the homesteader's trust while Wildcat watches for trouble from a distance ensuring all is clear for our attack. We will leave no witnesses."*

Wildcat joined the gang. They made their way southwest and eventually reached the Red River up into the Oklahoma territory. On a raid Spike lost his left eye and was now totally blind. He was robbed by his fellow gang members and abandoned on the trail to find his way in the dark. With no friends, food or water he stumbled on. He lasted less than a week before the wolves got him. Once on his back, his stomach and guts were easy pickings. TB caught a terrible cold, took a high fever and died under a tree. He too was stripped and left behind. Nobody noticed he was gone. Neither of them were ever mentioned again.

On their way the gang picked up a raccoon that asked too many questions. This raccoon proved himself to the badger by robbing a nest of blue jay eggs and was prized for his ability to climb even the tallest trees. The raccoon went by the name of Marcus. Marcus had defied his father and left on a journey beyond the sacred circle to explore and discover the unknown. Falling into bad company was not part of his plan. Being naive and young, this union almost proved fatal to the young explorer. In the end he just could not stand up to the pack of criminals and yielded his soul to do their evil biddings.

Once in Oklahoma the gang raided a defenseless village. The raid upon the village proved that the gang wasn't as tough as they thought they were. This time they had bitten off more than they could chew and were stomped into the ground by a force of Nature, the icon of the American Great Plains. The gang was finally held accountable for its crimes and met *Justice* on the southern plains. *"There will be a reckoning!"*

A Billion Stars; A Trillion Paths.

The Trails We Go Down.
Which Trail Will We Choose?
Will we find the trail that leads us to wonder?
Or follow the trail that carries us into damnation?

A Lost Trail is a Treasure Undiscovered.

MOTHER NATURE

PROTECT OUR PLANET

WE ARE WATCHING YOU!
WATCHING YOU!
WATCHING YOU!
WATCHING YOU!

440

Epilogue

Immortality

As long as the Cosmos exists there will be life somewhere in some form. From these forms of life intelligence will emerge. With intelligence will arise curiosity, wonder and the discovery of ourselves. We will learn to grasp and once we grasp we will hold on to what we discover and pass it to the next generation. We will recognize our being within its natural state and the state of being as it evolved from Nature.

Our spirituality is an extension of ourselves trying to be more than the physical and mortal beings that we are. The projections beyond our bodies are attempts to escape our humble fates as living creatures. We are just physical beings formed from a physical Universe.

We create myths and religions to sooth our fears and provide an escape from the unknown and death. Indifferent to our will, life and death does not ask for our permission. We exist and cease to exist in a continuum of matter and energy that moves without our consent.

Yet there are moments of escape when we leave our bodies through our imagination and wonder of the world and Universe that surrounds us. The majesty of the oceans, the awe of the world's highest mountains, the great and forbidding deserts, an emerald humming bird hovering over a beautiful flower, the brightness of a child's smile, the approval of a loving parent, ... We escape into an extension of ourselves, lost and found beyond our bodies within the wonder that surrounds us.

If we survive then our beings will pop up again and again within our families over time not knowing our previous existence but recognizing our common traits. Sons and daughters will see bits and pieces of their fathers and mothers within themselves; and the grandchildren will reflect all the generations of life that passed before them. When holding our grandbabies we will see ourselves, a brother or sister and/or a distant cousin or two.

If we dare feel the bond that binds us there will be peace on Earth. If there is peace on Earth there will be advancement toward the light. The light will represent the totality of our goodness and that goodness will again advance peace and enlightenment. Knowing our true place on this Earth will open the stars to our imaginations and good deeds; then again and again we will move forward.

For me I was a raccoon transformed into an eagle. An eagle that was nearly driven to extinction by the men who hunted us, then saved by the men and women who recognized the eagle's true worth and our mutual connection to this Earth and each other; one species saving another.

We are interconnected, bound together forever in life and in death, one with this Earth, one with the Cosmos, together joined under the light of knowing.

The Journey's End/Beginning
When landing on the mighty oak tree I realized that I had made it home and could finally let go; rest. Settling on the tree's branch I said to myself that I will only stop for a moment to ponder all that was, is and could be.

I had suffered and I had known happiness, I had known despair and joy and I had known love. I had known love on many levels; the love I had for my parents and brothers and sisters, the love of friends and mates and the precious love for and from my children. I have known the greatest gift of life and therefore I have traveled to the edge of the Universe and back.

I realized I had been on a great journey; a journey of wonder and discovery. Not the discovery of mighty rivers or of great mountain peaks; but rather the discovery of simple truths. First and foremost, we were born of and from this Earth and all the good or evil we do belongs to us.

Mankind has hidden this simple truth from us to advance their selfish wants. In spite of the overwhelming evidence that can be found everywhere on this planet they deny this basic truth.

They have created gods and demigods to explain our creation, denying the evidence at our feet. They have created these myths to hide and justify their own greed and lust for control. They seek to keep us confused and in conflict with each other; clouding our ability to see and discover this truth found everywhere on this planet.

The greediest and most selfish of the human race do not care about the planet or the misery of mankind and the species of creatures on the verge of extinction. They just want to satisfy their immediate lust for control and having more. More than they need, more than any one human being needs or deserves. They will not be happy until all the wild places and wild animals are gone.

They have cut down great and mighty forests and left ruin in their wake, depriving the Earth of its ability to cover itself exposing it to erosion. In their lust for wealth they have drilled, mined and polluted the Earth's precious streams and waterways and killed off untold numbers of aquatic creatures. They daily pile up heaps of garbage fouling the Earth's landscape, oceans and air. They have hunted hundreds of species into extinction and destroyed millions of acres of natural habitat. With no end in sight we are doomed; unless we listen to the Earth.

If we are to survive we have to rapidly change course, come about and redirect our activities to support the natural environment that gave us life and sustains us.

If we listen carefully, the Earth has been speaking to us about ourselves throughout history; about the planet we live on and the creatures we share this Earth with. There is clear evidence that tells us of the struggle and rise of all species including humans. We share a common heritage that is in direct line with the formation of our physical planet as it developed over time and through which it created multiple environments for life to be born in and evolve from.

From the streams, rivers and oceans, wherever water was found sprung life in one form or another. And from these sparks of life we have risen to consciousness and knowing.

Will we use this knowledge to gain wisdom and this wisdom to lead us into the future; a future in harmony with the Earth and all of its creatures, a planet in balance and at peace, a planet that is covered with sparkling blue waters, encased in a blue sky, surrounded by fresh and clean air and enriched with the movement and chatter of its many creatures? We were born of the Universe and are the children of this Earth. We can become the Keepers that inherit the Earth and hold it safe for future generations.

The Great Illusion (Life)

We believe we have found safe haven on a beautiful tropical island in the midst of a vast and dangerous sea; a sunny moment on an island full of warmth and plenty. We think we are safe, but it is just an illusion. The island (Life) itself is adrift, no longer attached to the Earth, but rather casted out onto a dark and unforgiving ocean that is itself adrift in a continuum of motion in time and space. The Cosmos and all that follows it, leaves itself behind while it speeds into the great unknown and future.

Time itself will be lost when this motion of the Universe expands into nothing or contracts into the beginning; again and again until eternity itself is bent into nothing.

The moments we desperately try to hold onto are passing by us as we ourselves are moving through this continuum of time and space. We are changing within ourselves as we desperately cling to life as our life passes before us and the world we live in. Within this continuum of motion, in time and space we exist.

Even while connected to each other and indeed all life, we are alone. The closest we ever come to knowing each other is through love. Touch, hugs, and kisses bridge the cosmic gaps between us; joining us in time and space stopping for a moment the continuum of motion. This moment is noted in time without meaning and cannot be erased by eternity.

Will we accept our fragile moment of life and bask in its warmth and light? Will we embrace this truth and accept our nothingness and fullness in the end? A circle within a circle that even eternity itself cannot comprehend.

Marcus

I was but a foot soldier bound by duty to serve my country. My delusionary duty took me to a far off land and to the death of a child. I have cried a thousand tears for a child that will never be, in a world that had gone completely mad. In a better world this war would have never been and that child would have grown old to love and care for her grandchildren. *So much Chaos and random destruction created by those who by now should know better.*

I had listened to the words of the spirit warriors and was falsely misled. Their gibberish and babble led me astray, but I believed them anyway. I wore a uniform and marched off to war, never to return. The storm had washed away the island and I was adrift alone in a dark and violent sea.

With my belief system shattered I needed the truth. *"Who are we? Where did we come from? Why do we exist? What is our purpose? Why does the hummingbird bring us so much joy?"*

I went on a long journey that took me years to complete. At first I was angry and wanted to throw out all the old beliefs and gods. The recital of old gibberish no longer made sense.

My mind was clouded and my soul was torn. Like sunlight through the forest the truths of our existence came beaming through the dark to illuminate my way. I settled on natural science and recorded history for many of the answers; our most solid ground. Both can be questioned, but their tangibles are real. There is evidence of both everywhere. Evidence of our being, of the Natural world that surrounds us, our physical evolution and the evolution of all species, ancient civilizations, the galaxies, the Universe, on and on and on and yet too few accept or believe…..

Reason and *wisdom* seem to escape us. Although we understand they exist we cannot seem to find them anywhere. They are the most endangered and elusive of our species, like looking for Big Foot in New York City.

Like UFOs and Big Foot, religion is everywhere and at the same time nowhere. There are sightings and crashes everywhere but not one true appearance or evidence anywhere. Not a tooth, body, craft or resurrection, yet too many believe…....

I slowly became a seeker, then a teacher and now a keeper. Ours is a world with so much promise that may never be. We could be living in a world guided by reason and compassion and a profound sense of being. A world filled with a boundless love for life and for our precious Earth.

I was nineteen years old in a war nobody wanted in a place and time that should have never been. How I yearned to return to the forest of my youth and to the arms of my loving parents. How good it would be to return to the world of my innocence before *Chaos* took me elsewhere, the *Chaos* and random destruction that we mindlessly create and sustain.

"Marcus, Wake up! Your mother and father love you. It is time to come home. You are dreaming again."

Author's Notes

States of Being
1. Hollow-ones; *Easily Led, Followers, Without Substance, Gullible*
2. Spirit Warriors; *Manipulators, Rabble Rousers, Extremist,*
3. Controllers/Elite; *the Powerful Who Seek to Control, Self-Serving*
4. Seekers; *Student, Driven by Curiosity, Adventurist*
5. Teachers; *Keeper and Sharer of Knowledge and Truth, Leader*
6. Spirit Guides; *Sharers of Wisdom, Goodness, Balance and Harmony*
7. Keepers-Seers; *Seek and Pass on Enlightenment, Embodies Wholesomeness and Purity of Being, Seer of the Future, (Possess the Traits of the Upper Four States of Being), Protectors of the Earth*

Characters; Roles & Traits
Mother Nature; *Giver and Sustainer of All Life, Mother Earth, the Cosmos*
The Oak Tree; *Home and Family, the Sacred Circle, Security*
Solomon and Sheba; *Mother and Father, Love and Warmth, Acceptance*
Vision; *the Healer, Visitor from the Future*
Romulus, Remus, Patricia, Isabela and Brutus; *Older Siblings and Baby Brother*
Marcus; *Seeker, Gullible, Naive, Curious, Student, Innocence, Wanderlust, Courage, Transformation*
Brutus; *Baby Brother, Bold, Courageous, Recklessness*
Eclipse; *Childhood Friend, Instigator, Atonement and Redemption, Dedication, Fidelity, Guardian*
The Crawler; *Seer*
Odysseus; *Trickster, Trust*
Oedipus Rex; *Fate*
Jetta; *the Black Widow, Wisdom, Seer of the Future*
Badger, Wildcat and Weasel; *the War Party, Bad Company, Criminals, Corruption*
Prairie Dog Villages; *the Southern Plains Tribes, Community, Bond with Nature*
Justice; *the White Buffalo, Justice, Reckoning, Conscience, Forgiveness*
Walking Moon; *Chief, Elder, Nobility, Courage, Wisdom*
Elk Horn and Falling Star; *Brother and Father of Walking Moon*
White Elk; *Marcus' Wife, Innocence and Purity*
Strong Heart, Gentle Touch and Morning Star; *Marcus' Children*
Father Coyote; *Saves White Elk, a Keeper, Compassion*
Midnight; *Teacher, the Truth, America*
Scorpion; *Teacher, the Universe*
Coyote; *Best Friend, Loyalty, Fidelity, Courage*

Characters; Roles & Traits

Gila Monster and Sidewinder; *Teachers, the Earth, Trust, Faith*
The White Ghost: *Guardian, Seer*
Heckle, Jekyll/Hyde; *Evil*
Otter; *Carefree Easy Going Beach Comber*
Seal; *Thrill Seeker, Dear Friend, Brotherly Love, Fellowship, Teacher*
Florence; *Saves Seal, Protector, Faithful, Salvation, Companionship, Mother Nature, the Garden Before Eden*
Mada; *The Young Islander, Saves Florence, a Guardian of Nature*
Wonder; *Seer, Perfection of Nature, Nature's Demise, Lust, Greed*
Oahu and Kil Auea; *True Love, Balance and Harmony*
Geo; *Teacher, the Structure and Formation of the Earth*
Rahoo and Hoora; *Seers and Protectors of the Forest, Spirit Walkers*
Crilu and Lucri; *Clan Elders Performing the Sacred Marriage*
Kralu and Lukra; *Clan Elders at the Ice Bridge*
Luway; *Overseer of the Destruction of the Ice Bridge*
David and Golith; *The Ancestors of the Marcus and Rahoo*
Mother, Father, and Sister Condor; *Adopted Family, Loyalty, Protection*
Mother Condor the Seer; *the Humans will Decide, Darkness or Illumination*
Father and Mother Grizzly; *Parents of Survival and Marcus*
Little River with Big Horns; *Battle of the Little Big Horn*
Plain Dwellers-Prairie Dogs; *the Sioux and Cheyenne,* (Nomadic Tribes)
Crazy Bear; *Crazy Horse* (Sioux Warrior)
Buffalo Crow; *Sitting Bull* (The chief and medicine man of the Sioux)
Strong Wolf; *Colonel Armstrong Custer, Arrogance,* (Seventh Cavalry)
Wild Goose; *Captain Frederick Benteen,* (Seventh Cavalry)
Whisky; *Major Marcus Reno,* (Seventh Cavalry)
The Keeper; *Marcus' Greatest Teacher, Wisdom, Truth, Purity of Being*
Shadow; *Eclipse, Remorse and Redemption, Guardian*
Chaos; *Lioness, Happenstance, Random Destruction, Fate*
Survival; *Brother Bear, Strength, Loyalty, Courage*
Ra and Cleo; *Solomon's Parents*
Sara; *Solomon's Baby Sister*
Stinky and Waddles; *Solomon's Friends, Tragedy, Orphans, Fellowship*
Scarface; *Saved by Marcus, Brutus and Eclipse*
Spike and Turkey Buzzard; *Members of the Gang*
The Great Divide; *Life and Death, Darkness or Illumination, the Great Unknown, Fate, Infinity and Beyond*

In the Beginning

"God gave man **dominion** over the fish in the seas and over the birds in the air, and over every living thing that moves upon the Earth. God said: "Be fruitful and multiply, and fill the Earth and **subdue it**.""

And mankind hunted the fish greatly diminishing their numbers while polluting the waters of the seas, and mankind drove many of the wild birds into extinction while fouling the Earth's air with toxins, and mankind killed off most of the large wild creatures and stripped the Earth of its protective forest destroying many of the Earth's natural habitats.

Mankind has killed millions of its own species with no end in sight.

Mankind continues to expand his **circle of pollution and destruction** around the Earth bringing this planet closer and closer to its doom.

"God created man in his own image."

The Void

Life's wonders come with life's burdens. The fear of the unknown, death, weighs heavy on our spirits. Remember, in the void there is nothing for us to fear.

Which Road Will We Take?

"Which road will we follow? One filled with light and promise or one filled with darkness and misery.

We must choose."

If we are to survive, the Keepers and our children will save and inherit the Earth; Nature's light will fill their lives with meaning and wonder.

The Cosmos gave birth to the Universe and from this birth all matter and energy came into being.

In time life evolved and with the passing of time came the comprehension of that which gave us life: the Cosmos.

We were born of and from the physical Universe and in that we are natural beings.

The Earth, our precious home, needs our protection.

Marcus

Which Path Will We Follow?

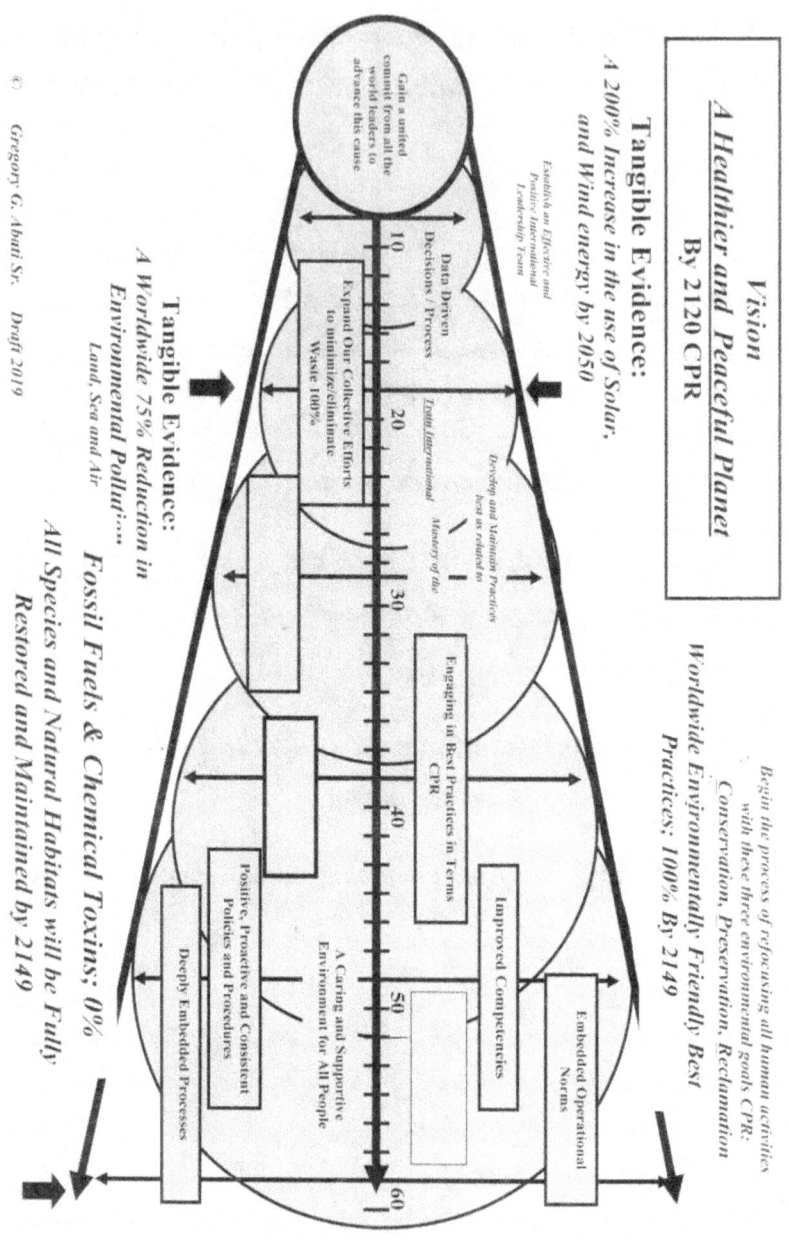

Vision
A Healthier and Peaceful Planet
By 2120 CPR

Worldwide Environmentally Friendly Best Practices; 100% By 2149

Begin the process of refocusing all human activities with these three environmental goals CPR; Conservation, Preservation, Reclamation

Tangible Evidence:
A 200% Increase in the use of Solar, and Wind energy by 2050

Tangible Evidence:
A Worldwide 75% Reduction in Environmental Pollution...
Land, Sea and Air

Fossil Fuels & Chemical Toxins; 0%
All Species and Natural Habitats will be Fully Restored and Maintained by 2149

Establish an Effective and Positive International Leadership Team

Gain a united commit from all the world leaders to advance this cause

Data Driven Decisions / Process

Expand Our Collective Efforts to minimize/eliminate Waste 100%

Develop and Maintain Practices best as related to

Train International Mastery of the

Engaging in Best Practices in Terms CPR

Improved Competencies

Positive, Proactive and Consistent Policies and Procedures

A Caring and Supportive Environment for All People

Embedded Operational Norms

Deeply Embedded Processes

10
20
30
40
50
60

Conservation, Preservation & Reclamation (CPR)

THE BEGINNING

My Journey Home from the Vietnam War 1968/69

In the Shadows of the Dead

Vietnam 1968-69

Copyright © January 28, 2014

www.amazon.com/dp/0991502922

<u>**MATURE AUDIENCE**</u>

In the Shadows of the Dead

This is a story of a young man's journey through the Vietnam War. It's a story about the impulsive nature of youth, the corruptive forces of war and the loss of innocence. It's a story of courage, honor, tragedy and brutality, self-sacrifice, compassion and heroism.

I was an eighteen year old Marine serving as a M60 machine gunner (MOS-0331) in Golf Company, 2nd Battalion, 26th Marines (2/26). Our unit operated from just north of Da Nang up into the Hai Van Pass to south of Chu Lai. The 2/26 was a combat unit deployed as a Battalion Landing Team (BLT) operating from the USS Okinawa, a helicopter platform, to engage and stop the Viet Cong (VC) and North Vietnamese Army (NVA) operating in this area. The 2nd Battalion, 26th Marines took part in Operations Meade River, Bold Mariner, Linn River and other significant engagements during my tour of duty.

This story takes place in the mud and the blood of South Vietnam. On January 28th, 1969 nine men were killed within 20-30 yards of my position. Alone, and in a bomb crater with my machine gunner lying dead behind me, I occupied the extreme right flank of my company. During this firefight two enemy soldiers were killed right outside of my gun position. After the initial assault these two enemy soldiers kept our forward unit pinned down for over an hour.

The 26th Marines lost 1,159 men killed in action (KIA) during its 44 months of service in Vietnam. This is one's man story of the war in Vietnam. I have lived my life **In the Shadows of the Dead**, the men, women and children who died in Vietnam. I shall never forget.

www.amazon.com/dp/0991502922

ISBN: 978-0-9915029-1-2